ELEVENTH HOUR

THE FBI THRILLERS

The Cove

The Maze

The Target

The Edge

Riptide

Hemlock Bay

Eleventh Hour

ALSO BY CATHERINE COULTER

Beyond Eden

Impulse

False Pretenses

G. P. PUTNAM'S SONS • NEW YORK

ELEVENTH HOUR

AN FBI THRILLER

Catherine Coulter

This is a work of fiction. Names, characters, places and incidents either are the product of the author's imagination or are used fictitiously, and any resemblance to actual persons, living or dead, business establishments, events, or locales is entirely coincidental.

While the author has made every effort to provide accurate telephone numbers and Internet addresses at the time of publication, neither the publisher nor the author assumes any responsibility for errors, or for changes that occur after publication.

G. P. Putnam's Sons
Publishers Since 1838
a member of
Penguin Putnam Inc.
375 Hudson Street
New York, NY 10014

Copyright © 2002 by Catherine Coulter

All rights reserved. This book, or parts thereof, may not be reproduced in any form without permission.
Published simultaneously in Canada

ISBN 0-399-14877-9

Printed in the United States of America

Book design by Deborah Kerner/Dancing Bears Design

TO PHYLLIS GRANN
YOU ARE A TREMENDOUS PUBLISHING TALENT.
THANK YOU FOR TWELVE INCREDIBLE YEARS.

CATHERINE COULTER

I would like to thank Producer and Assistant Director John Isabeau for his relentless pursuit on my behalf to see my FBI books made into films. When everything finally comes together, it will be because of his efforts.

Thank you, John, you're the best.

I would like to thank Inspector Sherman Ackerson and Spokesman Dewayne Tully for showing me around the main cop shop on Bryant Street (the San Francisco Hall of Justice), and answering every question.

I would like to thank Dr. Boyd Stephens, San Francisco medical examiner, who graciously showed me his facilities and answered all my questions, even the gruesome ones.

ELEVENTH HOUR

ONE

SAN FRANCISCO

Nick sat quietly in the midnight gloom of the nave, hunched forward, her head in her arms resting on the pew in front of her. She was here because Father Michael Joseph had begged her to come, had begged her to let him help her. The least she could do was talk to him, couldn't she? She'd wanted to come late, when everyone else was already home asleep, when the streets were empty, and he'd agreed, even smiled at her. He was a fine man, kind and loving toward his fellow man and toward God.

Would she wait? She sighed at the thought. She'd given her word, he'd *made* her give her word, known somehow that it would keep her here. She watched him walk over to the confessional, watched with surprise as his step suddenly lagged, and he paused a moment, his hand reaching for the small handle on the confessional door. He didn't want to open that door, she thought, staring at him. He didn't want to go in. Then, at last, he seemed to straighten, opened the door and stepped inside.

Again, there was utter silence in the big church. The air itself seemed to settle after Father Michael Joseph stepped into that small confined space. The deep black shadows weren't content to fill the corners of the church, they even crept down the center aisle, and soon she was swallowed up in them. There was a patch of moonlight coming through the tall stained-glass windows.

It should have been peaceful, but it didn't feel that way. There was something else in the church, something that wasn't restful, that wasn't remotely spiritual. She fidgeted in the silence.

She heard one of the outer church doors open. She turned to see the man who was going to make his midnight confession walk briskly into the church. He looked quite ordinary, slender, with a long Burberry raincoat and thick dark hair. She watched him pause, look right and left, but he didn't see her, she was in the shadows. She watched him walk to the confessional where Father Michael Joseph waited, watched him open the confessional door and slip inside.

Again, silence and shadows hovered around her. She was part of the shadows now, looking out toward the confessional from the dim, vague light. She heard nothing.

How long did a confession take? Being a Protestant, she had no idea. There must be, she thought, some correlation between the number and severity of the sins and the length of the confession. She started to smile at that, but it quickly fell away.

She felt a rush of cold air over her, covering her for a long moment before it moved on. How very odd, she thought, and pulled her sweater tighter around her.

She looked again at the altar, perhaps seeking inspiration, some sort of sign, and felt ridiculous.

After Father Michael Joseph had finished, what was she supposed to do? Let him take her hand in his big warm ones, and tell him everything? Sure, like she'd ever let that happen. She continued to look up at the altar, its flowing shape blurred in the dim light, the shadows creeping about its edges, soft and otherworldly.

Maybe Father Michael Joseph wanted her to sit here quietly with nothing and no one around her. She thought in that moment that even though he wanted her to talk to him, he wanted her to speak to God more. But there were no prayers inside her. Perhaps there were, deep in her heart, but she really didn't want to look there.

So much had happened, and yet so little. Women she didn't know were dead. She wasn't. At least not yet. He had so many resources, so many eyes and ears, but for now she was safe. She realized sitting there in the quiet church that she was no longer simply terrified as she'd been two and a half weeks before. Instead she'd become watchful. She was always studying the faces that passed her on the street. Some made her draw back, others just flowed over her, making no impact at all, just as she made no impact on them.

She waited. She looked up at the crucified Christ, felt a strange mingling of pain and hope fill her, and waited. The air seemed to shift, to flatten, but the silence remained absolute, without even a whisper coming from the confessional.

Inside the confessional, Father Michael Joseph drew a slow, deep breath to steady himself. He didn't want to see this man again, not ever again, for as long as he lived. When the man had called Father Binney and told him he could only come this late—he was terribly sorry, but it wasn't safe for him, and he had to confess, he just had to—of course Father Binney had said yes. The man told Father Binney he had to see Father Michael Joseph, no one else, and of course Father Binney had again said yes.

Father Michael Joseph was very afraid he knew why the man had come again. He'd confessed before, acted contrite—a man in pain, a man trying to stop killing, a man seeking spiritual help. The second time he'd come, he'd confessed yet again to another murder, gone through the ritual as if he'd rehearsed it, saying all the right words, but Father Michael Joseph knew he wasn't contrite, that—that what? That for some reason Father Michael Joseph couldn't fathom, the man wanted to gloat, because the man believed there was nothing the priest could do to stop him. Of course Father Michael Joseph couldn't tell Father Binney why he didn't want to see this evil man. He'd never really believed in human evil, not until the unimagined horror of September 11th, and now, when this man had come to him for the first time a week and a half ago, then last Thursday, and now again tonight, at nearly midnight. Father Michael Joseph knew in his soul that the man was evil, without remorse, with no ability to feel his own, or another's, humanity. He wondered if the man had ever felt truly sorry. He doubted it. Father Michael Joseph heard the man breathing in the confessional across from him, and then the man spoke, his voice a soft, low monotone, "Forgive me, Father, for I have sinned."

He'd recognize that voice anywhere, had heard it in his dreams. He didn't know if he could bear it. He said finally, his voice thin as the thread hanging off his shirt cuff, "What have you done?" He prayed to God that he wouldn't hear words that meant another human being was dead.

The man actually laughed, and Father Michael Joseph heard madness in that laugh. "Hello to you, too, Father. Yes, I know what you're thinking. You're right, I killed the pathetic little prick; this time I used a garrote. Do you know what a garrote is, Father?"

"Yes, I know."

"He tried to get his hands beneath it, you know, to try to loosen it, to relieve the pressure, but it was nice strong wire. You can't do anything against wire. But I eased up just a bit, to give him some hope."

"I hear no contrition in your voice, no remorse, only satisfaction that you committed this evil. You have done this because it pleased you to do it—"

The man said in a rich, deep, sober voice, "But you haven't heard the rest of my tale, Father."

"I don't want to hear anything more out of your mouth."

The man laughed, a deep, belly-rolling laugh. Father Michael Joseph didn't say a word. It was cold and stuffy in the confessional, hard to breathe, but his frock stuck to his skin. He smelled himself in that sweat, smelled his dread, his fear, his distaste for this monster. *Dear Lord, let this foul creature leave now, leave and never come back.*

"Just when he thought he had pulled it loose enough so he could breathe, I jerked it tight, really fast, you know, and it sliced right through his fingers all the way to the bone. He died with his damned fingers against his own neck. Grant me absolution, Father. Did you read the papers, Father? Do you know the man's name?"

Father Michael Joseph knew, of course he knew. He'd watched the coverage on television, read it in the *Chronicle*. "You murdered Thomas Gavin, an AIDS activist who's done nothing but good in this city."

"Did you ever sleep with him, Father?"

He wasn't shocked, hadn't been shocked by anything for the

past twelve years, but he was surprised. The man had never taken this tack before. He said nothing, just waited.

"No denial? Stay silent, if you wish. I know you didn't sleep with him. You're not gay. But the fact is, he had to die. It was his time."

"There is no absolution for you, not without true repentance."

"Why am I not surprised you feel that way? Thomas Gavin was just another pathetic man who needed to leave this world. Do you want to know something, Father? He wasn't really real."

"What do you mean he wasn't really real?"

"Just what I said. He didn't really ever exist, you know? He wasn't ever really here—he just existed in his own little world. I helped him out of his lousy world. Do you know he contracted AIDS just last year? He just found out about it. He was going nuts. But I saved him, I helped him out of everything, that's all. It was a rather noble thing for me to do. It was a sort of an assisted suicide."

"It was vicious, cold-blooded murder. It was real, and now a man of flesh and blood is dead. Because of you. Don't try to excuse what you did."

"Ah, but I was giving you a metaphor, Father, not an excuse. Your tone is harsh. Aren't you going to give me my penance? Maybe have me say a million Hail Marys? Perhaps have me score my own back with a whip? Don't you want me to plead with you to intercede with God on my behalf, beg for my forgiveness?"

"A million Hail Marys wouldn't get you anywhere." Father Michael leaned closer, nearly touched that evil, smelled the hot breath of that man. "Listen to me now. This is not a sacramental confession. You believe that I am bound by silence, that anything anyone tells me can go no farther than the confessional. That is not true. You have not made a sacramental confession; you are not contrite, you seek no spiritual absolution, and I am not bound to silence. I will discuss this with my bishop. However, even if he disagrees with me, I am prepared to leave the priesthood if I have to. Then I will tell the world what you have done. I won't allow this to continue."

"You would really turn me over to the cops? That is very impassioned of you, Father. I see that you are seriously pissed. I didn't know there was a loophole in your vow of silence. I had wanted you to be forced to beg and plead and threaten, but realize you're helpless and let it eat you alive. But how can anyone predict someone's behavior, after all?"

"They'll throw you in an institution for the rest of your miserable life."

The man smothered a laugh, managed a credible sigh, and said, laughing, "You mean to imply that I'm insane, Father?"

"No, not just insane. I think you're a psychopath—ah, I believe the politically correct word is sociopath, isn't it? Doesn't make it sound so evil, so without conscience. It doesn't matter, whatever you are, it's worse than anything doctors could put a tag to. You don't give a damn about anybody. You need help, although I doubt anyone could help the sickness in you. Will you stop this insanity?"

"Would you like to shoot me, Father?"

"I am not like you. But I will see that you are stopped. There will be an end to this."

"I fear I can't let you go to the cops, Father. I'm trying not to be angry with you for not behaving as you should. All right. Now I'm just mildly upset that you aren't behaving as you're supposed to."

"What are you talking about—I'm not acting like I'm supposed to?"

"It's not important, at least it isn't for you. Do you know you've given me something I've never had before in my life?"

"What?"

"Fun, Father. I've never had so much fun in my life. Except, maybe, for this."

He waited until Father Michael Joseph looked toward him through the wire mesh. He fired point-blank, right through the priest's forehead. There was a loud popping sound, nothing more because he'd screwed on a silencer. He lowered the gun, thoughtful now because Father Michael Joseph had slumped back against the wooden confessional wall, his head up, and he could see his face clearly. There was not even a look of surprise on the priest's face, just a flash of something he couldn't really understand. Was it compassion? No, certainly not that. The priest despised him, but now he was shackled for all eternity, without a chance for him to go to the police, no opportunity for him even to take the drastic step of leaving the priesthood. He was silent forever. No loophole now.

Now Father Michael Joseph didn't have to worry about a thing. His tender conscience couldn't bother him. Was there a Heaven? If so, maybe Father Michael Joseph was looking down on him, knowing there was still nothing he could do. Or maybe the priest was hovering just overhead, over his own body, watching, wondering.

"Good-bye, Father, wherever you are," he said, and rose.

He realized, as he eased out of the confessional and carefully closed the narrow wooden door, that the look on the Father's face—he'd looked like he'd won. But that made no sense. Won what? The good Father had just bought the big one. He hadn't won a damned thing.

There was no one in the church, not that he expected there to be. It was dead silent. He would have liked it if there had been a Gregorian chant playing softly. But no, there was nothing, just the echo of his own footsteps on the cold stones.

What did that damned priest have to look happy about? He was dead, for God's sake.

He walked quickly out of St. Bartholomew's Church, paused a moment to breathe in the clean midnight air, and craned his neck to look up at the brilliant star-studded sky. A very nice night, just like it was supposed to be. Not much of a moon, but that was all right. He would sleep very well tonight. He saw a drunk leaning against a skinny oak tree set in a small dirt plot in the middle of the sidewalk, just across the street, his chin resting on his chest—not the way it was supposed to be, but who cared? The guy hadn't heard a thing.

There would be nothing but questions with no answers for now, since the cops wouldn't have a clue. The priest had made him do things differently, and that was too bad. But it was all close enough.

But the look on the priest's face, he didn't like to think about that, at least not now.

He whistled as he walked beneath the streetlight on Filmore, then another block to where he'd parked his car, squeezed it between two small spaces, really. This was a residential area and there was little parking space. But that, too, was just the way it was supposed to be. It was San Francisco, after all.

One more stop to make. He hoped she'd be home, and not working.

TWO

WASHINGTON, D.C.

Special Agent Dane Carver said to his unit chief, Dillon Savich, "I've got a problem, Savich. I've got to go home. My brother died last night."

It was early, only seven-thirty on a very cold Monday morning, two weeks into the new year. Savich rose slowly from his chair, his eyes on Dane's face. Dane looked bad—pale as a sheet, his eyes shadowed so deeply he looked like he'd been on the losing end of a fight. There was pain radiating from his eyes, and shock. "What happened, Dane?"

"My brother—" For a moment Dane couldn't speak, and just stood in the open doorway. He felt in his gut that if he actually said the word aloud, it would make it real and true and so unbearable he'd just fold up and die. He swallowed, wishing it were last night again, before four o'clock in the morning, before he'd gotten the call from Inspector Vincent Delion of the SFPD.

"It's all right," Savich said, walking to him, gently taking his arm. "Come in, Dane. That's right. Let's close the door."

Dane shoved the door shut with his foot, turned back to Savich, and said, his voice steady and remote, "He was murdered. My brother was murdered."

Savich was shaken. Losing a brother to a natural death was bad enough, but this? Savich said, "I'm very sorry about this. I know you and your brother were close. I want you to sit down, Dane."

Dane shook his head, but Savich just led him to the chair, pushed it back, and gently shoved him down. He held himself as rigid as the chair back, looking straight ahead, out the window that looked out at the Justice Building.

Savich said, "Your brother was a priest?"

"Yes, he is—was. You know, I've got to go see to things, Savich."

Dillon Savich, chief of the Criminal Apprehension Unit at FBI headquarters, was sitting on the edge of his desk, close to Dane. He leaned forward, squeezed Dane's shoulder, and said, "Yes, I know. This is a terrible thing, Dane. Of course you have to go take care of it. You'll have paid leave, no problem. He was your twin, wasn't he?"

"Yes, an identical twin. He was my mirror image. But inside, as different as we were from each other, we were still so much alike."

Savich couldn't imagine the pain he must be feeling, losing a brother, a twin. Dane had been in the unit for five months now, transferred in from the Seattle field office, by his request, and strongly recommended by Jimmy Maitland, Savich's boss, who told Savich that he'd had his eye on Dane Carver for a while. A good man, he'd said, very smart, hard-nosed, tough, sometimes a hot dog, which wasn't good, but reliable as they come. If Dane Carver gave his word on something, you could consider it done.

His birthday, Savich knew, was December 26, two hours after midnight. He'd gotten lots of silly Christmas/birthday presents at the office party on the twenty-third. He'd just turned thirty-three.

Savich said, "Do the local cops know what went down? No, back up a moment, I don't even know where your brother lived."

"In San Francisco. I got two calls, the first just before four a.m. last night, from an Inspector Vincent Delion of the SFPD, then ten minutes later, a call from my sister, Eloise, who lives down in San Jose. Delion said he was killed in the confessional, really late, nearly midnight. Can you believe that, Savich?" Dane finally looked at him straight on, and in that instant there was such rage in Dane's eyes that it blurred into madness. He slammed his fist on the chair arm. "Can you actually believe that some asshole killed him in the confessional? At midnight? What was he doing hearing a confession at midnight?"

Savich thought Dane would break then. His breath was sharp and too fast, his eyes dilated, his hands fisted hard and tight. But he didn't. His breathing hitched, suspended for a moment, and then he made himself breathe deeply, and held himself together. Savich said, "No, it doesn't make sense to us, just to the person who killed him, and we'll find out who and we'll find out why. No, stay seated for a minute, Dane, and we'll make some plans. Your brother's name was Michael, wasn't it?"

"Yes, he was Father Michael Joseph Carver. I need to go to San Francisco. I know the reputation of the department out there. They're good, but they didn't know my brother. Not even my sister really knew him. Only I really knew him. Oh God, I thought I'd never say this, but it's probably better that my mom died last year. She'd wanted Michael to become a priest, prayed for it all her life, at least that's what she always said. This would have destroyed her soul, you know?"

"Yes, I know, Dane. When did you last speak to him?"

"Two nights ago. He—he was really pleased because he'd managed to catch a teenager who'd been spraying graffiti on the church walls. He told me he was going to make the boy a Catholic. Once he was a Catholic, he'd never do that again because he wouldn't be able to bear the guilt." Dane smiled, just for an instant, then fell silent.

"So you didn't sense anything wrong?"

Dane shook his head, then frowned. "I would have said no, that my brother was always upbeat, even when a local journalist tried to come on to him."

"Good grief, what was her name?"

"Oh no, it wasn't a woman. It was a man."

Savich just smiled.

"It happened quite a bit, but you're right, usually it was women. Michael was always kind, it didn't matter if it was a man or a woman doing the coming on." Dane frowned, fell silent again.

"Now that you think back, there is something, isn't there?"

"Well, I'm just not sure. He said something recently about feeling helpless, and he hated that. Said he was going to do something about it."

"Do you have any idea what he meant by that?"

"No, he wouldn't say any more. Maybe a confession that curled his toes, maybe a parishioner he couldn't help. But there was nothing at all that unusual about that. Michael dealt with lots of problems, lots of nutcases over the years." Dane curled his fist over the chair arm. "Maybe there was something there, something that frightened him, I don't know. I could have called him back and talked to him some more about it, pushed him when he clammed up. Why the hell didn't I?"

"Shut up, Dane. You're a cop. Don't freeze your brain up with guilt."

"It's hard not to. I'm Catholic."

A meager bit of humor, but a start. Savich said, "None of this was your fault. You need to find out who killed him, that animal is the only one to blame here, *the only one*. Now, I'll have Millie make the reservations for you. Tell me again, who's the lead inspector on this?"

"Vincent Delion. Like I said, he called me right before Eloise did last night, said he knew I was FBI, knew I'd want to hear everything they had. It isn't much as of yet. He died instantly, a shot through the forehead, clean in the front, you know, it looked like an innocent *tilak*, the red spot Hindus wear on their foreheads?"

"I know."

"But it wasn't just a red dot on the back of his head. Jesus, not on the back." His eyes went blank.

Savich knew he couldn't let Dane get sucked down into the reality of it, couldn't let him dwell on the hideous mess a bullet made of the head at the exit wound. It would just bury him in pain. He said very precisely, using his hands while he spoke to force eye contact, "I don't suppose the killer left the gun there?"

Dane shook his head. "No. The autopsy's today."

Savich said, "I know Chief Kreider. He was back here last year to appear in front of Congress on commonsense approaches to avoid racial profiling in the Bay Area. I met him down at Quantico on the rifle range. The man's a good distance shooter. And my father-in-law's a Federal judge out in San Francisco. He knows lots of people. What do you want me to do?"

Dane didn't say anything. Savich thought he was too numb with shock and grief to process what he'd said, but that would change. The good thing was that along with the rage and the pain he would have to deal with moment to moment, he would have his instincts and training kicking in. He said, "Never mind. Tell you what, head on out to San Francisco and talk to Delion, find out what they're doing. See if our office out there can help. Do you know Bert Cartwright, the SAC in San Francisco?"

"Yeah," Dane said, his voice flat as a creek-bed stone. "Yeah, I know him."

There was sudden animosity on his face. At least it masked the pain for a moment. "Yes, all right," Savich said slowly. "You two don't get along."

"No, we don't. I don't want to deal with him."

"Why? What happened between the two of you?"

Dane just shook his head. "It's not important."

"All right, you get yourself home and packed. Like I said, I'll have Millie take care of everything for you. Do you want to stay in the city or go to your sister's?"

"I'll stay in the city. Not at the rectory, either, not there."

"Okay, a hotel downtown, then. It'll be FBI approved, so you can count on it to be basic. You'll call if there's anything I can do."

"Yes, thank you, Savich. About my cases—"

"I'll see that they're covered. Go."

The two men shook hands. Savich watched Dane make his way through the large room with workstations for nine special agents, only six of them occupied at the moment. His wife, Special Agent Lacey Sherlock Savich, was in a meeting with Jerry

Hollister in the third-floor DNA analysis unit, comparing a DNA sample taken from a Boston rape-and-murder victim with a DNA sample from the major suspect. If they got a match, the guy was toast.

Ollie Hamish, his second in command, was in Wisconsin consulting with the Madison police on a particularly vicious series of murders, all connected to a local radio station that played golden oldies. Go figure, Ollie had said, and started humming "Maxwell's Silver Hammer."

Savich hated crazies. He hated unsolved craziness even more. It amazed and terrified him what the human mind could conjure up. And now Dane's brother, a priest.

He dialed Millie's extension, told her to make arrangements. Then he walked over and flipped on his electric kettle to make a cup of strong Earl Grey tea. He poured his tea into an oversized FBI mug and went back to MAX, his laptop, and booted up.

He started with an e-mail to Chief Dexter Kreider.

SAN FRANCISCO

At three-thirty on Monday afternoon, San Francisco time, after a five-hour-and-ten-minute flight from Dulles, Dane Carver threaded his way through the large open room toward Inspector Delion's overloaded desk. He paused a moment, studying him. The older man, with his bald, shiny head and thick handlebar mustache, was hunched over a computer keyboard, typing furiously. Dane sat down in the chair beside his desk and said nothing, just looked at the man at his work. It was like every other large cop shop he'd ever been in. Cops with their suit jackets hung over the backs of their chairs, their ties loosened, sleeves rolled up, a young Hispanic guy in handcuffs lounging in the side chairs, trying on sneers, a couple of lawyers in three-piece suits doing their best to intimidate—nothing at all unusual for a Monday afternoon. A decimated box of jelly donuts lay on a battered table in the small kitchen, a coffee machine that looked to be from the last century beside it, along with stacks of paper cups, packets of sugar, and a carton of milk Dane wouldn't touch in a million years.

"Who're you?"

Dane came to his feet and extended his hand. "I'm Dane Carver. You called me last night about my brother."

"Oh yeah, right." He rose, shook Dane's hand. "I'm Vincent Delion." He sat again, waved Dane to do the same. "Hey, I'm real sorry about your brother. I called you because I knew you'd want to hear what was going on."

The brothers had been close, Delion knew from Carver's sister, Eloise DeMarks. And Delion wasn't blind. The man was hurting, bad. He was also a Fed. All the Feds Delion had ever met hadn't seemed to feel much of anything. They all just wanted to press their wing tips down hard on his neck. Of course, he'd never seen a Fed in this situation before. Murder of a family member—something very personal, something over which he had no control at all. It couldn't get tougher than this.

Dane said, his voice effortlessly calm and compelling—it was a very good interview voice, Delion thought—"Yes, I appreciate that. Tell me what you have."

"I'm really sorry about this, but the first thing we need to do is go over to the morgue and you need to identify the body, not that there's any doubt, just procedure, you know the drill. Or maybe you don't. You ever been a local cop?"

Dane shook his head. "I always wanted to be an FBI agent. But yes, I know the drill."

"Yeah, I hear that's usually the way the thing works. Me, I always wanted to be local. Okay, Dr. Boyd did the autopsy this morning, and yeah, I was there. Your brother died instantly, like I told you last night. Boyd also says that was the case, if it's any comfort. I've spoken to your sister. She wanted to come up today, but I told her you would be here to handle things, that you'd fill her in. I'll need to speak to her, but in a day or two. I figured you'd rather take care of things."

"Yes. I've spoken to Eloise. I'll speak with her tonight. Now, about the gun—"

"No gun found at the murder site or anywhere in the church or within a two-block radius of Saint Bartholomew's, but the coroner extracted a twenty-two-caliber bullet from the concrete wall behind the confessional. So the bullet passed through your brother, out the confessional, and another six feet to the wall, not very deep, just about an eighth of an inch into the wall, and it was in pretty good shape. Our ballistics guy, Zopp—yeah, that's really his name, Edward Zopp—was on it right away. The thing is, you know, your brother was a priest, a very active, well-liked priest, and that's got priority over about everything else going on. The bullet was intact enough to weigh and measure, and Zopp was very happy about that. Usually it's not the case. Zopp said he counted the grooves and the land, and determined, of all things, that the gun is probably a JC Higgins model eighty or a Hi Standard model one-oh-one—both of those weapons are really close."

"Yeah, and they're also pretty esoteric. Neither of them is made anymore, but they're not hard to find, and they're not valuable. They're cheap, in fact."

"Yeah, that's it. Also Zopp told us it was weird because it's like the same gun the Zodiac killer used back in the late sixties and early seventies. Ain't that something? You remember, the guy was never caught."

"You're thinking there could be some sort of connection?"

Delion shook his head. "Nope. We're wondering if maybe our perp is an admirer of the Zodiac killer. Hey, it's a real long shot, but we'll see. Since we got the bullet, when we find the gun, we'll be able to match it for the DA."

Dane sat back in his chair and looked down at his wing tips. He hated this, hated it to his soul, but he had to ask. "Angle of entry?"

THREE

The killer was sitting right opposite your brother. They were looking at each other. The killer raised the gun and fired through the screen."

Jesus, Dane thought, seeing Michael, his head cocked just slightly to one side, listening so carefully to the penitent, trying to feel what the person confessing was feeling, trying to understand, wanting to forgive. But not with this guy, Dane was sure of that. His brother had been worried about this guy. The guy just raised the damned gun and shot him right through his forehead? For a moment, Dane couldn't even think, the horror of what had happened to Michael deadening his brain. He wished it would deaden the rest of him, but of course it didn't. He felt hollow with pain.

Delion gave Dane Carver some time to get himself together, then said, "We've already started checking local gun shops to see if they still carry either of these models or have carried them in the past, and if so, who's bought one in the last few years. Our local gun shop folk keep very thorough records."

Dane couldn't imagine using such a gun to murder someone, particularly if he'd bought the gun here in San Francisco. He'd get caught in no time at all if he bought it here, but it was an obvious place to begin.

"How was he discovered?"

"An anonymous call to nine-one-one, made only minutes after the murder."

"A witness," Dane said. "There's a witness."

"Very possibly. It was a woman. She claims she saw the man who shot your brother come out of the confessional, the proverbial smoking gun still in his hand. She says he didn't see her. She started crying—and then she hung up. Nine-one-one calls are taped, so if you'd like to listen to the call, we can do that. We haven't got a clue who the woman is."

"The woman hasn't called again?"

Delion shook his head.

"She didn't say whether or not she could recognize him?"

"Said she couldn't, said she'd call if she thought of anything helpful."

Great, okay, Dane thought. At least there was someone. Maybe she would call back. He said, "Have you spoken yet to the other priests at the rectory?"

For the first time Vincent Delion smiled beneath his thick

mustache, the ends actually waxed, Dane realized when he saw him smile. "Guess what? I figured you'd be ready to climb up my ass if I didn't let you in on that. So, Special Agent Carver, are you ready to move out?"

Dane nodded. "Thank you. I really appreciate this. I'm officially on leave from the FBI, so I've got time. Father Binney's got to be first. When we exchanged e-mails last week, Michael mentioned Father Binney."

"Oh? In what way? Something pertinent to this?"

"I'm not sure," Dane said, shrugged. "He just wrote of problems with Father Binney. There's something else," Dane added, raising his head, looking straight at Delion's mustache. "My brother said something to me on the phone the other night—something about how he felt helpless and he hated that. I'm hoping that Father Binney will have some ideas."

They passed the small kitchen area with microwave, coffeepot, and three different bowls of peanuts.

"Hey, you hungry? Want some peanuts, a cup of coffee?"

"Peanuts, not donuts?"

"Cops living on donuts, all sporting a big gut—that's a myth, that's just television," Delion said. "We're not big on donuts here, all of us are into fitness. We like peanuts in the shell from Virginia. Sometimes even the spicy ones."

"What's that then?"

"Well, that's just one jelly donut, probably the cleaning guy brought it in."

It was hanging off a paper plate, ready to make its final leap to the floor. Dane thought it more likely that the cleaning guy wouldn't touch it. He smiled, shook his head. "I ate on the plane. Thank you, Inspector."

The god-awful reality of it hit Dane when he saw his brother through the glass window in the very small viewing room at the morgue. Dr. Boyd, a tall, white-haired, commanding man, with a voice to make a sinner confess, had taken them through the security door, down the short hall into the room, and drew back the curtains. There was Michael, a sheet pulled up to his neck, only his head visible. Dane felt a lurch of pain so deep he almost gasped. He felt Delion's hand on his shoulder. Then he saw the red dot on Michael's forehead; it looked so fantastical, like it had just been painted on, nothing more, just a dab of makeup, some sort of fashion statement or affectation. He wanted to ask Dr. Boyd why they hadn't cleaned it off, but he didn't.

Dr. Boyd said very gently, "He died instantly, Agent Carver. There was just the slap of the bullet, then he was gone. No pain. I'm very sure of that."

Dane nodded.

"You know that we've done the autopsy, taken fingerprints and DNA samples."

"Yes, I know."

Delion stepped back, his arms folded across his chest, and watched Special Agent Dane Carver. He knew what shock was, what anguish was, and he saw both in this man. When Dane finally nodded and stepped back, Delion said, "Chief Kreider wants to see us now."

Chief Dexter Kreider's secretary walked them into the chief's office. The room wasn't all that big, but the view was spectacular. The entire side wall was windows, looking out toward the Bay Bridge, a huge Yahoo! sign and a neon-lit diet Coke sign the other landmarks in view. There was a large desk, and two large cabinets filled with kitsch, something that made Dane smile, for a moment. Just about every higher-up's office he'd been into had had at least one display case. And here, there was also a touch of whimsy—in a corner stood a colorful wooden carousel horse. Utilitarian and whimsical, a nice combination.

Dane knew that Chief Kreider could never sit on that carousel horse. He was a huge man, at least six-foot-four-inches, a good two hundred sixty pounds, not much of it excess, even around his belly. He had military-short hair, steel gray, and lots of it, wore aviator glasses, and looked to be in his mid-fifties.

He wasn't smiling. "Carver? Dane Carver? Special Agent?"

Dane nodded, shook the chief's hand.

"It's good to meet you. Come, sit down. Tina, bring us some coffee."

Delion and Dane sat at the small circular table in the center of the room. The chief still didn't sit, he stood towering over them, his arms crossed over his chest. Then he began to pace, until Tina, an older woman, with the same military precision as the chief, poured coffee, nodded to the chief, and marched out. Finally he said, "I got an e-mail from Dillon Savich, your boss back at Disneyland East."

"That's a good one," Delion said.

Kreider said, "Yeah, fitting. Savich writes that you're smarter than you've a right to be and you've got great gut instincts. He asks that we keep you in the loop. Delion, what do you think? You want to cooperate with the Feds?"

"No," Delion said. "This is my case. But I'll accept Carver in on the case with me, as long as I'm the boss and what I say goes."

"I don't want to take over the case," Dane said, "not at all. I just want to help find my brother's murderer."

Kreider said, "All right then. Delion's partner, Marty Loomis, is out with shingles, of all things, laid up for another couple of weeks. Inspector Marino has been in on this since Sunday night with Delion. I've given this some thought." He paused a moment, smiled. "I knew Dillon Savich's father, Buck Savich. He was a wild man, smart enough to scare a crook off to Latvia. I hear his son isn't wild—not like his father was—but he's got his father's brains, lots of imagination, and is a professional to his toenails. I respected the father and I respect the son. You, Carver, I don't know a bloody thing about you, but for the moment I'll take Savich's word that you're pretty good."

"Like I said," Delion said, "I don't mind him tagging along, sir. Hey, maybe he'll even say something bright every now and again."

"That's what I was thinking," Kreider said. He paced a couple more times, then pulled up right in front of Dane. "Or would you rather go off on your own?"

Dane looked over at Delion. The man wasn't giving anything away at all. He just stared back. Dane wasn't a fool. He slowly shook his head. "No, I'd like to work with Delion."

"Good." Chief Kreider raised his coffee cup, took one sip, and set it down. "I'll have the lieutenant reassign Marino. Delion, I expect twice-daily updates."

After they were dismissed, Delion said as they walked to the garage, "Lots of the guys wonder how Kreider makes love since the guy is always pacing, back and forth, never stopping. Tough to get much done when you can't hold still."

"Didn't you see that old movie with Jack Nicholson—*Five Easy Pieces?*"

Delion rolled his eyes and laughed as he pulled the 1998 Ford Crown Victoria, white with dark blue interior, out into traffic on Bryant Street. Delion headed north, crossed Market Street, and weaved his way in and out of traffic to Nob Hill. They found a parking slot on Clay.

Delion said, "Dispatch sent a field patrol officer from the Tenth District. He notified Operations, and they called me and the paramedics. Here, our paramedics are the ones who notify the medical examiner. Because it's very high profile, Dr. Boyd himself came to the church. I don't know how well you know San Francisco, but we're near one of the gay districts. Polk Street, known for lots of action, is just a couple of streets over."

"Yes, I know," Dane said. "Just in case you're wondering, my brother wasn't gay."

"That's what your sister told me," Delion said. He paused a moment, looking up at the church. "Saint Bartholomew's was built four years after the earthquake in 1906. The other church burned down. They made this one of red brick and concrete. See that bell tower—one of the big civic leaders at the time, Mortimer Grist, paid for it. It's a good thirty feet above the roof."

"Everything seems well tended."

"Let's go inside the church first," Delion said. "You need to see where everything is."

He needed to see where his brother's life was ended. Dane nodded, but as he walked down the wide central aisle, closer and closer to where Michael had been shot, in the third confessional, Delion had told him, the one that stood nearest to the far wall, each step felt like a major hurdle. His breathing was hard and fast. As difficult as it had been to see his brother lying dead on that gurney, this was harder. He suddenly felt a vivid splash of color hit his face and stopped. He looked up at a brilliant stained-glass window that spewed a spray of intense colors right where Dane was standing. He didn't move, he just stood, looking up and then beyond the colors, to the scene of Mary and Joseph in the stable, the baby Jesus in the manger in front of them. And angels, so many of them, all singing. He could practically hear the full, brilliant chorus of voices. He drew in a deep breath. The air began to feel warmer, and the crushing pain eased just a bit. He couldn't see the confessional. Rather than a yellow crime-scene strip, they'd rigged up a tall black curtain that cut off the confessional from prying eyes and curious hands. Delion moved the black curtain aside to reveal the confessional—all old, dark wood, tall and narrow, a bit battered, with two narrow doors, the first for the penitent and the far door for the priest. The dazzling colors from the windows were shining down on it now, making it look incandescent.

Slowly, he opened the door and sat down on the hard bench. He looked through the torn mesh netting. His brother had been just there, speaking, listening intently. He doubted the man had used the kneeler, not with the angle of the bullet. Did Michael know the man would kill him?

Dane rose and walked to the other side. He opened the door and eased down on the cushioned seat where his brother had sat. He didn't know what he expected to feel sitting there where his brother had died, but the fact was, he didn't feel any fear, nothing cold or black, just a sort of peace that he let flow deeply into him. He drew a deep breath and bowed his head. "Michael," he said.

Delion stood back, watching Special Agent Dane Carver walk out of the confessional. He saw the sheen of tears in his eyes, said nothing.

"Let's go talk to the rectory people," Dane said, and Delion just nodded.

They walked around to the back of the church to the rectory, which was set off by eucalyptus trees, a high fence, and more well-tended grounds. It was quieter than Dane thought it would be, the sounds of traffic distant. The rectory was a charming two-story building, with ivy trailing over the red brick walls, the tinkling of a small fountain in the background. Everything smelled fresh.

Michael was dead and everything smelled fresh.

FOUR

Father Binney immediately rose to greet them from behind a small reception desk. He was very short, and on top of his neck sat the head of a leprechaun. Dane had never before seen hair that red, without a single strand of white. Not even Sherlock could match this. Father Binney was also nearly sixty years old. Amazing.

He stuck out his hand when he saw Delion, but in the next instant he looked like he was going to faint. He grabbed the edge of a chair, staring at Dane.

"Oh, you gave me a start." He grabbed his chest. "You're Father Michael Joseph's brother, that's it. Our sweet Father in Heaven, you're so much alike, you scared me there for a moment.

Ah, do come in, gentlemen, do come in. Inspector Delion, it is good to see you again. You must be exhausted."

"It was a long night," Delion said as he followed Father Binney. He said to Dane, "I visited briefly with Father Binney this morning about eight o'clock, after the forensics team finally cleared the church for use again."

And you didn't say a word about it to me, Dane thought. He would have been surprised, though, if Delion hadn't been camping on the rectory's doorstep as quickly as possible.

"He spoke to everyone," Father Binney said. "You didn't find anything in Father Michael Joseph's room, did you, Inspector Delion?"

"Nothing that one wouldn't expect."

Father Binney was shaking his head as he led them into a small parlor. It was packed with dark-grained Chinese furniture, old and scarred and graceful, sitting on an ancient Persian carpet that was so frayed in spots that Dane was afraid to walk on it. The heavy red drapes had black dragons woven into them. "Do sit down, gentlemen." He turned to Dane. "I am very sorry for your loss, Mr. Carver. Everyone is. We loved Father Michael Joseph, it's a horrible thing. Oh my, you look so much like him, it's a shock even though I've seen a picture with the two of you—peas in a pod, the same smile. Oh my, this is very difficult. As I told Inspector Delion this morning, I'm the one who's responsible. If only I hadn't agreed to let that man come to the church for confession so late."

Father Binney sank down onto an overstuffed red brocade chair, all black against all red, except for his white clerical collar. Suddenly he covered his face with his hands. There were red hairs on the backs of his hands. Finally he looked up. "Please excuse me. It's just that I have to get used to looking at you, Mr. Carver, you're just so much like Father Michael Joseph. To have him gone, just gone, it's too much. Nothing like this has ever happened here at Saint Bartholomew's, and it's my fault."

Dane said in his deep, calm voice, "It isn't your fault, Father. It isn't mine either. It's this madman who killed him—he's the only one to blame here. Now, please, Father, tell us what you know about this man."

It steadied Father Binney. Slowly, he raised his head. He shuddered one more time as he looked at Dane. Dane saw that his feet barely reached the threadbare carpet, probably a good thing, since the thing was so tatty.

"As I told Inspector Delion, the man phoned late Sunday night, around eight o'clock, I think it was. I was on the desk for that hour, which is why I took the call. He said it was urgent, said he was very ill, that if he didn't speak to Father Michael Joseph, then he might go to hell if he died. He was very fluent, very believable. You understand, we have set times for confessions, but he pleaded with me, didn't let up."

"What was the man's name, Father?" Dane said.

Father Binney said, "He said he was Charles DeBruler, promised me he'd confessed to Father Michael Joseph two previous times, that Father had really helped him. He said he trusted Father Michael Joseph."

"What did my brother say, exactly, when you told him of the call?"

Father Binney frowned, his brow pleating deeply. "He was very angry, truth be told. He said he knew this man, that he didn't want to speak to him, not ever again. I was surprised, told him that I had never known him to fail to minister to anyone who asked for help. He didn't want to, but you see, I made him feel as if he was failing in his duty if he didn't see the man. I also told him that I never knew him to turn down a person who wanted confession, no matter the time requested, no matter what he thought of the penitent. Father Michael Joseph didn't wish to discuss the man with me, but he said he would see him one more time. If he couldn't do anything to change the man, it was the last time. Then he said something about having a decision to make, a decision that could change his life forever." Father Binney fell silent.

"What do you think he meant, Father, by 'change his life'?" Dane asked.

"I don't know," said Father Binney. "I can't imagine."

Dane slowly nodded. "The man asked for my brother three times. Why? If he didn't come to repent, then why did he want to see my brother, specifically?"

"I have asked myself that over and over," said Father Binney. "Three times he saw Father Michael Joseph. Why didn't Father Michael Joseph want to see him again? Why did he talk about making a decision that night that might change his life?"

"It sounds to me like this man had no intention of repenting his sins," Delion said. "Maybe it's possible that the man came to brag to your brother, you know, maybe he wanted to brag to someone about his crimes who was helpless to do anything about it. That's why your brother was angry, Dane, why he didn't want to see this man again. He knew the man was playing games with him. What do you think? It explains why Father Michael Joseph didn't want to see him again. Hey, am I off the wall here?"

"I don't know," Dane said. "The man came three different times." He fell silent. "The third time he killed my brother."

Father Binney's eyes filled. "Ah, but why would the man taunt Father Michael Joseph? Why?" Father Binney rose, began pacing. "I'll never see Father Michael Joseph again. Everyone is immensely saddened, and yes, angry. Bishop Koshlap is distraught. Archbishop Lugano is extremely upset by all of this. I believe he met with Chief Kreider this morning."

"Yes," Delion said. "He did." He turned to Dane. "The janitor, Orin Ratcher, found Father Michael Joseph just before the police came, right?"

"Yes," Father Binney said. "Orin has trouble sleeping, keeps odd hours. He said he was mopping in the vestry, thought he heard a pop, ignored it, then finally he came in and found Father Michael Joseph in the confessional."

"He didn't see anyone?"

"No," Father Binney said. "He said there was no one, just dark silence and Father Michael Joseph, still sitting in the confessional, his head back against the wall. Just a moment later a patrol officer came, said there'd been a call about a murder. Orin showed him Father Michael Joseph's body. Orin is in very bad shape, poor man. We have him staying here for the next couple of days. We don't want him to be alone."

Delion said, "I already spoke to him, Dane. He didn't see the woman who phoned in the murder either. Nothing. Zip."

"Father Binney, do you have that list of Father Michael Joseph's friends?"

"There are so many." Father Binney sighed and reached into his pocket. "At least fifty, Inspector Delion."

Delion pocketed the list. "You never know, Father," he said.

"Father Binney, could you tell us the dates and times of the two other visits my brother had with this Mr. Charles DeBruler?"

Father Binney, pleased that he could do something, was only gone for five minutes. When he returned to the sitting room he said, "Father Michael Joseph heard confession last Tuesday night until ten p.m. and last Thursday night until nine p.m."

Dane asked to look through his brother's room even though Delion had already searched it. At the end of nearly an hour, they had found nothing to give them any sort of clue. There was a pile of Dane's e-mails to his brother, beginning from the previous January, which he'd printed and kept, just over a year's worth. That was when Michael had finally gotten himself on-line and went e-mail mad. "Have your guys checked out my brother's computer?"

"Yes. They haven't found anything hidden on the hard drive, if that's where you're headed. No coded files, no deleted files that look like anything."

They spoke to two other priests, to the cook, the maid, three clerical assistants. None could add anything relevant. No one had ever spoken to or seen Charles DeBruler.

"He knew his murderer," Delion said when they were back in the car. "There's no doubt about that. He knew he was a monster, but he wasn't afraid of him."

"No," Dane said, "not afraid. Michael was repulsed by him, but he wasn't afraid of him. Charles DeBruler spoke two other times to my brother, last Tuesday and last Thursday, both in the late evening." Dane took a deep breath. "For Michael to be that upset, for him to be angry about seeing this man, it's my best guess that the man must have done something horrendous around both those other times. Delion, were there any murders committed here in San Francisco on those days or perhaps a couple of days before?"

Delion hit the steering wheel with his hand and nearly struck a pedestrian who was stoned and walk-dancing across Market Street. He gave them the finger, never breaking stride.

"Yes," Delion said, turning the Ford sharply to make the guy jump out of the way. "Damn. It makes sense, doesn't it? Why the hell didn't I think of that?"

"You're exhausted, for a start."

Delion blew that off, fingered his mustache. "Okay, Dane, let me think. We've had three murders, one a couple of weeks old. We've got the guy—a husband we believe who just wanted to collect on his wife's life insurance. That was Donnie Lunerman's case. He just shook his head when he walked out of the interview with the man. It boggles the mind what some people will do for fifty thousand dollars.

"I've got it. Last Monday night—just one night before the first confession—there was an old woman, seventy-two, who lived alone in the Sunset District, on Irving and Thirty-third. She was murdered in her home. No robbery, no forced entry, no broken windows. The guy clubbed her to death in her bed and took off. Thing's a dead end so far."

"He didn't shoot her," Dane said thoughtfully, bracing one hand against the dashboard as Delion took a sharp turn into the police garage.

"No, he bludgeoned her to death. Then, last Wednesday, and this is the one that everyone is all up in arms about, a gay activist was murdered, outside a bar in the Castro. Lots of witnesses, but no one close and no one can agree on what the guy looked like. He was straight, he was gay, he was fat, thin as a rail, old, young— you get the picture. That's not my case. The chief formed a special task force, that's how high profile this guy was."

"How was he killed?"

"Garroted."

"Okay. Blunt force, strangulation, bullet. The guy is all over the board."

"If," Delion said, "if—and this is a really big if—if the guy killed both those people and taunted your brother about them, then why would he kill him?"

"I don't know," Dane said. "I'm really not sure, but I'll betcha that our profilers would have an idea about that."

"Oh man," Delion said, screeching into a parking place in the garage, "the Feds are coming to roost on my head after all."

"They're good people, Delion." Dane paused a moment, then said, "You know, I'm wondering about that woman—the one who called in my brother's murder—why she was there at midnight on Sunday?"

"Yeah, everyone was wondering about that. No way to find her. Let's hope she calls us again."

"I wonder what she really saw."

"We'll probably never know. I don't think we'll have any luck finding her."

Dane said, "Maybe she'll be on Father Binney's list."

Delion glanced over at him. "You ever find anything out that easy?"

FIVE

She stood on the bottom step of the ugly Hall of Justice building on Bryant Street.

It was a beautiful Tuesday morning, gloriously sunny, with just a nip in the air, actually a typical winter day in San Francisco, as she'd been told many times. Yes, the air was so clear and sharp you couldn't breathe in deep enough.

She'd only been here about two weeks, and there had been other days like this. But this morning, this incredibly crisp, clear morning, she felt little pleasure. She walked slowly to the top step, people streaming around her, most of them moving fast, focused on where they were going. No one paid her any attention.

She was scared, really scared. She didn't want to be there, but she didn't have a choice. She'd tried for a solid two minutes to convince herself that Father Michael Joseph's death had nothing to do with her, but of course that was not going to work.

It was time to step up.

She went through the metal detector, made her way through the crowded lobby, and took the elevator to the fourth floor.

She'd been to the police station once before, when she'd first arrived in San Francisco. She'd had a weak moment, thought she would just waltz in and tell someone what had happened, see if someone would help her. But she realized soon enough that she was dreaming. She'd snuck away. That first time she hadn't noticed the series of black-and-white photos that lined the walls, many of them taken before the earthquake. She walked through the door to Homicide, into the small reception area. There was no one behind the high counter. She paused a moment, then walked through the door. She'd seen a lot of homicide rooms on TV and this one looked much the same except it was smaller, about a dozen big, scarred light oak desks shoved together in pairs, heavy old side chairs beside each one. There was a computer on top of each desk, stacks of loose paper, folders, books, a phone, and what looked like mounds of just plain trash. What struck her was that there wasn't much noise, no cursing, no yelling, no chaos. Just the steady low hum of a dozen simultaneous conversations. On one side of the main room were two small interview rooms, with no windows, that looked like soundproofed coffins. Finally, from one of those rooms, she heard some raised voices.

There were eight or so men in suits standing or seated at their desks, speaking on phones, working on computers. She didn't see any women.

Half a dozen other people stood around the room, some of them thumbing through the ratty metal file cabinets that lined every wall, some just studying their fingernails, some looking really worried. She wondered if they were criminals or lawyers, or maybe some of each. One young guy with purple hair and pants so low she could see that his navel was an outie, sauntered out of one of the interview rooms, winked at her, and smacked his lips. He must be really desperate, she thought, ducking her head down, to come on to her.

Other than the kid with the purple hair, no one paid her a bit of attention. She wondered if anyone would be willing to take the time even to listen to her. Everyone looked harassed, too busy—

"Can I help you, miss?"

It was a uniformed patrol officer. There wasn't a smile on her face. On the other hand, she didn't look like she was ready to chew nails either.

"I need to speak to the detective who's investigating Father Michael Joseph's murder."

The woman lifted a dark brow a good inch. "They're not detectives here in San Francisco. They're inspectors."

"I didn't know that. Thank you. May I please see the inspector? Really, I'm not here to waste anyone's time."

The officer looked her over, and she knew what the officer was seeing. It wasn't good. Finally, the officer said, "All right. I see that Inspector Delion is at his desk. I'll take you to him."

There was a man seated in the chair beside Inspector Delion's desk, his back to her. The set of his shoulders, the color of his hair were somehow familiar to her. A criminal being interviewed?

The officer said, "Hey, Vince, I've got a woman here to see you about Father Michael Joseph's murder."

"Yeah?" He looked as harassed and as impatient as every other man in the room. Then he grew quiet, his dark eyes on her face.

She knew what she looked like. Was he going to sneer at her? Tell her to get lost? No, he just sat there, staring at her, fingering his mustache. He didn't say anything else, just waited.

"Yes, I need to speak to you, sir."

The man seated in the side chair rose and turned to face her. She stared at him, unable to take it in. She had to be dead, there was no other conclusion. She didn't feel dead, but who knew? Here he was, looking at her, and he was dead, she had seen the bullet hole through his forehead, seen his eyes.

She squeaked, nothing more than that, and folded up on herself, fainting for the first time in her life.

Dane caught her before she cracked her head on the edge of the desk behind her. The inspector sitting there jerked back and said, "Hey!"

"I've got her, it's okay," Dane said.

"What the hell's wrong with her?" Delion shoved back his chair, splaying his hands on his desktop. "Damnation, it's only eight o'clock in the morning. Here, Dane, take her into the lieutenant's office. She and the captain are in a meeting with Chief Kreider, so it's free."

Dane hauled her up in his arms and carried her into a small glass-walled office. Like every other free space in the area, it was lined with old gray file cabinets that had seen better days a half century before. He laid her on the rattiest, ugliest old green sofa he'd ever seen. No, there was one just as ugly in the rectory at St. Bartholomew's.

"You got some water, Delion?"

"Uh? Oh yeah, just a moment."

Dane went down on his haunches next to her. He gave her a cop's once-over, quickly done, assessment made. She looked homeless—torn jeans, three different sweaters, one on top of the other, all of them on the ratty side, not dirty, just old and tattered. She wore no makeup, not a surprise. Her hair was a dirty blond with a bit of curl, longish, tied in the back with a rubber band. Even with all the bulky layers of sweaters, it was easy to tell she was thin, pale, no more than twenty-seven, -eight, max. Not doing well in life, that was for sure. She looked like she'd been in a closet for too long without a glimpse of the sun, or tucked away in a homeless shelter. She also looked like she needed a dozen good meals. She'd been carrying a wool cap. Even unconscious, she still clutched it in her fingers.

They had a homeless woman for a witness?

Of course, that was just the outside. What a person was like on the inside was what was important, what was real. But if her outsides gave any clue at all, it was that something bad had happened to her. Drugs? An abusive husband? Alcohol?

Why did she faint? Hunger?

"Here's some water. She show any signs of life yet?"

"Soon." Dane lightly slapped her cheeks, waited, then slapped her again.

A couple of inspectors stuck their heads in. Delion waved them off. "She'll be okay, don't call the paramedics, okay?"

A woman officer said, "She looks really down on her luck. The last person she should want to see is you, Delion."

Her eyelashes fluttered. Slowly, she opened her eyes, blinked a couple of times, and focused on Dane's face above her.

"Oh no," she said, so low he could barely hear her. She tried to get away from him by pressing herself against the back of the sofa. "Oh God, am I dead?"

Dane said, "No, you're not dead. I'm not dead either. You knew my brother, didn't you? Father Michael Joseph?"

"Your brother?"

"Yes, my twin brother. We're identical twins. My name is Dane Carver."

"You're not a priest?"

"Nope," said Delion. He brought his face down close to hers, which made her shrink back even more. Delion backed off, said, "He's the other end of the scale."

"You're a criminal?"

"No, I'm not. That was just a bit of police humor. Here, drink a bit of water."

He cupped the back of her head, brought her up a bit, and put the paper cup to her mouth. She sipped at it, then said, "Thank you, no more."

Delion pulled up one of Lieutenant Purcell's chairs, straddled it, waved Dane to the only other chair in the small room. Dane pulled it up next to the sofa.

Delion said, "You here to tell us about Father Michael Joseph? You know something about his murder? You wouldn't be the woman who phoned in the murder about midnight Sunday night, would you?"

"Yes," she said, unable to look away from Father Michael Joseph's brother. She lifted her hand, touched her fingertips to his cheek, the small cleft in his chin. Dane didn't move. She dropped her hand, swallowed tears. Dane saw that her fingernails were as ragged as her sneakers, her hands chapped. "You're so like him," she said. "I only knew him for two weeks, but he was always kind to me, and I know he cared about what happened to me. He was my friend. I'm not Catholic, but it didn't matter. I was there Sunday night, in the church, when that man shot him."

Delion said, "Why the hell didn't you come forward right away? Good God, woman, it's Tuesday morning. He was murdered midnight Sunday."

"Yes, I know. I'm sorry. I had to call you from a public phone, and I finally found one that worked by a convenience store about two blocks from the church. I called nine-one-one, told the operator what I'd seen. But I couldn't stay, I just couldn't. This morning I knew I had to come and talk to you, that just maybe I could help, but I really don't think so."

"Why couldn't you stay and talk to us on Sunday night?"

"I was just too scared."

"Why?"

She didn't say a word, just shook her head.

"Okay," Delion said, backing off for the moment. "I want you to take a deep breath. Get a hold of yourself. Now then, I want you to tell us everything that happened Sunday night, and don't leave out a single detail. We need everything. Can you do that?"

She nodded, closed her eyes a moment against the fearsome pain, the terror of Father Michael Joseph's violent death.

Dane watched her twist the old red wool cap between her long fingers, thin and very white.

She stared down at that woolen cap as she said, "All right, I can do this. I was sitting in one of the front pews on the far side of the church, waiting for Father Michael Joseph to finish."

"So you came in after the man had already gone into the confessional?" Delion asked.

"No, I'd been speaking to Father Michael Joseph, and he wanted me to stay, to talk to him when he'd finished hearing this one confession."

Dane said, "Was anyone else in the church?"

"No, it was empty, except for the two of us. It was very dark. Father Michael Joseph left me, walked to the confessional, and went inside."

"You saw the person come into the church?"

"Yes, I saw him. I didn't see him clearly, mind you, but I could see that he was slender, lots of black hair, and he had on a long Burberry coat, dark. I wasn't really paying all that much attention. I saw him go into the confessional."

"Could you hear either Father Michael Joseph or the other person speaking?"

"No, nothing. There was pure, deep silence, like you'd expect in a church at night. A good amount of time passed before I heard a popping sound. I knew instantly that it was a gun firing."

"How'd you know it was a gun?" Delion asked. "Most people wouldn't automatically think *gun* when they heard a popping sound."

"I went hunting a lot with my father before he died."

"Okay, what next?" Dane said.

"Just a moment later the man came out of the confessional. I think he was smiling, but I can't be sure. He was holding a big ugly gun in his hand."

SIX

She took another sip of water, trying to get herself together. She was shaking so badly she spilled some of the water on the woolen cap in her lap. She stared at it, and swallowed.

"You okay?" Father Michael Joseph's brother said.

She nodded. "Yes, I think so."

"Do you think he saw you?" Dane asked.

She shook her head. "I was in the shadows, down under the pew. No, he didn't see me."

"Okay, when you're ready, tell us the rest," Delion said.

"When I heard the gun fire, I slipped down beneath the pew. I was terrified that he'd come out, see me, and kill me. He looked around, but like I said, I'm sure he didn't see me. I watched him unscrew a silencer off the end of the gun—he did it very quickly, like he was really proficient at it—and he slipped both the silencer and the gun into his coat pocket. Then he did something strange, and it nearly scared me to death. He pulled the gun back out of his pocket. He held it pressed to his side. I think he was whistling as he walked out of the church.

"I didn't move for a real long time, just couldn't, I was just too scared that he was waiting behind the side door to see if anyone would come out, and then he'd kill me, quick and clean, just like he killed Father Michael Joseph.

"I finally went to the confessional." She swallowed, closed her eyes for a moment. "I looked at Father Michael Joseph's face. His eyes were open wide and I could see that he was gone. Oh God, he had such beautiful eyes, dark and kind, he saw so much. But his eyes were blank, vague in death, and there was a small red hole in his forehead. It looked so harmless, that little hole, but he was dead. There was something else, something in his expression. It wasn't fear or terror, you know, from knowing in that instant he was going to die; it was something else. He looked somehow pleased. How could that be possible? For God's sake, pleased about what?"

"Pleased," Delion said. "That's odd. You're sure?"

She nodded. "Or maybe like he was finally satisfied about something. I'm sorry, I'm just not sure."

"Okay, go ahead."

"Then I heard someone coming out of the vestry off to the left. I froze. God, I thought it was the murderer and he was coming back. I thought he'd see me because I wasn't hiding in the shadows anymore. He'd know that I saw him kill Father Michael Joseph, he'd believe that I could identify him, and he was coming back to kill me, too.

"I ran as fast as I could to the side door, flipped up the dead bolt, and managed to slip outside without making much noise. I waited there, it seemed like forever, but I didn't hear or see anything. Then I ran to try to find a phone."

"Where'd you go after that?" Delion asked.

"Back to the shelter on Ellis, near Webster, Christ's Shelter."

"That's a long way from Saint Bartholomew's," Delion said.

"Yes, it is. Father Michael Joseph was very involved in the shelter's activities and the people who stayed there. That's where I met him. He, ah, was very fond of history, particularly the thirteenth century. His hero was Edward the First."

"Ah, you know about that," Dane said, and felt his voice seize up. He swallowed, knowing they were looking at him. "He loved history. I never had the knack for remembering dates, but Michael could. I remember he'd talk me into a coma, going on and on about the Crusades, particularly the one with Edward."

"That's all well and good," Delion said, "but let's get back to it, all right?" He watched Dane collect himself, and lightly gripped his shoulder.

"Are you sure you didn't see more?" Delion said. "Anything else?"

"No, I'm sorry. The man was in the confessional when he shot Father Michael Joseph. The light was real dim—you know how the light is really soft and almost black at midnight? And the shadows, they were thick, deep, all over the church."

Dane nodded.

"It was like that. I'm sorry, but I got only a vague impression of him. The Burberry, the black hair, nothing else, really."

Dane said easily, "Do me a favor. Close your eyes just a moment and picture yourself standing inside Saint Bartholomew's. Can you see that incredible stained-glass window that shows the stable scene of Christ's birth? It's just behind the confessional."

"Oh yes, I can see it. I've stared at it many times, wondering, you know, how something made of glass could make you so aware of just being."

Yes, he thought, satisfied, she knew the window well. He said, "I saw it for the first time yesterday, stared at it, felt all those colors seep into me. It made me feel close to something bigger than I am, something deep inside that I'm rarely aware of, something powerful."

"Yes. That's it exactly."

"I can imagine how, even when it's dark in the church—that midnight dark you spoke about—how that window still shines like a beacon when just a hint of light comes through it. It would make all that black, all those shadows, take on a glow, a pale sort of shine, concentrated, as if from a long way off. I can see that. Can you?"

"Yes," she said, her eyes closed. "I can."

Dane sat forward on the chair, his hands clasped between his legs, his voice lower now, smooth as honey. "You feel like you're bathed in that light and it makes you feel warm and safe. It allows you to see everything around you more clearly because of that beautiful spray of colors."

"Yes. I hadn't realized how incredible it was."

"Which hand was he holding the gun in?"

"His right hand."

"He used his left hand to unscrew the silencer?"

"Yes."

"Was he a young man?"

"No, I don't think so. He didn't move like a young man moves, like you move. He was older, but not old, close to Inspector Delion's age, but he wasn't carrying any extra weight. He was slightly built but straight as a conductor's wand. He stood very straight, military straight. He had his head cocked to the right side."

"What was he wearing?"

"A long trench coat—you know, the Burberry. It's exactly the same sort of overcoat my father used to wear."

"What color?"

"Dark, real dark, maybe black. I can't see it all that clearly."

"Was he tall?"

"Not terribly, maybe five-foot-ten. I know he was under six-foot."

"Bald?"

"No, like I said, he had dark hair, lots of it, really dark, maybe black, just a bit on the long side. He wasn't wearing a hat or anything."

"Beard?"

"No beard. I remember his skin was light, lighter than anything else about him; it was like another focal point, a splash of white in all that gloom."

"You said he was smiling?"

"Yes."

"What did his teeth look like?"

"Straight, very white, at least they looked very white in all that darkness."

"When he walked away, was he limping? Did he favor one leg over the other? Did he walk lightly?"

"He was fast, his stride long. I remember that his trench coat flapped around his legs, he was walking so fast, and he was graceful, yes, I can remember how graceful he was."

"Did he ever put the gun back in his pocket?"

"No, he just kept it held down, close against his right side."

Her breathing hitched.

Dane leaned forward and patted her hand. Her skin was dry, rough. She blinked, so surprised at what she'd remembered so clearly, seen so clearly, that she just stared at Father Michael Joseph's brother.

She said, "Your name is Dane Carver?"

He nodded.

Delion waited another couple of seconds, saw that it was over, and said, "Not bad, ma'am."

"Yes, you saw quite a lot," Dane said, and now he leaned forward and lightly touched his fingers to her shoulder. It felt reassuring, calming, that touch of his, and she realized that he knew it and that's why he'd done it. Dane said, "That was really good. Inspector Delion will call up a forensic artist next. Do you think you could work with an artist?"

"Yes, certainly. I really don't think I can identify him if you ever catch him, though."

"Now back up a minute," Delion said. "Why were you in the church at midnight?"

"Father Michael Joseph told me that he had to meet this man really late for confession, but he said he wanted me to stay, he wanted to talk to me, see if maybe he could help me work things out."

"Help you with what?"

She shook her head.

"Maybe we could help you," Dane said.

She shook her head again, lips seamed together.

"You know," Delion said, "life has a funny way of changing things around. People you don't particularly trust one day, you can confide in the next."

"Look," she said, "I don't want any help. I don't want to tell you what I was going to speak to Father Michael Joseph about. I don't want you to keep asking me about it, all right?"

"But maybe we could help," Dane said.

"No. Leave it alone or I'll disappear."

Delion and Dane looked at each other. Slowly, Dane nodded. "No more questions about you and your situation."

"Okay. Good." Suddenly she started crying. Not a sound, just tears running down her face.

Delion looked like he wanted to run.

Dane grabbed a couple of Kleenex off the lieutenant's desk and handed them to her.

"Oh goodness, I'm sorry, I—"

Dane said, "It's okay. You've had a couple of tough days."

She wiped her face, her eyes. "I'm sorry," she said again, tears thick in her voice.

She clutched the Kleenex in her right fist, sat up, and swung her legs over the side of the sofa. She took a very deep breath, looked down. She paused a moment, sniffed, swallowed, then said, "This sofa is really ugly."

Dane laughed. Somewhere deep down, there was still laughter in him. "Yeah," he said, "it's butt ugly."

"Yeah, yeah," Delion said, scooting his chair forward, crowding Dane out of the way, easy since the office was very small. "We've got a lot to talk about, Ms.—Hey, we don't know your name."

She blinked at him. "My name is Jones."

"Jones," Delion repeated slowly. "What's your first name, Ms. Jones?"

"Nick."

"Nick Jones. As in Nicole?"

She nodded, but Dane thought it was a lie. What was going on here? Was she wanted by the police in some other city? Maybe she was wanted here, in San Francisco. Maybe that was why Michael had wanted to help her. Michael had always been able to sniff out folks who were in trouble, and he always wanted to help them. He gave her a long look but didn't say anything.

"Well, Ms. Jones," Delion said, "I could arrest you, send your fingerprints off, and find out what you've done."

"Yes," she said. "You could."

She was a good poker player, Dane thought.

Delion folded first. "Nah, we'll pass on that. No more questions about your background, your own situation. You got a deal. Now, tell us, Ms. Jones, did you meet other people that Father Michael Joseph knew?"

Nick nodded. "Yes, there was another woman he was trying to help. Her name is Valerie Striker. I think she's a prostitute. She was in the church when I got there. She'd just stopped by to speak to Father Michael Joseph for a moment. I remember she left maybe five minutes before that man came in."

Delion said, "Oh, shit. Whatcha bet he saw her?"

"It's possible," Dane said.

"Did you see her when you ran out of Saint Bartholomew's, Ms. Jones?"

She shook her head.

"Valerie Striker," Delion said and wrote the name down in his book. "We'll check on her. Just maybe she saw something."

"Or maybe he saw her," Nick said. "Dear God, I hope not."

SEVEN

Nick said, "I'm really sorry you lost your brother, Mr. Carver."

Dane's hands were clasped in his lap. "Thank you," he said, but didn't look up. He said after a moment, "You said that you and my brother were friends. How close were you?"

"Like I told you, we only met two weeks ago. Father Michael Joseph was visiting the shelter a couple of days after I arrived. We got to talking. We got off onto medieval history. I don't remember how it came up, to be honest. Father Michael Joseph was very kind, and very knowledgeable. We got to talking, and it turned out that he is—he was—fascinated by King Edward the First of England, particularly that last Crusade Edward led to the Holy

Land that led to the Treaty of Caesarea." She shrugged, tried to look self-deprecating, but Dane wasn't fooled for a moment. Who was she?

"He took me for a cup of coffee at The Wicked Toe, a little café just off Mason. He didn't care how I looked, didn't care what anyone else would think—not, of course, that the area is any great shakes."

She looked over at Dane, stared at him, and then she started crying again.

Dane didn't say anything this time, couldn't say anything because his throat was all choked up. He wanted to cry himself, but he wouldn't let himself, not here. All he could do was wait, and listen to her sobs.

When she'd stilled, he said, "Did my brother give you anything to keep safe for him?"

"Give me something? No, he didn't. Why?"

"Too bad."

Delion came into the lieutenant's office and said, "Valerie Striker lives on Dickers Avenue. I'm outta here. You want to come, Dane?"

Nick was on her feet. "Please, please, let me come with you. I met Valerie, she's so beautiful, and really nice. She was unhappy, didn't know what to do. There was this man who was threatening her. Please, let me come with you. Maybe if she sees me, she'll agree to talk to you."

"This is police business, ma'am. You're a civilian, for God's sake, you can't just—"

"Please," Nick said, and grabbed Delion's sleeve. "This is so important to me, please, Inspector. I won't get in the way, I won't say a thing, but—"

"I'm an outsider, too, Delion," Dane said. "Maybe she can be helpful if Ms. Striker doesn't want to talk to us." His unspoken message that Delion got real fast was that Ms. Jones might just disappear on them again.

Delion said low to Dane, "If this was FBI business, would you let her tag along with you?"

"Sure, no problem."

"Yeah, right." He said on a sigh to Nick, "All right, Ms. Jones, just this one time. Dane, she's your responsibility."

"Sure, no problem."

"Hey, wait. Before we head on over to Valerie's place, let's just wait for the forensic artist here before Ms. Jones starts to forget."

An hour later, Jenny Butler, one of two forensic artists on staff, held up her sketch for everyone to see.

"Is that him, Ms. Jones?" Delion asked.

Nick nodded slowly. "It's as close as I can get. Will it help?"

"Remains to be seen. Thank you, Jenny. How's Tommy?"

"He's just ducky, Vince. The older he gets the more of a handful he becomes." She added to Dane and Nick, "He's my husband. See you, Vince."

"Thanks. Ms. Jones, this sketch will be printed up and distributed, and there will be no mention of you."

Delion grabbed his jacket and headed out the door, Nick and Dane close on his heels.

Fifteen minutes later, he pulled the Ford next to the curb only a block from the address they wanted on Dickers Avenue.

The three of them stood a moment staring up at the old Victorian where Valerie Striker lived.

Delion looked at Ms. Jones—homeless woman, fake name—and said, "This is great, just great. I've got a Fed and a civilian with me to interview a witness. Great."

"He's all bark," Dane said.

They watched Delion stomp up the six stairs to the front door of the Victorian, which was painted four shades of green. He turned. "Hey, come on, you guys, enough chitchat. Let's see what Valerie's got to say."

The place looks terrific," Dane said, touching a pale lime-green gargoyle, one of three hovering over the lintel of the front door, looking down at them. "Business must be good."

"I talked to one of the inspectors in Vice; he said eight hookers live here. Everything very discreet, very respectable, doubtful even the neighbors know anything. There's a back way in, and it's all sorts of private."

Delion rang the bell to 4B. "There's four apartments on each floor."

There was no answer.

He rang again.

There was still no answer.

"It's pretty early," Dane said. "She's probably still asleep."

"Yeah, well, we're her wake-up call." Delion pressed his thumb on the bell and kept it there.

Three minutes later, he rang the bell to 4C.

"Yes? May I help you?"

"Very polite, very discreet," Delion said under his breath, then continued into the intercom, "This is Inspector Vincent Delion of the SFPD. I know I got you up, but I'm a cop and we need to talk to you. This isn't a bust, nothing like that. We're not here to cause you any trouble. We just need to talk."

A pause, then the buzzer sounded.

The entrance was old-fashioned, dripping with Victoriana,

the dark red carpeting rich and deep. Everything was indeed very upscale.

Dane glanced over at Nick Jones. She looked fascinated. Must be her first time in a hooker's nest. Come to think about it, it was his first time, too. Business, he thought, stroking his hand over the beautifully carved newel post on the stairs, was good.

They walked up one flight of stairs, turned right. The lush red carpeting continued. There was wainscoting along the walls of the wide corridor, and well-executed watercolors of the Bay were hung along the walls.

A woman in a lovely black kimono stood in the open doorway to 4C. She was young, with artfully mussed long black hair tossed over one shoulder. She wore almost no makeup. Delion looked at her, appreciated her, and guessed that five hundred bucks wasn't out of the question.

"Ms. . . . ?"

"Elaine Books. What do you want? Hey, she isn't a cop, she's homeless. I know . . . Valerie told me about you, told me you sort of hid in the shadows whenever somebody came around, that you'd only talk to this priest. And you, you're no local, just look at those wing tips; they're a cut above what local guys wear. What are you, a lawyer? What's going on here?"

Delion said, "They're with me, no problem. You really think his shoes look more expensive than mine? Nah, forget it. We need to speak to Valerie Striker, your neighbor in 4B, but she's not answering her doorbell. You seen her this morning?"

"No." Ms. Books frowned, tapped her lovely French manicure against the door frame. "You know, I haven't seen Valerie in a couple of days. What's going on with her?"

Dane said very slowly, "I really don't like the sound of this, Delion."

Delion said, "Right. Ms. Books, we'd like you to come next door with us, watch us open the door, okay?"

"Oh God, you think something's happened to Valerie, don't you?"

"Hopefully not, but we'd like you to verify that we're concerned, and that's why we're going in."

Delion knocked on 4B. There was no answer. He pressed his ear to the door. "Nothing," he said.

Delion put his shoulder to the door of 4B and pushed hard. Nothing happened. "Well made, solid wood, I should have guessed," he said. Both he and Dane backed up, then slammed their shoulders into the door. It flew inward, crashing against the inside wall.

A beautiful apartment, Nick thought, looking past them, all light and airy, so many windows, sunlight flooding in.

Where was Valerie Striker?

Dane stopped suddenly. He became very still. He turned, said very low, his voice urgent, "Ms. Jones, please stay right here. Thank you, Ms. Books. We'll take it from here."

"Hey, what's that smell?" Elaine Books jerked her head back. "Oh God, oh God."

"Stay back," Delion said. He turned to Dane. "Keep them here, all right?"

But it was too late. Before Dane could force Elaine Books and Nick Jones back out of the apartment, Nick saw two white legs sticking out from behind the living room sofa, a really pretty sofa, all white with even whiter pillows strewn across it. All over that white were dark stains, as if someone had dipped a hand into a paint can and just sprinkled the paint everywhere.

"Oh no," Nick said. "It's not paint, is it?"

"No," Dane said, "it's not. Don't move from this spot, you understand me?"

Delion went behind the sofa and knelt down. When he straightened, he looked hard, sad, and angry.

"I think we've found Valerie Striker. She's been strangled. I'd say she's dead a couple of days at least." He nodded to Dane, who herded the two women back into the hallway. He heard Delion on the phone, speaking to the paramedics.

Elaine Books leaned against the corridor wall and started crying. "I'm so sorry," Nick said. "She was your friend. I'm so very sorry. I liked her. She was kind to me, despite—despite how I look." Very slowly, Nick drew the woman into her arms and let her cry on her shoulder.

Nick looked up at Dane. "He killed her. He must have seen her, worried that when she found out about Father Michael Joseph's murder, she'd remember seeing him. He either knew who she was or he found out, came here sometime during the night on Sunday and killed her. That's exactly what happened, isn't it?"

Dane nodded. "Yes, that's probably right."

Elaine Books continued to weep, softly now, her head still on Nick Jones's shoulder.

Valerie Striker was dead. Chances were that she hadn't seen a thing, but that hadn't mattered. She couldn't tell them anything now. Nick closed her eyes as she rocked Elaine Books against her and thought, I'm the one who's supposed to be dead, not her. If only she'd waited for the cops, she would have remembered to tell them about seeing Valerie Striker, and they would have come here, maybe before the killer did, and they could have saved her.

It was her fault.

EIGHT

"She can't stay in the shelter," Dane said. "Do you have a safe house where we can stash her?"

"Yeah," Delion said, "but I don't know if the lieutenant will approve it for her. There's no real threat of danger here."

"You're wrong, Delion. When our guy sees this description—and I bet he will—he'll try to find out about the person who gave it, knowing that if he's ever caught, she can identify him. She'd be a sitting duck at the shelter."

"If she would just tell us her real name and address, we could send her little ass home."

Dane looked over toward the small kitchen where Ms. Nick Jones stood waving a tea bag in a paper cup of hot water, the cuffs of her ratty thick red sweater falling over her fingers. He could still see the tear streaks on her cheeks.

"Look, Dane," Delion said, "you're a cop. You know that since she isn't a teenage runaway, it means she's running from something or someone. That, or she's a druggie—that's the most likely. You notice she's wearing all those sweaters? She's probably hiding needle tracks on her arms.

"Maybe she's wearing them to keep warm. Whatever, it's unfortunate because our Ms. Jones seems bright and speaks well. She's well educated. It was just her bad luck that she was in Saint Bartholomew's on Sunday night, that is, if you believe the story she told us about why she was actually there."

Dane didn't say anything, kept looking at Nick Jones. "She has very nice teeth," he said. "Good dental hygiene."

"Yeah, I noticed. And that means she hasn't been on the street all that long. What? A couple of weeks? Not a month, I'll bet. She doesn't smell and her clothes aren't stiff with dirt."

"No."

"All right, Dane, I'll ask the lieutenant. Now, we've got four murders, all possibly committed by the same perp. We have a pretty fair description of him. Now we need to figure out why he did this."

"Well, we think he meant to do the first three—the old woman, the gay activist, and finally, my brother. Valerie Striker was just in the wrong place at the wrong time."

"Yes, and once we have the why, we'll have him. Let's go meet with the chief, tell him about Valerie Striker. It could have been one of her johns that killed her."

"You don't believe that for a second."

"All right, I don't."

"If the ME pins her murder down to sometime Sunday night, then we know with about ninety-eight percent certainty that the same guy killed her," Dane said. "You go see the chief. I'll speak some more with Ms. Jones."

"You know, I've always wondered why folks can't come up with better aliases. Jones, for God's sake."

"Nick is her real first name though," Dane said. "But it's not short for Nicole."

"You picked up on that lie as well, huh?"

"Oh yes. I wonder what it really is."

A few minutes later, Dane strolled over to the small kitchen. The single donut was gone. Finally tossed? Or was Ms. Jones so hungry that she ate it? He hoped she hadn't. From the looks of that critter, it would have given her food poisoning.

"Would you like some peanuts? Inspector Delion tells me that's the snack of choice here."

"But I just saw one of the men snag a donut that looked like it died last week."

Good, she hadn't eaten it.

"At least the ME is close. Peanuts?"

She shook her head and kept waving the tea bag in the water. "It's nearly black."

"I like tea strong," she said, but pulled out the bag and tossed it in the open trash bin. "It's hard to get really strong tea unless you do it yourself."

"You know I'm Father Michael Joseph's brother, Dane Carver. There's something else, something I don't think you've caught on to yet. I'm also a special agent with the FBI."

She dropped the cup. It splattered hot tea all over her, him, and the Virginia peanuts.

"Oh no, look what I've done. Oh no." She was grabbing paper towels, wiping him down, finally on her knees, wiping up the floor. "I'm sorry."

"It's all right," he said, pulled off another paper towel and joined her. "It's all right, Nick. I'm the one who's sorry."

"Not your fault," she said, staring down at that towel wet through with tea now.

"Hey," an inspector said, coming around the corner, "who took that last donut?"

Dane laughed, just couldn't help it. She didn't.

No can do," Lieutenant Purcell said, standing in her doorway. "No clear and present danger to her. You know that our budget's stretched to the limit, Delion. I'm sorry, but she's on her own."

Dane wondered if it was because she was homeless, and had less worth than someone who had a job and a bit of standing in the community. He didn't say anything. He'd already known the answer would be no and he'd also known what he was going to do.

He hadn't let Nick Jones out of his sight. She looked, quite simply, like she was ready to run. After he left the lieutenant, he went back to the small kitchen. She was still wiping up tea from the counter. "Enough," he said, took her arm, and guided her over to Delion's desk. Delion was in the lieutenant's office. Dane could see him gesticulating through the glass windows. He sat her down, came down beside her on his haunches. "Okay, tell me why you freaked out when I told you I was FBI."

"It was just a surprise, that's all. Your brother is a priest. You're at the other end of the spectrum."

She'd had time to come up with an answer, not a bad one either.

"That's true. What's your real name, Nick?"

"My name is Nick Jones. Just look in the phone book, you'll see there are tons of Joneses. Lots more Joneses than Carvers, that's for sure."

"How long have you been in San Francisco?"

"Not all that long."

"Two, three weeks?"

"Something like that. Two and a half weeks."

"Where did you come from?"

She just shrugged. "Here and there. I like to travel a lot. But it's winter, so it's best to stay in cities that don't get all that cold."

"How old are you?"

"Twenty-eight."

"Where'd you go to school?"

She didn't say a thing, just looked down at her hands, chapped and dry, and her ragged fingernails. Dane sat back in the side chair, crossed his arms over his chest. Finally, she said, "We had a deal here. No questions about me. You got that, Agent Carver? No questions or I'm out of here. I figure you need me, so leave it alone. All right?"

"It's too bad you feel that way," Dane said. "I have the FBI behind me, and you knew my brother. If you're in trouble, I can help you."

Her head came up with that. She seemed stiff all over, but it was hard to tell with all those layers she was wearing. She said, "It's your choice, Agent Carver."

"All right."

"What you need to do is find this man who killed Father Michael Joseph. Is there a death penalty in California?"

"Yes."

"Good. He deserves to die. I was very fond of Father Michael Joseph, even though I only knew him for a short time. He cared about all of us, didn't matter if you were rich or poor or a basically shitty person, he still cared."

Delion came up, shaking his head at Dane. "I had to try again. No go."

Dane said, "Inspector Delion means that there isn't a safe house for you. Given that I firmly believe you need to be kept out of harm's way, I'm taking you with me, back to my hotel. You'll stay with me until we find this guy."

"You're nuts," Nick said. "I'm homeless. No hotel would even let me through the door. Look at me, for God's sake. I look like what I am. Besides, I don't want to stay at a hotel. I'm just fine where I am."

Delion said, "The FBI undoubtedly has a safe house in the area."

"Nope, I don't want to involve them in this. Trust me, Delion, you don't either."

"The camel's-nose-under-the-tent sort of thing? That's fine by me. We don't want Ms. Jones to end up like Valerie Striker. I'm heading to a meeting with the chief now. We're organizing a task force, then we'll have more than enough manpower of our own to catch this creep."

Dane waited to say anything else until Delion was out of earshot. "You're safe for the moment. But, Ms. Jones, when the guy who murdered my brother and three other people realizes his description is out there, you know as well as I do that he'll try to hunt you down. You want to be in that shelter when you hear his footsteps coming up the stairs? There isn't anyone there who could help you."

She went nearly as white as his shirt. "I'll leave San Francisco, go south."

"No, going on the run isn't the answer. If you force us to, we'll arrest you as a material witness."

But evidently Delion wasn't out of earshot. He stopped, said over his shoulder, "You've obviously got a lot of crap going on in your life, Ms. Jones. I'd go with the big Fed if I were wearing your shoes. Let him watch out for you." Delion fanned his hands. "You don't have to worry about our asking you any more questions about your past, okay?"

"No," she said. "I'm stupid for staying this long. I've told you what I know. I'm outta here." She was out of her chair and heading toward the door in a flash.

Delion made a grab for her, but missed.

Dane sighed, said over his shoulder, "She moves fast."

One of the inspectors called out, "She must have learned that in the Tenderloin."

Dane stomped after her. He saw a flash of her red sweater as she ran past the elevator toward the stairs. He caught her just before she made it to the third-floor exit.

He didn't know what he expected, but she fought him like her life depended on it. She kicked and punched and didn't make a single sound while she was trying to kill him.

Why didn't she yell at him?

He finally managed to get behind her and force her arms against her sides. He pulled her back hard against him so she couldn't move.

"Hold still, just hold still."

She was breathing hard, but still she struggled and tugged and heaved. She was strong, workout strong. He simply held on as tightly as he could. She couldn't gain enough leverage to hurt him, but she tried.

A couple of cops came out onto the third-floor landing. "Hey, what's going on here?"

"I'm Dane Carver, FBI," Dane said. "She's trying to escape. Go ask Delion up in Homicide."

"You need any help?"

"No," Dane said. "I wish you'd come about five minutes ago, though."

"Yeah, I can see how you'd have trouble with a perp who's fifty pounds lighter than you. You want us to get Delion? Tough guy, Delion. He can stop a perp, no matter how big."

"Nah. I've finally got her pinned."

She'd quieted, just a bit, but he'd no sooner got the words out of his mouth than she went wild again. She took him by surprise this time, twisting sharply inward, and his hold on her loosened just a bit. She drove her elbow into his belly and was off again, as the air whooshed out of him.

"Yeah, you've got her, all right," one of the officers said, laughing.

Dane caught her again on the second floor just before she ducked into the women's room. "Okay, enough."

He pressed his back against the wall and jerked her back against him. "Let's try this again. That was a good move, that twist. Where'd you learn that?"

She was heaving, panting. She didn't say anything, just stood there, her head down, breathing hard. She didn't say anything for a very long time, but Dane was patient, he'd learned to be. Finally, he said, "Are you afraid the media are going to catch up with you and there'll be a photo or a video?"

"Another word about me, and, believe this—I'm gone. You have no right to question me, no right at all. No more, Agent Carver. No more."

He didn't want to drop it, but he knew he had to. They needed her. Dane sighed. "There just isn't anything easy in this life, you know? Why couldn't you have sold lingerie at Macy's? Something nice and normal?"

"I was nice and normal," she said, realized she'd let something out, and seamed her lips together.

"Oh? Maybe you were in real estate? Advertising? Maybe you were married and your old man knocked you around? All right, you got it, there won't be another word out of me."

"You've got words just waiting to spill out of you. Forget it." She leaned down and bit his hand, hard.

Dane yelled, just couldn't help himself. There were a good dozen folks on them then, half of them cops. She was homeless. There was no question who the good guy was. One uniformed officer grabbed her hair and yanked her head back.

The officer said, "She didn't draw blood, but it was close. You want some help here?"

"Yeah, could I have a pair of cuffs?"

The officer handed them over without even asking for an ID and Dane knew it wasn't because they were careless. He looked like a cop. He pulled her arms behind her and cuffed her wrists. "There," he said. "Now my body parts are safe. Thank you, ah, Officer, ah, Gordon. I'll leave the cuffs with Inspector Delion, up on four."

"No problem. You gotta watch yourself with these people. You might want your hand checked out, you never know what diseases she might be carrying around."

"Yeah, thanks, I will."

He barely understood Nick say "bastard" she had her jaw locked so tight.

"I'm not a bastard. I've got a pedigree. Now, what are we going to do with you?"

"Let me leave. I'll come back, I swear it."

"Nope. Let it go, Ms. Jones. You're with me now. Think of me as your own personal bodyguard. Just let it go. Can you do that?"

As he spoke he turned her around to face him. There was a line of freckles across her nose he hadn't noticed before, quite visible since she was so pale. But what he really saw, and hated, was defeat. She looked crushed, flattened.

He clasped her upper arms and shook her slightly. "Listen to me. I won't let anyone hurt you, I promise."

"You look so much like him."

"Yes, I know, but my brother and I were very different people. Very different. Well, not in all things, but in many."

"Maybe not," she said. "Maybe not. He promised he wouldn't let anyone hurt me either." She bit her lip. "But he's dead. Please, I wasn't responsible for his death, was I?"

She stood there, her arms pulled behind her, her wrists handcuffed, tears streaking down her cheeks.

"No," Dane said. "You weren't responsible. I do know one thing for certain—Michael's murder had nothing at all to do with you. Believe it."

"Oh shit," Delion said, coming to a dead stop about three feet from them. "I don't need this."

NINE

"What size do you wear?"

"I don't want any new clothes. Listen to me, Agent Carver, I just want to stay the way I am now. I have to, don't you understand?"

"You're going to be safer if you look like a reasonably dressed woman rather than a bag lady. This is a very ordinary, inexpensive store, Inspector Bates told me. She said we could get you a couple of things here that look like what everyone else is wearing. Don't give me any more trouble, Ms. Jones. I'm so tired I could sleep leaning against that taxi sign, and I know all the way to my wing tips that I need your help. Don't think of it as a favor to the cops. Think of it as a favor to my brother, you know, the man you really liked and admired. I need you to help me catch his killer."

He knew then that, finally, he'd touched her. He'd made her feel guilty, made her feel beyond selfish if she ran away. She wanted to catch the monster who murdered his brother. Good, whatever worked. It had taken him long enough. Maybe it would help her get over the idea that she was responsible.

What made it even better was that it was only the truth. He did need her.

"All right. Let's get some inexpensive things, then."

"And then some better things."

"I thought you said you were really tired."

"I am. But I'm staying at a good hotel, the Bennington, just off Union Square. I'd like to remain low profile. Having a bag lady on my arm would make everyone think I was some sort of pervert."

"They'd think you didn't have much money, that's for sure."

Dane didn't know where it came from, but he smiled.

Thirty minutes later, they walked out of *The Rag Bag*, a woman's retread clothes store just off Taylor and Post, not far from the Bennington Hotel. Of course in San Francisco, nothing was very far from anything else. She was wearing a decent pair of jeans, a white blouse, and a dark blue pullover V-necked sweater. The cap was gone from her head, her hair ruthlessly brushed back and clipped at the back of her neck.

They didn't get a single look from any of the tourists or staff at the Bennington. Once they were in Dane's room on the fourth floor, he said, "You still don't look like you're quite up to snuff. But better, much better. Would you like to shower and wash your hair or have an early dinner first?"

No big surprise. She opted for dinner. When it arrived twenty minutes later, he waved her to the small circular table with its two chairs and the room-service dinner he'd ordered up for them.

She said, "I look fine, really. No one noticed me at all. I'll just wear these clothes until you can catch this guy."

"Oh? And then you're going to trot back to the shelter? Or maybe panhandle on Union Square?"

"Yes. Whatever."

"I threw away your homeless clothes."

She gave him a long, emotionless look. "I wish you hadn't done that. They were all I had."

"When this is all over, you're not going back to a homeless shelter." He took a bite of his BLT, sat back, looked at her thoughtfully, and said, "No, you weren't going to do that in any case, were you? You're planning to hotfoot it out of town once this is over, aren't you?"

She didn't raise her head, just slowly and steadily ate her way through the pile of french fries on her plate. They were well done, brown and crispy, just the way she liked them.

She said, "You're right, yes. When this is over, I'm gone. I'm thinking about the Southwest. It's really warm there during the winter months."

"At least you're telling me some of the truth now. Hey, you like french fries."

"It's been a while since I've had any. They're wonderful."

"Michael loved french fries, too, claimed they helped him concentrate better on the football field and made girls think he was wearing a really nice aftershave lotion. Who knows?"

She raised her head. "Do you mind if I use your bathroom now?"

He nodded, took another bite of his sandwich, watched her eat one more fry, sigh, and push the plate away. She looked like she wanted to cry. "They're so good, but I just don't have any more room. I didn't know Father Michael Joseph liked french fries. It never came up."

"No, it probably wouldn't have. Do you want to go back to the shelter? Do you have anything there you need?"

"No, thank you. The fact is, if someone does have anything of value, they learn to strap it to their bodies or it's gone in five minutes."

"Sort of like car parts in a bad part of town?"

He wondered what she had strapped to her middle. Papers that would tell him who she was? What or who she was running from?

He listened to the sound of the shower running. He rose and walked to the phone. He'd nearly dialed his sister's number when he slowly laid the receiver back down. No, he couldn't imagine Eloise dealing with Ms. Jones. It would be unfair to both of them. Too much grief on Eloise's part, too much fear on Ms. Jones's. Not a good mix, too much, certainly, to ask of his sister. He'd have to trust her to stay there in the hotel while he was out with Delion. He carefully wrapped her water glass in a handkerchief. There was, at the very least, a nice clear thumbprint.

When she walked out of the bathroom nearly an hour later, Dane nearly dropped his coffee cup. The bag lady was gone. She was scrubbed, her hair clean and blow-dried, and the recycled clothes looked just fine on her.

She looked like a college kid with that fresh face of hers. He hadn't realized it, but her hair was more blond than brown now that it was clean, but there were lots of different shades, and it was on the curly side. She had it clipped again at the back of her neck. Her eyes, clear and sharp with intelligence, were a mix of gray and green. She was, he saw, quite nice-looking.

"You look fine now," he said, satisfied that he sounded only mildly pleased. The last thing he needed was for her to fear that he'd jump her. "I've got to go back to Homicide. I want you to stay here, in this room. Watch TV, or, if you want, go downstairs and buy some paperbacks, whatever. Just don't leave the hotel. Okay?"

He gave her fifty bucks even though she just kept shaking her head until he stuffed it in her jeans pocket. He realized then that she hadn't answered him.

He said again, "Listen to me. Promise you won't leave the hotel."

Finally she said, "Oh, all right. I promise."

He really hoped that she wasn't a liar.

He called his sister on his cell phone on his way back to Bryant Street, listened to her arrangements for their brother's funeral.

Michael was dead. They were actually talking about burying him. Dane couldn't stand it. Instead of going to the Hall of Justice, he drove back to St. Bartholomew's, at his sister's request, to see that everything was being handled. Father Binney, red-eyed, a slight tremor in his veiny white hands, had spoken to Bishop Koshlap and Archbishop Lugano. Everything had been arranged, everyone notified. Father Michael Joseph's funeral would take place at St. Bartholomew's on Friday afternoon, since there was another funeral already scheduled for the morning, and the wake Wednesday evening. "I am so sorry," he said over and over. "If only I hadn't talked him into seeing that man, that monster. I'm so very sorry."

Dane wished he could tell Father Binney again that he wasn't at fault here, that it was the monster who had murdered four people here in San Francisco, but the words just wouldn't come out of his mouth.

He drove too quickly to the Hall of Justice and was pulled over just south of Market by a motorcycle cop.

When he handed over his FBI shield, the officer just stared down at it, laughed, then said, "Hey, you on a big case?"

Dane just nodded.

"No ticket this time, Special Agent. Just watch the speed."

Dane thanked the officer and continued to speed to the Hall of Justice, despite the choking traffic.

He was shown into the task force room, which was actually the conference room next to the chief's office. Kreider's assistant, Maggie, told him the chief wanted lots of say on this one, wanted to be the first one to know if anything broke.

There were fifteen people crowded in the room. Dane stood leaning against the back wall and listened to Delion finish up.

". . . Okay, everyone knows the drill. The guy who just came in, over by the door, is Special Agent Dane Carver, FBI. His brother was Father Michael Joseph. He's not here as a Fed, just as a cop, and so he's a part of this hunt. Anybody got anything to say? No? Okay, that's it."

Dane looked up at the time line thumbtacked to the wall, at the photos of the four people murdered. Chief Kreider squeezed Dane's shoulder on his way out.

Delion said to Dane, "I'll bet our guys even have their moms working on this thing, Dane. We'll nail the guy, you'll see. Now, we're scheduled to see the medical examiner. Dr. Boyd promised he'd do Valerie Striker first thing. How's Ms. Jones?"

"She's fine. She swore to me she wouldn't leave the hotel."

An eyebrow went up. "You believed her?"

"Short of locking her up, I really didn't have a choice, but yeah, I do."

"You get her cleaned up?"

"Oh yes. She looks like a grad student."

"A grad student? You know, maybe that's a possibility. She looks brainy, speaks real well."

Dane shook his head. "She's smart, she's too scared to hide that. Graduate student? She seems a bit old for that, but who knows?"

Delion said, "I'm told by my sister—she's a professor of anthropology over at UC Davis—that there's a lot of cutthroat stuff in academia, more vicious, she says, than the business world. Of course, she doesn't really know what she's talking about but do you think our girl could be running from a badass professor?"

"Could be," Dane said, and burst out laughing, just couldn't help himself. "A killer professor. I like that, Delion. Let's stop by and see whose fingerprints are on this glass."

"Ms. Jones?"

"Yes, a beautiful clear thumb. If she won't tell us who she is, just maybe her prints are on file. You never know. And, Delion, thanks for making me laugh."

"No problemo."

Dr. Boyd met them at the morgue counter. "Valerie Striker was garrotted," he said. "Nothing more, nothing less."

Dane said, "Can you give us a time, sir?"

"It's difficult, but I'd say it was toward the middle of the night, Sunday night."

"Good enough."

Dr. Boyd said, "Same man who killed Father Michael Joseph?"

Delion nodded. "Yeah, if that's when she died, then it was probably him. She was a loose end."

"Now for my good news, gentlemen. Ms. Striker didn't go easily. She may have got some of him under her fingernails, probably skin from his neck."

"DNA," Delion said, and did a little dance.

"Get me a match and we'll fry the guy, Inspector Delion."

They watched Dr. Stephen Boyd walk away, pause to speak to one of his investigators, then continue toward his office.

"Hot damn," Delion said. "You know, no one ever even makes a joke about that man? No Sawbones, no Doctor Death, nothing like that. He's a straight arrow, smart, does what he says he'll do. When the pressure builds, the brass are really heating things up, Dr. Boyd never panics, just lowers his head and keeps marching."

"Good for him," Dane said. "On the other hand, if he did panic, the person on the slab wouldn't be able to tell anyone about it."

"True enough. Now, if that sample's got DNA in it, it's our first real break."

TEN

CHICAGO

Nick had never been so happy in her life. Well, maybe when she'd had her Ph.D. diploma placed reverently into her hand, but that was more a huge sense of relief than pure, unadulterated happiness. It was because of her fiancé, John Kennedy Rothman, senior senator from Illinois. "No relation," he'd told her, a lowly new volunteer in his reelection campaign three years before. That was before his wife, Cleo Rothman, disappeared, just up and ran away with one of his senior aides, Tod Gambol. Because everyone knew he loved his wife dearly, her abandoning her husband had given him an incredible sympathy vote and he'd been swept back into office by a 58/42 margin over his opponent, who'd been portrayed as too liberal for the fiscal health of both Illinois and the country, though he really hadn't been at all. Truth was, John's overpowering charm, his ability to look straight at a person and have that person believe that he would be the best at whatever he tried, was the overriding reason he was voted in.

And now she was going to marry him. It was heady. There were nearly twenty years separating them, but she didn't care. She had no parents to gainsay her decision, only two brothers, both Air Force pilots, both in Europe, both younger than she.

She knew all about campaigning now, what it would be like to live in a fishbowl. But the media really hadn't come after her yet, and she prayed they wouldn't, at least not until after they were married and she'd be able to simply step behind John as she smiled and waved.

It was a dark night, the wind whipping her hair back from her face, because it was, after all, Chicago. When you were walking the deep canyons, buildings soaring up on either side, and the wind swept off Lake Michigan, funneling through those buildings, whipping the temperature down, it could make your teeth chatter and your bones rattle. She ducked her head and walked faster. One more block and she'd be home. Why hadn't she taken a taxi? No, ridiculous. When she got home, she'd sit in front of her small fireplace, pull over her legs the heavy red afghan that her mom had knitted eight years before, and read some essays from her senior medieval research class.

She looked both ways, didn't see a single soul, and stepped into the street. It happened so fast, she wasn't certain what had actually happened after she was safely back in her apartment. A black car, a big job, with four doors, swept up the street, lights off, and veered straight at her. She saw that it was accelerating, not slowing, not swerving out of the way. No, it was coming straight on, and it was going to hit her.

She hurled herself sideways. She hit a fire hydrant and went crashing down on her hip. She felt the hot air, smelled the sour rubber of the tires as the sedan sped by. She lay there, pain pulsing through her hip, wondering why no one was around. Not a single person was stupid enough to be out in this weather. Oh God. Would the car come back?

She got up, tried to run, but ended up hobbling back across the street. She saw a bum in the alley just next to her condo building. He'd seen everything.

"Crazy bugger," the guy said, lifted a bottle to his mouth, and drank down a good pint.

She fumbled with her building door key, finally got it to turn, and almost fell into the lobby, so afraid that she just hung there, leaning against a huge palm, breathing hard. There was a neighbor, Mrs. Kranz, standing there. The old lady, a widow of a Chicago firefighter, helped her to her condo, stuffed aspirins down her throat, and sat her down as she built up the fire in the fireplace.

"What happened, dear?"

Dear God, it was hard to speak, hard to get enough saliva in her mouth. She finally got out, "Someone—someone tried to run me down."

Mrs. Kranz patted her arm. "You're all right, aren't you?" At Nick's nod, because she really couldn't speak, Mrs. Kranz said, "A drunk, more like it. Right?"

Nick just shook her head. "I don't know. I really don't know." A drunk? She'd felt all the way to her bones that it was someone who wanted to hurt her. Maybe even kill her. Was that unlikely? Sure it was, but it didn't change how she felt. A drunk. That might be right. Damn.

She thanked Mrs. Kranz, forgot the papers she was going to

grade, and went to bed. She shuddered beneath the covers, cold from the inside out.

When she finally slept, it was only to see that big dark car again, then another and another, all around her. She saw a man driving each car, and each man was wearing a ski mask pulled over his face. There was a kaleidoscope of madness in each man's eyes, but she didn't recognize any of them. There were so many, she didn't know where to look. She was spinning around, with all the cars coming toward her. She woke up screaming, breathing hard, soaked with sweat. She jerked up in bed. As she sat there in the predawn gloom, she saw those eyes again with their stark light of madness and thought they looked somehow familiar. When she was breathing more easily, she got up, went to the bathroom, leaned over the sink, and drank from the faucet. No, that didn't make any sense. There was no one who wanted to hurt her. She didn't have any enemies except for maybe one of the ancient professors at the university who didn't believe women should know anything about medieval history, much less teach it. Her hip throbbed with pain, and putting any weight at all on that leg made her groan. She took three aspirins and crawled back into bed.

She managed to sleep another hour, then awoke feeling groggy, her hip aching something fierce. She downed more aspirins, looked at herself in the bathroom mirror, and nearly scared herself to death. She looked pale, sick, like she'd been in a really bad accident. A drunk, she said to the image staring back at her. It had to be a drunk. She stripped off her pajamas, looked at the huge purple bruise covering her right hip, wished she had something stronger than aspirin, and got under the shower. Ten minutes later she felt a bit more human. It had to be a drunk, not an old relic of a professor, not a wild teenager out to scare her, no, a drunk, a simple up-front drunk.

The eyes, the madness, that was just a dream spun out of fear.

She didn't bother reporting it to the police. She had no license plate, so what could they do? She told John about it, and he held her close, stroking her hair. He repeated what Mrs. Kranz had said. "A stupid drunk, that's all. It's all right, Nicola. It's all right. You're safe now."

She didn't sleep well after that night, not until her first night wrapped in a blanket atop a very hard, narrow cot in the upstairs dorm of a homeless shelter in San Francisco.

SAN FRANCISCO

Wednesday evening, after a day of endless interviews, trying to find any connection between the murdered gay activist, the murdered old woman, and his brother, with no luck at all, Dane realized he had no choice but to take Nick with him to his brother's wake. He'd had her with him most of the day, primarily because he just didn't trust her to stay put in his room at the hotel, and she'd been a silent partner, saying very little and ordering more french fries for lunch at a fast food place in Ghiradelli Square.

But before he could take her to the wake, they had to stop at Macy's in Union Square and buy her a black dress, both for the wake that night and for the funeral to be held on Friday afternoon. And black shoes. Neither of them wanted to, but it had to be done.

They didn't arrive at the kind of Irish wake filled with a sea of voices, boisterous laughter, even louder sobs, lots of hair-raising stories about the deceased, lots of food, and too much booze.

This wake was attended by more men wearing black than Dane could count, all of them somber, and only two women, Ms. Jones and Eloise DeMarks, his sister, both wearing simple black dresses, both looking pale.

Father Binney greeted them in a hushed whisper, told them that both Archbishop Lugano and Bishop Koshlap were there. Dane didn't care, but Father Binney seemed to believe it was a great honor to Michael. So be it.

Eloise, tall and thin, her lipstick looking garish on her too-pale face, was dark-haired and dark-eyed just like her brothers. Grief bowed her shoulders, and she was as silent as their mother had been for those six long months before she finally left their philandering father. Dane didn't know if their father knew one of his sons was dead. They hadn't been able to reach him. Their mother had died of a ruptured appendix while traveling on safari in western Africa. Dane remembered that they hadn't heard a word from their father then.

Dane didn't want to view his brother's body again. He simply couldn't bear it. He waited at the back of the rectory chapel, his arms hanging at his sides, not moving, just wishing it was over.

His brother was dead. He'd forget for minutes at a time, but then it would smack him again—the terrible finality of it, the viciousness of it, the fact that he would never see his brother again, ever. Never get another phone call, another e-mail, another stupid joke about a priest, a rabbi, and a preacher . . .

How did people bear this pain?

Nick was standing just behind him. She picked up his hand,

smoothed out the fist he'd made. Her skin was rough but warm. She said, "They're honoring Father Michael Joseph, doing the best they can, but it's so very hard, isn't it?"

He couldn't speak. He just nodded. He felt her fingers stroke his hand, gently massage his fingers, easing the muscles.

She said, "I want to see him one last time."

He didn't answer her, and didn't look at her, until she returned to stand beside him.

"He's beautiful, Dane, and he's at peace. It's just his body here, not his spirit. I firmly believe that there is a Heaven, and since Father Michael Joseph was such a fine man, he's there, probably looking down at us, so happy to see that you're here and that you're safe. And he knows how much you love him, there's no doubt at all in my mind about that. I know he must feel sorry for your pain. I'm sorry, Dane, so very sorry."

He couldn't find words. He squeezed her hand. "Just three weeks ago—Christmas was just three weeks ago, can you believe that? Michael and I went down to San Jose to be with Eloise, her husband, and our nephews. Michael gave me an autographed Jerry Rice football. It's on my fireplace mantel. Only odd thing about it was that Jerry's an Oakland Raider now. Michael thought that was a hoot. Jerry in silver and black. I never saw him after I flew out on the twenty-seventh."

"What did you give Father Michael Joseph for Christmas? I'm sorry, but I don't think I'll ever be able to call him just Michael."

Dane said, "It's all right. I gave him a Frisbee. I told him I wanted to see his robes flapping around when he ran after the thing. And I gave him a book on the Dead Sea Scrolls, a topic that always fascinated Michael." He fell silent, wondering what would happen to Michael's things. He had to remember to ask Father

Binney. He wanted to look at that book that Michael had touched, read, and see his inscription to his brother in the front. He'd written something smart-ass, but he didn't remember exactly what.

Michael should have lived until he was at least eighty, maybe as an archbishop, like Lugano, that venerable old man with his mane of white hair. But he was dead because some madman had decided to kill him. For whatever reason.

Dane stood, back against the rectory wall, watching with Nick beside him, silent now, still holding his hand. It seemed that every priest in San Francisco had come, and each of them walked in his measured way over to Dane, each with something kind to say, each telling him what a shock it was to see how much he looked like Michael.

The whole time, Dane was wondering how they were going to catch the man who killed his brother and the other people. There wasn't a single good lead, truth be told, even though Chief Kreider had told the media that all avenues were being explored, and some looked very hopeful. All of that was advanced cop talk for *we haven't got diddly,* Delion had said under his breath.

Delion came up to him, nodded to Nick, and stood silently beside him. All three of them stood there in black, just like all the priests.

Dane said to Delion, "I've been thinking. Three murders in San Francisco—and no tie-in among the victims that anyone can find."

"True, unfortunately. But that doesn't mean there isn't a connection. We just have to find it."

Dane looked toward his brother's coffin, surrounded by branches of lit candles. "It seems like it was all well rehearsed, no mistakes, and that got me to wondering. Do you think this man has killed before?"

Delion frowned as he said, "You mean has he done this same sort of thing in another city?"

"Yes."

"He's some sort of serial killer? He comes to a city and randomly selects victims, then leaves to go someplace else?"

"No, not really that," Dane said. "He targeted my brother, no question about that, maybe even before he killed the old woman and the gay activist. Chances are they were random. What do you think, Nick?"

She blinked, and he saw her surprise that he wanted her opinion. She said, "If that's true, then Father Michael Joseph must have been the focus, don't you think? Maybe the whole point of all this was so the guy could tell Father Michael Joseph what he'd done, and dare him to say anything. Maybe it was some sort of game to him, his selection of Father Michael Joseph, at least, determined before he did these horrible things. I don't know. This is what you were talking about earlier and I thought a lot about it. I think you're right."

Dane said, "Yes, I still feel that way. I think it was all about the priest to him. There was planning here, his selection of my brother, at least, determined before he began killing. Or maybe any priest would do and Michael was a random choice, too."

Delion said, "So the guy thinks one day, I want to murder a priest, but before I do, I'm going to kill other people and rub the priest's nose in it when I confess it to him, watch him squirm because he's bound to silence. Do you think the perp is that sick?" Dane saw that Delion had included Nick in the question. She looked intent, like she was thinking ferociously. He didn't know why, but he liked that.

Dane said, "That may be close enough."

"Jesus, Dane. Then we've got to look for any other murders involving priests."

Nick said slowly, her brow furrowed, "I just don't know. That makes it sound pretty unlikely."

None of them said anything more. Dane watched Archbishop Lugano stare down at his brother, his lips moving in a prayer. Then he crossed himself, his movements a smooth ritual, leaned down, and kissed Michael's forehead.

Dane felt tears film his eyes. He nodded to Delion and turned abruptly away, realizing that Nick was still holding his hand. "I just can't stay any longer," he said, and she understood. They made their way through the waves of black-garbed priests and walked together from the chapel.

CHICAGO

Nick's eyes were wide open, she knew they were, but she couldn't see anything. No, wait. She was in a room, dark, almost black. She could feel how thick the blackness was, how heavy it was settling around her, with not a shred of light coming in. She lay there, on her back, looking up at a ceiling she couldn't really see, wondering what was happening, hoping she wasn't dead.

She tasted something sour, something that made her want to gag, but she knew she shouldn't gag or she'd start to choke. At least she was alive.

There was something in her mouth, something at the back of her throat. Then she remembered.

It had been a lovely evening in December, just a few days before Christmas, not too cold, no snow for the past three days, and the winds were fairly calm. Such a splendid occasion, perfectly orchestrated, naturally so, since John's private assistant had arranged it. Albia's birthday dinner was at John's magnificent Rushton Avenue condominium penthouse, looking out on Lake Michigan. It hadn't been just the three of them, no, Elliott Benson was there, a man she didn't trust, didn't like. He was rich and charming, supposedly a friend of John's, and she'd been told they'd known each other since college, but the truth was, whenever she had to spend time with him, she always wanted to go home and take a shower. She'd wanted it just to be the three of them, no aides, no other important people to coddle who had been or would be of assistance to John's career, but Albia had wanted him there.

Albia was John's older sister, an elegant, articulate woman, rich in her own right from ownership of several successful men's boutiques. Albia had been in John's corner since their mother had died when he was only sixteen and Albia twenty-three. She was turning fifty-five, but she looked a dozen years younger. She'd married when she'd turned thirty, been widowed just a year later. Albia had always been reserved, even standoffish with all the campaign volunteers, but since John had begun dating Nick, she'd warmed up considerably. Nick felt very close to her, indeed she was becoming a confidante.

Tonight, there was so much excitement, a feast on the dining table, a gorgeous diamond bracelet, presented by John to his sister, around Albia's wrist, winking and glittering in the soft glow of the half dozen lighted candles on the table. Elliott Benson had charmed and joked and flattered Albia, presenting her with diamond earrings that easily rivaled the bracelet John had gotten her. They were in her ears, gorgeous earrings. Elliott was trying to outdo John, it was easy enough to see, at least to Nick. Why had Albia wanted him there?

Nick's gift to Albia was a silk scarf imprinted with a Picasso painting that she'd found in Barcelona. Albia, exclaiming over that lovely scarf, had said, "Oh, I remember that Mother had a scarf very similar to this one. She loved that scarf—"

And her voice had dropped like a stone off a cliff.

Nick, filled with Albia's pleasure, pleased that her scarf had reminded her of John's mother, said, "Oh, John, you've never spoken of your mother."

John shot a look at his sister. She shook her head slightly, as if in apology, and looked back down at her plate.

"That's right, John," Elliott said, "I never even met your mother. Hey, didn't she die? A long time ago?"

"That's right," John said, his voice curt. "Nicola, you knew, didn't you? It was a car accident. It's been many, many years. We don't often speak about her."

She said, "A car accident? Oh my, I hadn't realized. I'm so very sorry. It must have been such a shock to both of you."

"Not to my father," John said.

Elliott started to say something, then chewed thoughtfully on a medallion of veal and stared at one of the paintings on the dining room wall.

Albia said, "It was a bad time. Would you please pass me the green beans, Nicola?"

Elliott told stories of college days. All of them involved girls that both men had wanted. His stories were funny, utterly charming, and many times he made himself the dupe, but still, it was a very strange thing. "Then, of course," he said, "there was Melissa—no, let's not speak of her this evening. I'm sorry, John. Another toast. To Albia, the loveliest lady in Chicago." And while he drank the toast, he looked at Nick and she wanted to slap that oily look off his handsome face.

Over a dessert of crème brûlée, Nick felt a sudden cramp, then another, this one stronger, more vicious. She had to excuse herself to run to the bathroom, where she got sick, and soon felt so ill, so utterly miserable, that she just wanted to curl up and die.

The pain was ghastly, her belly twisting and knotting. She threw up until she was shaking and sweating and couldn't stand. She remembered hugging the toilet with Elliott, John, and Albia standing next to her, not knowing what to do until Albia said, "I think we should call an ambulance, John. She's really sick. Elliott, go wait downstairs for them. Go, both of you! Quickly!"

And here she was in a hospital bed and they'd pumped her stomach. She remembered now that they'd told her about that before she fell asleep again, thanks to something very nice they'd given her. At least her stomach was calm. In fact, her belly felt hollow, scooped out, shrunk down to nothing at all. It hurt, but it was a dull ache, as if she'd been hungry for too long.

She remembered now that after they'd pumped her stomach, she lay on the hospital gurney feeling like she'd been bludgeoned with several baseball bats. Just on the edge of blissful drugged sleep, she remembered all those mad eyes staring at her from behind ski masks in her dreams, breathed in the smell of the exhaust from the big dark car that had nearly flattened her into the concrete.

It was so very dark. She turned her head just a bit and saw a flashing red light. What was that?

Then she heard a movement. Someone was in the room, close to her. She nearly stopped breathing.

She whispered around that miserable tube down her throat, "Who's there?"

A man, she knew it was a man, and his breathing was close to her, too close.

"Nicola."

Thank God, it was John. Why had she thought it could be Elliott Benson? There was no reason for him to be here.

She started crying, she couldn't help it.

She felt his hand on her shoulder. "It's all right, Nicola. You'll be fine. You must stop crying."

But she couldn't.

He rang the bell. In just a moment, the door opened, flooding the hospital room with light from the hallway. Then the overhead light in the room went on.

"What's the problem, Senator?"

"She's crying and she'll choke if you don't get that tube out of her throat."

"Yes, we have an order for that, once she is awake." She was standing over Nicola now, saying, "This isn't fun, is it? Okay, this won't be pleasant, Nicola, but it's quick."

After the tube came out, her throat felt like it was burning inside.

The nurse said, "Don't be alarmed about the pain in your throat. After all that's happened, it'll be sore for a couple more days." The nurse took a Kleenex and wiped her eyes, her face. "You'll be just fine now, I promise."

She got the tears under control. She took a dozen good-sized breaths, calmed her heartbeat. "What happened?"

"Probably food poisoning," John said. "You ate something bad, but we got you to the emergency room in time."

"But what about you? Albia? Are you ill?"

"No, we're fine. So is Elliott."

"It appears," the nurse said as she took Nicola's pulse, "that only you ate whatever was bad." She eased Nicola's arm back under the covers. "The senator believes it might have been a raspberry vinaigrette. You've got to sleep now. Senator Rothman will see to everything."

And she wondered, why hadn't John or Albia or Elliott gotten ill from the food?

John kissed her forehead, not her mouth, and she didn't blame him a bit for that. She wished she could have something to get rid of the dreadful taste, but she was so tired, so empty of words and feelings, that she just closed her eyes.

She heard John say to the nurse, "I'll be back in the morning to speak with the doctor, see that she's discharged. Oh, no, I can't. I have a meeting with the mayor. I'll send one of my people to see to things."

They continued speaking, in low voices, into the hallway. The overhead light clicked off. The door closed.

She was shut into the blackness again. But she knew this time she was alone and it was warm here, nothing to disturb her except that small nagging voice in her head: food poisoning from vinaigrette dressing? What nonsense. She'd eaten so little of everything because she was excited about Albia's birthday, the gift she'd given her, and she wanted desperately for Albia to be her friend, to accept her. She wondered as she fell back into sleep if she would have died if she'd eaten more.

She'd had food poisoning before, on a hunting trip with her dad, when she'd eaten bad meat. It hadn't been like this.

The next morning, the doctors couldn't say exactly what had made her sick. They'd taken blood tests, said they would analyze what was in her stomach and tested both the senator and his sister, but nothing was found.

Unfortunately, Mrs. Beasley, John's cook and housekeeper,

had already thrown all the food away, washed all the dishes. No way to know, the doctors said. Finally they'd let her go.

She'd nearly died. For the second time in a week and a half.

SAN FRANCISCO

Nick touched her fingertips to her throat, remembering how it had hurt for a good two days after she'd left the hospital in Chicago. She turned on her side, saw Dane's outline on that wretched too-short sofa not more than twelve feet from her, sighed, and finally fell asleep in her bed at the Bennington Hotel. She was afraid, afraid those mad, dark eyes would come gleaming out of the darkness at her, just over her head, hovering just out of reach. She prayed she wouldn't have any more nightmares.

Dane, sprawled on the sofa across the room, never stirred. He awoke with a start at 7 a.m. to see Nick Jones dressed in the blue jeans and white shirt he'd bought her, feet bare, pacing back and forth in front of him. He realized he'd slept hard, which was unexpected since the damned sofa was too short and hard as the floor. The TV was on, he could see the reflection of the colors in the mirror over the vanity table, but there was no sound.

"Thank God you're awake."

For as long as he could remember, when Dane woke up, he was instantly alert, and he was now. "What's the matter, Nick?"

She blew out her breath, splayed her hands in front of her. She took a step closer to him and said, "I know what's going on. I know."

ELEVEN

Dane swung his legs over the side of the sofa and stood quickly, the blankets falling to the floor at his feet. "You know what?" His sweatpants were low on his belly, and he quickly pulled them back up. He grabbed her hands, covered them. "What, Nick? What do you know?"

"Yes, okay. Listen, you were out like a light last night. I woke up, then couldn't go back to sleep and so I watched TV, turned down really low. It's a show, Dane, a TV show on the Premier Channel, a new one, just started probably a couple of weeks ago. It came on at eleven o'clock, called *The Consultant*. It was about these murders in Chicago and how this special Federal consultant comes in and solves them. It was kind of *X-File*-y, you know, unexplained stuff that gives you goose bumps and makes you look toward the window if it's really dark outside. I wasn't really paying too much attention until there was this creepy guy in a confessional, and I realized he was talking to a priest about what he'd done, taunting him about the people he'd killed, and then when the priest was pleading with him to stop, he laughed and shot him through the forehead. Dane, it wasn't about murders in Chicago, it was like the murders right here, in San Francisco."

Dane rubbed his forehead, dashed his fingers through his hair. He couldn't get his brain around what she'd just said. It didn't seem possible. He said finally, "You're telling me that some asshole murdered my brother because he was following the script of some idiotic TV show?"

"Yes. When the show was over, I watched all the credits and wrote down everything I could."

Dane dragged his fingers through his hair again, drew a deep breath, and said, "I'm going to order some coffee, then you're going to tell me everything, every little detail. Oh damn, let me call Delion. You're pretty sure about this?"

"I'm positive. I just couldn't believe it. I nearly woke you up, but realized that there wasn't much of anything you could do at midnight. And you were so tired."

"It's okay."

LOS ANGELES

After arriving at LAX on the 9 a.m. Southwest shuttle from Oakland airport, Inspector Delion, Special Agent Carver, and the woman they introduced as Ms. Nick Jones, with no designation at all, stepped into Executive Producer Frank Pauley's office with its big glass windows that looked across Pico toward the ocean. You couldn't see it because the smog was sitting heavy and gray over the city, but you could see the golf course.

Mr. Pauley was slightly built, tall, pleasant looking, and very pale. Surely that shouldn't be right, Nick thought. Wasn't everyone in LA supposed to be tanned from head to toe? He looked to be somewhere in his forties, and had a nice smile, albeit a nervous one when he met them. She couldn't blame him for that.

He shook hands all around, offered them coffee, and pointed them to the very long gray sofa that lined half the wall. It must have been at least eighteen feet long. There were chairs facing that sofa, all of them gray, and three coffee tables spaced out to form separate sitting groups.

Frank Pauley said, waving toward the sofa, "I just took over. I inherited this office and all the gray from the last executive producer. He said he liked a really big casting couch." He grinned at Nick, who didn't grin back, and said, "You called, Inspector Delion, because you believe that the murders in *The Consultant* that played last night are similar to murders that were committed in San Francisco over the last week and a half."

"That's right," Delion said. "But before we discuss any more of this, we'd like to see the show, compare all the points, make a final determination. Ms. Jones is the only one of us who's seen it so far."

"This is, naturally, very disturbing. Just a moment, please." Frank Pauley turned to the gray phone, punched in a couple of buttons.

Nick said, "Thank God you've only aired two of the shows."

Dane said, "We'll watch both episodes, Mr. Pauley. If we've got a match with San Francisco, we'll find out whether there have been any crimes that follow the first episode. We have no way of knowing whether the murderer would continue if you stop showing the episodes. But I presume the studio will announce that the show's been canceled?"

Frank Pauley cleared his throat. "Let me be up front here. Our lawyers have recommended that we immediately cancel the show and provide you with complete cooperation. Naturally, the studio is appalled that some maniac would do this, if, indeed, we discover that the episode does match the murders in San Francisco."

Dane said, "We appreciate it. Naturally you will have to be concerned about legal action."

"We always are," Frank Pauley said. "They're waiting for us in room fifty-one."

"Room fifty-one?" Nick said.

"A little joke, Ms. Jones, just a little film joke. It's our own private theater. We can see the first and second episodes now, if you wish."

Delion said, "Later, perhaps we can see the third episode as well."

"That's not a problem," Pauley said, waving a left hand that sported four diamond rings. Dane felt a man's instant distaste. Hey, maybe four different wives had given them to him, one never knew, here in LA.

They sat in the small darkened theater and watched the second episode of *The Consultant*. The city was Chicago, the church, St. John's, the priest, Father Paul. Dane watched Father Paul as he listened to a man telling him about the murder he'd just committed—an old woman he'd bludgeoned to death, no sport in that, was there? But hey, she was another soul lost from Father Paul's parish, wasn't she? Two nights later, a black activist was garroted in front of a club, ah, yes, yet another soul lost from Father Paul's parish, and what was the priest going to do about it? The murderer mocks the priest's beliefs, claims the Church is the perfect calling for men who can't face life, that the priest is nothing but a coward who can't even tell a soul, because he's bound by rules that really don't make a whole lot of sense, now do they?

In the fourth and final meeting, after two more murders, the priest loses it. He sobs, pleading with the murderer, raging against God for allowing this monster to exist, raging against his own deeply held beliefs, hating his own helplessness. The murderer laughs, tells him you live like a coward, you die like a coward, and shoots the priest in the forehead.

Dane leaned forward and shut off the projector. He said to Pauley, "Your writers made a mistake here. A priest is bound to silence only when it is a real confession, that is, when the penitent truly means to repent. In a case like this, where the man is mocking the sacrament itself, the priest isn't bound to silence."

Pauley stared at him. "But I thought—"

"I know," Dane said. "Everybody believes that. But the Church makes that exception. Now, if you'll excuse me, I'll be out in the hall."

The truth was, he couldn't bear the show another minute. He leaned against the wall, his eyes closed, trying to get a grip on himself. But he kept seeing the man firing that gun, shooting the priest in the forehead.

He felt her hand on his arm. They stood still, saying nothing, for a very long time. Finally, Dane drew several deep breaths and raised his head. "Thank you," he said.

She only nodded.

Delion came out of the small theater. "You didn't miss much. We have this big-shot consultant dude with some mythical agency in Washington, D.C., come riding into town—the guy's real sensitive, feels people's pain, all that crapola—he cleans the whole mess up because the local cops are stupid and don't have any extrasensory abilities, and he can 'see' things, 'intuit' things that they can't. It ended good except for five dead people."

Dane said, "He killed two more people in the show than he did in San Francisco."

"Yes. And maybe that means then that your brother didn't stick to the script and that's why the guy shot him after the two murders. Remember, your brother told Father Binney that he was going to make a decision that would change his life forever. There's only one threat your brother could have made to shut this guy down."

"Yes," Dane said. "Michael told the killer that he was going to tell the police about what this man had done."

Nick said, "And the guy had no choice but to shoot him. Father Michael Joseph wrecked the guy's script. He stopped him."

"Your brother must have told him what he was planning to do on Sunday night and the guy had no choice but to kill him. The other two people in the show were a guy who owned a bakery and a prominent businessman. If it hadn't been for Father Michael Joseph, there might be two more dead people in San Francisco."

"The guy kept saying that this Father Paul had lost another soul from his parish," Dane said. "Do we know if the two victims in San Francisco attended Saint Bartholomew's?"

"They're not on the membership list," Delion said. "But if the guy was following the script, the chances are good that they did attend mass occasionally. That would tie it all up with a pretty bow, wouldn't it?"

"Yes," Dane said, "it would. Not that it's any help."

Delion just shook his head. "I don't believe this. A damned script. The guy's copycatting a damned TV script."

"Not copycatting," Dane said. "Don't forget, the murders took place before the show aired. Look, at least we know for sure the guy has to be here, has to be somehow involved with the show. No outsider would know the scripts that well."

Savich typed on MAX's screen: *Episode One of* The Consultant—*set in Boston, three murders: a secretary, a bookie, and an insurance salesman, about two to three weeks ago.* "Dane, I'll check— Hey, wait a second. Ah, Sherlock, who was reading over my shoulder, just said these murders were not in Boston, but actually happened two and a half weeks ago, in Pasadena, California."

"Bingo," Dane said. "I'll tell Delion and he can call the cops in Pasadena. Nice and close to Los Angeles."

"Dane, the guy's officially taken this show on the road. You're now formally FBI, working this case. If you want to use the San Francisco field office, call Bert Cartwright, coordinate with him. You will remain in charge of the Federal part of the investigation, all right?"

"Yes, all right, but the thing is, Savich, the killer has to be here in Los Angeles, someone working for the studio, someone working on this specific show, or with access to it."

"Yes, of course, you're right. I'll let Gil Rainy know—he's the SAC down in LA—that you'll be coordinating with him. But you'll be calling the shots. I'll make sure everyone's clear on that."

"Thanks, Savich."

There was a brief silence, then a chuckle. "And that means you've got MAX at your disposal."

There was incredulity in Dane's voice. "You mean you're going to send MAX out for me?"

"Get a grip here, Dane. Deep-six that fantasy. No, let me know what you need and I will—personally—set MAX to work."

"Oh, so I didn't catch you in a weak moment."

"Never that weak." A pause, then, "How are you holding up, Dane?"

"Michael's funeral is on Friday afternoon."

The words were spoken with finality, cold and frozen over.

Savich said, "We'll be thinking about you. Just call when you need something."

"Thanks, Savich." Dane closed his cell phone and walked into the West LA Division on Butler Avenue. It was a big blocky concrete box with an in-your-eye bright orange tile entrance, evidently someone's idea of cheering up the place. Truth be told, the building was old and ugly, but humongous, nearly a full city block, with a parking lot beside it for the black-and-whites. Across the street was another lot and a maintenance station. It was in an old part of town, with lots of weeds, old houses, and little greenery anywhere.

Dane flipped open his shield for the officers standing at the front desk, got a nod from one of them, and walked to the stairs. He heard a loud mix of voices before he even saw the signs. He met Patty, a nice older lady who was a volunteer receptionist, kept chocolate chip cookies on a big plate on her desk, and tracked all the detectives. She told him they had three homicide detectives and Detective Flynn was inside with the two cops from San Francisco. Dane assumed Delion had just rolled Nick into the mix.

He walked into the large room, much bigger than the homicide room in San Francisco. All the detectives here were stationed in this room filled with gnarly workstations and funky orange lockers against the rear wall.

Patty had told him Detective Flynn's desk was down three rows. He walked past a man whose shirt was hanging out, past a woman who was shouting to another detective to *shut the fuck up,* and then there was Flynn—impossible to miss Flynn, he'd been told, and it was true. He saw Nick sitting quietly in the corner, reading a magazine. Well, no, she wasn't reading, just using it as a prop. What was she thinking?

Dane walked up to Delion and told him, "The murders from the first episode of *The Consultant,* they were in Pasadena. Two, two and a half weeks ago."

Detective Mark Flynn didn't wait for an introduction, just lifted his phone and started dialing.

Ten minutes later, he hung up. He was about fifty, black, and looked like he'd been a pro basketball player until just last week. He said, "You must be Agent Carver." The men shook hands.

Flynn said, nodding toward Nick, who'd come up to his desk when Dane arrived, "The murders in Pasadena took place before, during, and just after the first show. They sound pretty much identical to the murders on the first episode."

"That would mean, then," Delion said, "that our guy went back and forth to San Francisco, maybe he even flew back and forth a couple of times. Or drove, what with the waits at the airports. We'll have to match the exact times of the murders in both cities."

"And then we check the airlines," Flynn said. "Looks to me, boys, like we're stuck with a real ugly case. What do you say we go back to the studio and round up everyone who had anything to do with those scripts? I'll just bet the studio honchos are shitting in their pants, what with the possibility of lawsuits they'll face from the families of the victims."

"They have assured us of their complete cooperation," Delion said.

Flynn said, "Well, that's something. Hey, it's kinda neat having a Fed around. You bite?"

"Nah, never."

"That's good, because I bite back," Flynn said.

Dane said, "I'll be heading up our involvement with the local agents. Ms. Jones is a possible witness and that's why she's here with us. We want her to look at everyone who had anything to do with this show. Just maybe we'll get lucky."

"I say it's the writer," Delion said. "He dreamed it all up. Who else could it be?"

Detective Flynn just gave Delion a mournful look. "Sorry, son, but the writer—poor schmuck—yeah, he could be the one to start the ball rolling, maybe come up with the concept, a couple of show ideas, maybe even a rough draft for the first show, but is he our perp? You see, depending on the show, there can be up to a dozen writers with their fingers in the plot. Then there's all the rest of those yahoos—the director, the assistant directors, the script folk, the producers, the actors, hell, even the grip. I know all this because I live here and my kid is an actor. He's been on a few shows so far." Detective Flynn drew himself up even taller, if that was possible. "He's a comedian."

"Which shows?" Nick asked.

"He was on *Friends* and *Just Shoot Me*."

Nick nodded. "That's fantastic."

Flynn smiled down at her from his six-foot-six height and

said, "I wonder how many more episodes of *The Consultant* it would have taken before someone somewhere noticed."

"Needless to say," Dane said, "they've stopped the shows."

"The studio heads might be morons," Flynn said, "but not the lawyers. I'll bet they had conniption fits, ordered the plug pulled the instant you guys called."

Nick said, "How do they select which episode is played each week? Or are they aired in a specific sequence?"

"Since this show isn't about the ongoing lives of its main characters," Flynn said, "I can't imagine that the order would be all that important. Normally, though, I understand that they're shown in the order they're filmed. We'll ask."

Delion said, "Then that means our guy knows which episode is going to play next. And that means he's here in LA for sure."

"Yeah, over at Premier Studios," Flynn said.

TWELVE

Premier Studios was on West Pico Boulevard, just perpendicular to Avenue of the Stars. Across from the studio was the Rancho Park Golf Course. Dane was surprised at the level of security. There was a kiosk at the entrance gate, armed security guards, and dogs sniffing car interiors. Past the initial kiosk, the driveway was set up with white concrete blocks forming S-curves to force cars to drive slowly.

Detective Flynn flashed his badge and told them that the Big Cheese was expecting them, at which point the woman smiled, checked her board, and said, "Have at it, Detective."

There were giant murals painted on the studio walls: Marilyn Monroe in *Seven Year Itch,* Luke fighting Darth Vader in *Star*

Wars, Julie Andrews singing in *The Sound of Music,* and cartoon characters from *The Simpsons.* There was also advertising for new shows. Nick stopped a moment to stare at the building-size paintings of Marilyn Monroe and Cary Grant.

"They've been up forever," Flynn said. "Neat, isn't it?"

The head of Premier Studios, who was second only to the owner, mogul Miles Burdock, was on the fifth floor, the executive level of a modern building that didn't look at all fancy and was close to the entrance of the studio lot.

The Big Cheese's name was Linus Wolfinger and he wasn't a man, Pauley told them when he met them in his office on the fourth floor, he was a boy who was only twenty-four years old. He believed himself a genius, and the arrogant Little Shit was right.

"Does this mean you don't like him?" Delion said.

"You think it's that noticeable?"

"Nah, I'm just real sensitive to nuances," Delion said.

"The problem," Frank Pauley said, waving that hand with the four diamond rings on it, "is that the Little Shit is really good when it comes to picking story concepts, and God knows there are zillions pitched each season. He's good at picking actors, at picking the right time slots for the shows to air. Sometimes he's wrong, but not that often. It's all very depressing, particularly since he has the habit of telling everyone how great he is. Everyone hates his guts."

"Yeah," Delion said. "Even as delicate as I am, I can sure see why."

"Twenty-four? As in only two dozen years old?" Detective Flynn asked.

"Yep, a raw thing to swallow," Frank Pauley said. "On the other hand, most of the top executives in a studio are only around for the short term—maybe three, four years. You can bet their entire focus is on how much money they can pocket before they're out. This is a money business. There are simply no other considerations. You'll have an executive producer getting his paycheck, then he'll decide to direct a show and that means he gets another paycheck. It's all ego and money."

"Why are you telling us all this, Mr. Pauley?" Flynn asked.

Frank Pauley grinned, splayed his hands. "Hey, I'm cooperating. It's better if you have some clue what motivates people around here."

"You direct shows, Mr. Pauley?" Nick said.

"You bet. I sometimes also earn a paycheck for inputting on the actual writing of an episode."

"Three paychecks?" Nick asked.

"Yes, everyone does it who can. You know what's even better? For direction and writing, I get royalties or residuals. I've got no complaints."

Flynn rolled his eyes, said, "I've got to make sure my son is clear on all of this."

Delion said, "You're telling us that money, power, and ego—are the bottom line here in sin city? How shocking."

Pauley smiled. "I hesitate to say this so cynically, but I want to be totally up front with you. This is a very serious mess we've got on our hands. If it gets out, and you can bet the bank it will, I don't want to think what's going to happen. The media will be brutal. I've kept quiet about this, just as you asked. To the best of my knowledge, no one involved in *The Consultant* has left town because the cops were here this morning. Wolfinger is expecting us on the fifth floor. That's where the Little Shit's castle is. It was a regular office until Mr. Burdock hired him on. This way."

"What do you mean a 'regular' office?" Nick asked.

"You'll see."

"Tell us about Miles Burdock," Delion said.

"He likes everyone to think he's hands-on, that if he personally doesn't like a show, it's gone, but to be honest about it, it's really Linus Wolfinger who's got all the power around here. Mr. Burdock has so many irons in the fire—most of them international—and hell, you come right down to it, we're just a little iron. He really likes Linus Wolfinger, met him here at the studio, watched him over a couple of months while Linus did nearly all the planning and execution of one of our prime-time shows when both the producer and the director proved incompetent. Then he promoted him, put him in charge of the whole magilla just like that." Frank Pauley snapped his fingers. "It caused quite a furor for a while."

They went through three secretaries, all over fifty, professionals to their button-down shirts, with not a single long leg showing, and not a single long red nail.

Frank Pauley just waved at them and kept walking down the wide corridor. Flynn said, "I would have bet no self-respecting studio honcho would have secretaries like these."

"You mean like adult secretaries? Linus fired the other, much younger secretary the day he moved in. Fact is, though, everyone needs slaves who will work eighteen-hour days without much bitching. That means young, and so usually the secretaries aren't older than thirty. That's why Linus hired three secretaries. Let me tell you, the place really runs better now."

Nick said, "How long has Mr. Wolfinger been here?"

"Nearly two years in his current position, maybe six months before that. Let me tell you, it's been the longest two years in my life."

A man of about thirty-five, so beefed up he probably couldn't stand straight, put himself in their faces, barring their way. He looked like he could grind nails with his teeth. "That's Arnold Loftus, Linus's bodyguard," Pauley said under his breath. "He never says anything, and everybody is afraid of him."

"He's got lovely red hair," Nick said.

Pauley gave her an amazed look.

"You're here to see Mr. Wolfinger?" Arnold Loftus asked, his arms crossed over his huge chest.

"Yes, Arnold, we're expected," said Flynn.

Arnold Loftus waved them to a young man of not more than twenty-two who was walking toward them. No, "strutting" was a better word. He was dressed in an Armani suit, gray, beautifully cut. He stopped, and also crossed his arms over his chest. They were coming into his territory.

"Mr. Pauley," he said, nodding, then he looked at the three men and the woman tagging behind him.

"Jay, we're here to see Mr. Wolfinger. These are police and FBI. It's very important. I called you."

Jay said, "Please be seated. I'll see if Mr. Wolfinger is ready to see you."

Ten minutes later, just an instant before Delion was ready to put his foot through the door, it opened and the assistant nodded to them. "Mr. Wolfinger is a very busy man, but he's available to see you now."

"You'd think he'd be a little more interested, what with the studio lawyers going nuts," Frank said. "But it's his way. He always likes to show he's above everything and everyone."

They trailed Frank Pauley into Linus Wolfinger's office.

So this was the Little Shit's castle, Dane thought, looking around. Pauley was right. This was no ordinary executive office. It didn't have a scintilla of chrome or glass or leather. It wasn't piled with scripts, with memorabilia or anything else. It wasn't anything but a really big square room with a highly polished wooden floor, bare of carpets, windows on two sides with views toward the golf course and the ocean beyond, and a huge desk in the middle. On top of the desk looked to be a fortune in computers. There was a single chair, without a back, behind the desk.

Linus Wolfinger wasn't looking at his visitors, he was looking at one of the computer screens, and humming the theme from *Gone with the Wind*.

The assistant cleared his throat, loudly.

Wolfinger looked up, took in all the folks staring at him, and smiled, sort of. He stepped around from behind the huge desk, let them assimilate the fact that he did, indeed, look more like a nerd than not, what with his short-sleeve white shirt, pens in his shirt pocket, a black dickey that covered his neck and disappeared under the shirt, and casual pants that hung off his skinny butt. He said, "I understand from all of our lawyers, Mr. Pauley, that we have a problem with *The Consultant*. Someone has been copying the murders in the first two episodes."

"Yes," Frank said. "That appears to be the case."

"Now, I suppose you're all police?"

"Yes, and FBI," Detective Flynn said, "and Ms. Nick Jones."

Wolfinger pulled a pen out of his shirt pocket and started chewing on it. He said, "Did Frank tell you that the show is now, officially, closed down?"

"Among other things," Delion said. "We wanted to ask you first if you have any idea who the real-life murderer is, since it's very likely someone closely connected to the show."

"I do have some ideas on that," Wolfinger said, and put the pen back in his pocket. He opened a desk drawer, which was really a small refrigerator, and pulled out a can of Diet Dr Pepper. He popped the lid and took a long drink.

"Why don't we go into a conference room," Dane said. "You do have one, I assume? With chairs?"

"Sure. I've got seven minutes," Wolfinger said, drank down more soda, and burped.

"With all your reputed brains," Flynn said, "we should get this resolved in five."

"I expect so," Wolfinger said, and waved them into a long, narrow, utterly plush conference room just down the hall. Manning the coffeepot and three plates piled high with goodies was the second of the three secretaries, Mrs. Grossman.

All of them accepted cups of coffee.

Once they were all seated, Linus Wolfinger leaned forward in his chair and said, "Have you seen the third episode, the one that was scheduled to air this Tuesday night?"

"Not yet," Delion said.

Linus Wolfinger said, "It's about two particularly brutal murders that take place in western New York. There's an even more *X-Files* type of situation than there was in the first two. It's got this talking head that keeps appearing just before the victims get chopped up. It's pretty creepy. DeLoach loves shit like that. He's very good at it."

Dane and Delion looked at each other. When they'd first heard the writer's name, they'd been flabbergasted. "Why would the jerk advertise like this?" Delion had wondered aloud.

Dane said, "DeLoach? The main writer's name is DeLoach?"

Wolfinger nodded. "Yes, he's smart. Ideas keep marching out of his brain like little soldiers. He really knows how to manipulate the viewer well. I'm sure, however, that all of you already knew the head writer's name."

"Could be," Delion said.

"Sounds like you like the guy," Flynn said.

Wolfinger shrugged. "What's not to like? He's creative, has a brain, and best of all, he has a modicum of a work ethic. Why are you so excited about DeLoach's name?"

Delion, seeing no reason not to, said, "DeBruler is the alias our guy used in San Francisco, at the rectory."

"That's very close," Wolfinger said, tapping his pen on the tabletop. "But you know, despite the names being close, there's no way DeLoach is your guy."

"Oh?" Flynn said, raising an eyebrow.

"The thing is that DeLoach is a weenie. I once saw him throw away an ice cream cone when a fly buzzed near it. He—well, I guess you could say that he lives in his head, he's really out of place here, in the real world. He's got a real rich fantasy life, and that's good for Premier. As I said, he's also got a work ethic, so all of it works to our advantage. But is he a man who'd commit brutal murders? No, definitely not DeLoach."

Dane said, "It's possible that DeLoach is a dangerous weenie, that this rich fantasy life of his has somehow imploded and pushed him out of his head and into the real world. Tell us more about DeLoach. Is he the one who came up with the concept for *The Consultant*?"

"Yes," Wolfinger said. "Yes, he did. His full name is Weldon DeLoach. He's been responsible for two very successful shows in the last ten years. Well respected is Weldon, even though he's pretty old now."

"Define 'pretty old,'" Flynn said.

"He's probably early thirties, maybe even older than that."

"Glory be," Delion said. "He's nearly ready for assisted living."

Wolfinger said, "Despite what I've told you, you still think he's the primary suspect?"

"It sure looks possible," Delion said. "We'll have to look at everyone. We'll need lists from Personnel of all the writers who've been involved with the show, all the technicians, everyone who's even sniffed around the sets."

Dane said, looking thoughtfully at Linus Wolfinger, "DeBruler and DeLoach. The killer would have known his name, whoever he was. It doesn't mean much."

Delion shook his head, back and forth. "That would be just too easy. Makes the guy stupid, and Mr. Wolfinger here says he's got a brain. Ain't no road ever that straight. But we'll talk to him, the other writers as well and all those folks involved with making the show. Get us those lists, Mr. Wolfinger. I got detectives ready to go. The FBI is sending agents here to interview, do background checks, go over alibis, that sort of thing."

Linus Wolfinger nodded. He was tapping a pen on the tabletop. Dane knew it was a different one from the one he had been chewing on in his office because it didn't have teeth marks in it. "You didn't ask me who I thought was behind this."

"Well, no, we haven't," Flynn said. "And what do you know about it?"

THIRTEEN

Hey, it all stays in this room?"

"Sure, why not?" Flynn said. "Give it your best shot, Mr. Wolfinger."

Linus Wolfinger smiled at all of them impartially, tapped his pen one more time, and said, "I think it's Jon Franken. He's the assistant director for *The Consultant*. He's too good to be true, you know? Mr. Hollywood down to his tasseled Italian loafers. He knows everyone, is just so good at A-list parties. I know there's got to be something really nasty about him. No one that good is what he seems to be, you know?"

Delion rose, the others with him. He said, "Thank you, Mr.

Wolfinger. We'll really look close at Jon Franken. Me, I can't stand a guy who's too good at his job. It motivates me to nail his ass."

Flynn said, "Now, Mr. Wolfinger, do contact either me or Inspector Delion or Special Agent Carver here if you come up with something or if you find out anything that could be useful." All of them passed their cards to Wolfinger, who didn't take them, just let them pile up in front of him, close to that still-tapping pen that was driving everyone nuts.

Dane said, wishing in that moment that he could haul the little jerk up by his dicky and throw that damned pen out the window, "It would be easier if the murderer had stayed in the same city, but he didn't. At least now no more episodes will be aired."

Wolfinger said, "I've already slotted in *The Last Hurrah*, another new show about lottery-ticket winners and what becomes of them."

"Sounds innocuous enough," Flynn said.

Pauley said, "Maybe it's someone who's out to sabotage the show itself. I've been in the business a long time, made enemies. Maybe it's someone who hates me personally, wants revenge, knows that this one is my particular baby. I've got a lot on the line here."

Dane said, "You think a man would kill—what is the count now that we know of—eight people, just to get revenge on you?"

"Put that way, it doesn't sound too likely, does it," Pauley said.

"Were there problems getting the show off the ground, Mr. Pauley?" Flynn asked. "Someone specifically who put up roadblocks?"

"There are always problems," Wolfinger said, batting his hand at Pauley to keep him quiet, "but on this one there were fewer than usual. Mr. Pauley is right that he's got a lot to lose. He's married to *the consultant's* girlfriend on the show. He pushed to have her star. If the show closes down, then so does she." Wolfinger didn't sound sorry at all.

Dane glanced over at Pauley and knew he was thinking, *Little Shit*. Pauley said, "He's right—having the show shut down won't be wonderful for my home life, but Belinda will understand, she has to. But having the media go nuts over a script murderer will be a disaster for my reputation and the studio's. We won't even mention the lawsuits."

"Certainly everyone's reputation is on the line here," Flynn said.

"Unfortunately, yes," Wolfinger said. "I trust you gentlemen will try to encourage everyone interviewed to keep quiet about this?" He laughed. "Hey, it won't matter. This is far too juicy to keep quiet about. It'll be out before the day is over." Wolfinger looked down at his pen, frowned a moment, then said, "Then there's Joe Kleypas, the star. Interesting man. A bad boy, but nonetheless, an excellent actor. Maybe you want to put him up there on your suspect list."

"Why would he kill people to ape the show he's starring in?" Delion asked. "He has to know the show will be shut down."

Wolfinger shrugged. "He's a deep guy, never know what he's thinking. Maybe he's got mental problems."

Flynn said, "All right. We'll be speaking to you later, Mr. Wolfinger. Thank you for your time and your ideas."

When they left exactly seven minutes later, Nick said, "He's an interesting man. I didn't think he was a shit. Well, all that pen tapping was obnoxious."

"That's vintage Little Shit," said Pauley.

Frank Pauley stopped to frown at a framed black-and-white photo of Greta Garbo on the wall. He carefully straightened it, then nodded. "You're right. He acted like an adult. I've seen him do it before. But I've also seen him throw a soda can—full—at somebody who said something he didn't like."

Dane said, "Mr. Pauley, are they still shooting any of these episodes?"

"No. Eight shows were shot last summer and into early fall. The way it works is that if the show is picked up, that is, if the network decides to continue with more shows, they get everyone back together and shoot six to thirteen more. They usually make this decision after three, four shows. If the ratings are good, they pay for us to write more episodes. If it's a huge success, everything is given the go-ahead and things move really fast. Oh yes, I called the AD—assistant director—Jon Franken for you."

"This is the guy Wolfinger thinks is the psychopath?"

"Yeah. Wolfinger is cute. Can you believe the damned head of the studio was talking like that? Making accusations? But again, Wolfinger does just as he pleases, usually the more outrageous the better. As for Franken, the man has both feet firmly planted on the ground, knows how to squeeze money out of the sidewalk, and if something needs to happen yesterday, he's the guy you go to. He's trusted, something so unusual in LA that people come up to pinch him to see if he's real. He also works his butt off."

"Exactly what does he do on the show?" Dane asked.

"Actually, it's Franken who has to know more about the actual show than just about anyone, including the line producer. He's in charge of setting up off-studio sites, getting everyone together who's supposed to be shooting, setting up the actual shooting schedule, holding everyone's feet to the budget fire. He listens to the stars whine about the director or sob about their latest relationship gone bad, stuff like that. He's got the big eye. Oh yes, Franken's really big into anything otherworldly; he goes for that stuff. He and DeLoach are really in sync on this one."

"Did they develop the idea together?" Dane said.

"I'm not really sure about that. I do know that they've always got their heads together."

Delion said, "I hope he's older than twenty-four."

"Yes, Jon's been around for a long time. He might even be forty or so. An adult. He started out sweeping off sets when he was just a kid. He's expecting us."

They found Jon Franken on the sound stage for a new fall sitcom that wasn't doing well titled *The Big Enchilada*. He was talking to one of the actors, using his hands a lot, explaining something. From twelve feet away, they could see that he was buff, tanned, and dressed very Hollywood in loose linen trousers and a flowing shirt, his sockless feet in Italian loafers. He looked to be in his forties.

Pauley waved to him, and in a few minutes he joined them. He was polite, attentive, and when they asked him about the order of the episodes, an eyebrow went up. "I've been hearing some rumors, something about some murders that are similar to an episode of *The Consultant*. Is this true?"

Delion said, "Well, so much for discretion."

Jon Franken was incredulous. "You honestly believe that this could have remained a secret? This is a TV studio. There isn't a single secret anywhere within two miles of this place."

Dane said, "Yes, you have it right, and we need your help. Frank Pauley said you know everything and everyone."

Franken said, appalled, "The higher-ups must be shitting their pants. A murderer who's copying a TV show? Incredible." He shook his head, "Only in Hollywood. I'll do my best."

"Thank you," Dane said. "We understand you're close to DeLoach. How much of the actual writing was his?"

"Depended on the episode. The first two, however, were ninety percent Weldon, since it was his idea to begin with. Oh, Jesus, I can't believe that."

Nick said, "Are the episodes to be shown in a certain order?"

"Yes, that's usually the way it's done. There's not too much week-to-week carryover, so it really doesn't matter, but yes, the episodes would remain in the order they were filmed."

"Have you seen him, Mr. Franken?" Flynn asked.

"No, he isn't working right now. He called me a couple of days ago, said his brain was tired and he was taking some time off. He said not to expect him anytime soon. He's done this before, so no one gets cranked about it, but he never calls in and I don't think anyone knows where he went. Listen now, even though the first two episodes are Weldon's, that doesn't mean he would do something this heinous. It just isn't him."

Dane asked, "Is the same episode shown all over the country on the same day at approximately the same time?"

Franken said, "The first two *Consultant* episodes were shown on Tuesday night everywhere, but Wolfinger slotted them a little differently, depending on the demographics, or maybe because of it, so they'll probably okay some more scripts. Beginning with the third one, it's not that heavily Weldon's work. Do you agree, Frank?"

"You're right," Pauley said.

Delion said, "Who can tell us what Weldon's travel schedule's been the past month?"

"That would be Rocket Hanson. She makes all the arrangements for the writers, and for everybody else for that matter."

"Rocket?" Nick said, "That's a wonderful name."

"Yeah, she was trying to break into films thirty years ago, thought she needed something unusual to get her through the door. It stuck."

Flynn said, "Has Weldon DeLoach been out of town a lot very recently?"

Franken just shook his head. "I haven't been working directly with him for several months now. You'll have to speak to other folks. We e-mail a lot and speak maybe once a week if we're not working together on a show. I heard someone say he was off to see some relatives, maybe in central California, but I'm not sure about that."

Dane said, "I don't suppose the relatives are near Pasadena?"

"I haven't a clue. Listen, believe me, you're wrong about Weldon. I know it looks bad, but you're way off course here."

Dane asked, "What is Weldon writing now?"

Franken said, "He's been writing for *Boston Pops* for about four months now."

Delion looked pained.

Franken nodded, said, "Yeah, I agree with you, Inspector. It's a dim-witted show that has somehow caught on. Lots of boobs and white teeth, and one-liners that make even the cameraman wince. It's embarrassing. Weldon keeps trying to sneak in some weird stuff, like some Martians landing on the Boston mayor's lawn, just for an off-key laugh, but nobody's buying it."

Frank Pauley nodded.

They spoke to a good dozen writers. Nothing promising on any one of the group, just a bunch of really interesting men and women who didn't have a life, as far as Dane could tell. "Oh yeah, that's true," one of the female writers said, laughing. "All we do is sit here and bounce ideas off each other. Lunch is brought in. Porta Pottis are brought in. Soon they'll be bringing beds in."

Dane said when they were walking down Pico back to their two cars, "It's time for a nice big meeting, mixing Feds with locals. There's lots of folks that need very close attention."

Flynn nodded, saw some kids shooting baskets, took three steps toward them before he caught himself.

FOURTEEN

ST. BARTHOLOMEW'S
SAN FRANCISCO

Dane and Nick were seated in the second row in St. Bartholomew's, Nick staring at Father Michael Joseph's coffin, Dane staring at the wooden cross that rose high behind the nave, both waiting silently for the church to fill up and the service to begin. They'd come back from LA the previous evening for Michael's funeral.

It was an overcast early afternoon in San Francisco, not unusual for a winter day. It was cold enough for Dane to wear his long camel hair coat, belted at the waist. The heavens should be weeping, Father Binney had said, because Father Michael Joseph had been so cruelly, so madly, slain.

Dane had taken Nick to Macy's again on Union Square. In two hours flat, he'd come close to maxing out his credit card. She kept saying, "I don't need this. I don't. You're making me run up a huge debt to you. Please, Dane, let's leave. I have more than enough."

"Be quiet, you've got to have a coat. It's cold today. You can't go to the—"

He broke off, just couldn't say it, so he said finally, "You can't go to the church without a coat."

She'd picked out the most inexpensive coat she could find. Dane simply put it back and handed her another one in soft wool. Then he bought her gloves and boots. Two more pair of jeans, one pair of black slacks, two nightgowns, and underwear, the only thing he didn't help her pick out. He just stood by a mannequin that was dressed in a sinful red thong and a decorative bra, his arms crossed over his chest.

At noon, she'd finally just stopped in the middle of the cosmetics section on the main floor. Salespeople swarmed around them. A woman was closing fast on her to squirt her with perfume, when she said, "This is enough, Dane. No more. I want to go home. I want to change. I want to go to Saint Bartholomew's and say good-bye to Father Michael Joseph."

Dane, who'd never in his adult life shopped for more than eight minutes with a woman, said, "You've done well—so far. All that's left is some makeup."

"I don't need any makeup."

"You look as pale as that mannequin in lingerie, the one with the blood-red lips and that red thong that nearly gave me a heart attack. At least some lipstick."

"I'll just bet you noticed how pale she was," Nick said, and turned to the Elizabeth Arden counter.

And so Dane found himself studying three different shades of lipstick before saying, "That one. Just a touch less red. That's it."

Dane finally turned in the pew to look over his shoulder. So many people, he thought. Not just priests today, like at the wake, but many parishioners and friends whose lives Michael had touched. Archbishop Lugano and Bishop Koshlap both stopped and spoke to him, each of them placing his hand on Dane's shoulder, to give comfort, Dane supposed. He was grateful for their caring, but the truth was he felt no comfort.

He watched Bishop Koshlap stand over Michael's coffin, and he knew his eyes were on Michael's face. Then he leaned down and kissed his forehead, straightened, crossed himself, and slowly walked away, head bowed.

Dane stared down at his shoes, wondering how well they had hidden the bullet hole through Michael's forehead.

Michael was gone forever, only his body lying in that casket at the front of the church. A huge sweep of white roses covered the now-closed coffin, ordered by Eloise because Michael had loved white roses. Dane hoped, prayed, that Michael knew the roses were there, that he was smiling if he could see them, that he knew how much his brother and sister, and so many people, loved him.

But Michael wasn't there and Dane didn't think he could bear it. He focused on his shoes, trying not to yell his fury, his soul-deep pain out loud.

DeBruler, DeLoach—he just couldn't get the names out of his mind, even here, at his brother's funeral mass. A sick joke? His anger shifted to the murderer who was somewhere down in LA, someone connected with that damned TV show. He turned when he heard his sister Eloise's voice behind him. He rose again, kissed and hugged her, shook her husband's hand, hugged his nephews. They sat silently in the row behind him.

Archbishop Lugano spoke, his deep voice reaching the farthest corners of the church. He spoke spiritual, moving words, words extolling Michael's life, his love of God, the meaning of his priesthood, but then there were the inevitable words of forgiveness, of God's justice, and Dane wanted to shout there would never be any forgiveness for the man who killed his brother. Suddenly, he looked down to see Nick's hand covering his, her fingers pressing down on him, smoothing out his fist, squeezing his hand. She said nothing, continued to look straight ahead. He looked quickly at her profile, saw tears rolling down her face. He drew in a deep breath and held on to her hand for dear life.

Other priests spoke, and parishioners, including a woman who told how Father Michael Joseph had saved not only her life, but her soul. Finally, Father Binney nodded to him.

He walked to the front of the church, past Michael's coffin, hearing gasps of surprise throughout the church, for he was the very image of his brother. It was difficult for people to look at him and accept that he wasn't Michael. He went up the steps to stand behind one of the pulpits. It was only then that he saw that the church was overflowing, people standing three and four deep all around the perimeter, filling the south and north transepts, even out beyond the sanctuary doors.

And Dane thought, Is the murderer out there somewhere, head bowed so people won't see him gloat? Did he come to witness what his madness had brought about and delight in it? Dane had forgotten to say anything to Nick about keeping an eye out, just in case.

Then he saw his friends, Savich and Sherlock. Dane felt immensely grateful. He nodded to them.

Dane looked down at his brother's coffin, the white roses blanketing it. He cleared his throat and fastened his gaze just over the top of Savich's head because he just couldn't bear to speak looking directly at anyone. He said, "My brother loved to play football. He was a wide receiver and he could catch any ball I could get in the air. I remember one of our last high-school games. We were behind, twenty to fourteen. There was only a little over a minute left in the game when we got the ball again.

"All the fans were on their feet and we were moving down the field, me throwing passes, Michael catching them. Finally, we were on the eighteen yard line, with only ten seconds left to play. We had to have a touchdown.

"I threw the ball to Michael in the corner of the end zone. I don't know how he kept a foot inbounds, but he actually caught that ball just as he was tackled hard, and he held on. He won the game, but the thing was, that hit tore up his knee.

"He lay there, grinning up at me like a fool, knowing he'd probably never play another football game, and he said, 'Dane, it's okay. Sometimes the bad things don't touch you nearly as much as the good things do. We won, you can't get gooder than that.'"

Dane's voice broke. He vaguely heard scattered small laughs. He looked down again at the roses that covered Michael's coffin. Then, suddenly, he felt warmth on his face, looked up, and saw that brilliant sunlight had burst through those incredible stained-glass windows. He felt the warmth of that light all the way to his bones. He said, voice firmer now, "Michael appreciated the good in everyone, rejoiced in it; he also understood that the bad was a part of the mix, and he accepted that, too. But there was one thing he wouldn't accept, and that was evil; he knew it was here among us. He knew the stench of it, hated the immense tragedy it brought into the world. The night he was shot, he knew he was facing evil. He faced it, and the evil killed him.

"Michael and I shared many things: Two of them were Sunday football games and tenacity."

Dane paused a moment, and this time he scanned all the faces around him. He said in a low voice, filled with despair and promise, "I will find the evil that destroyed my brother. I will never give up until I do."

There was a moment of absolute silence.

The silence was broken by a soft popping sound. Even as slight a sound as it was, in the dead silence it echoed to every corner of the church. A man yelled, "This woman's hurt!"

People jerked around, trying to see what was happening.

Nick yelled, "Oh God, it's him, Dane! He tried to kill me! It's him!"

Dane saw blood streaking down her face, felt fear paralyze him for an instant. Then he raced down the steps toward Nick, as she shoved her way through bewildered knots of mourners, yelling at them, "Stop him! There, he's wearing that black coat, that black hat. *Stop him!*"

People were turning and grabbing anyone in black, but since nearly every person was wearing black, including a good three dozen priests, there was pandemonium, people shoving, people yelling, people grabbing other people. It was madness.

Dane reached Nick, looked at the blood snaking down her face, and yelled, "Dammit, Nick. Are you all right?"

"I'm okay, don't worry. Just a graze, I guess. We've got to get him. Dane, hurry, I saw him running that way."

Dane thought he saw the man then, moving fast, darting around people or pushing through them, his head down, heading to the narrow side door of the church.

Dane shoved two priests out of his way, saw the man disappear out the side door and the door swing closed again. He nearly burst with fury. The bastard had come here, to his brother's service, probably laughing behind his hand, in madness, and triumph. And he'd tried to murder Nick.

Dane made it to the door, shoved a good half dozen people out of his way, and threw it outward. He saw Savich, a blur, he was running so fast, saw him leap, left leg extended, smooth and easy, saw his foot strike the man's kidney, solid and hard. The man fell forward, flailing his arms to keep his balance. He managed to fling himself about, to face his attacker, and that was a mistake. Savich hit him three times, in the neck and head. The man gasped with pain, shock on his shadowed face, went limp and dropped. Savich went down beside him, checked his pulse and yelled, "I've got him!"

Dane couldn't believe it. Neither could Delion or Nick, who now stood over the man.

Dane said, "He's the one, Nick?"

"I think so," she said. "Can you turn him over, please?"

Savich pulled the man onto his back, got the hat off his head.

Dane said, "This is Dillon Savich, he's my boss at the FBI. Savich, this is Nick Jones, our only eyewitness."

Savich nodded. "You'd better see to that head wound she's got. This guy's down for the count. Go ahead, take care of her, Dane. Nice to meet you, Nick." Savich looked up at his wife, gave her a good-sized grin. Sherlock put her hand on his shoulder. "That was rather dashing," she said, smiling down at him. "It's lucky you guys don't have to wear high heels." She punched him in the arm, looked over at Dane. "This is the maniac who killed your brother? This is the man who just shot Nick? Oh goodness, look at your face." Sherlock pulled a handkerchief out of her jacket pocket, gave it to Dane, and watched him very gently pat Nick's forehead. "It looks like the bullet just grazed you, but scalp wounds really bleed. What do you think, Dane? I think it's okay, just looks really bad. I'm Sherlock."

Delion glanced at Nick's face, nodded, then stared again at Savich, who was still on his haunches beside the man. He shook his head back and forth. "I don't believe this, I just don't fucking believe this." He grabbed Savich's hand, pumped it up and down. "I always thought the Feds were pantywaists. Hey, good job."

Savich checked the guy's pulse again, rose, and dusted off his suit pants. "You must be Inspector Delion. Have you called this in?"

"Yeah, it's done," Delion said.

A group of black-garbed priests were pressing in, Archbishop Lugano at their head. He said in a voice that carried nearly to California Street, "I have a cousin who's in the DEA. She's not a pantywaist either. Well done, sir, thank you."

Savich merely nodded. "Dane, get the blood out of Nick's eyes and see if she can identify this bozo."

Dane stared at the narrow furrow the bullet had made at her hairline just above her temple. It was still bleeding sluggishly. He pulled away Sherlock's handkerchief and took out his own, folded it up, and said, "Nick, press this hard against the wound. We'll get you to a doctor in a minute."

"Let me take another look at the guy, Dane." She was still breathing hard, and there was rage in her eyes as she looked down at the unconscious man who was Father Michael Joseph's murderer. She said, "I was sitting there, listening to you, and then the light came through that stained-glass window and I knew I was going to cry. I bowed my head; then in the very next instant I felt this shock of heat on my face. I looked up and saw the light from that window was shining directly down on that man. I saw him looking at me, and then I knew, just knew."

Delion was searching his pockets. "No gun. Well, it's got to be around here somewhere." He called over two uniformed officers who had just arrived and told them to start the search.

The man groaned, tried to pull himself up onto his knees. One of the officers grabbed his left arm, another grabbed his right. They cuffed him and hauled him toward a police car at the curb.

Dane said, "Look at this crowd. How are we ever going to find that gun?"

"I think perhaps I can help," Bishop Koshlap said. He flung back his head and yelled, "Everyone please listen to me. There is a gun somewhere to be found. Please help our priests form search groups. If any of you saw this man shoot this woman, please step forward."

Dane watched all those people, at least four hundred of them, grow silent and calm because the bishop himself had given them a task, a task that really mattered. He saw Archbishop Lugano speak to the priests, saw them divvy up the crowd and set to work. Dane looked down at Nick, frowned, and took back his folded handkerchief to press it himself against Nick's face, "You weren't pressing directly on the gash. You're still bleeding. But no matter, it's nearly stopped. I can see it's not bad, thank God.

"You know what, Nick? My brother would have been very pleased about this."

Savich said to Delion, "I'm not so sure there's a gun to find. If I were the shooter, I'd have another guy here so I could hand the gun off to him."

Delion knew he was right, but they had to look, just in case. "Yeah, I know." He heard sirens, and quickly went to Nick. "The paramedics are nearly here. You can bet the media will be right behind them. I want you to go with the paramedics back to Bryant Street. The last thing we need is photos of you in the *Chronicle*. We'll meet you there."

"But Dane, I've got to go with him to the cemetery."

Dane said, "It's okay, Nick. Delion's right. If the media see you, it will be a nightmare. I'll see you back at the police station." He paused just a brief moment, lightly touched his fingertips to the wound on her forehead. "I'm sorry."

FIFTEEN

When Delion called a halt to the search, all the mourners formed a car processional that wound a mile to the west, to the Golden Gate Cemetery. The sun was shining, although the day remained cold, and there was the heavy scent of the ocean in the air. Dane looked down at the rich earth that now covered his brother's grave and said, "We just might have gotten him, Michael. I pray that you know that." He stood there a moment longer, staring down at the mound of earth that covered his brother's body. Michael was gone and he would never hear him laugh again, hear him tell about the drunk guy who tried to steal the bishop's miter and ended up hiding in a confessional.

He didn't approach his sister, couldn't look at the pain in her eyes and say something comforting. Eloise, her husband, and her kids were clutched together, and that was good.

When at last Dane turned away from his brother's grave, he saw Sherlock and Savich. He hadn't noticed that they'd flanked him, not saying anything, just there, solid and real.

Dane drove his rental car to the police station on Bryant Street, Savich and Sherlock following. Delion had wanted Savich to go downtown with them immediately, but Savich had just smiled, shaken his head. "Important things first," he'd said, nothing more, and taken his wife's hand in his and followed Dane to the cemetery.

When Dane walked into the homicide room nearly two hours later, he immediately saw Nick, seated in the chair beside Delion's desk. He said her name and she turned. "You look like a prisoner of war with that bandage on your hair."

"It's not nearly as bad as it looks. No stitches necessary. The paramedics couldn't stop talking about what had happened, and I think they lost it with the gauze."

"All right, but you just try to relax, all right?"

She nodded.

"It still shakes me to my toes that I didn't protect you better. If you hadn't bowed your head at just that moment, the bullet would have hit you square on and you'd be dead. Jesus, I'm sorry, Nick."

Nick realized this very well, in an abstract sort of way. It hadn't really sunk in yet, which was probably a blessing. When it did, she'd probably shudder and shake herself to the nearest women's room. She said, "I wish you wouldn't try to take credit for this. Just stop beating yourself up, Dane. This wasn't your fault. Do you think this means God doesn't want me to die just yet?"

"You mean that it isn't your time? Fate rules?"

"Yes, I guess so."

"I don't have a clue. I'm just really glad he didn't succeed."

"I bowed my head because I was crying and I didn't want you to see."

He gulped, but didn't say anything more.

"What you said about Father Michael Joseph, it was very moving, Dane. Did he really catch that touchdown pass? Really tore up his knee?"

He nodded, got a grip on himself. "Yes. You know, this thing about Fate or whatever—if you like, we could get drunk one night and discuss it."

It was a slight smile, he saw it. It made him feel very good.

"Yeah," she said, "I'd like that."

Lieutenant Linda Purcell came up to them, looking resigned. "We found the bullet. That's the good news. Unfortunately, it shattered against a concrete wall. No way to know if it was from the same gun that killed Father Michael Joseph. No matter. It'll all come together anyway. Delion's doing his thing. Just hang around and listen, don't interrupt. We decided to let the guy think about the wages of sin and left him downstairs in the tank for a couple of hours. We just brought him up here. We don't have any one-way mirrors here so keep back from the doorway so he doesn't focus on you."

Dane looked toward the guy who'd shot Nick. His head was down between his arms on the scarred table. He was sobbing, deep gulping sobs that sounded like he believed life as he knew it was over. And he was right, Dane thought, the bastard.

Nearly all of the inspectors hanging around in the homicide room were close enough to the interrogation room to hear. They all looked exactly the same, excited and on the edge. Dane imagined that if they were in an FBI field office, there would be no difference at all. Women agents, in particular, didn't cut any slack to a murderer who broke down in tears. That had surprised Dane when he was new in the FBI, but over the years he'd changed the opinions he supposed he'd absorbed by osmosis all through childhood and adolescence.

Delion sat across from the sobbing man, not saying a word, just watching, arms crossed over his chest, his mustache drooping a bit. Patient, like he had all the time in the world. They watched him examine a thumbnail, heard a soft whistle under his breath, watched him trace a fingertip over a deep gash in the scarred wooden table between them.

They'd taken the guy's long dark woolen coat, hat, and gloves, which left him in a gray sweatshirt and wrinkled black pants. Dane couldn't tell if he was just like the man Nick had originally described. But he saw he was slight of build, looked to be in his forties, and had a full head of dark hair—just as she'd said. And she'd recognized him from across the church.

Finally, the guy raised his head and said between gulps, "You've been holding me for a long time, haven't spoken to me, and now I'm up here in this crappy little room with cops standing outside the door watching. What do you want from me? Why did that big guy try to kill me? I'm gonna sue his ass off. His pants'll fall right off him."

Sherlock snickered.

Both Dane and Nick drew in their breaths. The guy's face was really white, like he hadn't seen the sun in far too long. Just as Nick had said.

Delion said, "We asked you before if you wanted a lawyer and you said you didn't. You want a lawyer now, Mr.—? Hey, why don't you tell us your name."

The man tilted his head back, as if he were trying to look down his nose at Delion. He sniffed, swallowed, and wiped his hand across his running nose. "You already know my name. You took my wallet hours ago and then you just left me alone to rot."

"Your name, sir?"

"My name's Milton—Milt McGuffey. I don't need no lawyer, I didn't do nuthing. I want to leave."

Delion reached over and took the guy's forearm in his hand, shook it just a little bit. "Listen to me, Mr. McGuffey, that guy who hit you is a cop. He just wanted to keep you from running away from the scene of a crime. He was being efficient, just doing what he was supposed to do, you know? Trust me on this: You really don't want to sue him or his ass. Now, why don't you tell me why you tried to kill Nick Jones at Father Michael Joseph's funeral mass."

"I didn't try to kill no Nick Jones! Is that the broad who was bleeding all over the place? Hey, I was just standing there listening and then everything went wild and I heard her yelling. I just wanted to get out of there and so I pushed open that side door and ran. Then that big guy tried to kill me."

"I see," Delion said. "So then, tell me, Milton, why you were at Father Michael Joseph's funeral. You a former priest, or something?"

He wiped his nose again, rubbed his hand on his sweatshirt sleeve, and finally mumbled something under his breath.

"I didn't hear you, Milton," Delion said.

"I don't like Milton. That's what my ma called me just before she'd whack me aside the head. I said that I like funerals. So many people sitting there trying to act like they give a shit about the deceased."

Savich touched Dane's arm to keep him from going into the room. "Easy," he said in his slow, deep voice, right against Dane's ear. "Easy."

"I see," Delion said. "So you just wandered into Saint Bartholomew's like you'd walk into a movie, any movie, didn't matter what was playing?"

"That's right. Only a funeral's free. Wish there was some popcorn or something."

"So you didn't know the star of this particular show?"

Milt shook his head. His eyes were drying up fast now.

"Where do you live, Mr. McGuffey?"

"On Fell Street, right on the Panhandle."

"Real close to Haight Ashbury?"

"That's right."

"How long have you lived there, Mr. McGuffey?"

"Ten years. I'm from Saint Paul, that's where my family still is, the fools freeze every winter."

"Hey, my ex-wife is from Saint Paul," Delion said. "It's a nice place. What do you do for a living?"

Milton McGuffey looked down at his hands, mumbled something. It was getting to be a habit.

"Didn't hear you, Milt."

"I'm disabled. I can't work. I collect benefits, you know?"

"What part of you is disabled, Mr. McGuffey? I saw you run, saw you turn around, ready to fight. You were fast."

"I was scared. That guy was really big. He was trying to kill me, I had no choice. It's my heart. It's weak. Yeah, I've decided I'm going to perform a public service—I'm gonna sue that cop; he's dangerous to everybody."

"Where did you get the silencer for the gun?"

Very slight pause, then, "I didn't have no gun. I don't even know what a silencer looks like."

"We'll find that gun, Milt, don't ever doubt that. Was it the same gun and silencer you used to kill Father Michael Joseph?"

He nearly rose right out of his chair, then slowly sank down again, shook his head back and forth. "I didn't kill no priest! I'm nonviolent. All we gotta do is respect and love each other."

"Do you prefer a gun to taking a poker and striking an old woman dead?"

"Hey, man, I don't know what you're talking about. What old woman?"

"You remember that piece of doubled-over wire? Do you like that the best, Milt? Pulling that wire tighter and tighter until it's so tight it cuts right through to bone?"

"Stop it, man. I'm nonviolent, I told you. I wouldn't hurt nobody, even a parole officer. Hey, you think I shot that broad in the head? Not me, man, not me."

Delion rolled his eyes, mouthed toward the open door, *Prime asshole.*

"What were you in jail for, Milt?"

"It was just one mistake, a long time ago, a little robbery, that's it."

"There was a guy whose head you bashed in along with the robbery. Don't you remember that?"

"It was a mistake, I just lost it—you know, too much sugar in my diet that day. I served my time. I'm nonviolent now. I don't do nuthing."

"Do you watch the show *The Consultant?*"

"Never heard of it." The guy looked up then, and there was no doubt about it, he was puzzled by the question. Genuinely puzzled. He had no clue what *The Consultant* was, dammit. That, or he was an excellent actor, and unfortunately Delion didn't think that was the case. Well, shit. That was a surprise, a bad one.

Delion leaned forward, delicately smoothed his mustache with his index finger. "It's about this murderer who kills people and then taunts a priest about it, all in the confessional, so the priest can't turn him in. He kills the priest, Milt. This guy's a real bad dude."

"Never heard of it. Not a word. I don't like violent movies or TV shows."

Delion looked up at Dane, then beyond him, to Savich. Slowly, after but a moment, he nodded.

Savich walked into the small interrogation room, took a seat beside Delion, and said, "How are you feeling, Mr. McGuffey?"

The guy pressed himself against the back of his chair. "I know who you are. You're that big fella who tried to kill me."

"Nah, I wasn't trying to kill you," Savich said, a smile on his face that would terrify anyone with half a brain, still in doubt in McGuffey's case. "If I'd wanted to kill you, trust me, you'd be in the morgue, stretched out on a nice cold table, without a care in the world. What did you do with the gun?"

"I didn't have no gun."

"Actually, yes, you did and you gave it to that other guy. You know, Milt, the thing is that I saw you. I was watching the crowd, that was my assignment from the lieutenant, to watch, because just maybe the guy who killed Father Michael Joseph would be there, to get his jollies, to make him feel really proud of himself. Sure enough you came. But you weren't there just because you were proud of your work; nope, you were there to kill Nick Jones because she can identify you. You really moved fast, didn't you? It's only been a couple of days since she gave your description to the forensic artist and the drawing of you was in the newspaper. How'd you find out it was Nick Jones?"

"Look, man, I did see that drawing in the paper, that's true, but I didn't know who the guy was. Wait, you can't really think that guy was me. No way, I don't look nuthing like that dude. Mean fucker, that's what I thought when I saw his picture and read the story."

"Yeah, right, Milt," Savich said. "Whatever. Now, don't get me wrong. That was a real slick move you made—you palmed the gun, silencer still attached, and handed it off to your partner as you ran past him. He slipped it into his coat pocket. You never broke stride. It really was well rehearsed and well executed. Only thing—I was watching. You weren't lucky there."

Savich leaned forward until his nose was an inch away from McGuffey's.

He said very slowly, *"I saw you do it.* They're looking for him right now. I gave a really good description. They'll bring him in and he'll rain all over your picnic." Savich looked over at the door, knew that Sherlock was close.

McGuffey's eyes followed.

Sherlock stepped right up into the doorway, gave Savich a big smile, nodded in satisfaction, and stuck her thumb up.

"Ah," Savich said, "at last. Didn't take our guys too long, did it? Just over two hours. I told you I gave them a great description. Now we have him."

"I don't know what you're talking about! I didn't do nuthing, do you hear me? Nuthing! You couldn't have caught no guy because there wasn't a guy."

Savich rose suddenly. "You can go back to your cell now, Milt. You're tiresome, mouthing all that crap, crying, for God's sake. Just look at poor Inspector Delion. He's nodding off, your lies have bored him so much. You need lessons, Milt. You weren't really all that good a show."

Savich leaned over and splayed his hands on the tabletop, got right in McGuffey's face. "We're going to hold you on the attempted murder of Nick Jones. After your accomplice talks—and he'll fillet you but good, Milt, don't doubt it—the DA is going to have a solid multiple-murder case against you. He's going to enjoy parading you in front of a jury—talk about a slam dunk. He's even got a witness, you know who she is, all right—Nick Jones. You saw her standing out there, didn't you? The white bandage around her head? She sure sees you, and believe me, she knows who you are.

"Yeah, the DA's really going to be happy about this one. You know what else is great about California, Milt? California's got the death penalty. Killing a priest and an old woman, now there's just no excuse for that at all—rotten childhood, too much sugar, chemical imbalance in your brain; none of that will work. They'll drop-kick you right into San Quentin's finest facilities. You can appeal for years, but eventually you'll exhaust everything our sweet legal system has to offer you, and then you're toast."

Savich snapped his fingers in McGuffey's face. "Dead. Gone. And everybody will be real happy when you're off the face of the earth. See you at your trial, Milt. I'll be waving at you from the front row."

Savich walked out of the room, whistling.

McGuffey rose straight up and yelled, "Wait! Dammit, wait! You can't just walk off like that!"

Savich just flapped his hand toward McGuffey, not turning around.

"Wait!"

SIXTEEN

Savich smiled at Dane, and very slowly turned, a dark eyebrow raised, obviously impatient.

McGuffey said, nearly falling over his own words he was talking so fast, "He's a liar, he'd roll on his own mother, I didn't do nuthing, do you hear me? You can't believe a word he says. Old Mickey's a king shit, got no sense of right or wrong, a real moral asshole."

"Mickey seems just fine to me," Sherlock said, coming to stand beside Savich, leaning against the door frame. "I spoke to him for a good ten minutes. He seemed real upright, not a lying bone in his body. I think everyone's going to believe what he has to say, Mr. McGuffey, you know? I believed him."

"No, no, you gotta listen to me. I didn't kill no priest. I didn't kill no old woman or any gay guy. It was Mickey who hired me. I didn't hire him, I didn't. I wasn't going to kill her, just make a big noise, right? I was just supposed to scare her good, make sure she was on the next flight to China. I never murdered nobody! You've got to believe me, you've got to." McGuffey was scrambling away from the chair, trying to shove the table out of the way so he could get to Savich. Delion simply clapped his big hand on McGuffey's forearm and said very quietly, "No, Milt, you just sit right back down here."

McGuffey yelled at Delion, "Mickey Stuckey's a damned liar! Don't believe him. He set the whole thing up."

Sherlock said, "Mr. Stuckey told me you hired him, just to be his palm guy, to stand there, keeping his eyes on everything and take whatever you passed to him. He claims he didn't have a clue about what you were going to do. He's really against shooting a lady."

Sherlock shut up and stepped back, no reason to lay it on too thick. The guy looked white now, not just pale, actually white.

Milt was on his feet, trying to pull away from Delion, who'd really clamped down on his forearm and wasn't about to let go. "No! Man, you gotta listen to me. I told you, Mickey's a liar."

Savich sighed deeply, crossed his arms over his chest, and said, frowning, "All right, since I'm still here, why don't you tell me your side of it. But don't lie about it being Mickey who was the shooter because I saw you pass the gun to him. What you tell me better be right on target because I'll tell you, Milt, I'm really leaning toward Stuckey's story and I haven't even heard him tell it yet."

"Okay, okay, you gotta listen, okay? I'll tell you the truth. Here it is."

"Just a moment, Milt," Delion said. "I want to tape-record this. You okay with that?"

"Sure, sure, let's get on with it."

Delion flipped the record button. He gave his name, the date, and McGuffey's name, said, "You're willing to make this confession, no one's coercing you?"

"Dammit, yes. Let's go!"

"You don't want a lawyer present?"

"No, I just want you to hear the truth!"

Delion gave him his Miranda rights, asked him if he understood, to which Milt spewed out more obscenities before he said yes, he understood his rights, to the tape recorder.

"Okay, Milt, tell me what happened."

McGuffey said, "Look, Stuckey called me a couple days ago, said this guy down in LA wanted me to scare this broad at a priest's funeral. Stuckey said he'd give me ten grand, but I had to do it in the middle of the service, for God's sake, in front of hundreds of people, which sounded real stupid to me, but he said that was the way it had to be. I didn't want to do that, but Stuckey had me by the short hairs, you know? I owe him money, some bad investment decisions, you know? So I had to take the job or he might have broken both my legs. But it was never murder, oh no.

"Stuckey had a gun for me, and a silencer, and said the shooter had to be me, it just had to. When I asked him why, he laughed and said, 'You look just right, Milt, that's what the guy said. You look just right, maybe even perfect for the role.' Whatever the fuck that means."

He really did look just right, Dane thought. A good physical resemblance. Damn, nothing was ever easy.

"You really expect me to buy this?" Savich said, lounging back in the uncomfortable chair, looking bored.

Milt sat forward, clasping his hands in front of him, like he was ready to pray. "Look, Inspector, like I told you, I had to have the money. I had to pay off Stuckey or I was in really deep shit. Then there's my disability and that jerk of a landlord is nearly ready to throw me out. Hey, I was just three days away from sitting on Union Square, leaning against the Saint Francis Hotel, begging for money. I had to take the job. A man's gotta survive, you know? A man's gotta pay off his bad investment decisions."

Delion had sat back in his chair, his arms folded over his chest, a sneer on his face. "You want us to believe that this guy specifically told Stuckey it had to be you because you just looked right? You were perfect for the role?"

"I swear it. Hey, Stuckey told me the LA guy's name was DeFrosh—weird name—you'd never forget that stupid name.

"Stuckey said the guy faxed him a photo of the lady I was to give scare to, you know, shoot her just a little bit but not kill her, I wouldn't ever do that. Yeah, the guy told Stuckey that the broad was homeless, but hey, she sure didn't look homeless in the church, but what do I know? How would the guy in LA know about that? Stuckey didn't tell me nuthing else, I swear it."

Dane looked down at Nick, who was as white as the bra he'd watched her pick out in their marathon shopping spree. It was just this morning. Amazing.

Savich said, "What did you do with the photo he faxed of the lady?"

"Stuckey has it, just showed it to me, then took it right back."

"What did it look like?"

"She was coming out of this police station with that guy who's standing beside her out there, you know, that dead priest's brother. It didn't look like no police station I've ever seen in San Francisco. Yeah, Stuckey's got it. She's a looker, I wasn't about to forget her. Like I said, she sure didn't look homeless in the church so for a while there I wasn't sure it was really her."

The bastard took the photo in LA. Dane couldn't believe it.

"So you recognized the priest's brother?"

"Oh yeah, heard people talking about how he and Father Michael Joseph looked identical and it really shook some people up. Everybody was real quiet, you know? Everyone was focused on that guy and what he was saying. Lots of them were crying just listening to him. Then she had the nerve to move—no reason that I could see, she just lowered her head right when I pulled the trigger. Jesus, I could have killed her, but thank the good Lord that it went just like it was supposed to. Yeah, the bullet just grazed her."

"Tell us more about this guy from LA."

"I don't deal with people I don't know, at least usually, and neither does Mickey Stuckey. He said he knew the guy, knew he was good for the money. Hey, he gave me five thousand up front. He told me his name was DeFrosh—I already told you that. Really weird, man."

Milton McGuffey put his head down on his folded arms and began to cry again. Everyone heard him say over his sobs, "I don't want to go to jail, but now I'll have to do time just because I put a little crease in the broad's forehead." He raised his head. "I want Stuckey to go down. I never should have agreed to do it in the church."

Delion said, "You didn't realize there would be cops there?"

"Stuckey told me there'd probably be a couple there, but if I got my timing right, I'd get away, no problem. Damned bastard, that Stuckey. I really want him to go down, he set the whole thing up."

Savich said as he himself smiled down at McGuffey, "Yes, he'll go down, all right, Milt, just as soon as we catch him."

McGuffey's jaw literally dropped open. He stared at Savich for a very long time.

He said, "Shit, man."

Then he yelled at the top of his lungs, "I want a lawyer!"

Delion looked over at Savich, who was speaking to Lieutenant Purcell. They heard her say she'd already put out an APB on Mickey Stuckey, aka Bomber Turkel, the most creative of all his aliases. Delion said, "That guy is something else, Dane. He's your boss?"

"Yeah, I've been in his unit for about five months now."

"Smooth as butter," Delion said. "I was thinking about letting you have a go at Milton, but he knew you, knew you weren't a cop, so that wouldn't have worked. And there was Savich, looking ready, even smiling a little, and I knew he had something up his sleeve. He did good, didn't he?"

"Oh, yes."

"His wife, her name is really Sherlock?"

Dane nodded, smiled. "Yes, they're quite a team."

"You know," Delion said, "I've been in court with Sherlock's dad. Now there's a tough, high-powered dude. Defense lawyers hate his guts. They bitch about having the rotten luck to end up with the only law-and-order judge in San Francisco. Cops love him, needless to say."

"Yes," Dane said. "Too bad that Milton McGuffey isn't a bit more stupid. The DA'll have trouble proving attempted murder. We need Stuckey. At least Milt verified—and it's probably the only thing he said that was true—that the guy who hired him lives in LA and his name's DeFrosh. Damn, Milton isn't the killer, Delion."

"Yeah, I know, but we're getting there, Dane. I'm going to call Flynn, tell him what happened. He's gonna love it that the creep who set this all up told Milton his name was DeFrosh."

Dane said, "Maybe he thinks we're slow—DeFrosh even rhymes with DeLoach. What is he trying to prove? Is it his goal to get up close and personal with us? Or maybe he just wants us to believe that Weldon DeLoach is the killer?" Dane stopped when he saw Nick leaning against a wall, actually against a gray file cabinet since there was no wall showing. "Hey, you okay, Nick?"

She said as she lightly touched her fingertips to the bandage on her forehead, "In this case, it really does look worse than it really is. I'm okay, just resting a bit."

Delion said, "I don't know, Nick. I think you look kind of cute. In a pathetic sort of way. If you want a safe house now, I'll bet the lieutenant will spring for it."

Dane said, "No, I'm keeping her with me. Are you in, Delion? We're all going to LA tomorrow."

"I'm ahead of you, boyo," Delion said. "I already called Franken. He said there was still no sign of Weldon. He's got everybody looking for him, but he doesn't hold much hope of finding him. Since the police are looking, too, maybe someone will see him. Franken's going to meet us at the studio at ten o'clock tomorrow morning. He's got some video of Weldon DeLoach."

"We'll finally see what the man looks like," Nick said.

"Yep," Delion said. "And there's lots of stuff to go over with Flynn. He's got a small army of people working on the personnel lists, interviews, checking alibis, possible motives. We've got a lot to tell him as well."

He looked over at Savich and Sherlock and rolled his eyes. "More Feds. It always starts with a single Fed—sort of like reconnaissance—then you look up and the Feds are converging, multiplying like rabbits until soon they're everywhere and they've taken over. Hey, FBI Director Mueller will be out here before long. He comes from here, you know. Hey, you guys coming with us to LA?"

"Count us in," Sherlock said, coming to stand by Nick.

Savich said, "What's this about the gun that killed Dane's brother being like the two possible guns in the Zodiac killer case? What was that—some thirty years ago?"

"Ain't that a kick?" Delion said. "It's got our ballistics guy, Zopp, nearly drooling he's so excited, telling one blonde joke after another." At Sherlock's raised eyebrow, he grinned. "Yeah, Zopp says blonde jokes help his synapses fire. But you know, it has to be a coincidence, has to be."

"Hmmm," Sherlock said. "Yeah, it's a coincidence, but it's a strange one."

Delion said, "Hey, Sherlock, you as tough as your daddy?"

"He likes to think so," Sherlock said, and smiled real big. There were three other inspectors standing close by, grinning like loons at her.

"Local cops really like her," Savich said, and just shook his head, and Delion thought, *Boy, that guy's proud of her.*

Savich said, "So you don't mind if we tag along to LA with you, Delion?"

"More the merrier," Delion said. "Hey, Lieutenant, any word on Stuckey yet?"

"Not yet, but we'll get him." Lieutenant Linda Purcell looked around at all the assembled homicide inspectors and said, "Everyone saw how Savich worked the guy around? How he got Stuckey's name out of him?"

There were boos and hisses from the cops. A couple of inspectors threw some peanuts.

Before Dane left, Delion motioned him aside to tell him that Nick's fingerprints weren't on file.

"Hey, at least we know she's not a criminal."

"I already came to that conclusion for myself," Dane said.

SEVENTEEN

LOS ANGELES

Jon Franken, assistant director of *The Consultant,* said, "We couldn't find any photos, but as I told you on the phone, Inspector Delion, we did find something every bit as good. He flipped a switch on the video feed and pointed. "That's Weldon—second guy on the left, the one just standing off to the side, arms crossed over his chest, watching everyone be idiots. He watches a whole lot, just stands back in the shadows, claims it gives him ideas. Whatever, he does have brilliant ideas."

"Freeze it," Dane said and looked at Nick as the screen held the image. The fact was she already looked frozen. She had to be afraid, looking at the man who very possibly hired Milton McGuffey to murder her, the man who might have killed his brother. Dane lightly touched his fingers to her forearm. "Nick?"

"I don't know, I just don't know." She turned to look up at Dane. "Maybe the bone structure is similar." She shrugged. "It's pretty scary."

"I know. Now, Nick, I want you to forget the hair, the tan, the eyes—it could all be cosmetic alterations. Study his face, the way he moves, how he talks using his hands."

She said finally, "Maybe, I just don't know. I just can't be sure. He looks so different."

Delion said, "Milton McGuffey—would you have spotted him if he hadn't shot you?"

"You want brutal honesty here? The answer is I'm just not sure. Probably. Yes, I probably would have said something."

Flynn said, "From everything you've told me, the reason our perp selected McGuffey is because of the way he looks—that is, he looks a lot like him. Now, Mr. Franken, you still don't have a clue where Weldon DeLoach is."

Franken shook his head. "Sorry, like I already told you, he'll be here when he wants to be here. If he's in LA, he'll be coming around. Weldon is a man of very set habits."

"Mr. Franken," Nick said, "has Mr. DeLoach always looked like this? Darkly tanned, really light hair?"

"Why, yes," Franken said. "As long as I've known him. And that's about eight years now. Why do you ask?"

Dane said to Nick, "If our guy is DeLoach, then when you saw him, he was most certainly wearing a wig, contacts. As for losing the tan, I'm not sure how that would be done except with makeup."

"But why would he bother?" Nick said. "He sure didn't expect me to be sitting in the church."

"Yeah, but he would have seen a lot of people while he was in San Francisco. Maybe the disguise was for any- and everyone."

Franken said, rubbing his elegant long fingers over his chin, "I don't think Weldon DeLoach is the murderer. He—he's just not the type to kill anyone. As I told you before, it's just not in him."

Dane remembered Wolfinger had called DeLoach a weenie. "You mean you believe he's a coward?"

"No, nothing like that. It's just—no, not Weldon."

Nick said, "The killer wanted McGuffey to look like him, Dane, and that's why he hired McGuffey to kill me. So he has to be dark and really pale-skinned."

"You're probably right, Nick." Dane asked them to zoom in to get a close-up of Weldon DeLoach, which Franken did. Wolfinger had said DeLoach was around thirty. Well, he didn't look thirty. He looked forty, maybe more. He looked like he'd lived hard, that, or certainly a lot of stress. According to other writers interviewed, he wasn't a cocaine neophyte. "But those years are over," one of the lighting guys had told them. "Weldon hasn't done bad stuff in a long time. He's been really straight."

DeLoach's dark tan really stood out against his white shirt and white pants. His eyes were a pale blue. He had thinning hair—nearly white it was so blond.

Dane said, "Do you have anything with Weldon DeLoach speaking?"

"Why?" Delion said. "Nick never heard him speak."

"Maybe she'll recognize some of the moves he makes when he's animated and speaking. Besides, I want to hear his voice, too."

When Franken ran some more footage, there was Weldon DeLoach at a birthday party being held on a set, giving a toast. He had the softest voice Nick had ever heard, soft and soothing, without much expression or accent. She studied him carefully—

the way his arms moved, his hands clenched and unclenched around a cup of booze he held aloft as he spoke, the way he held his head.

When it was over, she shook her head. "I'm sorry, I can't be sure. But you know, if the San Francisco police can catch Stuckey, maybe he'll identify DeLoach's voice."

"Good idea," Dane said, and jotted it down in his small notebook. "Could you give us a copy of the tape?"

Franken nodded, said, "No problem. You're really hoping that Weldon DeLoach is the madman who's copying the scripts for *The Consultant*, aren't you?"

"Fact is," Delion said, sitting forward, "when we find him, we really want to sit down with him and have a nice cozy chat. We'll see."

"It's not Weldon," Jon Franken said again.

"Now, Mr. Franken," Flynn said, "you said the first two episodes of *The Consultant* were Mr. DeLoach's scripts, almost exactly, right?" Dane noticed that Flynn's left hand always moved slightly up and down when he concentrated, as if he were dribbling a basketball.

"Yes," Franken said, "DeLoach was really excited about the series." His cell phone rang and he excused himself. When he came back, he said, "That was my assistant. She said one of Weldon's friends just told her that Weldon was going up to Bear Lake to spend time with his dad. Said he was going to take at least three weeks and he wanted to do some fishing, too. His father's in a home up there, *Lakeview Home for Retired Police Officers*."

Delion said, "You mean DeLoach's father is a retired cop?"

Franken said, "Yeah, I guess so. I do know his dad's been there a long time. Once Weldon told me that his father was confused most of the time."

Flynn said, "We already knew Weldon didn't ask the people here at the studio or anyone else to make him any airline reservations. If he did fly somewhere, we would have found a record, what with all the security."

"Bear Lake," Delion said thoughtfully. "That's up in the Los Padres National Forest, isn't it? In Ventura County?"

"That's right," Flynn said. "Just an hour north on I-5, over the Tejon Pass. Well, maybe more, what with our god-awful traffic."

"And that means, of course, that DeLoach could have easily driven up to San Francisco anytime he wanted. And Pasadena," Nick said.

"Yeah, that's right," Flynn said.

"Thank you, Mr. Franken," Delion said, rising. "Detective Flynn's people have interviewed all the other writers and employees of *The Consultant*. Everyone checks out, at least on the first pass, which is admittedly shallow. Oh yes, Mr. Franken, where were *you* last week?"

Jon Franken was gently swinging his foot with its Italian loafer tassel falling to one side, then to the other. He raised an eyebrow, but answered readily enough, and with good humor, "I was right here, Inspector Delion. I'm working on *Buffy the Vampire Slayer* at present. Very long days."

Delion nodded, then turned away, saying over his shoulder, "Oh yes, what's the name of Mr. Frank Pauley's wife? You know, the one who plays the girlfriend on *The Consultant*?"

"Belinda Gates."

"We'd like to speak to her. And the star of the show, Joe Kleypas."

"Of course. Watch it with him, Inspector. Joe isn't always mellow, particularly when he drinks. He's got quite a temper, actually. If you accuse him of being a murderer, his smile might just drop off his face." He looked Savich and Dane up and down, smiled to himself, and said, "Of course, it would be interesting to see what would happen if he went at it with you guys."

Jon Franken took Savich and Sherlock to the commissary for lunch. "Belinda's working a soap this week," he said as he chewed slowly on a single french fry. "A guest slot. There were some problems, so I know they were shooting today. Maybe she'll be here. If she doesn't show, I'll take you to her trailer. It's pretty rare that the bigger stars come in here. They hang out in their trailers most of the time. You probably noticed trailers scattered all over the lot." He shook his head. "What a life, not much glamour sitting in a trailer."

Sherlock said, looking around the big rectangular room, "I guess I expected a big buffet, cafeteria-style. I do like all those 1930s murals on the walls."

"I like all the ape characters from the new *Planet of the Apes* you've got set around this big room," Savich said. "They're really lifelike."

"This is Hollywood," Jon said. "We never stop advertising or patting ourselves on the back. Actually, though, this commissary doesn't compare to the one over at Universal. You can catch some really big stars over there because the place is so opulent."

Belinda Gates walked in some ten minutes later. Sherlock said, "Goodness, she's got rollers in her hair, Dillon, those big heat rollers. Do you remember the last time I used them to straighten my hair? You helped me roll them in?"

He said as he wrapped a long red curl around his finger, "Let's do it again. It was fun."

Sherlock paused a moment, remembering very clearly what they'd done just after pulling the rollers out. She said to Franken, "That's really Belinda Gates? She's very beautiful."

"Yes, that's her," Franken said, and smiled as he chewed another french fry. "She is beautiful, and most important, the camera loves her face."

Both Savich and Sherlock realized in that instant that Jon Franken had slept with her.

Sherlock said, "Tell us a bit about her, Jon."

Franken ate another french fry, shrugged his elegant shoulders. "Belinda is basically a lightweight. She learns her lines, takes direction well, and has enough talent to keep the wolves at bay—of course, now that she's nailed Frank Pauley she doesn't have to worry. She works when she wants to, which probably means that her head's less screwed up than it was. The thing is, she doesn't have much fire in the belly; she just doesn't have it in her to go for the jugular. If you're looking at her as a suspect in this mess, all disguised and made up to look like a man, I'd say she wouldn't be able to make it through the first audition. Now, if you're interested in Frank Pauley as your murderer, maybe Belinda will give you something incriminating. Pauley just might have enough acid in his gut to do something like this. The thing is, I just don't know why he'd sabotage his own show."

"And you could? Make it through the first audition?" Savich said. He ate a carrot out of his huge salad.

"Oh yes, believe it. Listen, I'd still be sweeping the studio floors if I didn't have it in me to take out a few jugulars, if I didn't want to move up in this business more than I wanted to eat, which was in question in those early years." And then he smiled again, wiped his hands on a napkin. "I'll introduce you and let you at her. A few years ago, Belinda had some problems with the cops. She might not be all that easy for you."

Jon Franken rose. "Forget what I said about Pauley. Even if his worst enemy were backing this show, he still wouldn't have the guts or the imagination to try to bring it down through this convoluted, god-awful violence. Ah, Belinda is taking her lunch out. This should be a good time. She doesn't tape for another hour or so; I checked."

Sherlock and Savich met with Belinda Gates in a small green room connected to a talk show stage. She didn't look friendly. She looked suspicious, her lips tightly seamed together.

A challenge, Sherlock thought, smiling at her, remembering what Franken had said. She introduced herself and Savich, carefully showing Belinda Gates their FBI shields up close.

"You're both FBI?"

"Yes, that's right," Savich said, sitting back so he wouldn't overwhelm, so just maybe she would relax.

"Partners?"

"Sometimes," Sherlock said, sticking out her hand so Belinda Gates was forced to shake it. "Actually, we're partners all around—we're married and we're FBI agents. Isn't that a kick?"

Belinda said, looking back and forth between them, "You're really married? To each other?"

"Oh yes," Sherlock said. "We've got a little boy, Sean's his name. He's nearly a year old now. He's walking, but he can also crawl as fast as I can walk. Besides being good parents, we're good agents. We're here to catch this killer and we need your help. We assume you know all about this, Ms. Gates?"

Belinda Gates leaned toward Sherlock, less wary and suspicious now. "Oh yes. Your husband—he looks like he could star in that new series Frank just dreamed up. It's about a sports lawyer who's a real looker and a hunk, stronger than most of his athlete clients. His clients are always getting him into trouble." Belinda cleared her throat. "Listen, I'll do whatever I can to help you find this horrible person. Is your name really Sherlock?"

"Yes, it is."

"Cool."

"Thank you," Sherlock said. "We really appreciate speaking with someone who knows the ropes and all the players. I was very impressed with your role on *The Consultant*. I only saw the first two episodes, but you were really good. Your Ellie James character was believable, sympathetic, and beautiful, of course, but you can't help that." She paused a moment, and Belinda smiled.

"It's unfortunate that the show has to stop, at least until we catch the maniac who's causing all this grief. We're hoping you can give us some ideas."

EIGHTEEN

Belinda nodded, said, "I'll certainly try, but I really don't know anything. I do know that poor Frank is really upset about the show's cancellation, but what can he do? He told me that DeLoach or some other writer involved in the scripts is killing people to match the murders in the first two episodes. Frank started calling it *The Murder Show.*"

"Catchy title," Sherlock said. "Yes, that's the essence of it."

"Well, I think that actually Weldon DeLoach came up with that title, but the powers-that-be didn't like it, preferred *The Consultant*. More uptown, you know what I mean?"

"Yes," Sherlock said. "More Manhattan than Brooklyn."

"Exactly," Belinda said, smiling. "That was Frank's take on it as well. He's been in the business a long time. He was an actor back in the early eighties, never made it big, and that was okay because he realized he wanted to make shows, not star in them. He didn't ever want to do movies. He loves TV. He's at his happiest when he's the mover behind the scenes, you know, getting scripts actually made into shows, selling the networks, doing the budgets, lining up the actors and directors. Kicking butt to keep everything moving and reasonably on budget.

"The first show he produced was *The Delta Force,* back in the mid eighties, ran for about four years. Maybe you've seen some reruns?"

Savich nodded. "It was a good show."

Belinda Gates seemed to light up from the inside, gave him a big smile and pulled one of the big rollers out of her hair. A long fat curl flopped out. "I'll tell him what you said. You know, Frank tells me everything so I know probably as much as he knows about this murderer."

Sherlock said, "You're smart, Ms. Gates, you're on the inside. We know that you've given this some thought. We need your help. Do you have any idea who could have orchestrated all this?"

Belinda pulled out another roller, gently ran her fingers through the big loop of hair, decided it was cool enough, and nodded to herself as she said, "If I had to guess, I'd say it was the Little Shit, you know, Linus Wolfinger. He's very smart. But it's more than that." She paused a moment, scratched her scalp, and said, "It seems like every single day he has to prove that he's the smartest guy on the planet, the biggest cheese. It doesn't matter what it is, he's got to be the best—the fastest, the smartest—and everyone has to recognize it and praise him endlessly."

Savich sat forward, clasped his hands between his knees, and said, "Other than his need for everyone to know how great he is, can you think of a reason why he'd actually follow a TV script to murder people?"

"Because it's weird, it's different, that's why. The Little Shit really likes to think up things to show his scope, all his abilities that are so much more impressive than, say, yours or mine. A murder would be a different kind of challenge for him. If he is the one killing these people, then he had to know that the police would catch on soon enough. Hey, I bet he even set it up to get the police pretty close to him, and that would put him center stage, right in the spotlight. Does that make sense?"

"Not really," Sherlock said.

Another roller came out and Belinda scratched her scalp. "Of course it doesn't, I'm just being bitchy. If I really had to vote, though, I'd pick Jon."

"Jon Franken?" Savich said, and he knew a moment of real surprise and recognized it for the mistake it was. Everyone in this bloody studio was a suspect. Still, he hadn't put Jon Franken in the mix, not really, because he was just—what? He was too together, he was focused. He was very Hollywood, yes, that was it; he was normal in that he fit just right into this specific environment. Savich just couldn't see him at ease in a murderer's world.

He said to Belinda Gates, "Why do you think it's Jon Franken?"

"Well, Jon is one of the sexiest guys who's not an actor in LA. He's slept with more women than even Frank knows about, and believe me, Frank knows just about everything. Jon's sexual prowess has helped him really plug in to everything in LA that counts. He knows everyone, knows who's on the A list at any given time for the past ten years, and that's because he's slept with them. He knows stuff he probably shouldn't know, knows all the players, intimately, most of them, including me, not that I'm a big player, mind you. Sex is powerful. Maybe sometimes even more powerful than money."

Savich thought that was probably true. The good Lord knew that if he chanced to look at Sherlock—it didn't matter where they were or what they were doing—the chances were he wanted her right at that very minute. He remembered just the week before they hadn't even made it into the house. They'd made love against the garage wall. But to have sex color every encounter, to make it the cornerstone of your success, to have sex as a major building block to help you get what you wanted and to get you *plugged in*—no, he really couldn't relate to that.

Belinda said, "I know that all makes it sound like Jon is a real Hollywood predator, and he is, but I'm using 'predator' in the good sense."

Sherlock laughed. "I've never before heard a person described as a predator in a good sense."

"As sort of the real insider," Belinda said, no offense taken. Then she frowned. "But then there's another side to Jon. He's got a mean streak, and it's really deep inside him."

Sherlock said, "Tell us about this mean streak. We haven't seen it."

"Well, when I stopped sleeping with him, I was the one to break it off—not him. Normally it's Jon who wants to move on, but the word is that he does it very smoothly, doesn't leave a woman wanting to cut his— Well, doesn't leave a woman wanting revenge. Nope, he manages to keep his women as friends.

"Don't get me wrong, he would have been the one to move on from me, too, but it just so happened that I met Frank." Belinda leaned closer. "It still scares me when I think about it. I told Jon the truth. I remember he just stood there, right in front of me, and his hands were fists at his sides. He didn't hit me. He just said in this really soft voice that I was a bitch and no woman dumped him. I think he slashed my tires, but since I didn't see him actually do it, I can't prove it. I'd call that pretty mean."

"I would, too," Sherlock said. "But that isn't the end of it, is it?"

"Right. Then there was Marla James, a young, real pretty girl who actually had some talent. I don't know what went on between them, but whatever happened, Jon saw to it that she was kicked off her show. I heard she was pregnant—by Jon? I don't know, but she left LA."

Sherlock took down all the facts Belinda knew about Marla James.

"Then there was the guy who aced Jon out of an AD spot—that's assistant director—on this new show he really wanted. That was *Tough Guy,* lasted four years. Anyway, the guy ended up with two broken legs, couldn't do the job. Jon got it. Was he responsible? You betcha, but there wasn't any proof."

Savich said, "Are you upset that *The Consultant* has been stopped?"

Belinda smiled, shrugged, pulled out another roller, and scratched her scalp. "Poor Frank, he's the one who's really upset. This was his baby. He has a lot of ego on the line here."

Sherlock said, "Can you think of anyone who would be pleased to see the show closed down?"

Belinda pulled out the final roller, dropped it, and all three of them watched it roll across the floor.

"Pleased enough to murder people according to a prewritten script? Now that's something I haven't thought about," she said, frowned at the fallen roller, then ignored it. All the rollers were arranged like little smokestacks in front of her. She ran her fingers through her hair, over and over again. Her hair, Sherlock decided, didn't need to be combed. It looked tousled and thick and utterly beautiful, more shades of blond than she could count.

"You know," Belinda said, her voice low, all confidential now, "Wolfinger's bodyguard. He's this big guy, never says a word. His name's Arnold Loftus. I think he and Wolfinger sleep together."

"You're saying that Wolfinger is gay?" Savich said.

Belinda just shrugged.

A boy with a bad complexion stuck his head in. "They need you on the set, Ms. Gates."

Belinda took one final swipe at her hair, nodded at herself in the mirror, rose, and smiled at them. "Sean's his name? I'd like to have a little boy," she said, nodded to both of them, and walked out of the green room.

Savich said, "I got turned on watching her with those rollers, Sherlock. What do you say we buy some of our own?"

"Some really big ones?"

"Oh yes," he said, "bigger than the ones we used before," and Sherlock laughed.

CHICAGO

My poor darling, how are you feeling?"

Nicola looked up at John Rothman, heard three of his aides speaking in the hospital corridor because he'd left the door ajar. His face was ruddy from a stiff Chicago wind and thirty-degree weather, his blue eyes bluer than a summer sky. She thought she'd first fallen in love with his eyes, eyes that could see into people's souls, at least see deep enough that he always knew the right things to say when he was campaigning.

"I'm okay now, John, just a sore throat and my stomach feels hollowed out."

"I'm here to take you home. I was thinking, Nicola, maybe you should just move in with me now. The wedding is in February, so why not speed some things up a bit?"

She hadn't slept with him. The one night she'd decided she was ready, they were caught making out just outside one of John's favorite clubs—*The High Hat*—his tongue in her mouth, his hands on her butt, and there'd been photos in the *National Enquirer*. Very embarrassing.

He'd only given her light pecks on the cheek after that incident.

She said, "If I move in with you, people will find out. Don't forget what happened before."

He shrugged. "All right, then. Let's move up the wedding. How about the end of the month?"

She was silent.

"I want us to begin our life together, Nicola, as soon as possible. I want to make love with you."

She was still silent.

"I saw you naked, you know. You're really quite beautiful."

She smiled up at him as he took her hand, squeezed it lightly. "When did you see me naked?"

"I came over to get you, a couple of weeks ago. I rang the buzzer but you didn't answer. I had a key, and so I let myself in. I heard the shower, and I watched you step out and dry yourself.

You didn't know I was there. I don't know why I'm telling you this now, except to say I'd like to see you that way again. I'd like to lick you all over, Nicola."

Maybe it was because she still felt utterly empty inside, but she didn't say what she probably would have said with a smile two weeks before—*Licking goes both ways.*

"I'm very tired, John. Really, too tired to even think straight. I want to go home, lie in my own bed, get myself back together. Then we can talk about it. Did the doctor say anything more to you? About the food poisoning?"

"After speaking to each of us extensively, we figured out that only you had the raspberry vinaigrette dressing."

"Dressing can cause food poisoning?"

John shrugged. "Would you like me to come back and take you home?"

Before she could say anything, one of John's aides appeared in the doorway. "Senator, excuse me, but there's a call from the mayor. He's looking to speak to you."

"Go, John. I'll be all right."

He leaned down, kissed her cheek. "You're so pale," he said, and lightly touched his fingertips to her cheek. "Shall I get you a bit of lip gloss from your purse?"

She nodded.

She watched him walk to the small table on the opposite side of the hospital room, open her purse, and pick up the lip gloss. He looked at it, frowned. "It's really light," he said. "You need something to make you look healthier."

"I'll put on some colorful stuff when I get home. Will I see you later?"

"I'm sorry, but I've got a meeting with a very important lobbying group tonight. I put off my lunch with the mayor so I could grab a little time to come see you. Albia is coming by to take you home. I'll see you tomorrow."

She watched him walk out, tall, slender, so very elegant. Interestingly enough, he ranked nearly as high with male as with female voters. She heard the buzz of voices surrounding him, disappearing finally down the hall.

Albia arrived two hours later, sweeping into her room, two nurses behind her, not to chastise, but to bow and scrape and give her anything she asked for. Albia had that effect on people. She was a princess, well, perhaps now that she was in her fifties, she was a queen. She was regal. She was so self-confident, so self-assured, that sometimes even John would back down in the face of a single word from his sister's mouth. She had been his hostess before he married Cleo, and then after she ran off with Tod Gambol. She was an excellent campaigner. It was rare that a reporter would ever ask her an impertinent question.

"Albia," Nicola said.

Albia Rothman leaned down, kissed Nicola's cheek. "Poor little girl," she said. "This is so awful. I'm so very sorry." She ran her finger over Nicola's cheek.

"It was hardly your fault, Albia."

"That doesn't lessen my being sorry that it happened during my birthday dinner."

"Thank you."

Albia straightened, walked to the window, and looked out toward Lake Michigan. "This is a very nice room. John didn't even have to insist. You were brought here right after they released you from the emergency room." She looked at Nicola, then away again. Albia was a very tactile person, and now she was running her hand over the drapes, less institutional than in most of the rooms that had drapes, but still.

"I've had food poisoning before, Albia. This wasn't like that other time."

A sleek eyebrow went up a good inch. "Oh? How very odd. I suppose this sort of thing can affect a person in different ways."

"I'm just having trouble understanding what I ate that could have caused it."

"I see. Do you wish to pursue it any further then?"

Nicola wanted to pursue it all the way to the moon, if necessary, but she knew when something simply wasn't possible. She shook her head.

Albia pulled a chair close to Nicola's bed and sat down. She crossed her legs, quite lovely legs, sheathed in stockings and three-inch black Chanel heels.

"John tells me that he wants to marry you as soon as possible. He reminded me about that car that almost hit you, and now this. He wants you safe and sound, and to a man—to John—that means you're in his house, in his bed, and he's looking after you. When he's there, that is."

And Nicola said, without hesitation, "I don't know, Albia. I don't think I'm ready to rush things."

"What is this? John is an excellent catch. He has more women chasing him—both here and in Washington—and he is charming to all of them, but it's you he wants. And that is a miracle, to my mind."

"A miracle? Why?"

"He loved Cleo so very much, loved her nearly to the point of obsession. When she ran away, I thought he would simply shut down he was so devastated. I was very worried about him, for months on end."

"I remember. I felt so very sorry for him, all of the staff did as well as the volunteers." Nicola remembered how stoic he appeared whenever anyone mentioned his wife's name, how stiff and remote he became.

Albia said, shaking her head, her voice incredulous, "To think that Cleo actually ran off with Tod Gambol. Sure, he was something of a hunk, a lot younger than John, but for her to want him more than John, well, it still doesn't seem possible to me."

"I wonder where they are," Nicola said. "It's been three years and still no word?"

"No, not a thing. I'll never forget how he met her. He was taking one of his very rare vacations, a long weekend really, and she was there at the hotel, some sort of manager, and there was the fire in his room and she came to apologize. And, well, they were married one week later. I was very surprised, as was the rest of the world. They kept it all very private."

"They were together for five years," Nicola said, remembering Cleo Rothman's voice, her incredible talent for organization and management. The staff had loved her.

She said, "I remember wondering why John hadn't married until he was, what? Nearly forty?"

"That's right. He and Cleo were married when he had just turned thirty-nine. Didn't he tell you? Well, he fell in love with a girl in college—this was at Columbia. Her name was Melissa and they were going to get married when they graduated. Our father was against it, of course, because John's life was planned out for him, and that included three years of law school, and a nice long wait until our father could find him the right sort of wife, you know what I mean, but John didn't care. He wanted Melissa and he wasn't going to wait."

"What happened?"

"She died in an auto accident at the end of her senior year. John was distraught, didn't recover for quite a number of years.

Actually, I don't think he recovered until he met Cleo. But look, Nicola, it's only been three years, and he wants to marry you. That is a miracle. He is very much in love with you, don't you think?"

"So much tragedy," Nicola said, aware that she wanted to cry, that her throat hurt so badly she didn't think she could speak another word. She was so hungry she wanted to gnaw her own elbow. She wanted to get out of there, she wanted to go home and curl up in her own bed. And she didn't want anyone at all to come into her condo and see her naked in the bathroom.

"I'm so tired, Albia. I believe they're going to release me soon."

Albia rose. "Yes, I've taken care of it. If you'd like to dress now, I'll take you right home."

"Thank you. I would like that very much. But, Albia, I want to go to my own place. I'm just not ready to move in with John."

NINETEEN

BEAR LAKE, CALIFORNIA

Dane had volunteered to drive the two hours up to Bear Lake to see what they could find out about Weldon DeLoach from the staff and, they hoped, from his elderly father. "Hey, maybe," Flynn had said, "old Weldon will be hiding in one of the rest home's closets."

Dane pulled onto the freeway, then turned to Nick. "I forgot to tell you. Flynn got a search warrant and went over to Weldon's house. Unfortunately they didn't find anything to either implicate DeLoach or give a clue as to his whereabouts. And just before we left, Delion checked in with Lieutenant Purcell. They haven't caught up with Stuckey yet, so we have no gun. There wasn't anything in Milton McGuffey's apartment either that gives us a clue to the man who called Stuckey. But it's early days yet."

She nodded, stared down a moment at her clasped hands. She had a jagged fingernail and began worrying it. "I wanted to tell you that I was really sorry I couldn't be with you at the cemetery. I wanted to say good-bye to Father Michael Joseph, too, but they rushed me off so fast I didn't have a chance to speak to you about it."

"I'm sorry you couldn't come, too. At least the media didn't catch up with you. But you can bet some enterprising souls are trying their best to put this all together. Something will leak soon from the studios, if it hasn't already. Then it's going to be really rough, with you at the epicenter."

She looked, quite simply, terrified.

Dane, impatient, said, "Look, Nick, you know this is an international story. For God's sake, you're the eyewitness to my brother's murder."

"Not really. I haven't been any help at all."

"We'll see. Now, the media thing. It's going to happen. You really need to reconsider telling me what's going on with you."

"No, I don't." She still hadn't come to a decision about what to do. She knew she couldn't be a homeless person forever; it wasn't any sort of solution at all, but what she would do, she just didn't know yet. "You made a deal. Keep your questions to yourself."

He shrugged, and she knew he was irritated, probably more than irritated. He changed lanes to avoid being stuck behind an eighteen-wheeler. He looked over at her, his expression serious. "I'm sorry, but the shit will hit the fan. It's coming. Okay, no more questions, but when you're ready to tell me, just let me know."

She said nothing, just stared at the dashboard.

"I want to thank you, Nick, for the way you've stuck with me over the last days. It's—it's been difficult, and you really helped me."

She nodded. "It's hard to believe that so little time has passed. It's been very hard for you."

"Yes." He was silent, to keep control. Damnation, it was so hard. He said, "It's been difficult for you as well."

She said, surprising him, "I remember when my father died—it was in a hunting accident—some idiot took him for a deer up in northern Michigan. Death like that, so sudden, so unexpected, you just can't figure out how to deal with it."

"Yes," Dane said, eyes on the road in front of him. "I know. How old were you when your dad died?"

"Nearly twenty-two. It was really bad because my mom had died just two years before. Sure, I had lots of friends, but it's just not the same thing."

He said slowly, "I never really thought of you as a friend."

She felt a punch of hurt at his words. "I would have thought that we've been through enough to be friends, haven't we?"

"You misunderstand me," Dane said. "No, I didn't think of you as a friend precisely, I thought of you as someone who was there for me, who understood, someone important."

She was silent for a moment, but to Dane it seemed an aeon had passed before she said, "Maybe I agree with you."

Dane smiled as he slowed for a car coming onto the freeway. "Hey, you got any relatives at all?"

"Yes, two younger brothers, both Air Force pilots. They're in Europe. All these questions. Are you trying to trip me up? Is this one of your famous FBI strategies to make a perp spill her guts?"

"Nah. If I wanted to interrogate you, I'd be so subtle, so con-

181

summately skilled that you wouldn't even be aware of what I was doing."

"I've also got two uncles who drill for oil in Alaska."

"I'm sorry about your folks."

"Thank you. I think they were both surprised when I ended up with a Ph.—Well, that's not important."

Yeah, right, he thought. "What do you think of Savich and Sherlock?"

"Sherlock showed me a photo of Sean. He's adorable."

"Sean is nearly a year old now, running all over the place, jabbering a language that Savich claims is an advanced code used in rocket science. I'm Uncle Dane, only it doesn't come out that way."

"They've been here less than twenty-four hours—it's like I've known them for much, much longer. Sort of like you, only not exactly."

"I know what you mean."

"How long have you been an FBI agent?"

"Six years now. I came out of law school, went to a big firm, and hated it. I knew what I wanted to do."

"A lawyer. I wouldn't have guessed."

"You mean I don't look slimy?"

"Close enough." A lawyer, that was all she needed. Both a lawyer and an FBI agent. She'd nearly spilled the beans about her Ph.D. It looked like he didn't even need to exert himself particularly to get information out of her.

Nick didn't tell him anything more about herself, eventually just looked out her window at the passing vegetation that was getting greener as they gained altitude.

They finally arrived at Bear Lake. Set amid groves of pine trees, up a beautiful long sloping lawn that stretched up about fifty yards from Bear Lake, was a lovely old two-story building of weathered wood, each room featuring glass doors and a small terrace that gave onto the lake. There were several piers that went some fifty feet out into the calm blue water, where half a dozen canoes and several power boats were tied up. Lovely white-painted chairs and benches were scattered over the manicured lawn. But it was winter, and even though it was in the high fifties today, no one was outside to appreciate it.

They left their rented cherry-red Pontiac Grand Am in a small parking lot set amid a grouping of pine trees and walked on a flagstone path to the discreet entrance. Nick looked up at the crystal-clear sky, at the cumulus clouds that were sweeping lazily overhead. She turned a moment to look at Bear Lake glistening beneath a noonday sun, snow glinting on the peaks in the distance. There was only a light spray of snow around Bear Lake.

Nick stood still a moment, staring out toward the lake. It was as still as a postcard. She said, "I think this is a beautiful place, but somehow, I don't know why, I just don't like it."

She turned, sped up, and entered the double glass doors, which led into a large lobby. In the center was a large wooden counter with offices behind it.

Behind the counter stood a stout woman with curly black hair and a very pretty smile. The name on her tag read Velvet Weaver. With the thin black mustache over her upper lip, she didn't look much like a Velvet.

Dane introduced both himself and Nick, showed her his FBI shield.

"Oh dear, I hope there's nothing wrong."

"This is just routine, Ms. Weaver," Dane said easily. "Just a couple of questions we hope you can help us with. Could you please tell us about one of your patient's sons, a Mr. Weldon DeLoach?"

Velvet nodded. "I suppose there's nothing wrong with that. Yes, a lovely man, Mr. DeLoach, a wonderful son. You know, he's this big TV writer in Hollywood and so it's only the best for his father."

"Is Mr. Weldon DeLoach here right now? Visiting with his father?"

"Oh no, Agent Carver, Weldon hasn't been here for a week, at least not that I know of. Of course, he could have visited when I wasn't on duty. I'll ask around for you. I was wondering just the other day when he was coming to see his father again. Not that Captain DeLoach knows when his son is here, poor man. Dementia, you know, for about the last six years now. Is something wrong with Weldon?"

Dane shook his head. "Nothing at all. As I said, this is just routine, Ms. Weaver. Now, I understand that Captain DeLoach is a retired police officer?"

"Yes, he was the captain of this small-town police department in the central valley for nearly forty years."

"Do you remember the name of the town?" Dane asked.

"Dadeville. It's a good-sized town now. Not all that far from Bakersfield. Poor man, but he's eighty-seven years old and human parts break down. It's sad, but Captain DeLoach doesn't seem to be in any particular distress about it. It's usually that way. What you can't remember doesn't hurt you."

"He's that old?" Nick said.

"Yes. Weldon was his only child, born when Captain DeLoach was already well into his forties. Captain DeLoach, when he remembers, tells everyone that it was his third marriage, and his wife was much younger.

"She died, I believe, in some sort of accident when Weldon was only four years old. Captain DeLoach never remarried. He raised Weldon. And he's a very good son; he's paid for his father to be here for nearly ten years now. Never complains about any of the extras, always comes to visit."

Ms. Weaver paused, looked a bit worried. "May I ask you why you're here, Agent Carver? I know you said it was just routine, but still—would you like to speak to our manager, Mr. Latterley? He isn't here right now, but I could have him call you."

"That's not necessary, but thank you, Ms. Weaver. We'll speak to Mr. Latterley later. We're really here to see Captain DeLoach. Will that be a problem, Ms. Weaver?"

"Not at all, but let me warn you not to expect much. Captain DeLoach normally just sits about, looking out at the lake and the mountains. It's very peaceful here, very soothing for the soul. I know he enjoys watching people water-ski. Of course, now that it's winter, there's not much of that."

Nick said, "What does Weldon look like, Ms. Weaver?"

"A lovely man, is Weldon. Let's see, I suppose he'd have to be in his early forties. He's fair-skinned, light hair, although, you know, he's always really tanned, told me once that he was real proud of that tan. And he's very creative. Always has ideas for the old folks here, things to keep them involved, to keep their brains going."

"Yes, I see," Nick said, and looked over at Dane. How could Weldon DeLoach possibly be the man she'd seen in the church? But then, why had the man used aliases that were so like Weldon's name?

Dane walked down the long, wide, very pleasant corridor. Landscapes lined both sides of the white walls. He wondered about Weldon DeLoach. How was he involved in all this? Did someone hate him so much as to implicate him so directly in the murders?

Nick said quietly so Ms. Weaver wouldn't hear, not looking at him but at the soft watercolor landscapes, "How can Weldon be the monster? Can he be that good with disguises?"

"We'll find out."

"Here's Captain DeLoach's room," Ms. Weaver said, and raised her hand to knock. They heard a groan from inside. Dane didn't hesitate, he was through the door in under a second.

TWENTY

The old man was on the floor beside his overturned wheelchair, moaning softly, a small rivulet of dried blood on his face that had dripped off his chin and onto the floor.

Dane turned to Nick, but she was already gone, probably with Velvet Weaver, to the nurses' station to get help.

"Captain DeLoach," Dane said, leaning close, "can you hear me, sir? Can you tell me what happened?"

The old man opened his eyes. He didn't look like he was in pain, just dazed.

"Can you hear me, sir? See me?"

"Yes, I can see you. Who are you?"

"I'm Special Agent Dane Carver, FBI."

Slowly, very slowly, the old man lifted his trembling, deeply veined hand, and he saluted.

Dane was charmed. He saluted him back. Then he gently wrapped his hand around the old man's and slowly lowered it. "You fell out of your chair?"

"Oh no, Special Agent," he said in a voice that sounded otherworldly it was so whispery thin. "He was here again and I told him I wouldn't keep quiet anymore, and he hit me."

"Who, Captain? Who hit you?"

"My son."

"Hey! What happened here?"

A nurse fell to her knees beside Captain DeLoach, feeling his pulse, cupping her hand around his ancient face. "Captain, it's Carla. You fell out of your chair again, didn't you?"

The old man groaned.

"All right. Now, let me clean the blood off your face, see how bad it is. You've got to be more careful, you know that. If you want to run around the room, just call one of us and we'll steer you. We'll even hold races if that's what you'd like. Now, just lie still, Captain, and I'll take care of everything."

Captain DeLoach's eyes closed. Dane couldn't rouse him.

His son?

Weldon DeLoach had hit his father and knocked him out of his chair? But Velvet had said Weldon hadn't been around for a week. She also said that the old man usually didn't know his own name. Dane held the old man's hand until Carla came back into the room. An orderly, a big Filipino man, lifted him in his arms and carried him to the bed. The old man looked like a bunch of old bones barely knit together, his pale, veined flesh wrapped in a bright blue flannel shirt and baggy pants. There were thick socks on his feet, and only one bedroom slipper. The other slipper was lying near the TV. The orderly laid him on his back, very gently straightening all those old limbs.

"All right, I understand from Velvet that you're FBI agents," Nurse Carla said, not looking at either of them. "Would you mind telling me what's going on? What do you want with Captain DeLoach?"

Dane said, "We came to the door, heard moans, and I immediately opened the door and came into the room. Captain DeLoach was lying on the floor, just as you saw."

"He's always falling out of the chair, knocking it over," she said. "But this is the first time he's hurt himself. Nasty cut on his head, but it won't need stitches. I hope he doesn't have a concussion. That could really take his brain right out of commission."

Dane and Nick watched her wash out the cut, then apply an antibiotic and a bandage. Nick patted her own Band-Aid that covered the graze made by the bullet and flopped her hair back over it.

Carla said, "Captain DeLoach? Can you hear me? Open your eyes."

The old man didn't answer her, just lay there, occasionally moaning.

"He spoke to me," Dane said. "He was quite lucid. He said that someone hit him. Is it possible that that cut isn't from his fall?"

Carla snorted. "Not likely. His only visitor is his son, and Weldon was here last week. Weldon's like clockwork, never more than two weeks go by before he comes to visit." She frowned up at Dane. "You say he was lucid? How could that be? He hasn't been lucid in days now."

"He was. Excuse me a moment, I'm going to have a look around."

"Suit yourself," Carla said. She looked over at Nick. "Did you hear him speak lucidly?"

"No. When I saw him on the floor, bleeding, I came to get you."

"Well, this is all very interesting. Captain DeLoach? Come on now, open your eyes." She lightly slapped the old man's cheeks, once, twice, yet again.

He opened his eyes, blinked.

"Do you hurt?"

He moaned again, closed his eyes.

Carla sighed. "It's really hard when their minds go. Hey, what are you doing?"

Nick said, "I was just checking the chair; it's really sturdy. How does the captain manage to turn it over? It's quite heavy."

"Good question, but he's done it before. No one's seen him actually topple over, just the aftermath. Okay, I've got this wound bandaged. When the doctor comes around I'll have him look at it. Let me give the captain a sedative to help him rest."

"He looks pretty quiet to me right now," Nick said, inching a bit closer to look at the old man's pale face.

Carla said, arms crossed over her chest, eyes suspicious, "You don't know anything about it, do you, so your opinion doesn't count. Now, tell me why two Federal agents are here to see Captain DeLoach."

"Sorry," Nick said, "it's on a need-to-know basis and you're not in the loop."

Nurse Carla harrumphed and laid the palm of her hand on Captain DeLoach's forehead, nodded, pulled a small notebook out of her pocket, and scribbled something down. She didn't say anything else.

Nick wished Dane would come back. She knew he was looking to see if there was any sign of an intruder, any sign that Weldon DeLoach had been there.

Ten minutes later, they were in Mr. Latterley's office with its long glass windows looking onto Bear Lake. He'd just returned, and was still breathing hard.

"Have you seen Weldon DeLoach recently, Mr. Latterley?"

"No. I understand he visited a week or so ago, but I didn't personally see him. He's very dependable, as I'm sure everyone's told you. Once every couple of weeks, he's here to see his father, make sure he's got everything he needs. Sometimes Weldon comes more often."

Dane sat forward. "Have you seen anyone, any stranger, around lately? Today, to be specific?"

Mr. Latterley shook his head. "Well, I was in town for a couple of hours, so you'll have to ask the staff. But I'll tell you, Agent Carver, there's no reason for someone to come here. Oh, we get an occasional hiker in the summer or a tourist who takes a wrong turn, but today? Not that I know of, Agent Carver."

Nick said, "The glass doors in Captain DeLoach's room weren't locked, Mr. Latterley. Someone could have simply opened them and walked in."

"Well, yes, they could, but why? You don't think that someone actually came in and struck Captain DeLoach, do you? He's a very old man, agents. Why would anyone seek to hurt him?"

"I asked him who hit him and he told me it was his son."

Mr. Latterley blinked. "You must have misunderstood him," he said. "Or the old man was just weaving in and out and that was what came out of his mouth. No, not Weldon. That's ridiculous."

He was shaking his head, an interesting head, Nick thought, staring. Shiny, bald, and pointed. She'd never seen a bald head quite so pointed before.

"No," he said again, more forcefully this time. "Impossible. You didn't see any sign of anyone, did you, Agent Carver?"

"I can't be certain. We would like to speak to all the staff who work near Captain DeLoach's room."

Dane spent the next hour doing just that. To a person, they shook their heads and looked bewildered by his questions.

Nick sat beside Captain DeLoach's bed, holding his hand, speaking quietly to him, hoping for a sensible response, but he didn't speak. She said to Dane when he came in, "He did open his eyes a couple of times, but he looked right through me, didn't respond at all. I've been speaking to him, about lots of silly things, but he hasn't answered me."

Just before they left, the doctor came out to say, "I examined Captain DeLoach's head wound. He seems to be all right. To be perfectly honest, I can't tell if it happened because he hit his head when he fell or if someone indeed struck him. But on the face of it, it seems strange to even consider that some miscreant from the outside would come into the old man's room and smack him around."

Dane said as he walked beside Nick toward their car, "Captain DeLoach said that he told his son he wouldn't keep quiet anymore and his son hit him. I wonder what he meant by that?"

"I'm beginning to think we should try the Oracle at Delphi."

He laughed. "Not a bad idea."

"I just realized, I'm really hungry. Do you think we could stop at a Mexican place on the way back to LA?"

"Sure can."

Dane walked into Nick's connecting room at the nicely updated Holiday Inn, not far from Premier Studios on Pico.

She was on the phone. She hadn't heard him, she was so intent on the call.

He stopped cold. Who was she speaking to?

"Listen," he heard her say, "I'm calling from the *Los Angeles Times*. My editor asked me to check out for sure whether he was traveling west. Does his schedule include either San Francisco or Los Angeles?"

She sensed him, there was no other word for it, and whipped around. She met his eyes, and quietly eased the phone back into the cradle.

"I can get the number from the hotel clerk, but it would be easier if you just broke down and told me what's going on."

Nick felt a corrosive fear leap to life. She wanted to cover up with a dozen blankets, run as fast as she could.

"Go away."

He sat down beside her on the queen-size bed, picked up her hands, and held them between his. She had nice hands, short nails, no rings. The skin was smooth again. Her hair was half-dry and she was wearing a bit of lip gloss. Nice mouth, too. No, he wouldn't go there. He said, looking at her straight in the face, "Listen to me, there's a lot going on here, and on top of it all, here you are scared out of your mind about—whatever. Why won't you let me help you? My brain can handle more than one thing at a time. I can multitask as well as a woman. Come on, trust me, Nick."

She suddenly looked very tired, and flattened, yes, defeated. She looked desperately alone.

Very slowly, he pulled her against him. He felt the panic rise in her, but he didn't do anything at all but hold her, give her what comfort he could. He said against her damp hair, which smelled just like his, since they both had used the hotel shampoo, which had a girlie-girl smell, floral and soft, "You've seen firsthand that there's lots of bad stuff and bad people in the world. But you know what? Some of it we can actually do something about. We're going to catch the man who killed all those people, my brother included." He stopped. If and when she was ready to tell him about herself, then she would. Maybe it was all a matter of trust. So be it. No more pushing. He said only, "I'm here for you, Nick."

"Yes, and so is the murderer, and he's already tried to have me killed. I want to leave, Dane. You don't need me anymore."

"It's too late, Nick." He raised his finger and lightly touched it to the Band-Aid that covered the bullet graze. "That's the whole point. Milton failed so the guy who hired him will try again, count on it. You need me, if for nothing else, as a bodyguard."

"Everything is rotten," she said. "All of it, just plain rotten."

"I know. But we'll take care of things. Trust me on that. Hey, rotten is my stock-in-trade. I get a paycheck because of rotten. It gives me motivation."

She fell silent. She didn't move either, just let him pull her close and hold her. She felt the core of steadiness in him, felt how solid he was, physically, and his heart, that was solid, too. She knew he was a rock, that once this man gave his word, you could bet the bank on it.

She thought of Father Michael Joseph, his face identical to Dane's, but he was dead now. She knew Dane was alone with that and she knew he was battling each hour, each day, just to get through. Here she was leaning on him, and he was comforting her. Who did he lean on?

"I'm all right," she said, slowly pulling away from him. She looked at him then and lightly laid her palm against his cheek. "You are an estimable man, Dane. I am so very sorry about your brother."

He closed down, and his face went blank, because he had to hold himself together.

"I would appreciate it," she said, standing, straightening the sweater he'd picked out for her the previous Friday, a lovely V-necked sweater, deep red, that she was wearing over a white blouse, "if you wouldn't try to find out who I was speaking to."

She saw in his eyes that he wasn't going to ask the front desk. At least he was still willing to give her some leeway. He said, "I will find out sooner or later, Nick."

"Later," she said.

He said nothing to that, just shrugged back at her. "Are you ready? We're all meeting for dinner to exchange information."

"I'm ready," she said, and picked up the wool coat he'd bought her. He'd done too much for her, far too much, and he was offering to do more. It was hard to bear. She ran her hands over the soft wool. It felt wonderful. She kept stroking it even as she said over her shoulder, "I was always scared. I'd lie in one of the small cots on the second floor of the shelter, the allotted one blanket pulled to my ears, and I'd listen to people moving about downstairs. Sometimes there'd be yelling, fighting, screaming, and always, I huddled down and was afraid because violence seemed to be part of the despair, and the two always went together. Sometimes they'd bring their fights upstairs and they'd throw stuff or hit each other until some of the shelter staff managed to get things back under control.

"There were drug users, alcoholics, people who were mentally ill, people just ground down by circumstance, all mixed together.

There was so much despair, it was pervasive, but the thing was—everyone wanted to survive."

"And then there was you."

"Yes, but I suppose you could say I was one of those who'd been ground down by circumstance."

She stopped, looked down at her left hand, still stroking her wool coat. "The alcoholics and the addicts—they were self-destructive. It's not that I didn't feel sorry for them, but they were different from the other homeless people because they'd brought their misery on themselves. And they never seemed to blame themselves for what they'd become. It was the strangest thing. One of the shelter counselors said it was because if they ever had to face what they really were in the mirror, they wouldn't be able to bear it. Everyone there had so little. But they were the ones responsible for what had become of them, responsible for where they were. And because they wouldn't face the truth, there was no hope for them.

"The mentally ill people—they were the worst off. I truly can't understand how we as a society allow people who are so ill they can't even remember to take their medications or even know that they need medication, to just roam the streets. They suffer the most because they're the most helpless."

Dane said, "I remember when one of the New York mayors wanted to get the sick people off the streets and into safe houses, but the ACLU went nuts."

Nick said, "I remember. The ACLU cleaned up this poor woman, dressed her like a normal person, fed her meds so she could pass muster, and they won. Except that poor woman lost. Within days she was back on the street, off her meds, cursing and spitting at people, vulnerable and helpless. I wonder if any of the lawyers at the ACLU lost a bit of sleep over that."

"Who are you, Nick?"

She grew very still, didn't move, just stood there when he opened the door to the Grand Am. She said, "My name is Nick, short for Nicola. I don't want to tell you my real last name. All right?"

"You mean, if you tell me your real name I would have heard of it?"

"No. It means that you have a computer and access to information."

So there was something on her, something to be found, something other than just who she was. What had happened to her?

When he was seated in the driver's seat, the key in the ignition, he turned to her and said, "I want to know who you are, not just your name."

She looked straight ahead, saying nothing, until he pulled out of the Holiday Inn parking lot onto the street.

She said, "I'm a woman who could be dead before the first day of spring."

His hands tightened around the steering wheel. "Bullshit. You're just being dramatic, and you're wrong. I think by the first of spring, you'll be doing what you were doing last month. What were you doing in December, Nick?"

"I was teaching medieval history." She didn't know why she said that. Well, he already knew she had a Ph.D., this much more wouldn't tell him anything.

"Are you by any chance Dr. Nick?"

"Yes, but you already guessed that. You know that your brother loved history."

"My brother was an impressive man, he was a very good man," Dane said, and shut up, really fast. He could feel himself breaking apart, deep inside, where his brother's blood and Dane's own pain flowed together. He remembered Archbishop Lugano at Michael's service, his hand on Dane's shoulder, telling him to take it just one day at a time.

He concentrated on driving. He was momentarily distracted by a girl on roller skates, wearing shorts that showed half her butt cheeks, and she was waving to him, grinning and blowing him kisses over her shoulder. He waved back, grinned a bit, and said, "That's some presentation."

"Yes indeed, you're right," Nick said. "I agree, she does skate very well."

Dane jerked around, surprised. "That was funny, Nick."

She smiled. It was a small smile, but a smile nonetheless.

"Where are we going?"

"We're all meeting at *The Green Apple,* over on Melrose."

Nick sighed. "Doesn't sound like they'll have tacos, does it?"

"I just hope they don't serve fried green apples. I'm an American, I love fat, but you know—my belly rebels fast if I eat even two pieces of KFC. It's a bummer."

"Don't whine. It means you won't ever have to worry about your weight."

He smiled at her, then said, "I sure hope someone has found out something useful. The bottom line is that what you and I found out just leads to more questions."

As it turned out, Sherlock and Savich had struck gold.

TWENTY-ONE

Sherlock said between bites of a carrot stick, "We dug up a guy who's a real good friend of Weldon DeLoach's. His name is Kurt Grinder. He's a porn star. Yeah, yeah, I know—the name. I just couldn't help myself so I asked him. He said it was, actually, his real name. He's known Weldon for some eight years, ever since he came to LA. He said he saw Weldon DeLoach two and a half weeks ago at the Gameland Bowling Alley in North Hollywood. Said he and Weldon went bowling together every week, on Thursday night, said Weldon told him that bowling always relaxes him. He was getting worried because Weldon hadn't called him and he couldn't get an answer at Weldon's apartment."

Detective Flynn said, "I can see by that gleam in your eyes,

Agent Sherlock, that there's more to it than that, and you're just leading us slowly down the garden path."

"Enjoy it," Savich said. "Let her string it out. I promise, it's worth it."

Sherlock waved her carrot stick, sat forward a bit. "Turns out that Kurt Grinder had some problem with his bowling shoes and had to stay awhile. Weldon left before he did. When Kurt came out of the bowling alley he saw this guy stop Weldon before he got to his car. They talked for a couple of minutes. Before Kurt could catch up, Weldon and this man went off together, in this man's car, not Weldon's."

Delion said, thumping his fingers on the tabletop, "All right, Sherlock, what man?"

"Kurt said he'd never seen him before, but he got a real good look at him." She dropped her voice so everyone had to lean forward to hear her. "Kurt said he looked to be in his thirties, had dark hair, lots of it. But what really stuck in his mind was that the guy's skin was as white as a whale's belly."

"And that means," Savich said, "that if Kurt is telling the truth, and as far as I could tell he had no reason to lie, that De-Loach could be connected to the killings."

"Or maybe," Dane said slowly, "someone's setting him up. Don't forget. We can't find him. And him being the killer has always been too obvious."

Savich nodded. "One of the first things we asked Mr. Grinder was had he ever seen Weldon with black hair and no tan. He laughed, said Weldon was always changing his look, that he loved disguises, but he'd never seen him go that far. Okay, Sherlock, the *pièce de résistance*."

Everyone at the table leaned forward again.

"Kurt got his license number."

"Jesus," Flynn said, "Kurt Grinder can come work for the LAPD."

Delion said, "Okay, so who owns the damned car?"

Savich said, "Belinda Gates. Frank Pauley's wife, the costar of *The Consultant*."

No one said a word for a good three seconds.

"But it was a man who met Weldon at the bowling alley," Flynn said slowly. "The car belongs to the actress?"

"Yes," Sherlock said. "Savich was thinking that just maybe we could pay a little visit to Belinda and Frank this evening."

Nick, who'd been silent, said now, "Do you think Belinda Gates disguised herself as a man?"

"Ah, Jesus," Delion said. "My brain's getting constipated. Hey, at this point I'm ready to believe in aliens landing in the Hollywood Bowl."

"The question is, where is Weldon DeLoach?" Savich said. He looked over at Nick and Dane. "Okay, let's look at this again. Dane, tell us what you make of all those events at the nursing home."

"Captain DeLoach is demented," Dane said. "No question about that. But I swear to you, when I first spoke to him, he was lucid. Do you know that when I told him I was FBI, he saluted me? Maybe he really did fall out of his chair, maybe he really did make all that up. I just don't know."

Dane turned to Nick, who was sitting with her hands in her lap, just staring down at the remains of her chicken salad, and said, "Nick? What do you think?"

Nick nodded. "Everyone at the nursing home believed Captain DeLoach had fallen, and no one had been around. I don't want to agree, but what else can we believe? That's a lot easier to swallow than a son trying to kill his own father."

"If," Sherlock said, raising another carrot stick, "if Weldon really did bang him on the head and toss him out of his chair, the question remains, what wasn't the old man going to keep quiet about?"

"About the fact that Weldon was murdering people according to his own scripts," Flynn said. "That's pretty obvious."

"Maybe," Sherlock said, but she was frowning. "Maybe. But you know, that's just too easy."

"He wasn't going to keep quiet any longer about what his son was doing," Dane said slowly, spacing out each word. "It sounds possible that Weldon was telling his father he was a murderer, and the old man finally freaked."

Nick said, "But the thing is, who would believe Captain DeLoach if he told everyone that his son was murdering people? His only audience is the nursing home staff, and they all think he's demented. They'd just shake their heads and say how sad it was. They'd just give him more medication. Weldon would have to know that. Why would he hurt, maybe even try to kill, his own father when there was no downside for him?"

Over coffee and tea, Flynn told them his snitches were plugged in and would send juice his way if they found out anything. As for the writers and crew on *The Consultant,* as well as two supervising producers, there was nothing on any of them to raise red flags.

"Typical stuff," Flynn said. "An arrest for prostitution, some drugs, rehab, parking and speeding tickets, a couple of spousal abuse calls, but no charges pressed, nothing to start my gut dancing."

"Yeah?" Delion said. "What? The rumba?"

"Nope," Flynn said, "straight salsa. My wife tells me she likes to see me play basketball, but she loves to see me salsa."

Nick looked at Flynn and said, "I'm pretty good myself, Detective Flynn."

Flynn's eyes gleamed. "We'll have to try it sometime."

Savich said, "Yeah, yeah, now, what about Pauley and Wolfinger?"

"Mr. Frank Pauley has been knocking around Hollywood for going on twenty-five years. He's been married four times, and the current Mrs. Pauley, Belinda Gates, according to insiders, is in for the duration. There's nothing unusual about him, nothing we can find hiding in his closet."

Sherlock said, "Surely if Belinda is involved, her husband has to at least suspect something."

"Agreed," Flynn said. "Now, Belinda Gates. She came to LA five years ago, got some minor roles, did some commercials, a couple of soft porn flicks, even did makeup for several sitcoms. Landing Pauley really made her career.

"From what we can tell, Linus Wolfinger is indeed a boy wonder. An arrogant little prick, evidently likes boys, but that's gossip, not fact. He came from nothing; an orphan in and out of foster homes. Put himself through college—UC Santa Barbara—went to work in various production jobs at Premier Studios a year after he graduated, and somehow managed to impress Burdock at the tender age of barely twenty-three, and the rest, as they say, is history. There's nothing on him, just one damned speeding ticket—and that was on the first day he was driving his new Porsche."

"What was he doing that year after he graduated?" Savich asked.

Flynn's eyes lit up. "Don't know yet. We're checking it." He pulled a small black book from his inside jacket pocket and wrote in it. "One thing's for sure, no one involved in *The Consultant* will be making a move without our being aware of it." Then he smiled at everybody. "How about some dessert?"

Flynn and Delion ordered slices of apple pie, with French vanilla ice cream. When the two servings of dessert arrived, Flynn looked around the table. "All you pantywaist Feds, you nibble around like birds. No wonder you need the locals—we provide not only the brains, but the bulk."

Sherlock, head cocked to the side, her red hair corkscrewing out, said, "You mean that's our problem? A simple lack of sugar? I never thought of it like that." She grabbed up her fork and cut a big piece of apple pie from Flynn's slice.

Nick laughed. Dane joined in. It felt good.

Frank Pauley and Belinda Gates actually did live in a glass house, Dane thought, staring up at the monstrosity atop a cliff off Mulholland Drive. It was filled with lights, and if someone was wandering around inside naked, people five miles away could enjoy the view.

Five cops and one civilian trooped up to the gigantic double wooden doors. Flynn knocked.

A woman answered the door wearing a French maid's outfit, replete with stiletto heels and stockings with seams up the back. She had a sexy little white cap on her head. The only thing was, she had to be at least fifty and a good twenty pounds overweight, her dark hair sprinkled with gray and cut butch.

Everyone managed to keep it together, even when she asked them to follow her into the living room.

"Sir, you have visitors. I believe they're all police officers."

Then she nodded, perfectly serious, to each of them in turn and glided out on those three-inch black heels.

Once the door closed behind her, Delion said to Frank Pauley, "Nice house."

"Thanks. My second wife was an architect. She designed it and it was built to her specifications. Since my third wife and Belinda both really liked it, I haven't made any changes." He cleared his throat. "The only thing is, Belinda picks the staff and doesn't like anyone to be younger than fifty, and so we have FiFi Ann, who really is a very nice person, frighteningly efficient, and something of an exhibitionist."

"FiFi Ann?" Sherlock said, an eyebrow up a good inch.

"She decided that was the name she wanted. She's a former actress. She, ah, picked out her French maid's outfit herself, said she wanted to adjust her image. Now, why are you all here at nine o'clock at night?"

"We would like to speak to Belinda," Sherlock said. "Is she here?"

"Certainly. Her partying days are over unless she's on my arm." Pauley walked to the phone, punched a couple of buttons, and called, "Cops in the living room. Come save me."

"Cute," Flynn said.

Belinda came in not five minutes later, wearing black leggings and a sweatshirt, no sneakers. Her face was shiny with sweat, her hair plastered to her head. She was wiping her face with a towel.

"Hi, Agent Sherlock, Agent Savich. Frank, you don't need help from them. They've got a little kid who's adorable. Who are these other folks?"

Introductions were made. As usual, Dane included Nick, making her seem to be just another Federal agent.

"Are you here to arrest Frank?" Belinda said.

Flynn reached for the handcuffs in his back pocket, pulled them out, and waved them toward Pauley. "You want me to take him to the floor, ma'am? We officers of the law like to be obliging."

Belinda laughed, continued to wipe sweat off herself. She suddenly pulled off her sweatshirt. Underneath it she was wearing only a little workout bra.

The men in the room nearly expired on the spot. Nick laughed. "That was very well done. I'll bet you Detective Flynn has already forgotten the handcuffs."

Belinda just smiled. "Frank, why don't you get us all a soda?"

When everyone was seated on the stark white leather chairs, love seats, and huge long sofa, facing a fireplace Nick couldn't ever imagine using in LA, Sherlock said, "Belinda, please tell us why you met Weldon DeLoach two and a half weeks ago at the Gameland Bowling Alley, why you were dressed like a man, and where you went."

Frank Pauley jumped to his feet and walked fast to a huge set of floor-to-ceiling glass windows. Actually, since the entire living room that faced out toward the ocean was glass, he had no place else to go.

Belinda drank down her soda and said after a moment, "Isn't it strange how easily you can get tripped up?"

"Yeah, but that's how we make our living," Delion said. "What were you doing meeting Weldon DeLoach? Why were you dressed like the perfect description of our murderer?"

Frank whirled around. "I knew it, I just knew it. Weldon is crazy about you, wants to make you a star and—"

Four wives, Nick thought, getting a glimmer of reality in the glass house.

Belinda smiled toward her husband, who looked ready to break into small pieces he was standing so rigid. She didn't seem at all perturbed. "Actually, sweetie, he's not. Weldon isn't my type, you are. Now, Weldon and I had arranged to meet that night, at the bowling alley, and I was to pick him up. We went to *La Pomme* in Westwood, sat at a booth and brainstormed story ideas. He wanted my role in *The Consultant* to be bigger." She shrugged. "Yes, I was dressed like a man. Weldon asked me to, told me what to wear, what disguise to use. Of course, now that's academic since Weldon is nowhere to be found and the show's been yanked."

Sherlock said, "Weldon wanted to change your role to a man's? This doesn't make a whole lot of sense, Belinda."

"He was thinking about another idea, a woman who was a spy and had the international community believing she was a man. He wanted to see if I was a good enough actress to fool people into believing I was a man. Nothing more than that. I think I did well. Nobody gave me a second look. Weldon laughed and laughed, he was so tickled. You know, Frank, how he acts when he's excited."

"How did you carry it off?" Sherlock said. "You're beautiful and you've got lots of hair."

"Well, you see, I used to do makeup back in the bad old days, and I'm really good at it. That disguise wasn't much of a challenge."

Nick felt her heart crash to the floor. It sounded so reasonable the way Belinda, the actress, told it, even the wretched disguise. Thing was, Nick believed her.

"She's a hell of an actress," Flynn said to the group as he walked to his car in the large circular driveway. "We can't forget that. God, she's gorgeous, isn't she?"

TWENTY-TWO

CHICAGO

Nicola arrived home with a bad headache after a two-hour, very contentious staff meeting at the university. At least she no longer felt like she'd been starved and kicked around. It had been three days since the food poisoning. A week since she'd begun to see everything in a different light.

She dropped her mail on the small table in her entrance hall, went to the fridge and pulled out a bottle of diet tonic water, and got three aspirins from the medicine cabinet.

When at last she sorted through her mail, she found a single letter without a return address. Her name was written in bold cursive. The handwriting looked vaguely familiar.

Nicola picked up her two-hundred-year-old Chinese dragon

letter opener that John had given her for Christmas and slit the envelope open. She pulled out three sheets of closely written pages. She read:

Dear Nicola, I bet you're surprised to hear from me.

Me who? Nicola skipped to the last page of the letter and read the clean-cut, crisp signature: *Cleo Rothman*. No, it was impossible. Why would Cleo write to her after three years of silence?

There's no easy way to say this, Nicola, but since I was always very fond of you, I'll just come out with it. Don't marry John or you'll be very sorry. He isn't what he seems. You believe, like everyone else, that I skipped town with Tod Gambol, don't you? I didn't. I have no idea where Tod Gambol is, but I wouldn't be surprised if he was dead. I ran, Nicola, I ran. John was going to kill me. You want to know why? Because he believed that I was sleeping with Elliott Benson, that longtime crony of the mayor's and friend of John's. Are they really friends? I don't know.

Actually, I've heard the rumors that you're also sleeping with Elliott. Does John know about them? I'd bet on it. Maybe you've already realized that whatever woman John has, Elliott has to take away from him. You know, I heard he's really good in bed. Are you sleeping with him, Nicola? It doesn't really matter because John undoubtedly believes you are.

You're thinking I'm nuts, but let me tell you what happened three years ago. John was in Washington and I needed something that was in his library. I saw that his safe was open. He's the only one who knows the combination. I was curious so I looked inside. I found a journal, John's journal, and I took it. I've copied a couple of pages for you so you can see what he really is, Nicola. I don't know if he killed his mother, but I do know that he killed Melissa, the girl in college that John wanted to marry until he found out she'd slept with his best friend. And guess what? His best friend was Elliott Benson. How many other women has he killed?

Here are the journal pages, Nicola. You can read for yourself, and not just take my word for it.

Have things already started happening to you?

Run, Nicola, run. John is quite insane. Stay alive.

Cleo Rothman

Slowly, Nicola picked up the final two pages in the letter. John's journal. She read.

Enough, Nicola thought when she finished reading. It was enough. She grabbed her coat and was out the door and on her way to John's condominium in three minutes flat.

She was going to get the truth, tonight.

LOS ANGELES

The star of *The Consultant*, Joe Kleypas, lived on Glenview Drive in a small redwood-and-glass house set on stilts in the Hollywood Hills, surrounded by dead brush, almost-dead mesquite bushes, and straggly pines. After the third knock, Kleypas came to the door wearing only pale blue drawstring sweatpants that had seen better days. He'd tied them loosely, letting them hang low on his belly, showing off his famous abs, which looked like he'd polished them to a high shine. His hair stood up in spikes, and he looked close to snarling. He was also drunk. He weaved just a bit in the doorway, waved a glass at them that was half-full of either water or straight vodka. "My, my, what have we here?"

Sherlock stuck her FBI shield in his face.

He took another drink and sneered even more. "Oh yeah, you're the Keystone cops."

"That's right," Savich said. "We're the Federal Keystone cops. We want to talk to you, Mr. Kleypas."

"Federal Keystone cops. Hey, that's funny."

"It's Mr. and Ms. Federal Keystone cops to you," Dane said.

"Very funny, hot shot." Joe Kleypas had planted himself firmly in the doorway, his arms crossed over his bare chest, a well-worked-out bare chest. Nick wondered how Dane would look if he polished his abs. She wondered if you just walked into a drugstore and asked for ab polish.

Kleypas said, "I already talked to Detective Flynn. I don't want to speak to any more Keystone cops, even Federal ones. Just get the fuck out of here now, all of you. Hey, you're awful pretty, you an actress? You want, maybe we could go someplace, have a little drink. My bedroom's got a good view of the canyon, the sheets aren't too bad."

Neither Sherlock nor Nick knew which one of them had struck his fancy. Nick said, "That's nice, but not today, thank you."

Joe Kleypas shrugged and his abs rippled a bit. "Then all of you can get out. Get out of my face." He drank down the rest of his drink, hiccuped, gave a slight shudder. Not good, Sherlock thought. The man looked about ready to explode.

They'd been told he had a violent temper. A mean drunk— no worse sort of man than that, Sherlock thought, and took another couple of easy steps back in case he did something stupid, like let loose on Dane or Dillon. Sherlock said low to Nick, "Let's go sit in the car," and tugged on her arm. "We're a distraction. Let the guys handle it." They watched Savich very smoothly force Kleypas back into his house and follow him. Dane closed the door behind them.

When Dane and Savich came out some fifteen minutes later, both of them looking disgusted, Sherlock said, "Dillon, please tell me he confessed. It really would make my day."

"Yeah, he did confess," Dane said, "to about a dozen different love-guests, all in the last month, most of the ladies married. He prefers married ladies; he told us that about four times. I think he'd like the two of you to add to his list. Charming guy. Oh yeah, he was drinking straight vodka."

"Dillon, look at your knuckles," Sherlock said, and grabbed his hand. "You hurt yourself. I don't like this."

"I didn't like his mouth," Savich said, shrugging, and flexed his hands. "He came at me, and I ended up shutting it." Nick saw him rub his knuckles, a very slight smile on his face. "Nothing out of his mouth but foul language."

"Now he can repent at his leisure," Sherlock said comfortably, and patted her husband's arm. She knew Dane wouldn't tell a soul that his boss had decked a big Hollywood jerk with shiny abs. She must remember to buy some iodine; she had some Band-Aids in her purse. She always carried them for Sean. Dillon must really have been mad to hit him with his fists.

After Sherlock finished doctoring him, Savich, with a grin at his hands that now sported two Flintstones Band-Aids, pulled the Taurus out of the narrow driveway that sat atop stilts a good thirty feet from the canyon floor, and said, "Kleypas is one miserable lad, but he's more pathetic than dangerous. He's too busy drinking to be doing much of anything else."

"The word over at the studio," Dane said, "is that Kleypas is having trouble getting work because of that drinking problem. *The Consultant* was more or less his last chance. He's really bummed that it's been pulled. He'd be the last one to submarine the show."

The following morning, Nick was blow-drying her hair—another item Dane had bought for her—half an eye on the local TV news. She dropped the hair dryer and yelled, "Oh, no!"

It bounced against the wooden dresser, then clattered to the floor.

Dane was through the door in a flash, zipping up his pants.

"What is it—" He came to a fast stop. She was standing there, clutching her middle, staring at the TV. She didn't say a word, just pointed.

There she was, in living color, walking beside him down Pico Boulevard toward their parked car. There was a close-up of her face and the newscaster said in a chirpy voice, a voice so carefree and pleased he could have been talking about how he'd gotten laid the previous night, "This is Ms. Nick Jones, the San Francisco police department's key witness in the Prime-Time Killer murders. Sources tell us that Ms. Jones was living in a homeless shelter in San Francisco and just happened to see the killer at Saint Bartholomew's Church."

"Well, damn," Dane said. "I'm not surprised that they've got something, but all this? They've got everything, including your name and a shot of you." He saw that Nick was as white as the bathroom tile.

He walked over to her and pulled her against him. "It will be all right," he said against her still-damp hair. "You've got the fastest guns in Hollywood on your side. We'll keep clear of the reporters. It'll be okay."

She laughed, a desperate laugh that felt like a punch to his gut. She raised her head to look at him and splayed her palms on his bare chest. "I've got to get out of here, Dane. There's no choice for me now."

"No. I said I'll protect you and I will. You want more Feds around? Fine, I'll speak to Savich. He'll arrange it."

"It was luck that saved me at Father Michael Joseph's funeral, not you."

"You're right about that, Nick." Dane hated to admit it. "I'll get more folks to guard you," he said again.

She just shook her head. Then, to his astonishment, she leaned her head forward and lightly bit his shoulder. Then she pulled away from him. "I hope I didn't break that very nice hair dryer you bought for me."

"You're not going to run, Nick."

She gave him a long look, then nodded as she said, "Very well," and of course he knew she was lying. She didn't do it very well.

He said nothing, just rubbed where she'd bitten him and left her room to finish dressing. He realized he'd never been bitten before. Did it qualify as a hickey?

Forty-five minutes later, they were in the Los Angeles field office, in the conference room with the SAC, Special Agent in Charge Gil Rainy. Sherlock said, "Sure the press found out about the murders being based on the first two episodes, but how did they find out about Nick? Not just her name, but that she was homeless."

"Maybe the murderer himself," Dane said. "He wants to flush her out, put her in the limelight."

Delion said, "Already the media idiots—oops, I'm being redundant—have labeled the murderer the Prime-Time Killer. I swear, even if it cost lives, the media would spit it all out, no hesitation at all."

Rainy said, "I bet they sat around and brainstormed to come up with the cute handle. But, bottom line, the leak isn't any big deal. The murderer already knows about her so who cares if everyone else does, too? Still, it's like the media wants to offer her up as the sacrificial goat."

Savich said, "I called Jimmy Maitland and told him what they showed, asked him to rattle some cages, find out how this happened. The thing is—where did they get the photo of Nick and Dane? To be honest, it seems to me like a plant. I think someone sent the photo in along with specifics."

"The murderer," Dane said, and looked over at Nick, who hadn't said a word. "Who else would have?"

Flynn said, "You're right. If a reporter had found them, he would have shot some video, not just taken a photo of them, so maybe Dane's right, it was the murderer."

Dane said, "Actually, that's not what's so bad about all this." He sat forward as Nick grabbed his arm.

"No, Dane, don't."

He ignored her. "Nick was in the homeless shelter in San Francisco because she's running from something or someone she hasn't told any of us about. So I think she's got two people after her, both dangerous. Being on TV was the worst thing that could have happened to her."

Sherlock said, "Okay, Nick, then it's time for you to level with us. We're the Feds. The perfect audience. Flynn and Delion are locals, but they aren't bad either, what with all the sugar they eat. We will do everything we can for you, count on it. Now talk."

Nick actually smiled. "Thank you, Sherlock, but I can't. I just can't."

Savich said, "We could lock you up, you know."

"No, you can't," Nick said. "I made a deal with Delion and Dane. Leave me alone. This is over." Then she simply pushed back her chair and walked out of the room.

"Well, hell," Dane said, and shoved back his chair to go after her.

"Not to worry," said Gil Rainy. He spoke into his cell phone. "She won't get out of the office."

Flynn said, "But we can't hold her, can we?"

"Sure," Delion said. "She's a material witness, in the flesh."

They heard some orders, a yell, and furniture crashing over. They ran out of the conference room to see four male agents holding Nick's arms and hands, trying to protect themselves. That left her the furniture to kick, which she was doing. She'd lost control. She was fighting as if her life depended on it. Dane realized he'd pushed too hard, but he hadn't felt he'd had a choice.

Delion yelled, "Don't hurt her, dammit!"

Three chairs lay on their sides, and a computer monitor was hanging off the edge of a desk. An agent grabbed it just in time.

"Give her to me," Dane said, although he knew she'd try to kill him, too. The agents gladly handed her over. This time she didn't bite him, she tried to kick him in the groin. He heard Rainy yell, "Hey, not that!" as he quickly turned to the side, just in time, and her knee struck his thigh. He pulled her back against him and closed his arms around her body, pinning her arms to her sides, her legs against his, giving her no leverage at all. But she just wouldn't stop. She heaved and jerked and didn't make a sound.

"Hey," Dane said finally, "anybody got any handcuffs?"

"Don't you dare, you jerk," Nick said.

He grabbed her shoulders and shook her. "Listen to me, Nick. You are not going to die, at least not in my lifetime. You really might try for a little trust here." He shook her again. Rainy handed him a pair of cuffs. Dane jerked her arms behind her and cuffed her.

He thought she was going to explode. She kicked and bit and twisted until Sherlock walked right up to her, got in her face, and said, "Stop it, Nick, or I'm going to belt you. The men won't because you're a woman. You're really pushing me here."

Nick believed her. She got control of herself, but it took a bit of time before the hideous panic subsided. She was white, shaking, her breath coming in gulps. "Don't hit me, Sherlock," she said, and just went limp. Sherlock held her up.

"Somebody give me the key to these ridiculous handcuffs."

One of the agents tossed Sherlock the keys. She opened them up, slipped them off, and rubbed Nick's wrists. Sherlock said, "Okay, don't you move or I'll coldcock you. Now, Nick—"

Dane said, "Her name's Nicola. At least she told me that much. And she's a Ph.D.—medieval history."

Nick lunged for him. Sherlock grabbed her and managed to hold her, as Nick yelled, "You just had to blab it, didn't you, Dane Carver? I'm going to bite you again really good, when you least expect it, damn your eyes, just like I did this morning when you were half-naked and I bit your shoulder!"

There was complete silence, at least twenty special agents frozen in place, all ears.

Sherlock blinked, eased her hold on Nick, who ran at Dane, her fists up, ready to kill him. He was fast, grabbed her, pulled her back up tightly against his chest, and held her arms against her sides. "This is familiar," he said, remembering how he'd saved himself in the police station in San Francisco by holding her immobile just this way.

She was still breathing too fast, but at last her muscles were beginning to relax. "I'm not going to let you go just yet. I really would like my body parts intact."

One of the special agents guffawed. "Hey, Agent Carver, speaking of body parts, let's see the bite on your shoulder."

"Ah," said another agent, "the perils of being an FBI agent. I think Dane should get combat pay."

Nick growled. At least her breathing was slowing down.

TWENTY-THREE

SAC Gil Rainy assigned two agents to protect Dane and Nick. Old geezers, Gil said, who needed to do something different because they'd just about burned out on bank robbers.

"Old geezers, hell," Delion said when he met Bo and Lou, neither of them over forty-five. "I'm gonna belt Rainy in the chops."

It was just after lunch, eaten at a KFC, Nick and Dane each eating only one piece of deep-fried chicken breast, when they headed back to Premier Studios to speak to Frank Pauley. The two special agents, Bo and Lou, were hanging a good ways back.

They were at the corner of Brainard and Loomis when out of nowhere a motorcycle came roaring up to the driver's side of the car. The rider was dressed in black leather, a helmet covering his head and face. He pulled a gun out of his leather jacket and began shooting. He was fast and smooth. The window exploded. Dane felt glass shower over his head and face, felt the sting of a bullet that came too close to his ear.

"Nick, get down on the floor! Now!"

She was down instantly. The bullet missed her by no more than an inch, and shattered the passenger-side window, spewing glass shards all over her.

"Jesus, keep down!"

Dane jerked the steering wheel to the left, trying to smash the Trans Am into the motorcycle. He nearly managed it, but the bike swerved hard left, then pulled back. Dane jerked out his SIG Sauer and held it in his left hand, waiting, while he tried to control the car and not kill anyone. Suddenly, the bike came back up again, the guy firing rapidly, at least six shots, emptying his clip. He stuffed it inside his black leather jacket, pulled out another, and fired again. Dane fired back, still wrestling with the car. He felt a smack of cold against his left arm, ignored it, and fired again. In the next instant, they were at a side street. Dane jerked the steering wheel sharply right. They screeched on two tires as the Trans Am barreled onto the street, barely missing three cars whose drivers were sitting on their horns and yelling curses.

Dane managed to bring the Trans Am to a stop next to a curb in front of a small 1940s bungalow. He was breathing hard, adrenaline flowing so fast his heart was nearly pumping out of his chest.

The motorcycle flew past, revving hard and loud. The guy fired two more shots, both high and wild. Then Dane just couldn't believe it—the guy turned a bit and waved to them. In the black leather gloved hand he waved, he held a gun.

Nick was stuffed on the floor, her head covered with her hands. Blood trickled over her hands from the glass shards that had struck her. He reached out his right hand and lightly touched her head. "Nick, are you okay?"

"Yes, just some glass in my hair. Oh dear, my hands are cut a bit, but nothing bad. Are you okay?"

"Sure."

"Where are Bo and Lou?"

"They're coming up behind us right now." Dane opened the door and got out. Then he looked down at his shirt. "Well, shit."

She yelled from behind him, "You're shot, dammit, Dane Carver. How could you?"

He heard her voice shaking, felt the shock building in it, and said calmly, "I'm all right. A through-and-through shot, a flesh wound, nothing broken, everything works. I've cut myself worse shaving. It's hardly worse than what Milton's bullet did to your head. Take it easy, Nick. We're okay, both of us, and that's what's important."

"The guy waved to us. Did you see that? He actually waved to us as he was holding the gun!"

"Yeah, I know. Some balls, huh? How did you see that? I told you to keep way down."

"I just looked up there at the end. The bastard." She was starting to tremble, then shudder. He took off his bloody jacket and wrapped it around her, pulled her against his side. "It's okay. Just hang on, breathe deeply. That's right, nice and deep. Bo and Lou will be here in a minute."

"I thought we were going to be bored out of our gourds," Lou said when he trotted up. "I'm sorry, guys. We were really hanging back. We won't do that again." He looked at the shattered windows, closed the driver's-side door, and waved away the six or so civilians who were closing in on them.

"Everything's okay here, folks. Just go about your business. Hey, what's all that blood? Jesus, Dane, you got hit."

Bo said, breathing hard, "The guy clipped you, Agent Carver. Okay, let's get you over to Elmwood Hospital, it's the closest, good emergency room. I took Lou there just last month."

Dane said, "What was wrong with Lou?"

"I ate too much fat over a couple of days and got a gallbladder attack," Lou said. He moved Dane's hand and pressed his own palm hard over the wound. After a few minutes, he tied his handkerchief around Dane's upper arm. Dane thought about his single piece of KFC and hoped he'd never have a gallbladder attack.

"There," Lou said, "that should slow the bleeding down. Try to remember to give it back to me. My wife gave me that handkerchief for my birthday just three days ago. It's real linen and she embroidered my initials on it. If I lose it, my goose is cooked."

"It won't be lost, Lou," Dane said, "but it will be bloody."

"My wife is used to blood. That's okay."

"I'll keep an eye on it," Nick said, looking up a moment from picking glass out of Dane's hair. She said to him, "You just have a few nicks where some glass got you. Hold still. Bo, if you'll take care of our rental car, Lou can take us to that hospital, okay?"

Bo gave Dane the once-over, nodded, then saluted. "Lou, try to get him a different doctor than the one you had." He loosened the handkerchief a bit as he added, "The guy wanted to cut Lou up right there."

"Didn't happen," Lou said. "I started feeling better and got the hell out of there. Your jacket's ruined, Dane. Hey, Nick, you got yourself together?"

"I'm nearly together, thank you," she said.

Lou looked at her more closely, seemed satisfied. "All right, we're out of here. Bo has already called in. He'll secure the crime scene until someone gets here. Dane, I don't suppose you saw the shooter? Maybe a license plate?"

Dane just shook his head. "The guy wasn't in a car, he was riding a Harley. I didn't even get a good look at the gun. I was too busy trying not to get a bullet through my head. Nick, are your hands still bleeding?"

"No, hardly at all," she said. "I'm just fine. Be quiet now, and let's get you to the hospital."

She'd regained her balance, held the shock at bay. He was proud of her.

Special Agent Lou Cutter got them to Elmwood Community Hospital in under eight minutes. He used the siren and traffic disappeared in front of them. It was an experience Nick had never had. It was, she told him, very cool.

Dane was breathing lightly through his mouth, the pain sharp and hot now, and he didn't like it one bit. It was the first time he'd been shot. By a guy on a damned motorcycle. He said to Lou, "He was probably planning to come up along the passenger side and shoot Nick. We were lucky. He couldn't get up on the sidewalk next to her, too many people. He still tried it from my side."

"If he shot you," Nick said, "you would have lost control of the car and crashed. Then he could have shot me really easily. Or maybe the car crash would have killed me."

Lou said, "Thanks to you, Dane, you kept it together and pulled both of you through. Good job. Now, you do realize that this little show is way over the top. None of us expected anything like this. It's completely different from what he's done to date."

Dane sighed. "Like you said, Lou, this performance was over the top. The guy's desperate, he's losing it. Nick, I'm sorry."

"You're the one he shot."

Lou took care of all the administrative hassles with the emergency room staff, which was a relief since Nick was focused entirely on Dane.

She supposed that Dr. John Martinez thought she was Dane's wife and so didn't kick her out of the cubicle.

"Went right through your upper arm, Mr. Carver," he said after cleaning and examining the wound, poking around while Dane watched him, his mouth tightly closed. "You were very lucky. Not anywhere near any major vessels. It isn't bad at all, when you think about how bad it could have been. How did it happen? Were you cleaning your gun or something? You know that I'm going to have to tell the cops about this."

"You already have," Dane said. He pulled his FBI shield out of his inner pocket and flipped the case open.

"FBI. I've never treated an FBI agent before," Martinez said as he injected Dane's arm. "Let's just give that anesthetic five minutes to kick in. Then, just a few stitches and that'll be it, apart from a tetanus shot." It felt to Dane like ten years passed before Dr. Martinez sank his first stitch.

Dane stared straight ahead, felt the push of the needle, the pull of the thread through his flesh. He focused on the array of bandages on the shelf in the cubicle. All sizes of gauze. In and out—it seemed like a hundred times—then, thank God, Dr. Martinez was done. Dane looked down at his arm as they bandaged it, then watched a nurse clean and bandage the backs of Nick's hands.

"The stitches will resorb, but I want you to have them checked in a few days," Dr. Martinez said. "We're going to give you some antibiotics to take for a while. Any problems at all—fever, heavy pain—you get your butt either back in here or to your own doctor." He looked over at Nick. "Hey, you a special agent, too?"

"She's above just an ordinary special agent," Dane said and sucked in his breath when the nurse jabbed a needle into his right arm.

"That's your tetanus shot," Dr. Martinez said. "Now, just one more for the pain. It should keep you smiling for a good four hours. And you're going to need some pain pills, enough for three days. Don't be a macho, take them."

"He'll take them," Nick said, her bandaged hands on her hips, as if ready to belt him if he got out of line. She was still wearing his bloody jacket. She looked ridiculous.

The nurse said something and the doctor nodded. "Since you're not his wife, you need to step out, ma'am. She's got to give him a shot in the butt."

"I've seen a lot of him already," Nick said, "but not his butt."

When Dane walked out of the cubicle, his left arm well bandaged and in a dark blue sling, he was trying to get his pants fastened with just his right hand.

Nick shoved his hand out of the way. "Hold still." She zipped the pants the rest of the way up, fastened the button, then got his belt notched. "There, you'll do." She smirked, no other word for it. "Hey, did you have Dr. Martinez check the teeth marks on your shoulder?"

"He said I didn't have to worry about infection, the antibiotic should cover the teeth marks, too. If you're rabid, that could, however, be a problem."

She smiled, a small, stingy one, but still something of a smile.

She straightened in front of him, studied his face for a long time. She picked out the last of the glass and stroked her fingers through his hair to neaten it. "You're pale, but not bad. Thank you for handling that so well, Dane. I owe you."

"Yeah," he said. "You do." He leaned down, kissed her, then straightened again. "Debt paid."

She laughed, looked off-kilter for a moment, which pleased him, then took off his jacket and draped it over his back. He was about to kiss her again when Lou came up. "Everything's taken care of. Everyone's excited to have a real FBI agent in here with a bullet wound. They get LAPD occasionally, but never a Fed. I think that woman over behind that desk wants to jump your bones, Dane."

"My bones wouldn't jump back," Dane said. He felt slight nausea now even though his arm throbbed only a bit. The nurse had shot him up with Demerol. Whatever it was, it was working.

"We're going back to our Holiday Inn and I'm going to watch Dane rest until tonight."

"All right," Lou said, "but you can expect everyone to come over and see for themselves what happened."

"Oh dear," Nick said. "We'll be needing another car."

"Not to worry," Lou said. "Bo is already working on it. You'll have another car there within a couple of hours, guaranteed."

You could have been killed. Very easily."

"Let it go, Nick. It's my job. The arm will be fine in just a few days, according to Bo, who, according to Lou, has reason to know. How are your hands?"

She waved that away. "I don't want you to get killed."

"I won't. Drop it. Give me one of those egg rolls. Oh, dip it first. Thank you."

She watched him eat. It was dark, almost seven o'clock in the evening. They'd been alone only for the past four minutes. Savich and Sherlock were the last to leave, Sherlock saying, "Remember, we're two doors down, in twenty-three, and it's the same phone number. Enjoy the Chinese."

"You need another pain pill," Nick said when she realized he wasn't going to eat any more. She fetched him one from the bottle on the dresser.

She didn't even take the chance that he'd try to be macho, just shoved it in his mouth and handed him a glass of water.

"That should help you sleep. You need rest, not any more talk." She stood up and stretched, then began pacing the small room, to the door and back again.

"That was really much too close."

"No," Dane said, shaking his head, "that bullet old Milton fired in the church was much closer."

"How many more times can we be lucky?"

"This second time wasn't entirely luck," Dane said.

"Yeah, yeah, you're Superman."

He said, "Promise me you won't run, Nick."

"Listen, you, I want you to stop looking into my head."

"You're real easy to read, at least right now. Running won't help you. You do realize that, don't you?" His brain was stalling out, working slower, beginning to fuzz around the edges. He couldn't be certain he'd make any sense in another minute. He felt bone tired, his body and his brain closing down.

She said, "Well, I'm not a jerk, so I won't leave you while you're down. So stop trying to figure out how you can get your paws on some handcuffs."

"Thank you," he said, and closed his eyes. At least Savich had gotten him out of his clothes. He was wearing a white undershirt and sweatpants, no socks. He liked to feel the sheets against his toes. Nick pulled the single sheet to his chest, then straightened it over him.

He had nearly died because of her.

TWENTY-FOUR

CHICAGO

She heard him unlock the front door, walk into the large entrance hall, and pause a moment to hang up his coat. She heard him mumbling something to himself about some contributor. When he walked into the living room, where she sat in one of the sleek pale brown leather chairs, his face went still, then lit up.

"Nicola, what a wonderful surprise. I was going to call you the minute I got my coat off. You lit the fireplace, that's good. It's very cold outside."

She rose slowly, stood there, staring at him, wondering what was in his mind, what he was really thinking when he looked at her.

"What's wrong? Oh God, did something else happen to you? No one told me a thing, no one—"

"No, nothing more happened. Well, actually, I did get a letter from your ex-wife, warning me that you are trying to kill me because you believe I'm sleeping with Elliott Benson."

"From who? You got a letter from Cleo?"

"That's right. She wrote to tell me you believe I'm sleeping with Elliott Benson, that you believed she slept with him, too."

"Of course you're not sleeping with him. Good God, Nicola, you won't even sleep with me. Besides, he's old enough to be your father."

"So are you."

"Don't talk like that. I'm nowhere near that old. You know I've wanted to sleep with you, for months now, but you put me off, and now you've begun to back away from me."

"Yes, I have, but that's not what's important here, John."

"Yes, I agree. Now, what's this nonsense about a letter from Cleo? That's impossible, you know that. She's long gone, not with Elliott Benson, for God's sake, but with Tod Gambol, that bastard I trusted for eight long years. What the hell is this about?"

"I got the letter just a little while ago. She warned me that you would try to kill me, just like you did her. She told me to run, just like she ran. I want to know what this is all about, too, John. She makes serious accusations. She wrote about your mother's supposed accidental death, and the death of your college sweetheart—both car accidents. Her name was Melissa."

His face flushed with anger, but when he spoke, his voice was calm, like a reasoned, sympathetic leader reassuring a constituent, the consummate politician. "This is nonsense. Ridiculous nonsense. I don't know who wrote you a letter accusing me of all this, but it wasn't Cleo. She's been gone for three years, not a single word from her. There's no reason she'd write to you, for God's sake. As I recall she didn't even like you. I think she was jealous of you because, truth be told, even back then I thought you were wonderful. Don't get me wrong. I loved Cleo, loved her very much, but I thought you were bright and so very eager and enthusiastic."

She wasn't about to go there. Yeah, she thought, she probably would have licked his shoes in those days, if he'd wanted her to. She said, "John, I could have dismissed this letter as a crank, but there was more."

"What the hell are you talking about?"

"She included several pages from your journal."

"My journal? Why would she do that?"

"She said she found it by accident one day in your library safe. She read it, read your confession about killing Melissa. It's right here, John, in your handwriting. How many women have you killed?"

He stood stiff as the fireplace poker, just three feet behind her, close enough to grab to protect herself if she needed to. He said slowly, his pupils dilated, "I don't know what you're talking about, Nicola. I have a journal, but writing something like that? What, as a joke? It's absurd. No, wait. Did Albia put you up to this?"

"Oh no, John, no joke. No Albia either. No, don't come any closer to me. Not even a single step. You see this?" She waved three pieces of paper at him. "This is Cleo's letter to me and two pages she copied from your journal. This is from the woman I knew when I first came to work for your reelection campaign, a woman I liked very much. When she left you, I believed, like the rest of the world, that you were devastated, but she tells me that she ran for her life. I remember how everyone felt so very sorry for you. No, stay back, John!"

He never looked away from the pages she held. She saw he wanted those pages, wanted them badly. He said, "Yes, Cleo left me, you knew that, Nicola. If you'll show me the letter, show me those ridiculous journal pages, I'll be able to prove that it's not even from Cleo. Really, that's quite impossible."

"I don't see why it's impossible. And yes, actually, it is from Cleo. I know her handwriting. God knows I read enough of her memos when I was volunteering. She wrote that you not only tried to kill her—that's the reason she ran, because of the journal—but you're trying to kill me because you believe I'm sleeping with Elliott Benson."

"Again, John, how many women have you killed?"

"For God's sake, Nicola. Somebody else wrote you that letter, someone who copied her handwriting, someone who hates me, wants to destroy us. Someone made up those journal pages. Don't let that happen, Nicola. Let me see that letter. Give it to me."

Nicola took a step back. She was nearly against the fireplace now. She felt the heat of the flames against her back. She said, "Cleo wrote that she doesn't want me to die. She wrote that I should run, just like she did. She didn't want to die either."

"This is utterly ridiculous." He looked dazed, as if he couldn't quite grasp what she was saying, and all through it, he was staring at those pages in her hand. "Let me see that goddamned letter."

"No, you'll destroy it and the journal pages. I can't allow you to do that."

"All right, all right. Listen to me. I didn't kill anyone—not my mother, not Melissa, not anyone. That's just insane." Still he stared at those sheets of paper, his pupils sharp black points of light, his face as white as his beautifully laundered shirt. "You've got to let me see that letter. It can't be from Cleo. She loved me, she wouldn't say such things."

"She left because you wanted to kill her and because she realized you were insane with jealousy. You believed she was unfaithful to you."

"She left me to be with Tod Gambol, everyone knows that. Listen, Nicola, let's sit down and talk this over. We can start at the beginning. We can work it all out. I love you."

"I'm going to the police, John. I suppose I wanted to confront you with the letter, hear what you had to say. I really hoped that I'd believe you—"

"Dammit, then listen to me," he said, but still he was staring at that letter. "Give me a chance. I had nothing to do with my mother's death. I was sixteen years old, for God's sake. She was an alcoholic, Nicola, and the decision at the time was that she ran her car off the road because she was drunk. As for Melissa, by God I loved her, and she slept with Elliott—the bastard has always wanted what I have—but I didn't kill her. I simply broke it off with her. It was a damned accident, it had to be. The letter and the journal—it's got to be a forgery. Give me the letter, Nicola, let me examine it."

"No. I think I'll give it to the police, let them figure it out."

"It would ruin me politically, Nicola, you must know that. Do you despise me so much that you want me to have to resign from the Senate? Spend my days being hounded by the press? I didn't do anything, dammit! You can't simply read a letter, some stupid pages from a make-believe journal, from God knows whom, and decide I'm a murderer, accuse me of killing my own mother? I was only sixteen! A boy doesn't murder his own mother!"

She said very quietly, "The boy does if he's a psychopath."

"A psychopath? Good God, Nicola, this is beyond ridiculous. Listen to me. You must realize how impossible this all is. You can't go to the police." He drew himself up, becoming the patrician gentleman, tall, slender, elegant, and he was angry, his hands clenched into fists at his sides. He looked from her to the letter, the pages still clutched in her right hand. He said softly, "You're not going anywhere, you stupid little ingrate. Just look what I've done for you—Jesus, I was going to marry you, make you one of the most sought-after women in America. You're young, beautiful, intelligent, a college professor, and not left wing, which was a big relief, let me tell you. With you at my side, with my coaching you, showing you what to do, we could have had just about everything, maybe even the White House. What is wrong with you, Nicola?"

"I don't want to die, John, I really don't. Were you driving that car, wearing that ski mask, trying to run me down?"

"The cretin who wrote you that letter, he's trying to turn you against me. Why can't you believe that? None of this is true. A drunk nearly hit you, nothing more than that."

"And the food poisoning, John? Was that all an accident, too?"

"Of course it was! Just call up the doctor and ask him again. That damned letter isn't from Cleo!"

"Why not? How can you be so sure that Cleo didn't write me? She wants to protect me, save me from you. You did want to kill her, didn't you, John? Did you really believe she was being unfaithful to you, or was that just a ruse, or some sort of sick fantasy?"

"I'm not sick, Nicola," he said, his voice shaking with rage. She was suddenly afraid, very afraid. She eased her hand into her jacket pocket, felt the grip of her pistol.

"The truth is that the bitch was sleeping with Tod Gambol,

my trusted senior aide for eight fucking years! He had the gall to sleep with my wife! They would go out to motels during the day when I was in Washington, or even when I was in Chicago and in meetings. I have the motel receipts. I'm the wronged one here, not Cleo. Dammit, you knew that, everybody knew that. Don't you remember how sorry you felt for me? You cried, I remember that. As for Elliott Benson, I don't know if she slept with him, it doesn't matter. And now you believe this insanity just because someone who hates me wrote you a letter, scribbled a confession. God, Nicola, that's just stupid."

"John, I told you. Cleo wrote that she never slept around on you, that she has no idea where Tod Gambol is, but she thinks he might be dead."

He said very quietly, "Nicola, why would you believe this letter when you've known me for four years now? I've always been kind and considerate to you, to everyone around me. Have you ever seen me lose my temper? Have you ever heard anything remotely this bad about me? Anything about my ever sleeping around on Cleo?"

"Then why didn't you tell me about your mother? About your dead fiancée?"

"Why the hell would I? They were very painful times for me, and no one's business. Maybe, after we were married, I'd have told you about them. I don't know."

"It's true that I always felt safe around you because no one ever even hinted that you played around like many of the other men in Congress, hitting on young women."

He faced her, palms spread out, and his voice softened, deepened, "Please, let's sit down and discuss this like two people who are planning on spending the rest of their lives together. It's all a misunderstanding. You've gotten ideas that simply aren't true.

We'll find out who tried to hit you in that car. It will be some drunk, you'll see. As for the food poisoning, it was an accident. There's no big conspiracy here, no mystery, other than who sent you that letter."

"I realize if I take these journal pages to the police that you and all your spin doctors could just claim I was a nutcase and wasn't it so sad, and everyone would probably believe it. If only she'd sent me the original journal pages and not copies, then maybe I'd have a chance, but not with these."

She paused. He said nothing.

"But I don't want to see you again."

Without warning, he ran at her, his hands in front of him, his fingers curved. Oh God. She whipped the Smith & Wesson out of her pocket, but he was on her, grabbing for the letter. He ripped it out of her hand, leaped back, panting hard. He stared down at the pages before he shredded each one. When he was done, he bunched the paper into a ball and threw it into the flames. He said, both his face and voice triumphant, "That's what your letter deserves."

His hands were still fists, the fingers curved inward. She would have been very afraid if she hadn't had her gun. She was shaking as she said, "I'm leaving now, John. Stay away from me."

She came awake that night at the sound of a noise. It was more than just a condo creak, more than just the night sounds she always heard when she was lying in bed alone, with nothing to do but listen.

She thought of Cleo Rothman's letter, now destroyed, about

that car with the accelerator jammed down coming straight at her, about the food poisoning that could have put her in her grave. She thought of John coming toward her, destroying that letter.

There was absolutely no doubt in her mind that he'd wanted to kill her. But there was no proof, not a single whisper of anything to show the police.

She heard it again, another sound, this one like footsteps. No, she was becoming hysterical.

She listened intently, for a long time, and it was silent now, but she was still afraid. She thought she'd rather be in the dentist's chair than lying there in the dark, listening. Her mouth was dry, and her heart was beating so loud she thought anyone could hear it, track the sound right to her.

Enough was enough. Nicola got out of bed, grabbed the poker by the small fireplace, turned on the light, and looked in every corner of her bedroom.

Nothing, no one was there.

But then she heard something again, something or someone running, fast. She ran to her living room, to the large glass doors that gave onto the balcony. The doors weren't locked, they were cracked open.

She ran to the railing and looked down at a shadow, and it was moving.

Then she smelled the smoke. She ran back into her condo and saw smoke billowing out of the kitchen. Oh God, he had set a fire. She grabbed up her phone and dialed 911. She ran into the kitchen, saw that there was no way to put out the fire. She had time only to pull on jeans, shoes, and a shirt, grab her purse and coat, and she was out of there, banging on her neighbors' doors as she ran. She knew he was waiting downstairs, probably hiding in the shadows between the buildings across the street, knowing that she'd get out alive since she'd been on the balcony looking down at him.

She stayed close to the building, huddling with the neighbors, watched the fire trucks arrive, watched the chaos, the evacuation of everyone in the building. No one died, thank God. Actually, only her condominium was destroyed, and the one next to it slightly burned and smoke-damaged.

But he hadn't cared if the whole building had burned. He just wanted to make sure she was dead. She heard a firefighter say to the chief, "The fire was set. The accelerant is in the kitchen of 7B."

She realized in that moment that Senator John Rothman had burned her condo, or had it burned, with the hope that she'd be burned with it. He wanted her dead.

Since she had nothing left, since she had only her purse, it wasn't hard to decide what to do.

She spent the night in a temporary Red Cross shelter, watching to see if John would come looking for her. She even gave them a false name. The next morning, the volunteers gave her some clothes. She had decided during the night what she was going to do. Before she left Chicago, she used her ATM card, then tore it up.

An hour later, she was headed for San Francisco.

TWENTY-FIVE

LOS ANGELES

Savich and Sherlock were back the next morning with coffee and bagels.

"Nonfat cream cheese," Sherlock said, pulling out a plastic knife. "Dillon refuses to allow any high cholesterol in his unit."

Savich, who'd been studying Dane's face, said, "We've decided that you two are going to stay in today. Sorry about that, Nick, but Dane will doubtless try to go find the bad guys unless someone with staunch resolve keeps him here. You willing to take on the job?"

"Yes, he will do as he's told," Nick said as she gave Dane a bagel smeared with cream cheese.

He took one bite and turned green.

"You're still nauseous?" Sherlock said. "Not to worry, it'll ease off soon."

"How do you know?" Dane asked, staring at Sherlock. "Don't tell me you've been around another gunshot wound?"

"Well, the thing is," Sherlock said, paused, looked at her husband, then quickly away. "I sort of got a knife thrown into my arm once—a very long time ago."

"Yeah, a really long time," Savich said. "All of two and a half years ago."

"Well, it was before we were married and it feels like we've been married forever." She gave her husband a fat smile and said to Dane, "True, it wasn't much fun, but I was up and working again within two, three days."

"I think she felt nauseous," Savich said, his voice emotionless as a stick, "because the doctor gave her four shots in the butt. I remember that I cherished every yell."

Sherlock cleared her throat. "That is neither here nor there, the whole thing's best forgotten."

Savich said, "Forget the four shots in your butt or the knife wound?" He was trying for a light touch, but Dane heard the fear in his voice, a fear he still hadn't gotten over. He'd felt that fear for his brother when they'd been younger, whenever Michael had put himself in harm's way, something both of them did playing football, white-water rafting, mountain climbing. They'd done so much together before and during college. Then came Michael's time in the seminary and Dane's trip to Case Western to become a lawyer, something he'd hated to his bones. At least it hadn't taken him all that long to realize he wanted to be a cop.

Sherlock said, "Okay, no more about that incident. We've got a murderer who's running scared, so scared that he tried an insane stunt yesterday. He's insane, desperate, or both. We've been trying to find out what Linus Wolfinger did during that year after he graduated and before he came to work here and met Mr. Burdock, the owner of Premier Studios."

"And not having much luck," Savich said. "MAX is pretty upset about the whole thing. He just can't seem to find anything, as of yet—no credit-card trail, no employment trail, no purchase of a vehicle."

Sherlock said, "So we've decided to ask him, straight up. What do you think, Dane?"

"Why not the direct approach?" Dane said and shrugged. "It'll give us a story to check, not that it'll matter. I'm beginning to believe that none of them is telling the truth."

"At least everyone is consistent," Savich said.

Sherlock's cell phone trilled the leading notes to the "X-Files" theme. "Hello?"

"This is Belinda Gates. We're in really deep trouble here. Maybe."

"What happened?"

"I was watching a cable station last night, nine o'clock. I saw *The Consultant*, the third episode."

"Oh no," Sherlock said, "we are in trouble."

Three hours later, LAPD Detective Flynn, feeling harassed, said to the group of ten people crowded into Dane's Holiday Inn room, "The program director, Norman Lido, of KRAM, channel eight locally, said Frank Pauley from Premier Studios sent him the episode and gave him permission to show it, told him they'd canceled the show, but maybe KRAM would like to pick it up. He liked the episode, showed it last night. This particular cable channel reaches about eight million people here in southern California."

"Didn't the idiot know why the show had been pulled?" Dane said. "The whole world knows."

"Claims he didn't know," Flynn said, shrugged. "Of course he's lying through his teeth. Why, I ask you, would any person with any sense of ethics want to air this show?"

The answer was money, of course, but it hung in the air, unspoken. He'd probably been paid a bundle to show the episode.

Flynn said, "When I told him it was all over the news, the jerk smirks and tells me he never watches the networks, they're a bunch of has-beens. I told him that even minor stations like his had it plastered all over their local news. The jerk just stood there and pretended to be surprised. It was really close, but I didn't slug him."

"Why didn't Belinda Gates call me last night?" Sherlock said. "Right after she saw the show?"

"We'll ask her," Delion said.

"She didn't know what her husband had done?"

Delion shrugged. "Don't know yet. But Sherlock and Savich are off to see Pauley. I can't wait to hear what he has to say. Depending on what he does say, I'm ready to haul his ass off to jail or stake him out in the middle of Pico Boulevard at rush hour."

"At least there haven't been any reports yet of any murders similar to the ones committed in episode three," Flynn said.

"No news is good news, I guess," Savich said. "When we spoke to Pauley by phone, he claimed he didn't know anything about this, that he never gave a copy of any episode to anyone. We're going to go see him again, and Belinda as well. Delion thought Sherlock would do best with her. Dane, you stay in bed and try to get yourself healed. Nick, you keep out of sight; the media is going to be crawling all over the studio."

"No," Dane said. "I'm okay, really. I want to come see Pauley with you." He paused a moment, then said, "I really need to do this, Savich."

After a pause, Savich said, "All right, Dane. We'll pick you up in about fifteen minutes. But I think this is the last time you guys should be out and about here in LA. There's just too much media interest, and I'd just as soon not take any more chances with Nick's safety. Or yours," Savich added, looking at Dane's arm.

Nick just looked at him and said, "I'll get your clothes together for you while you take a shower."

"Thank you."

"Be careful of your arm."

Frank Pauley stood in the middle of his office, his arms at his sides, and said without preamble to the four people who'd just been ushered into his office, "It's like I told you a couple of hours ago, I did not send that damned episode over to KRAM. I don't even know the program manager over there. I've never even heard of Norman Lido. Obviously, somebody got ahold of the tape— maybe the murderer, maybe not—and sent it over in my name to confuse things, to make you think I did it. But I did not. There's a little thing called liability, you know, and the studio will get its butt sued off if there are more murders. Jesus, I wouldn't ever do that. It's madness."

Sherlock said, "Why weren't you watching TV with Belinda last night?"

"What? Oh, I was playing poker with some guys in Malibu. It's a weekly game. There were five of us. You can check it out."

Savich waved to the very long gray sofa. "Do sit down, Mr. Pauley." He motioned Sherlock, Dane, and Nick to sit down as well. "Agent Carver was shot yesterday, so he needs to take it easy. It's likely that the murderer was trying to kill Nick."

Pauley just stared at Dane, then over at Nick. He said slowly, looking utterly bewildered, "I just don't understand any of this. It doesn't make sense. All of this is just plain crazy."

"I'm starting to agree with you," Dane said. He was feeling a bit green again. His arm was throbbing, a dull bite that just wouldn't stop. He cupped his right hand under his elbow, sat back in the comfortable gray leather chair, and held himself perfectly still.

Nick's hand hovered, then lightly touched his.

"Mr. Pauley," Sherlock said, "help us get a handle on this, please. When you got home last night from your poker game, did Belinda tell you about the show?"

Pauley looked at his fingernails, then down at the tassels on his Italian loafers. "I didn't go home last night."

"Oh?" Savich said. "Just where did you go?"

"We played poker until really late and I had too much to drink. I stayed over at Jimbo's house."

Savich raised a dark eyebrow. "Jimbo?"

"That's James Elliott Croft."

"The actor?" Nick said.

"Yes. He's also a lousy poker player. I won three hundred bucks off him."

Savich said, eyebrow raised higher, "And he still let you stay?"

Pauley said, "Hey, it's a really big house. I'm a quiet drunk, never bother anyone."

Sherlock said, not breaking the rhythm that she and Savich had set up, "When you saw Belinda this morning, she told you about the show?"

Pauley shook his head. "No, she was pissed at me because I'd told her I was coming home but I didn't. She'd left for a run before I even got back from Jimbo's house."

Savich said, "So you don't know why she wouldn't have called last night, the minute she realized she was watching episode three?"

"No clue. She's at home right now. I know that Detective Flynn spoke to her. What did he tell you?"

Sherlock gave him a nice smile. "I think I'll just keep that under my hat."

"You shouldn't wear a hat, ever," Pauley said. "It wouldn't look good on you."

"Depends on the hat," Sherlock said, still with a sunny smile.

The phone rang. Pauley shot a harassed look toward his desk, listened to it ring again. "I told Heather not to disturb me so it must be really important," he said, and picked up the phone, a fake antique affair in, naturally, gray.

When he hung up, he said, "That was Jon Franken. He says that his own personal copies of the next episodes of *The Consultant* are gone."

"What do you mean, gone?"

"Agent Savich, look, the episodes we taped of *The Consultant*—they're videotapes, and all over the place. Anyone who wants a copy can get ahold of it. All the producers, the editing department, the grips, anyone on set could get copies. They're not locked away. Jon said that someone evidently took his copies." He sighed. "Everyone knows that actual murders were committed using the scripts from the episodes. Who would steal Jon's copies?"

"How many of his episodes are missing?" Sherlock said.

"He said the next three. Look, there's just no way to hide the last three episodes we shot last summer. I'm surprised that Jon even noticed." He looked like he wanted to howl. Sherlock devoutly hoped he wouldn't.

"It seems," Sherlock said, "that the videotape was delivered by Gleason Courier Service. We spoke to the man who delivered the film and the letter. He said the package was simply left in their mail delivery drop at the North Hollywood office. Here's the letter."

She stuck it out to Pauley. He took it, stared down at it.

"Please read it, Mr. Pauley," Savich said. "Dane and Nick haven't heard it."

Frank read: *"Dear Mr. Lido, I'm enclosing an episode of* The Consultant. *We've decided to cancel the series due to many factors, and someone suggested that you might find it appropriate for your audience. Give it a try, see what you think, get back to me."*

Frank looked up. "He signed my name, and my title. It isn't my handwriting though, I can prove that." He was up fast, nearly ran to his desk and pulled some papers off the top. "Here," he said, shoving the pages into Savich's hand, "this is my handwriting."

"It's very similar," Sherlock said at last. "Even the letters are slanted the same way. It's hard for me to tell."

"Not for me."

Savich rose. "All right, Mr. Pauley. We will be in touch."

Nick just happened to look over her shoulder as she left Frank Pauley's office. He was standing in the middle of the room, his arms stiff at his sides, his hands fists. Just like he had been standing when they'd come in.

They were standing at the elevator doors when Dane said, "While we're here, why don't we drop in on Linus Wolfinger?"

"That's the plan," Savich said and punched the up button.

They went through the three secretaries, all of them the same adult crew, still showing no cleavage, just elegant suits in subdued colors. The place hummed with efficiency.

Nick nodded to Arnold Loftus, Linus Wolfinger's bodyguard, who was leaning against the same wall, looking buffed, tan, and bored. Sherlock picked up a magazine from one of the end tables and handed it to him.

Arnold Loftus automatically took the magazine. "Thank you. Hey, you guys are the FBI agents, right?"

"That's right," Sherlock said. "Does the FBI interest you?"

"Oh yeah, you guys get a lot more action than I do."

Nick smiled at him. "How's tricks?"

He shrugged. "Never anything going on. Wolfinger prances around, telling everyone what to do and how to do it, and people want to stick a knife in him, but they haven't yet because they're more afraid of him than they are of their mothers, at least that's how it looks to me. I guess if somebody got pissed off enough to go after him, I'd have to save him. Hey, thanks for the magazine."

"You're welcome. Is Mr. Wolfinger here?"

"Oh yeah, you just have to get past his guard dog."

"You're not the guard dog?"

"Nah, I'm the ultimate weapon."

Savich laughed, just couldn't help himself. "What's the guard dog's name?"

"I call him Mr. Armani, but his real name is Jay Smith."

"Now we've got a Smith and a Jones," Dane said, and looked toward Nick, who ignored him.

"I don't think," Sherlock said after they'd stepped away, "that Mr. Arnold Loftus and Mr. Linus Wolfinger are lovers."

"Agreed," Nick said. "Who was it who told us about that?"

"I'll have to look it up in my notes," Sherlock said.

Jay Smith, in a beautifully tailored pale gray wool Armani suit, frowned at them. "Mr. Wolfinger is very busy. There are a number of people waiting—"

Savich simply walked by him, paused a moment, and said over his shoulder, "Do you want to tell Mr. Wolfinger that we're here to speak to him or should I just go on in?"

"Wait!"

"Oh no, this is police business. I don't ever wait." Savich winked at Sherlock, and she put her palm over her breast and mouthed, "My hero."

Savich opened the door, stepped into the huge, bare office and stopped cold.

Linus Wolfinger was lying on top of his desk, and he looked to be asleep, unconscious, or dead.

TWENTY-SIX

"Shall we try CPR?" Nick said.

"It may be too late for him," Dane said. "Hey, he doesn't look bad, if he's dead. A real pity, he was so young."

"I think he looks very peaceful," Sherlock said. "Do you think I should maybe kiss him? See if he'll come around?"

"Like the Sleeping Prince?" Nick asked.

Jay Smith was wringing his hands behind them. He whispered, "That's not funny. He's not dead and you know it. He's meditating. For God's sake, you can't interrupt his meditation. He'll fire me if I allow it. Oh God, I'm still in hock to MasterCard for this suit."

Sherlock patted his Armani arm. "Good morning, Mr.

Wolfinger," she called out, then simply brushed past Jay Smith, who looked to be on the point of tears. "I'll be fired, for sure he'll bounce me out on my ear. What will I tell my mother? She thinks I'm a real big shot."

Linus Wolfinger didn't move, just lay still, looking dead.

Sherlock walked right up to the desk, leaned down, and said not an inch from his face, "Did you send episode three over to Norman Lido at KRAM?"

Linus Wolfinger sat up very slowly, and in a single, fluid motion, graceful as a dancer. He stood and stretched. Suddenly he looked just like an awkward nerd again, all sharp bones and angles, three pens in his white shirt pocket, tattered sneakers on his feet. "No," he said, "I didn't. I actually had no idea until Frank told me a while ago. He's very upset about it since some character pretended it was from him and forged his name."

Savich said, "Mr. Wolfinger, what did you do that year after you graduated from UC Santa Barbara?"

Linus Wolfinger pulled a pen out of his shirt pocket, listed to the right, and began tapping, tapping that damned pen against the desktop. "That was such a long time ago, Agent Savich."

"Yeah, all of two and a half years ago," Savich said. "Try to reconstruct the time for us."

Linus looked over at Dane. "What happened to you?"

"A Harley."

"A Harley hit you?"

"Nah, the guy on the Harley."

Linus looked thoughtful. "I've always thought of Harleys as being cheap Porsches, but every bit as sexy. Now, listen to me. I know you're confused, that you don't know your heads from your asses, but I don't know anything either. All of this is quite a shock.

I don't need to tell you that Mr. Burdock is pissed about the whole thing. The media is sniffing around big time, invading everyone's privacy, his in particular. And our lawyers are whimpering, hiding in their offices."

"Tell us what you did during that year after you graduated, Mr. Wolfinger."

Tap, tap, tap went the pen. Linus said on a shrug, "Nothing happened. I just bummed around the western states—you know, Wyoming and Nevada, places like that. I was trying to find myself."

Savich said, "What did you live on during that year?"

"Nothing much. I was by myself, didn't eat much, just drove around."

Nick said, "You said you were driving around Wyoming. My very favorite place is Bryce Canyon. Did you visit there? What did you think?"

"Gorgeous place," Linus said, nodding. "I spent a good couple of weeks there. What else can I do for you folks?"

Savich didn't have time to continue with Linus because the door burst open and Jon Franken came running in, his handsome face red.

He came to a dead stop when he saw the four people standing there, watching him. He drew up, sucked in a deep breath, and said, "What I meant to say is that I heard that those idiots over at KRAM showed episode three of *The Consultant* last night. Why did you okay such a thing?"

"Good morning, Mr. Franken."

"Oh, stuff it," Jon Franken said. "Why did you do it?"

"I didn't. Someone sent it over saying it was from Frank."

"That's bullshit," Jon said, and dashed his fingers through his beautifully styled hair. Next to Linus Wolfinger, Jon Franken looked like a model, one with style and good taste. He looked very Hollywood with his white linen slacks, dark blue shirt, and Italian loafers, no socks. He looked long and sleek and elegant. And royally pissed. He also didn't look the least bit intimidated by Linus Wolfinger, who could have him out on his ear in about two seconds.

Linus Wolfinger wouldn't stop tap, tap, tapping that damned pen.

Jon said to Savich, "I'm sorry for bursting in here like this, but I just heard. Belinda called me. What the hell happened? Please tell me there weren't any murders."

"Not yet," Sherlock said.

"Good. Maybe this was just a distraction," Jon said, and streaked his long fingers through his hair again. His hair was so well styled that it fell right back into place.

Wolfinger showed signs of life at that announcement. "Maybe Jon has a point there. Maybe this was just another planned detour for the police, to get you all panicked. What do you think?"

"I think you could be right," Savich said. "Dane, sit down before you fall down."

Dane went to one of the two very uncomfortable chairs in the huge, nearly empty office and sat down. He cupped his left arm with his right hand.

"What happened to you?" Jon asked.

Linus said, "A Harley."

"What?"

But Jon Franken didn't wait for an answer, just began pacing. "Look, this has got to come to an end. You've got to stop the maniac. Everyone is really freaked."

Savich said, "You told us, Mr. Franken, that Weldon De-

Loach is around thirty years old. When you showed us that tape, we all agreed that he looked older, forty at least."

Jon shrugged. "That's what he told me. He lives hard, what can I say? This town is really tough on some people, and Weldon's one of them. You don't understand—it sounds like a joke, but it's all too true. People who work in TV die young because they work their butts off—an eighteen-hour day is common. Lots of people just sleep here on the lot, on sets, in trailers. I found one guy sacked out in Scully's bed on stage five, his foot dangling over the side of the crib at the end of the bed. About Weldon—look, I never had any reason to doubt him. Are you saying he's a lot older than he told me?"

"He's forty-one, nearly forty-two," Sherlock said. "You've known him for eight years, right?"

"Yeah, about that. I really never paid much attention. Who cares?"

"A lot of things could hinge on that," Sherlock said. "We don't know yet."

Savich turned back to Linus Wolfinger. "It's time for a geography lesson, Linus. Bryce Canyon is in Utah, not Wyoming. So, what were you doing during that year?"

Jon Franken looked at Linus. "You don't know where Bryce Canyon is? Jesus, Linus, you're supposed to know everything."

Savich wished that Jon Franken would take himself off.

Linus just smiled and continued to tap his pen. "The agent over there told me how much she loved it and that it was in Wyoming. I wasn't about to make her look like an ignoramus. It wouldn't be very polite, now would it?"

Well, shit, Dane thought. The politicians in Washington could learn spin from these characters.

Dane's cell phone rang just as Nick was seat-belting him into the backseat of Savich's rental car, a big dark blue Ford Taurus. They were parked on the studio lot because the media couldn't get into the studio itself, thank God. He listened, didn't say a word for a good three minutes. Sherlock, Savich, and Nick were all staring at him, waiting.

"All right," Dane said. "I'll get back to you within the hour." He pressed the end button, stared at Savich, and shook his head. "That was Mr. Latterley, the manager of the *Lakeview Home for Retired Police Officers*—you know, the nursing home where Weldon DeLoach's father has lived for the past ten years."

"Mr. Latterley says that Weldon DeLoach called this morning. Said he wants to come see his father late this afternoon, and was that all right. He also said that when he'd called before they told him that his father fell out of his wheelchair and hurt himself."

"But no one told us that Weldon had called before," Sherlock said.

"That's right," Dane said. He sat back, leaned his head against the seat, and closed his eyes. "No one called at all to tell us. You know, of course, that I left my card with every sentient employee at the nursing home."

Savich didn't say anything else. He pulled out of the studio and onto Pico Boulevard, crammed with traffic and blaring horns. "First things first," he said.

Because of heavy traffic, it was forty-five minutes before they exited 405 and wound up Mulholland Drive to Frank Pauley's glass house. The surrounding hills were dry, too dry.

FiFi Ann, in her French maid's outfit, the little white cap on her hair, answered the door and stared at Dane's arm in its blue sling.

"Somebody bring you down, Agent?"

"Yeah, a Harley."

"Dangerous fuckers," FiFi Ann said, leaned down, and smoothed her black-latticed pantyhose.

"We'd like to see Mrs. Pauley," Sherlock said.

"Come with me," FiFi Ann said, straightening, and turned on her stiletto heels.

Belinda was drinking a cup of coffee by the blue swimming pool, wearing a very brief bikini, pale pink.

Both men froze in place for a good six seconds, eyes fixed on her.

Sherlock went right up to her and said, "Nice-colored Band-Aids you're wearing, Belinda."

"Yes, aren't they?" Belinda set down her coffee cup and rose, stretched a bit, knowing very well the impact she was having on the men. She grinned at Sherlock. "I like pink. It does wonderful things for my skin."

"All shades of pink look great with my red hair. Aren't we lucky?"

Belinda laughed, grabbed a cover-up, and slipped it on.

"That's better," Nick said. "Now the guys can breathe and get their pulses back down below two hundred."

"Okay, Belinda," Sherlock said, pulling her chair close, "tell me why you didn't call me last night the minute you realized episode three was on?"

She didn't say anything for almost a full minute. Then she got up and walked to the edge of the kidney-shaped swimming pool and stuck her foot in the water. She turned slowly, looked at each of them in turn, and said simply, with no attempt to excuse herself, "I wanted to see what would happen."

Nick nearly fell into a wildly blooming purple bougainvillea. "You what?"

Belinda shrugged. "You see, I never really believed that the first two episodes were blueprints for those murders. I thought it was at best a stretch, that the police and FBI had just latched onto them because they were close to actual crimes that they couldn't solve. Listen, my role in this show is a good one. It's a solid stepping-stone for me. With the show canceled nobody's going to see me, which means I'm going to have trouble getting another good part. Of course, you, Sherlock, knew I lied to Detective Flynn and Inspector Delion this morning when I told them that I'd taken sleeping pills before the show started and simply fell asleep even before the show was over."

"Yeah," Sherlock said. "They were very angry at you. I think Detective Flynn came this close"—she pinched her fingers nearly together—"to arresting you for malicious mischief. So what you're saying now is that you—just like that fool Norman Lido at channel eight—wanted to see what would happen."

"I wanted people to see me, to see what a good actress I am, to realize that they want to see more of me, not that meathead Joe Kleypas, who's always rubbing his fingers over his stomach so women will notice his abs. You know, the more I think of it, the more I think it was Joe who sent episode three to channel eight. He's hungry. He knew, just like I did, that *The Consultant* is a winner. He even laid off the booze he was so hyped about the role. Then all this happened. It isn't fair."

She toed the water, shrugged, but didn't look at them. "I'm really sorry if more people die, but who knows, maybe they would anyway."

"Don't even try to excuse what you did," Sherlock said. "It was a really low thing to do." She got up from her lounge chair, walked to Belinda at the side of the pool, looked her in the eye, and said, "I am personally very disappointed in you, Belinda." Sherlock shoved her into the water, and walked to the others, not looking back.

She heard a sputtering cough behind her, then, oddly, laughter. "Good shot, Sherlock," Belinda yelled out.

Sherlock still didn't turn around to look at her. She said, "I think it's time we went to Bear Lake. Weldon told them he wouldn't be at the nursing home until late afternoon."

Dane said, "Detective Flynn's got the place covered and Gil Rainy is there with a half dozen agents. If he shows early, they'll get him."

"I still want to go," Nick said. "I want to finally see Weldon DeLoach." She turned to Savich. "He really is over forty. Isn't that interesting? Why would he lie about his age?"

"Who knows?" Savich said. "Maybe ten years ago he thought it was necessary. Hollywood is a town for young people, after all."

"Maybe," Dane said. "But he may have had another reason to lie. I really want to look him right in the face and ask him."

Sherlock looked over her shoulder one last time at Belinda Gates, treading water in the deep end of the pool, her white coverup ballooning around her. Sherlock called out, "I was going to show you another photo of Sean at his grandmother's swimming pool. Dillon is holding him and he's in a swimsuit, too, and you just don't know who's cuter. But I'm not going to show it to you now, Belinda."

Belinda just kept treading water. She laughed again.

TWENTY-SEVEN

It was another beautiful day at Bear Lake. There was no more snow on the ground, and the air was winter-clear and smog-free. The calm water sparkled under the late afternoon sunlight. It had taken them just a little over an hour and a half to drive I-5.

"Not bad time," Dane said. "Considering."

"Considering what?" Sherlock said.

"Considering that it's LA and there are more cars per square foot here than any place in the country," Dane said. "You wouldn't believe some of the stories Michael used to tell me when he was just out of the seminary, living in a parish in East LA. I'll never forget how he'd say that—" Dane's voice fell off. His jaw tightened and he seamed his mouth together. Control, Nick thought, looking at him, keeping control was very important to him.

Savich said easily, "Gil Rainy was telling Sherlock and me that sometimes it takes him a good hour just to commute into the field office, and he only lives four miles away. Of course, Washington, D.C., ain't no picnic either, is it, Dane?"

Dane just nodded, not ready to speak yet.

"How about where you're from, Nick? Bad traffic?"

"No," Nick said. "Not bad at all."

"And you're Dr. Nick, a Ph.D. in medieval history. Do you teach college?"

Nick said, "Yes, I do."

"Ah. I thought college campuses were usually all jammed up with all sorts of gnarly traffic," Sherlock said.

"I guess it depends on the campus," Nick said, then turned to look out the window. Dane saw that her hands were stiffly clasped in her lap.

They parked in the small lot and walked to the entrance of the *Lakeview Home for Retired Police Officers,* founded in 1964.

They were met by Delion, Flynn, and Gil Rainy, all wearing buttoned-up sport coats, but still looking a bit chilly.

Flynn said, "No sign of him. Gil's got two agents posted out of sight at the turnoff. They'll call when he shows so we can be ready."

Dane said, "Anyone speak to Captain DeLoach?"

"No," Gil said. "A heavy woman with a mustache named Velvet Weaver said that Nurse Carla told her that he wasn't with it today, he was just sitting in his chair drumming his fingers on the wheels, humming to himself."

"I'd like to see him," Dane said.

"Go," said Savich.

As Dane and Nick walked down the long corridor, they heard laughter, lots of it. The laughter was coming from old voices, and sounded wonderful. They paused at the doorway to a big recreation room where there were several televisions, a quality Brunswick pool table, card tables, and a small library section with bookshelves loaded with paperbacks.

There was a pool competition under way, and half a dozen people were seated around, taking sides, cheering or booing. Mainly they seemed to be laughing because both players—an elderly woman in a loose-fitting loud print dress, and an old codger in gray flannel slacks and a Harry Potter T-shirt, high tops on his feet—were dead serious about the game, only they weren't very good. Dane smiled and said to Nick, "You think maybe we'll want to come here someday?"

"I don't know. I don't play pool all that well."

They walked past the rec room and down another fifteen yards to Captain DeLoach's room.

She hadn't laughed much in the past month, she thought.

The door was closed. Dane tapped lightly and called out, "Captain DeLoach?"

There was no answer from inside.

Dane called out more loudly, "Captain DeLoach? It's Agent Dane Carver here to speak to you again."

Dane opened the door, careful to keep Nick behind him, which was really stupid, she thought, what with his left arm in a sling.

The room was empty.

Dane breathed out real slow. "Right. Let's go see if he's one of the cheerleaders back in the rec room."

They found Captain DeLoach literally holding the eight ball, the old guy in the Harry Potter T-shirt trying to get it away from him.

Captain DeLoach was yelling, "Come on, Mortie, you lost to Daisy. She beat you fair and square. You can't throw the eight ball at her or I'll have to arrest you!"

"She deserves to eat it," an old woman yelled, and thumped her cane on the floor.

Dane realized then that at least a third of the old people were women. They were retired police officers? He didn't think things were so enlightened in law enforcement forty years ago.

Mortie wasn't happy, but he fell back, obviously still fuming. At that moment, Captain DeLoach tossed him the black eight ball, laughed, and said, "Make her eat it if you want to."

"Just let him try it," Daisy yelled, shaking her fist at Mortie.

"Excellent," Dane said. "Carla was wrong. Captain DeLoach isn't out to lunch. Looks like he's with us today, thank God."

In another minute, they had Captain DeLoach off to the side.

"Do you remember me, sir?"

Captain DeLoach looked Dane up and down, stared at his left arm in its blue sling, then very slowly raised his arm and saluted him.

Dane saluted back. He smiled at the old man.

"I've got a gun," Captain DeLoach said.

"Do you?"

"Yes, Special Agent, I do." His voice dropped to a whisper. "Don't want anyone to know, might scare 'em. I bribed Velvet to buy it for me. I told her no one could prove that I wasn't attacked, and as a senior law enforcement officer I should be armed. It's even registered in her name. It's a twenty-five-caliber Beretta. Eight rounds in the clip and one in the chamber. All I have to do is pull back the hammer and I can kill anyone in the blink of an eye." He pulled his hand from his pocket and in his arthritic old palm was the elegant small black automatic pistol.

"How long have you had the gun, sir?"

"Velvet got it for me yesterday. I didn't want my son coming back to try to kill me again."

"We heard that he called yesterday, said he was coming to see you in just a little while. We want to meet Weldon. Why don't you let me deal with him, Captain? I doubt you'll have to shoot him."

"Will you shoot the little cocksucker for me then?"

"Maybe," Dane said. "Just maybe I will. Why is it that he wants to kill you, sir?"

The old man just shook his head, stared down at his arthritic fingers.

"Captain DeLoach," Nick said, "how old is your son?"

Captain DeLoach looked over at the pool match, then down at his hands and said finally, looking up at Dane, "He's so young he's barely on this earth, but the thing is, Special Agent, he just won't stop trying to keep me quiet. It pisses me off, you know?"

Captain DeLoach looked toward Daisy, who was cheering because she'd just made the three ball in the corner pocket. "They've started another game. Old Mortie doesn't have a chance. Do you know that he was once a police commissioner in Stockton? Daisy was married forty years to a desk sergeant from Seattle who died the day after their anniversary, fell over with a massive heart attack. She's got spunk." He thought a moment, then said, "You know, if Daisy weren't so old, I just might be interested."

"Yeah, you're right, sir," Dane said. "I'd guess she's all of seventy-five."

"More like seventy-seven," Captain DeLoach said. He slipped the small Beretta into the pocket of his jacket. He was wearing the sports jacket over his blue pajama tops. "I'll bet she was hot when she was younger."

"Maybe so," Dane said, and thought of his own grandmother, who'd died some years before.

Suddenly, Captain DeLoach said in a soft, singsong voice, "I can feel him. He's near now. Yes, very close and coming closer. I always could tell when he was near. Isn't that interesting?"

"Your son, Weldon, Captain DeLoach, when exactly was he born? What year?"

"The year of the rat, yes, that was it. I really got a good laugh out of that. A rat." The old man threw back his head and laughed out loud. The pool match stopped. Slowly, all the old folks began turning to look at Captain DeLoach laughing his head off. "Or maybe," he said finally, wheezing deep in his chest, "it was the horse, yes, that was it. The year of the horse."

Daisy called out, "Hey, tell us the joke."

Captain DeLoach's head fell forward and he gave a soft snore.

Dane started to shake the old man, then drew back his hand. "I should take that gun," he said to Nick. "I really should."

"I'll bet you that Velvet would just buy him another one."

Dane nodded. "You're right. Let's go wait with Sherlock and Savich."

An hour later there was still no sign of Weldon DeLoach. Everyone stayed at their stations until it was dark. Then Detective Flynn and Gil Rainy called everyone in.

Sherlock said, "All a hoax. A distraction, to get us all focused on Captain DeLoach and away from him."

Gil Rainy said, "You feeling okay, Dane? You look better today than you did yesterday."

Dane just nodded. "Arm feels better. All I am is depressed. Captain DeLoach seemed fine, then he was laughing so hard I thought he'd choke on his own breath, then he was just gone, asleep, making light little snores like women make."

"I don't snore," Nick said. "You've slept close enough to me to know I don't snore."

Everyone turned to stare at her.

"Bite me," Nick said to everyone in general, and stalked off to the Taurus.

The phone rang in Dane's Holiday Inn room at ten o'clock that night.

"Yeah?"

"Dane, Savich here. Captain DeLoach—no, don't worry, he isn't dead, but he fired a gun at someone. Maybe it was Weldon, but nobody knows. When the staff got into Captain DeLoach's room, he was on the floor, unconscious, the gun beside him, and there was a big hole in the wall just behind that small sofa. The glass sliding doors weren't locked but they usually aren't, so that doesn't necessarily mean anything."

"Is Captain DeLoach going to make it?" Dane asked.

"I think so," Savich said. "I couldn't get exact information about his condition, only just what I told you. The people there are on top of it. We'll go out there tomorrow."

"What about the two cops Detective Flynn had out there covering Captain DeLoach's room?"

"They didn't see a thing. Didn't hear a thing until the shot."

Dane cursed again, real low so Savich wouldn't hear him. "He's our only lead, Savich."

"Maybe not. Now, get a good night's sleep. Sherlock says to tell you that tomorrow you'll be ready to rock and roll again."

Dane grunted into his cell phone, laid it on the bedside table, looked over at Nick, and told her what had happened.

"I've decided," Nick said slowly as she handed Dane two pills and a glass of water, "that Weldon DeLoach doesn't exist. Maybe he's just a name Hollywood made up, someone they've all created for us like some huge Hollywood production, an epic that pits reality against art, and reality loses. You know, lots of money, all big stars, lots of hoopla, a cast of thousands, murder and mayhem."

"You know," he said once he'd swallowed the pills, "that's something to think about."

"No," she said, "it isn't. I'm just talking, all blah, blah. I guess I'm just really tired, Dane."

She turned off the overhead light in his room and went through the adjoining door into her own.

TWENTY-EIGHT

BEAR LAKE

The doctor told me it wasn't an accident," Mr. Latterley said, looking distressed. His bald pointed head, Nick saw, was shiny with sweat. It was obvious he'd never had to deal with anything like this before.

"Evidently Captain DeLoach was struck just above his left temple. The doctor said that the wound wasn't consistent with his simply falling out of his chair. I've reported this to our local police and they've been interviewing everyone, but so far, we have very little. Every time they try to interview Captain DeLoach, he starts cackling like he's some old crackpot, shouts that he'll win and surprise everybody, but that's it. Over and over, that's all he says. I don't think he wants to talk to them. He won't give them the time of day."

Dane said, "We'll have two round-the-clock guards on him now."

"That's good. This is all very disturbing, Agent Carver. Violence at *Lakeview*. Not at all good for business." He shook his head. "And your suspect is his own son. I must say, Weldon DeLoach has always appeared to be a very nice man. Every time I have spoken to him, he's been solicitous of his father, very caring, always paid any and all charges on time. I've e-mailed him and spoken to him on the phone countless times over the years."

Dane handed Mr. Latterley a photo. "Is this Weldon DeLoach?"

Mr. Latterley looked down at the grainy black-and-white photo that they'd had shot off the VCR reel. He didn't say anything for a very long time. Finally, he raised his head, and he was frowning. "That's Weldon. Bad photo, but yes, Agent Carver. You know, it's entirely possible that it wasn't Weldon who was here today. In fact, I simply can't accept that it could have been him. He takes too good care of his father to want to hurt him."

"All right. If not Weldon, have you any idea who else it could be?" Dane asked.

Mr. Latterley reluctantly shook his head. "No, no one else visits him, at least I've never seen anyone else. We do have security here, but I suppose some criminal from Captain DeLoach's past could have gotten in."

"It would have to be a criminal with a very long memory," Dane said. He rose. "I want to speak to Daisy."

They found Daisy in the rec room, this time reading a very old *Time* magazine, chortling about Monica's semen-stained blue dress and how the president was dancing around that blow. "A hoot, that's what it was," Daisy said. "He wanted history to judge him as a great president"—she laughed some more—"now he'll be known as the moron who couldn't keep his pants zipped."

Daisy was wearing a different loose housedress today, sandals, her toenails painted a bright coral that matched her lipstick.

"I'm Special Agent Dane Carver and this is Ms. Jones." Dane showed her his FBI shield.

"I remember you two. You were here yesterday. I'm Daisy Griffith," she said, and grinned up at the two of them, a full complement of white teeth in her mouth. Nick believed they were hers. "Now, you're here because of poor old Ellison. Knocked himself out again, didn't he? Never did have a good sense of balance, did Elly. Always hurling himself about in that chair of his whenever he gets excited. Of course, he's old as dirt—hmmm, maybe even older." Daisy paused a moment, tapped her fingertips on a photo of Clinton shaking his finger at the media, and said, "I heard some of the nurses talking; they claimed it wasn't an accident, that his son tried to knock him off. Is that true?"

"We don't know," Dane said. "Have you ever met Weldon DeLoach?"

"Oh yes, nice boy. Polite and attentive, not just to Elly, but to all of us." She paused a moment, sighed. "Elly talks about him a lot, says he's real talented, with lots of imagination, a good writer. He's a Hollywood type, you know."

"Yes, we know. Did Captain DeLoach ever speak to you about his son, other than what he did for a living?"

"Well, sure. Elly said he was just too old when Weldon was born, that Weldon had been a big accident. The boy had needed a younger man to raise him, and then his mother up and died on the two of them. Here he was, an older cop, and he had a little kid to raise.

"Just last week I think it was, he said his boy hadn't turned out the way he would have liked, but what could he do? He said he was tempted, particularly now, to let everyone know what the real truth was. He said it would scare the hell out of me. I asked him what he meant by that, and he just threatened to throw a billiard ball at me. Mortie thought that was real funny, the old buzzard."

The old buzzard, Mortie, was scratching his forearms incessantly. He said, yes, of course he'd spoken to Weldon over the years. "Oh sure, Elly talked about him sometimes, but I got the idea there was no love lost between the two of them. Did you know that Elly used to be a wicked pool player? Then his hands started shaking and the arthritis got him." Mortie shook his head and scratched his forearms again.

"Would you like a pool cue, sir?" Nick asked. She chalked a cue and then handed it to Mortie. Mortie grinned and walked over to the pool table. He was hitting balls at a fine clip when Dane and Nick left the rec room.

"I thought it might keep him from scratching himself for a while," Nick said. "What do we do now?"

"Onward to Nurse Carla."

They found her at the nurses' station, scanning a chart, whistling *Silent Night*. "Oh, yes," she said, "all the staff know and like Weldon. He's a very good son—considerate, kind, always visits his father. To think that he'd strike his father—nope, I just can't believe that. It had to be an intruder."

"What does Weldon look like?" Dane asked.

Carla Bender thought for a moment. "He's real blond, practically white-haired, and he's pale—like he doesn't go outside enough. I joked with him about it once and he just laughed, said his skin was real sensitive and he didn't want to get skin cancer. You know, Agent Carver, anything his father needed, Weldon always okayed it without hesitation. Good son. I just won't believe that he struck his own father down."

"I don't think so either," Velvet Weaver said as she came out of a bathroom down the hall. "Weldon's really nice, soft-spoken, and I've never seen him as being remotely capable of any violence. And what could the old man possibly do to him to make him go into a rage and strike him?"

Dane showed her Weldon's photo.

"Yep, that's Weldon."

Nurse Carla agreed.

They spoke to orderlies, to two janitors, to a group of gardeners. Everyone knew Weldon DeLoach, but no one had seen him anywhere around the time his father was struck.

"I really wish that just one person had seen Weldon," Dane said as he steered Nick back to their new rental car, a Pontiac compact. "Within a mile of this place, that would be close enough." He sighed.

"If it was Weldon, he was super careful. Or he was wearing a disguise, like the one he just might have worn in San Francisco."

Dane didn't say anything, just drove toward LA, ideas flying about in his brain, none of them leading anywhere except fantasyland. He kept his eye out for Harleys.

Nick finally fell asleep a little before midnight and was promptly hurtled back to that night in Chicago when the dark sedan had tried to run her down. Her dreams skipped to the man she'd seen leaving her condominium, the man who'd set the fire. Then, suddenly, she was staring at the man on the Harley, firing nonstop at them.

Oh God, oh God. She gasped and bolted straight up in bed, panting. It all came together. She realized suddenly that all three were the same man.

All three times, the man was out to kill her, not because she was an eyewitness to Father Michael Joseph's murder, but because the man was sent from Senator Rothman, who wanted her dead. Odd how it had all come together in a nightmare, but she was completely certain of this.

She quietly got out of bed. She pulled off her nightgown. She put on her clothes, her shoes. She looked at the adjoining door, drew in a deep breath, and quietly turned the knob.

She heard Dane breathing evenly in sleep. She didn't think she breathed at all as she stole over to the bureau and took Dane's car keys out of his jacket pocket. She saw his wallet on the bureau and took a credit card. And finally, his SIG Sauer, and an extra clip. She looked back toward him. He was still sleeping.

She looked back at him one last time, then quietly closed the adjoining door again. He'd already been shot trying to protect her. She simply couldn't bear the thought of him dying—like his brother—a senseless, vicious death. She simply wouldn't put him in harm's way. She was a target and, as long as she was with him, so was he, for the simple fact that she knew to her soul that if she were threatened, he would give his life for her.

There was simply no way she could bear that. No way at all.

Besides, she had a plan. If it failed, she could disappear again. She slipped out the door, quietly closing it behind her.

It was Savich, in a room three doors away, on the edge of sleep, who heard a car's engine rev not far from their rooms. He was out of bed and standing naked in the Holiday Inn doorway, watching Dane's rental car disappear out of the parking lot.

TWENTY-NINE

Sherlock sighed. "Does she have any money?"

"She can't have much," Dane said. "And that means that she'll hitchhike. Oh damn, I take that all back. Nick's not an idiot. Let me check." He ran back into his room. After a couple of seconds he called out, "Does anyone have any handcuffs?"

"Not on me," Savich said.

Dane was back in a moment, breathing hard. "When I catch up with her, I'm not going to rely on reason anymore. It's time for brute force. Remind me to get some handcuffs from Detective Flynn. Here's the deal. She didn't just steal the car keys, she also has my AmEx and my SIG Sauer." He stopped, looked momentarily baffled. "Why did she sneak out? Nothing's really changed. Why?"

Within ten minutes, Detective Flynn had an APB out on the Pontiac, driven by a young woman with shoulder-length blondish-brown hair, gray eyes, weight around one fifteen. Well, not just gray eyes, Dane thought, they were pure gray and large, with dark lashes. But she was thin, still too thin, although she looked better than she had when he'd first met her. Good God, it was just last Tuesday. And she was wearing a pair of dark brown slacks and a light brown sweater, he'd checked. Purse? Her purse was black leather, just like her short boots. Size seven and a half, yes, that was her exact shoe size. It was important to be accurate for the APB, and so he mentioned that her eyebrows were a dark brown, nicely arched. Jesus, he was losing it. She was about five-foot-eight-inches tall—well, maybe taller because she came nearly to Dane's nose. Every officer in the LA area was alerted, in great detail.

She'd taken all her clothes—all the clothes he'd bought her. He discovered very quickly that he'd never been so scared in his life. She was out there alone and she didn't have any idea how to protect herself. She had his car and she had his gun. She wasn't helpless, thank God. He was going to tie her down when he found her and not let her up unless they were handcuffed together.

His healing arm itched. When his cell phone rang ten minutes later, he nearly fell over in his haste to get it.

Nick left the Pontiac three miles from the Holiday Inn, in the middle of a long row of cars parked in front of an apartment complex. She locked it and left the keys on top of the front driver's-side tire. Obvious place, but given Dane's resources, the chances were that the police would retrieve the car before a thief decided he was hard up enough to steal it.

His SIG Sauer felt heavy in her purse. She'd checked the clip. There was a full fifteen rounds in it. Other than that, she had twelve dollars and Dane's AmEx. She didn't quite feel like Rambo, but it was close enough.

It wouldn't be dawn for several more hours. No one had followed her from the Holiday Inn. It was dark and she was armed. With each passing minute there was more distance between her and both the bad guys and the good guys.

She saw some kids in baggy pants on the corner of Pickett and Longsworth. They were probably dealing drugs. She didn't even pause, just turned quickly and walked to the east. The freeway wasn't more than a mile away and she'd flag down an eighteen-wheeler. She'd gotten to San Francisco riding high above the ground in big trucks and keeping company with at least a half dozen truck drivers. She'd even learned how to operate a CB.

If she ran into a nut this time, she had the SIG Sauer. She flagged down a really big Foster Farms truck heading up I-5. A beefy guy named Tommy stopped because, he told her, he had to make it to Bakersfield, and he'd been driving without a stop for too long and was dead on his feet. Would she mind singing and talking to him until he let her out? She didn't mind at all.

He got her as far as Ventura County. "Hey," he said, "I think we sing a pretty mean *Impossible Dream.*"

An hour later, a smaller supply truck loaded with linens and bathroom supplies for one of the big ski lodges picked her up and began the climb to Mt. Pinos.

It was cold in the Los Padres National Forest, but down at Bear Lake elevation there wasn't much snow on the ground, just a white veil, and the air was clear, as it had been yesterday.

The driver dropped her off in front of Snow House, a small lodge where she could wait until the stores opened. She wasn't about to take a room. She knew they'd be tracking the card, would realize soon enough where she was.

Things had to happen soon or Dane would get to her. She sucked in a nice deep breath and walked into Snow House.

Her husband was driving up from LA a bit later, she told the desk clerk, and was meeting her here. This was where they'd spent their honeymoon and they wanted to come back. She was just here first. No, she didn't want to check in just yet. She'd wait in the lobby area, near that roaring fire. They didn't seem at all suspicious.

When the stores opened, she smiled toward the clerk behind the counter and walked out. She visited a small boutique, bought a cheap parka and gloves, and went to a general store at a filling station.

An hour later, she hiked to the Lakeview Home for Retired Police Officers.

She began to wonder if her great plan was going to lead to anything. She had to try it. She believed that Captain DeLoach had more answers than he'd given to them before. Now she was alone, and she knew she could get him to talk.

At least she prayed she'd get the old man to talk.

She walked straight to Captain DeLoach's double-paned sliding doors, and tapped on the glass. No answer.

She tried the door. It was locked.

She tapped harder on the glass and jumped when she heard a querulous old voice mutter, "Who the hell wants in now? That you, Weldon? You want to finish the job on me, you little bastard?"

The curtains were jerked back and she was face-to-face with Captain DeLoach. He looked pale, sported a small white bandage around his head, but his old eyes were clear and focused.

He stared at her a moment, nodded to himself, and unlocked

the doors. She watched him wheel his chair back before she opened the door and eased in. She relocked the door and drew the curtains.

She said, "I shouldn't be here, Captain DeLoach, but I think you're where all the action is, so consider me your bodyguard."

"You're a lot prettier than that idiot I kicked out of here last night. Overweight dolt, all he wanted to do was eat Carla's doughnuts and she was getting pissed, which means that she'd carp at me. Did you see any of the cops they put around to protect me?"

"Not a soul, but I was really careful."

"Yeah, yeah, I bet they're all asleep. Hey, I recognize you. You're an FBI agent, aren't you? The gal with Agent Carver?"

"Yes, that's right, I was with Agent Carver. I'm here to protect you. You don't need those other cops. But you've got to keep my presence here quiet, okay?"

The old man ruminated on this for a good five seconds and then slowly nodded. "I haven't had a girl around me without a needle in her hand in more years than I can remember."

"Do you remember back for a lot of years?"

"Yep. Do I salute you?"

"Yes," Nick said. Slowly, the old man saluted her and she saluted him back. She said, "Tell me about some of those years you remember, Captain."

Captain DeLoach paused again, then said in a dreamy voice, more singsong than not, "You know, young lady, some of those years are so clear in my head that it's like yesterday. I can feel what I felt then, the exhilaration, the excitement. I can see their faces as they were then, hear the yells, the screams, feel them score into me, deep, taste them, you know? I can feel all the joy and triumph, the pure sweetness of winning, and I loved that, you know?"

"No, sir, I don't know what it is you're talking about."

He gave her the sweetest smile. "So many people I knew, liked, but now they're mostly dead. All except me and mine, of course. Yep, just look who's left. That's a shame, isn't it?"

"Yes, sir, it's a real shame. Why do you call Weldon a little bastard?"

"I remember it was like yesterday that he was just a little tyke, couldn't even walk yet, and he was into everything. I was alone. What did I know about how to raise a baby?"

"I imagine it was very difficult, sir. What about Weldon?"

No answer this time. His head just fell forward. He seemed to be asleep. From one moment to the next, he was simply gone, someplace in the distant past when he'd known happiness. Poor old man. She wondered how it would feel to have your own son trying to kill you. She didn't know what Captain DeLoach had meant with all that talk about the yells and screams. It made no sense.

She straightened, looked around the large room. It was nice and warm in there. She shrugged out of her parka, walked around a bit, getting acquainted with everything. It was like a junior suite in a hotel, only it was personalized with some photos on the end table—none of Weldon, but she and Dane had already remarked on that. Maybe she'd ask Captain DeLoach if he had any pictures of his only son stashed somewhere. Beside his bed were a few more photos—of a baby, and then that baby as a toddler. Weldon? She didn't know. But wait—that couldn't be. There was a car in the background, and the car wasn't forty years old. It was around the mid 1980s. Okay, so it wasn't Weldon. Another family member had a little kid, that had to be it.

Nick turned away from the photo, realized that Nurse Carla or anyone who worked there, for God's sake, could come tromping through the door. Where could she hide?

There was a big walk-in closet six feet from the double bed. The wood doors were slatted so she could see Captain DeLoach clearly. She spread her parka on the carpeted floor and made herself comfortable.

She'd bought taco dip, a small box of Wheat Thins, and a Diet Dr Pepper—her favorites—in the small food market inside the filling station, using up four dollars and eight cents of her twelve dollars. Before she fell asleep, her stomach happy, she wondered how long it would take Dane to track her down.

At ten o'clock in the morning, Delion, Savich, Sherlock, and Dane were seated around Detective Flynn's desk in the detectives' room on the second floor of the West Los Angeles Police Department. Linda, today's volunteer receptionist, had given them all homemade cookies when they'd come in. "I've always admired the FBI," she'd said, patting Savich's bicep. "And you're so nice, too."

Sherlock had said, "What about me, Linda?"

"I think of you as their mascot, cute as a button with that red hair flying all over the place. As for you," she said to Dane, "you look a bit on the edge. The cookie will help get things in perspective, sugar always does."

"Thank you, Linda," Dane said. "That's what we've been hearing about, sugar."

The detectives' room was, as usual, a madhouse, which didn't appear to bother anyone. Savich settled down in a side chair next to Detective Flynn's desk, MAX on his lap. He looked up after ten minutes and said, "No indication that she's used the AmEx yet, either that, or folks are just too lazy to check. Since the card's in your name, Dane, and not hers, I can't imagine anyone not checking. We just wait, nothing else to do."

Sherlock said, "You know the deal you made with her not to delve into her past? Well, we've got to find her and protect her, we've got to find out who she is. The time has come. Dillon, can you have MAX find out who she is?"

"Yes," Savich said. "We know her name's Nicola, she's twenty-eight, she's got a Ph.D., and she's a college professor. This won't be anything for MAX. Everyone on board with this?"

Delion said, "Do it. Now isn't the time for irrelevant promises."

"Yeah," Dane said. "That's what I figured."

While Savich worked, Detective Flynn was sitting back in his chair, his hands laced over his belly, a basketball on the floor beside him. He said, "I just don't understand why she took off like this. She's pulling us away from the really important stuff—you know, multiple murders, silly things like that. I'd like to get in her face when we catch up with her."

Sherlock said, "Do you think she headed back up to San Francisco? To hide herself in the homeless population again?"

Dane shook his head. "No. And I don't think she's gone back home either, wherever home is."

"Then where did she go?" Flynn asked, sipped at the god-awful coffee. His phone rang. He picked it up, barked, "Yeah? Detective Flynn here."

He wrote something on a pad. When he set the receiver back into its cradle, he was grinning. "How's this for a bit of luck? Our girl hitched a ride with a trucker. He said he always listens to the police reports on his CB. Said when he heard the APB, he knew he'd given our girl a ride."

"Where?" Sherlock said.

"Up in Ventura County."

"Hog damn," Dane said. "She's gone to see Captain DeLoach."

"But why did she just run away like that?" Flynn asked.

"I'll be sure to ask her after I handcuff her," Dane said.

"I'll provide the handcuffs," Delion said.

"I'm still gonna burn her ass," Flynn said.

MAX chose that moment to beep. Savich looked down, smiled. "MAX just told me who she is."

Savich closed down MAX, rose, and stretched. "We can be at Bear Lake by midafternoon.

THIRTY

One moment there was only the sound of Captain DeLoach's soft snoring. The next there was a man's voice, speaking quietly, right there, right next to Captain DeLoach's wheelchair.

"Wake up, old man. Come on now, you can do it. It's Weldon, and I'm here to make sure that it's over, at least for you. Wake up, you old monster, wake up. I'm going to mete out the only justice you'll ever get in this world, and I want you awake for this."

Captain DeLoach jerked awake, snorted, looked up, and whispered, "Weldon, how did you get in here? There's cops out there protecting me, lots of them. And the Feds, they're everywhere looking for you. You'd better run while you've got the chance. How did you come in through the sliding doors? I always keep them locked."

"You old fool, I have a key to the sliding doors. Not a soul saw me, for sure not that one cop chatting up Velvet in the reception area. And the other one who's supposed to be protecting you—I saw him out in the parking lot smoking a cigarette. There's just the two of them, old man.

"It's finally time for you. For more than thirty years you've thumbed your nose at everybody. Now it stops. No more time for any big announcements to anyone else from you. It's simple justice, you know it."

"You think you can manage it this time when you didn't the last two times, you little wimp?"

"I was trying to scare you, not kill you, you monster. I didn't think I'd have to kill you then. Is your brain so far gone you can't remember that?

"But this time, I am going to kill you. All your threats to tell the world what you are will die with you. After that fall you took—I really hoped you'd die, but you're still tough, aren't you? Why didn't you make your big announcement?"

Captain DeLoach said, grinning widely, "Of course I'm tough, but no one could tell that by looking at you, you little pussy. I didn't say anything because I wanted to torture you more, boy. Make you wonder, worry when the blow was going to fall. Threatening your daddy, trying to scare him—nearly to death—that's not a nice thing, you know. And you left me there, lying on the floor, my head all bloody."

"Shut up. No more abuse from you, old man, no more."

"I'm still your only daddy, you puking coward. Jesus, I can't believe that you're actually part of me, although your mother was weak, always whining, just like you. And then she died, and it was just you and me, but you weren't strong, you weren't a man, you were just like her. And then you just up and left after high school, believed you'd escaped me. Well, I was sick of you, I wanted you out of there.

"But I kept tabs on you, boy. After all, you were the only one who knew. I wanted to make sure you wouldn't ever tell anyone. And now you want to kill your own daddy."

"Quiet! Just shut up, damn you. No more threats, no more lies. I'm going to send you to hell, where you belong."

Weldon paused a moment, then said, "What I really can't believe is just how long you've lasted." He reached into his pocket.

Nick said, "No, Weldon, you're not going to do anything to your father. Step away from him."

Weldon DeLoach jerked up, appalled and surprised as he looked into the muzzle of the SIG Sauer, held in the hand of that homeless woman he'd seen on TV. What the hell was she doing here? He straightened slowly, took a step back.

The old man laughed, rubbed his arthritic hands together. "She's my own personal bodyguard, Weldon. You thought there was only two cops. Not a chance. She's here, staying right in my room. What do you think about them apples? She sharp, or what? Salute her, Weldon, she's with the Federal Bureau of Investigation. She's a special agent."

Weldon kicked at his father's wheelchair, missed, and yelled, "You moron, she's not a cop. She's a homeless woman who just happened to see things that would make her a real danger to the murderer."

"What shouldn't she have seen, Weldon?"

"The murderer just after he killed the priest in San Francisco."

"Hey, does she think it's you?"

Weldon was still blond today, deeply tanned, his eyes a pale blue. Nick wasn't at all good with guessing people's age, but if she had to, she'd say he was easily in his forties. Was it makeup? Contacts? Or was this the way he really looked? Nick simply didn't know if he was the man she'd seen in the church. Maybe disguised, but she knew she'd be useless in court. She held the gun steady, knew she had to get him down to the floor, get him tied up so she could breathe again, so she could think, get help. She was scared, almost as scared as she'd been when she had faced John Rothman.

Still, she had to try. She said, "To be real accurate, Weldon, yes, I saw you." She continued, now looking back at the old man, "Sir, I saw Weldon in a church just after he'd murdered Father Michael Joseph. And he's killed other people as well. He wrote TV scripts, then copied them in real life. I'm sorry, but he is a very evil man."

Captain DeLoach said, "Hey, you really mean that? Nah, that doesn't make any sense. Weldon's a pussy. No spine in that back of his, just mush. You really a homeless woman? Fancy that, I won't have to pay you, will I? You don't expect anything because you're not an officer, right?"

"Right, this is for free," Nick said, not looking at the grinning old man, who really did sound pleased as punch.

"You said Weldon is a murderer? He's really a criminal?"

"That's right, sir."

The old man laughed. "Listen to me, girl, you're all wrong about this. Weldon couldn't kill a roach if it crawled over his bare feet and started gnawing on his toe. He's a coward."

"Sir, please be quiet." She adjusted her aim with the SIG just a bit and said to Weldon, "I want you to lie on your stomach on the floor. Now." It was aimed right at his chest.

"No," he said. "I can't. I haven't killed anyone. Don't you see? It's this filthy old man who's the monster. You can't believe the havoc he's wrought. This is justice, dammit."

"What are you talking about?"

Captain DeLoach laughed. "Yeah, tell her, Weldon. Tell her why you want to murder your dear old dad."

"No, she doesn't need to know. Listen, I've got no bloody choice. Believe me, sister, this crazy old man richly deserves it."

"Why does he deserve to die?"

Captain DeLoach started laughing again, spittle pooling in the corners of his mouth, flecked with blood.

Nick said, "Come on, Weldon, what on earth are you talking about?"

In that moment, Weldon grabbed the arms of Captain DeLoach's wheelchair and shoved hard. Nick had only an instant. As the chair rammed into her, she fired. The shot went wide, shattering the TV screen. Captain DeLoach's arm flew up to gain balance, and he struck her wrist. The SIG flew out of her hand and skidded across the floor to land just beneath Captain DeLoach's bed.

Nick froze, expecting Weldon to pull out his own gun and shoot both of them. There'd already been one shot, why not more? But he didn't have much time. Nursing home staff would burst in there in just a couple of seconds. She had to protect the old man. She raced around in front of Captain DeLoach's wheelchair.

But Weldon didn't try to shove her aside, didn't draw a gun to kill her. He just ran out through the glass doors, yelling back at her, "You've made the worst mistake you'll ever make in your life!"

Seconds later, Nurse Carla, a cop behind her, burst in to see Nick Jones racing out the glass sliding doors, a gun in her hand.

Captain DeLoach was sitting in his chair. He was smiling, looked happy as a clam, singing *Eleanor Rigby*.

Nick saw Weldon racing toward a small black car, Japanese, she thought, maybe a Toyota, but she couldn't be sure. Where was that cop who was supposedly out here smoking a cigarette? She didn't see anyone. She yelled, "Stop, Weldon! Or I'll shoot, I mean it!"

But he didn't. Nick raised the gun, then realized she didn't need to fire at him. She aimed at the tires of the black car just as he flung open the driver's-side door and threw himself in.

She fired, hitting both back tires just as he gunned the engine and roared out of the parking spot, rubber and smoke spewing out of the tires. Soon he'd be driving on the rims and that wouldn't last long.

Weldon was keeping his head down, afraid she'd shoot him. She saw the instant he knew she'd hit his tires. The car swerved madly to the left. As the rubber was finally stripped away, the god-awful screeching of steel against concrete filled the air.

Nick kept firing until she'd shot ten of the fifteen rounds in the SIG. She stopped, to save the remaining bullets. She'd hit the two back tires; that had to at least slow him. She started running. She wanted more than anything to pull him out of that car.

The car swerved wildly from side to side. The tires were smoking, grinding, the steel beneath raw on the concrete, tearing it up. The stench of burning rubber filled her nostrils.

She watched him suddenly jerk the car to the right and head it directly into the pine woods that began about forty yards from the east side of the rest home. He crashed it into a pine tree. Smoke billowed up, black and thick, and then it was quiet.

She saw him dragging winter clothes out of the car and running into the woods.

"Stop!"

Nick headed after him, the SIG still in her right hand. She realized then she wasn't wearing warm clothes. She'd run out of Captain DeLoach's room with nothing but her V-necked red sweater over a white blouse, jeans, and boots.

She didn't care. She wasn't going to fail now, she couldn't. This madness had to stop and she was the only one there who could stop it. She heard him crashing through the undergrowth ahead of her. How far? Twenty feet?

She saw Father Michael Joseph's face in her mind's eye, a beautiful face, open, rich with intelligence and humor. He was laughing at something he'd just told her about King Edward. And now, because of Weldon DeLoach, no one would ever see that smile again or hear that laugh. So like Dane, and so different, but not in the ways that counted. Both put themselves on the line for others, both had a core of honor. She realized in that instant that she didn't want to let Dane out of her life, ever.

Weldon had to be just ahead, not that far. Wait, she couldn't hear him crashing through the trees anymore. Had he fallen? Was he hiding, lying in wait for her?

Before she could react, he grabbed her around the neck and hauled her back against him. His other hand was on her arm, trying to pull the SIG out of her hand. But she wasn't about to let go. She pulled and twisted, but he pulled his arm tighter. "Damn you, be quiet. Let that gun drop. Now!"

Nick yelled at the top of her lungs, jerked as hard as she could, and drove her elbow into his stomach. He yelled, his hold loosened just a bit. She jerked the SIG down and pulled the trigger. She shot him in the foot.

He screamed, released her. He was dancing in place, trying to grab his foot, his eyes wild with pain.

Sherlock, Savich, and Dane saw the dance, saw her standing there, the gun dangling in her hand, breathing hard, staring at Weldon DeLoach. Flynn and Delion came up to stand beside them.

"Jesus, woman," Dane said, reaching her first. She turned, white-faced, and he forgot every curse word he'd stored up. "Ah, dammit, Nick," he said, and pulled her against him. "Just look at you. You're freezing, you twit."

"No, I'm not," she said against his shoulder. "Be careful, Dane, you might hurt your arm."

"My arm? You're worried about my fucking arm?" He couldn't help it, he started to laugh. He saw Flynn and Delion pull Weldon DeLoach to the ground, Flynn pulling off the guy's boot to wrap his parka sleeve around the wound.

Flynn looked up, grinned at her. "Congratulations, Dr. Campion, you brought down the perp. They don't exactly teach you that a foot wound is the way to go, but hey, I'm not about to argue with success. Okay, Weldon, shut your trap."

"You know," she said.

"Yeah," Dane said, "we know, but it's not important now."

"It hurts, dammit!"

"Yeah, I'll just bet," Flynn said, and came down on his haunches beside Weldon. He looked straight down into that face, and read him his rights.

"No, I don't need an attorney. I didn't do anything. You've got to listen to me."

Savich, who was standing over him, said in a quiet voice, "So now you didn't do anything?"

"I didn't commit those script murders! Yes, I came up with the idea for the series, but I had nothing to do with those murders. They're horrible. I don't know who's responsible. It may be someone at the studio, someone who worked on the series. But I don't know who."

Sherlock said, "I see. So it has nothing at all to do with the fact that you seem to be trying your best to murder your father?"

"No, dammit. Do you have any idea what he's done to me all my life?"

Weldon looked ill, but he held on, sucked in a deep breath.

"No, no one knows anything," Delion said. "Listen, Weldon, someone murdered four people in San Francisco. You hired that moron Milton to kill Nick at the funeral because she saw you in the church. Then there's Pasadena. It's times like this I'm really glad I live in California and we've got the death penalty. They're gonna cook you, Weldon."

The pain was glazing his eyes. He was holding his foot, crying, pleading. "No, listen to me, I wouldn't kill anybody. I'm not like that."

Savich said, "Tell us exactly why you tried to kill your father. This time in nice plain English."

Weldon's voice was soft now, so quiet it was like listening to him again on the video. He was getting himself back in control. He'd finally managed to regain some calm, control the pain in his foot. "I can't. There's too much at stake here."

"That's not a very good start, Weldon," Dane said.

Weldon lowered his head and moaned at the pain in his foot.

Delion snorted, stood, his hands on his hips. "Sherlock has called on her cell phone and rounded up a doctor for you. Let's get you back to the parking lot. Detective Flynn and I will help you."

Weldon DeLoach tried to get up on his own, but ended up moaning again, clutching his foot. Flynn and Delion got him up and half carried him back to the facility.

Dr. Randolph Winston, a geriatrician, was waiting for them

at the front entrance to attend to the foot, a thick black eyebrow arched. "A woman shot him in the foot? Here, at Lakeview?" The eyebrow went even higher when Detective Flynn just shrugged.

"No elderly person I've treated has ever been shot in the foot. Let's get him to the hospital."

Dane nodded. "We'll follow. We've got lots more to talk about with Mr. DeLoach."

THIRTY-ONE

Delion and Flynn read the riot act to the two policemen assigned to keep an eye on Captain DeLoach, then rode with Weldon to the hospital. The rest of them walked back to Captain DeLoach's room.

It appeared that Captain DeLoach's brain had faded into the ether again. Or it was all an act, one at which he excelled.

He was still singing *Eleanor Rigby*. Nurse Carla said, just shaking her head, "The fact that his son tried to kill him—I think it knocked him right off his mental pins again. I was with him several times during the morning and he was with it the whole time, but not now. Poor old man. How would you like to have a son who keeps trying to kill you?"

Nick moved away from Captain DeLoach and said, her voice low, "Something is very strange here. When Weldon was in the captain's room, he called his father a monster, said he had to stop him. But Captain DeLoach, he wasn't afraid at all. He taunted Weldon."

Savich walked to the old man, who was still singing softly, vacantly, in his wheelchair.

"Captain DeLoach? You've met me before. I'm Dillon Savich. I'm an FBI agent."

Slowly, the old man stopped singing *Eleanor Rigby* and raised his eyes to Savich's face. Then, slowly, he raised his hand and saluted.

Savich, without pause, saluted him back.

"I saluted that girl, too," Captain DeLoach said in a singsong voice. "I thought it was weird to have to salute a girl, but I did it. Respect for the Federal Bureau of Investigation, you know? It's a sign of the times that the Feds would allow a girl to join up. I always wanted to be an FBI agent, but I couldn't. And now it turns out she isn't a cop, just a girl who's homeless, leastwise that's what Weldon said. Hey, is that little redheaded girl a cop?"

"She certainly is, an excellent FBI agent."

The old man gave her a toothy grin and saluted her. Sherlock didn't salute him back, just gave him a little wave with her fingers. He gave a dry, cracking laugh, shook his head. "That girl over there, the homeless one, she saved me from Weldon, the little pissant. I don't think he would have killed me. You see, Weldon's a coward. I never could teach him to be a man. He's always hated blood, wouldn't ever go hunting with me. Once I tried to get him to butcher a buck, but he vomited all over his shoes and hid. He's never even used a gun as far as I know."

"How was he going to kill you, sir?" Dane said. "I believe he struck you the first time."

"Nah, that first time, I fell over all on my own. That last time he could only bring himself to shove my chair over."

The old man started laughing, more spittle spotted with blood sprayed on his chin. "What a hoot this all is, best time I've had in years. Nah, I don't think Weldon could have killed me. But I could tell he was going to try. He was going to strangle me with a string. The girl there thought he had a gun, but he didn't. He won't touch 'em. I saw the string hanging out of his pocket, you know, real stout with little knots tied along the length? Yep, just a string because there's no blood when you strangle someone. But it's still gross. Weldon just doesn't realize how gross it is to strangle someone—all the gagging, the eyes, my God, the eyes, they bulge, you know? And you can see all the terror, the fright—it all oozes out—then the final acceptance that they're going to die. It isn't a pretty sight. No, shooting's cleaner. Only thing is, though, that the eyes fade really fast with a bullet."

Nick closed her eyes, said, "I shot Weldon in the foot. You're right, it was easier."

"For a homeless girl, she knows stuff," Captain DeLoach said, and began humming *Eleanor Rigby* again.

"Are you trying to make us think you're senile, Captain DeLoach?" Sherlock said, her palm resting lightly on the old man's shoulder. She gently kneaded the flesh and bone and the flannel shirt, all that was left of him.

"Nah, I just like to sing. I was the only middle-aged guy who liked the Beatles."

Dane said, "But why did Weldon want to kill you, sir?"

The old man looked at Dane. "I think you're probably an excellent cop, young man. You're passionate, you stick tight, you don't screw around, all are important to be successful in any job."

Dane said again, "Why does your son want you dead?"

"The little pussy thinks he's safe if I'm dead. And he would be." The old man, now as sharp as any of them, stared at Dane, his faded eyes bright with intelligence. He said, his voice so proud, "Weldon's got to know that I'll talk now, and why not? I was the sheriff, and look at what I did, no one ever had a clue. Of course, like the saying goes, a dog never shits in his own backyard." He laughed, a wheezing, scaly sound that made Sherlock's skin crawl.

"Captain DeLoach," she said, "do you pretend to be senile? Is it all just an elaborate charade?"

The old man said, "Me, senile? Hey, I haven't seen you before, have I? Aren't you the cutest little thing. My wife had the look of you. All sprite and fire and that lovely hair, so red, like blood, one could say."

"Yes," Sherlock said slowly, "I suppose you could say that, but I doubt many people would. Now, Captain, you just made a little joke, didn't you? You know exactly who I am. You were just pretending, just continuing with your charade."

He said nothing.

Sherlock said, "What was your wife's name, sir?"

"Marie. Her name was Marie, French for God's mother's name, something that always made me smile, particularly when I'd come home and my hands would still have seams of blood in the cracks. Yep, my palms would look like road maps."

"I know you were a sheriff," Dane said, "but did you have blood on your hands that often?"

"No, not just *on* my hands, Agent. There was usually so much blood it would work its way into the lines and hunker down and live there. No matter how hard I scrubbed, I couldn't get it all out.

Then I really looked at my hands one day and knew I liked it. It was always a reminder to me of how much fun I had."

Nick stepped up to the wheelchair, leaned down, and clasped her hands on the wheels, got to within an inch of his face. "You killed people, didn't you, sir?"

"Well, of course, young lady. I was the sheriff."

"No, not as a sheriff. You killed people. You liked it. You liked seeing the remnants of their blood in your hands. You got away with it. And that's what Weldon doesn't want you to tell the world, isn't it?"

"Ain't you a cracker. Of course I got away with it. I might be old now but I'm still not stupid. It was easy. Once they even got a picture of me, but it didn't lead them even close to me. I was that good." He raised his hand and snapped two of his bony fingers together. "I'm eighty-seven years old. You think I care now if everyone knows? Hell, I deserve the attention, the recognition of what I did. What will they do? Put me on trial? Sentence me to the death penalty? Judging by the way I'm feeling these days, the blood I keep spitting up, I'm ready for the needle already. Not that they'd ever get the chance, a man of my age with cancer. Hey, you think I'm senile. Listen to this." And the old man started humming *Eleanor Rigby* again, saw the shock on their faces, and laughed.

Nick said, "And Weldon didn't want you to tell anyone, did he?"

"No, he claimed it'd ruin everything. He didn't want it known that his pop was a serial killer. Weldon was always afraid of me, terrified of me when he discovered what I was doing, but he kept quiet, particularly after I told him I'd nail him upside down to a tree and skin him alive if he ever told anyone. He didn't."

It was Dane who said slowly, "I remember when I first went

to San Francisco Homicide after my brother's murder. Inspector Delion said they'd found out from the bullet that the gun that killed my brother was like the gun the Zodiac killer used."

Captain DeLoach laughed again, whistled something no one knew through his teeth. "I'm impressed, Agent. I read about it at the time and it kind of got me started, you know? I wanted to be better than him. The least I could do was use the same kind of weapon he used. A fine gun—my JC Higgins model eighty."

Captain DeLoach sighed, rubbed his old hands together. "Nope, I wasn't the Zodiac killer. I was really a bit more basic than the Zodiac killer was. But I liked his style. Isn't that a kick? What a handle. Trust the media to always come up with a good sound bite. If only I'd been open about what I did, maybe I would have gotten a handle, too."

The old man frowned, looked off into nothing at all, said, "Hey, do you think he's still around? Maybe he's in a nursing home, just like I am. Maybe he's here, you think?"

No one said anything, just waited.

Captain DeLoach continued singing, then he said, his voice sharp, "Your guy didn't use my gun. Nope, mine's hidden, and I'll be glad to tell you where." He gave them a big smile.

Dane said, "Weldon knows. He has to."

Savich said, for the third time, "Tell us why your son wanted to kill you, sir."

The old man laughed, smacked his lips together, and started singing again.

Nick moved close and said right in his face, "I saved your life, sir. I figure you owe me. Tell us the truth."

Captain DeLoach gave her a big smile, raised his veiny old hand, lightly touched his fingertips to her cheek. "So soft," he said.

"You want to know, do you, little girl? Yeah, I guess I do owe you. Weldon wanted to protect his boy."

"His boy?" Dane said. "Weldon has a son?"

"Sure. Didn't let me near him when he was young, but then he came here to meet me. I took care of him really good, now didn't I? I got him all juiced up and now, here he is, following in his granddaddy's footsteps. Weldon wanted to protect his boy, didn't want to see him ruined, hounded by the media."

"Who is his boy, sir?" Savich said.

"You're FBI, son, it's your job to find out. I don't want to make things that easy for you." He coughed, and a trickle of blood snaked out of his mouth.

Sherlock said, "I don't want to salute you, sir."

Captain DeLoach said, head cocked to the side, "Well, after all, you're just a girl, when it all boils down to what's important."

"And I'd say that you're an evil old man."

"Oh yeah," he said. "Oh yeah, I really am. And I'm eighty-seven years old and sitting real pretty. Ain't life a kick?"

When they reached the Ventura County Community Hospital, they saw Weldon, who didn't look too good. He was pale, still in pain, and he knew the dam had burst. Everything he'd been struggling with was over now, and he knew it. Dane lightly laid his palm on Weldon's shoulder. "I'm very sorry, Weldon. We're all very sorry."

"You know," Weldon said, his voice dead. "That wretched old man told you all of it?"

Savich said, "Yes, your father finally got around to telling us in simple English, once I asked him to do it, with no crazy allusions or cover-ups. He's really quite mad. I don't think he's senile, not for a moment, but he's fooled everyone else. He's a fine actor."

"He's been mad all my life. So he's finally done it. I didn't know whether or not he really meant it."

"How old were you when you discovered what he was?" Sherlock asked.

"I was ten years old. I couldn't sleep one night, and he'd left early in the evening, supposedly on a call. I waited for him. I saw him drive into the garage. I heard the kitchen door open. I started to go to him, but something stopped me, something that had scared me about him for a good long time. I stayed hidden behind some of my mother's favorite curtains in the living room.

"I heard him come in and he was whistling. I crawled to the kitchen. I saw his clothes, saw his hands—he had blood all over him. So much red, and even as I watched, it was turning darker and darker, almost black. His shirt was stiff with blood. At first I was terrified that it was his, but not for long.

"I watched him scrub his hands in the kitchen sink, watched him strip to his underwear, wrap up his bloody clothes, and tie them up in a neat bundle. It was practiced, everything he did, like he'd done it many times before. He never stopped whistling. I watched him take that bundle of bloody clothes out in the backyard. He paced off six steps from a big old elm tree. He dug down and dumped the bundle in. I saw that there were maybe half a dozen bundles down there. Then he shoveled dirt over all of it. He never stopped whistling.

"When I was twelve, I wondered if he was the one they called the Zodiac killer. I saw all about the murders on TV, but they weren't on the same days he was gone. And that insane whistling—it was always the same, always *Eleanor Rigby*. He still hums or whistles that damned song now, only he uses it to fool people, to make them think he's senile."

"What did you do?" Dane asked.

"Oh man, I was never more scared in my life. I didn't know what to do. I was just a kid. He was my father."

Nick said, "You confronted him, didn't you? You just couldn't stand it anymore and you confronted him."

"Yes, and do you know what he did? He just stood there, looking down at me, and began to laugh. He laughed until there was spittle on his mouth. Then he just stopped and went cold. Like, with no warning, his body went perfectly still and his eyes were dead. There was no one behind those eyes and I knew it. I was twelve years old and I knew it." Weldon paused, took a shuddering breath. There wasn't a sound in that small room. "He told me in this cold, dead voice exactly what he would do to me if I said anything to anyone."

"You were brave to confront him," Nick said. "Very brave."

"Turns out I was a coward, turns out when I was old enough to kill the old monster, I didn't. I just wanted to scare him to keep him quiet. But I knew he wouldn't. This time I was going to strangle him. Would I have gone all the way until I knew that his heart was no longer beating?" Weldon shook his head, looked down at his bandaged foot, winced. He said finally, "What are you going to do?"

He looked at each of them in turn. From Inspector Delion to Detective Flynn, to the FBI agents, in a circle around him. The pain meds had finally kicked in completely and there was only a dull throb in his foot. He looked at Nick. "I don't blame you for trying to protect an old man. You didn't know."

"I wish I had shot him instead," Nick said. "But if I had, we wouldn't have learned the truth."

Weldon was shaking his head, back and forth, his eyes on each of their faces in turn. "I left home on the day I turned eighteen. I came to LA because I was a good writer and I wanted to write TV and movie scripts. I met a girl, Georgia, and we fell in love. I got her pregnant. We got married. A drunk driver killed her when our son was only three years old."

"You raised your son alone just like your father did you?"

"Of course, but I wasn't like my father, I really loved my boy. I would have done anything for him. It wasn't long before I got work writing for a TV sitcom and started making enough money so I didn't have to worry about it all the time." He paused a moment. "I kept up with the old man. Do you know that long after he was in his sixties, the people still wanted him to stay on as sheriff?"

"Why?" Dane asked.

"The old man was so mean he could face down drunk bikers. Once, I heard he'd pistol-whipped a man for hassling a woman, all the while yelling at him, 'No one fucks with my town!' That's what he always loved to say, and then he'd spit out a wad of tobacco.

"I'll bet you're all wondering why I've kept him in such a nice place for the last ten years."

No one had actually really thought about it yet, but Nick knew they would have, sooner or later.

She said, "Why did you?"

Weldon said simply, "He told me if I didn't keep him sitting real pretty until he kicked off, he'd contact the press and tell them where bodies were buried that no one even knew about, tell them where his gun was hidden, tell them all about the bundles he'd buried beneath that elm tree. There'd be so much proof, they'd have to believe him.

"I agreed. What else could I do? There was my own growing career to think about, but most important, there was my boy, my own innocent boy."

Nick said slowly, "I guess I can understand that, but was he still killing people? Didn't you realize you had to do something once you were an adult and out from under his thumb?"

Weldon said, "I tried never to think about it. He's right. I was a coward, and he knew I wouldn't say anything once I had my boy. He was still the sheriff thirteen years ago when something went wrong with an arrest, and a car ran over him, smashing his legs. He's been confined to a wheelchair ever since. So I knew the world was safe from him."

Savich started to say something, but Nick shook her head, said, "He started his threats recently, didn't he? He knew he was getting close to the end and he wanted recognition for what he'd done. He wanted the world to know just what had walked among them for years and years."

Weldon nodded, his hands clasped, so pale, so deadened, that it broke her heart. "Yes. After he told me what he was planning to do—you know, make his announcement to the press, tell everyone everything—I didn't know what to do. I reminded him that he'd sworn to keep quiet for as long as I kept him in that home. He just laughed, said he was going to croak pretty soon so it didn't matter. I knew his madness was beyond control then."

Weldon stopped cold. Then he seemed to look deeply inside himself, drew a deep breath, and said, "That's when he told me he'd had a nice little visit with his grandson. And that's when I hit him and knocked his chair over. I should have killed him then but I just couldn't do it. I threatened him, hoped to scare him into silence like I already told you, but I knew that wouldn't work. After

I left, I thought about it and knew I had to kill him, there was just no other way. I failed."

Dane said very gently, "Weldon, your father visited with your boy and confessed what he was to him?"

"Yes."

"Weldon, who is your son?"

Weldon shook his head. "Listen, Agent Savich, my son isn't a murderer, he isn't."

"But you believe he is," Sherlock said, "and it's eating you alive. You think your son killed the people in San Francisco and in Pasadena, copying the scripts you wrote."

Finally, Weldon DeLoach said, "I just couldn't make myself accept that he was like his grandfather, that his head wasn't right, that something was missing in him."

Dane said, "We've got to bring him in, Weldon, you must know that. You can't let him continue doing what your own father did for so many years."

Weldon was shaking his head. "Don't get me wrong. I didn't figure it out until just a couple of days ago. And even then I didn't figure it out for myself. The old man actually bragged about how he'd finally gotten a real man in the family, how he didn't have much to teach his grandson, because—like his granddaddy—he was born knowing what to do and how to do it. He told me that his grandson came to see him, brought a Christmas present, a nice tie with red dots on it. And how perfect that was, and so he told the boy he was going to die soon and he wanted to tell him all about himself. And he laughed and laughed at how stupid everyone was, the cops especially."

Weldon fell silent, looked at them again. He said at last, "I haven't known what to do. I just knew I had to kill that obscene old man, get him buried, and gone."

Sherlock said very gently, "But what were you going to do about your son?"

"Get him help. Stop him from doing any more harm. Turn him over to the police if I had to."

Sherlock said, "We're the cops. What's his name, Weldon?"

But Weldon just shook his head. "I couldn't let him continue, not like my father had done. He was a good boy, really. I know something must have happened to make him snap, to turn him into a monster like his grandfather. I don't know what it was, but there just had to have been something. He was doing so well. He's very smart, you know, extraordinarily talented. But then there were some signs—he struggled when he was in high school, didn't like his teachers, couldn't make friends—it was enough to make me pay attention. He was violent once, when he accidentally killed a girl in college, but it could have happened to any guy, you know? Things just got out of hand. It was involuntary manslaughter. I got him help. They made him well. My son promised me he was just fine, and I wanted desperately to believe him.

"Something happened. The old man did this to him, somehow."

He looked up at each of them in turn. "Do you know I still don't know how many people that old monster killed? There were people he killed that were never found by anyone. Oh Jesus."

He put his head in his hands and sobbed very quietly.

THIRTY-TWO

"Wait! You can't go in there!"

As she pushed past him, Sherlock said, "Jay, it's time for you to go away now. It's time to take your custom suits from Armani, get another job, and pay off your credit cards."

"But he's meditating! He specifically told me he didn't want to be bothered. And I love Armani. When I wear Armani everyone knows it's Armani."

Suddenly Arnold Loftus came roaring forward. He didn't try to bar their way, he rounded on Jay Smith. "Shut up, Jay. They're here for a reason. Don't try to stop them."

"You're the damned bodyguard. Don't let them go in there, you moron, you've—"

Arnold very gently picked up Jay Smith beneath his armpits and simply walked away with him. He said over his shoulder, "The Little Shit fired me. Whatever it is, go for it."

Dane gently turned the handle. The door was locked. He turned to Jay, still held up by his armpits, and held out his hand. "Key," was all he said.

Arnold let Jay down, watched him like a hawk as he went to his desk, got down on his knees, and untaped a key beneath the center drawer. He handed it to Dane.

"Thank you," Dane said.

Dane quietly unlocked the door, slowly pushed it open. The huge office was dark, like a movie theater, and indeed, there was a movie showing, on the far white wall. Linus Wolfinger was seated in the chair behind his desk, his chin propped up in his hands, watching.

It was an episode of *The Consultant,* one they hadn't seen. He didn't look away from the screen even after all six of the people who'd come into his office were standing around his desk.

He said in a calm, conversational voice, "My dear old dad blew the whistle, I take it?"

"No," Delion said. "Your dad told us about how he'd found out that his son was a murderer, but no, he didn't tell us your name."

"That crazy old pile of bones told you then."

Savich said, "Actually, we managed to figure it out. MAX, my computer, verified for us that you were born Robert Allen DeLoach, and you attended Garrett High School here in LA. Here's a photo of you."

Savich laid the photo faceup on Wolfinger's desk. Linus didn't bother to look at it.

Sherlock said, "We also found the real Michael Linus Wolfinger. Here's his photo. He isn't you."

Linus waved a hand. "The guy died in a skiing accident, nothing more. He was an orphan. Taking his identity wasn't a problem. I wanted to work in the studio. With the year in that institution, I knew no one would hire me." Linus shrugged. "Who the hell cares?"

"Tell us about the girl in college," Dane said.

Linus shrugged again, his fingers were tapping on the desktop. He couldn't seem to keep himself still. "Silly little twit, told me she wouldn't go out with a nerd. I twisted her neck until it broke. Unfortunately my father came in before I could get rid of her body. But he helped me, told me that I wasn't like my grandfather, that he was going to get me help. I argued with him but he told me I had no choice. For my own good, he was putting me in an institution. If I didn't agree, he'd turn me over to the police."

Linus looked at them again, shrugged. "I am very smart, you know. In fact, I'm more than smart. I'm a genius. That year in the Mountain Peak Institution, in the butt-end of nowhere—well, I used that year to plan out what I wanted to do with my life. It was right after that that Wolfinger died and I took on his name and his past. Dear old dad got me a job here at the studio. Then I met Miles Burdock and impressed the hell out of him, which was tough, but I told you, I'm a genius. I've proved it. I've made lots and lots of money for the studio. That's why all the old duffers around here call me Little Shit. They're all jealous. Hey, I'm the crown prince, the best fucking thing that's ever happened to this place."

He paused a moment, looked at Savich. "I don't suppose my daddy knocked off my grandfather?"

"No," Dane said, "but he really wanted to. He still does. How did you find out about your grandfather? How did you even know where he is?"

Linus laughed. "I was at my dad's house last month and came across a paid invoice to the old folks' home. I had never met my grandfather, but I did know that my dad hated him. He told me several times that he'd never put that old man in my life, never. I suppose my dad told you that?"

Dane nodded.

"I wanted to meet him, maybe find out why my dad hated him so much. I even took him a Christmas present. Do you know what I found out from that pathetic old man?"

No one said anything, just waited.

"He told me about what he'd done. At first I just didn't believe him, it was too fantastic. But he told me stuff that sounded too real to be made up. He called my dad a coward and a wuss. Then he asked me if I was really of his blood, if I'd ever killed anyone. I told him I had. I thought the old man would crawl out of his wheelchair and dance he was so pleased.

"He cackled, blood and spittle hanging off his chin. He wagged his finger at me, told me it was in my blood, told me I had the look of him when he was young, and the good Lord knew it was so deep in his blood that now it was coming out of him. He coughed again and more blood came out of his mouth.

"I realized then that I was just like him. I told him that I'd gotten bored, and then my dad had come up with this terrific idea for a series. As I listened to him, everything came together in my mind. I knew exactly what I was going to do. I added my own ideas to the first two or three scripts, and my dad was really pleased that I was so interested and that my ideas worked so well.

"When I told my grandfather what I was going to do, he

wanted all the details. He even helped me refine some of my plans. When I left, he laughed and wished me luck, said he wanted to hear how things actually went down because, he said, things never go exactly as planned, and that just makes it all the more fun. I told him he could read all about it in the newspaper." Linus shook his head, tapped his fingers some more on the desktop.

"Jesus, it was fun, particularly that priest in San Francisco, your twin brother, Agent Carver. He surprised the hell out of me. It gave me quite a start when you first came in here."

Dane wanted to kill the little bastard. He felt Savich's hand on his arm, squeezing very lightly. He fought for control, managed to keep it. He said, "It's over now, Linus, all over. You're dead meat."

Linus said, "You do know I'm the one who sent that picture of you and Miss Nick to the media. All I had to do was make a couple of calls to the SFPD to find out who she was. And now she was here, sniffing around, looking at everyone, but I knew she wouldn't recognize me."

Dane said, "But you hired Milton to kill her. You were afraid that she might recognize you eventually."

Linus shrugged yet again, his fingertips tapping a mad tattoo. "Why take a chance? Too bad Milton was such a lousy shot." He looked at Nick. "Pity he missed you. Just a graze. Bummer. But I would have gotten you, Miss Nick, oh yes, I would have killed you dead." He gave a short laugh, then turned back to the show. He pressed a button, lowering the volume even more. He said, never looking away from the episode playing on the wall, "Father Michael Joseph was my first big challenge. He told me he was going to blow the whistle on me, leave the priesthood if he had to. I was going to kill him anyway, but I had to speed things up." He looked at Dane and smiled. "It was a beautiful shot. But you know what? The damned priest looked happy, like maybe he realized that he'd saved some lives with his sacrifice. Who can say?"

Dane was breathing hard now, struggling to keep his hands at his sides, to keep himself from wrapping his hands around Linus Wolfinger's neck and choking the life out of him. He was a monster, maybe even more of a monster than his grandfather, but that would really be saying something.

"What did you do with the gun?" Sherlock asked.

He grinned at her. "Who knows?"

Dane smiled at him. "You're going to pay now, Linus. You're going into a cage and you're never going to come out except when they walk you down to the execution room to send you to hell."

"I don't think so," Linus said, lifted his hand, and in it was a gun, a derringer, small and deadly. He aimed it at each of them in turn.

"Don't even think about it, Linus," Savich said. "It's too late. We don't want to have to kill you. Don't make us."

Linus Wolfinger laughed. "Do you know running this studio isn't even much fun anymore? Nothing's much fun anymore." He said, in a very good imitation of Arnold Schwarzenegger, *"Hasta la vista,* baby." He stuck the derringer in his mouth and pulled the trigger.

THIRTY-THREE

They'd just returned to the Holiday Inn. Linus Wolfinger had been dead for only an hour. It seemed much longer.

Nick stood in front of the TV and watched John Rothman, senior senator from Illinois, face a slew of cameras and a multitude of shouting reporters.

"... We're told it's your wife, Senator, the one everybody believed ran away with one of your aides three years ago. They found her body, but where's your aide?"

"... Sir, how did you feel when they told you they'd found your wife's body?"

"... She's dead, Senator, not off living with another man. Do you think your aide killed your wife, sir?"

". . . How do you think this will affect your political career, Senator?"

Nick simply stared at the TV screen, hardly believing what she saw. She felt a deep pain, and rising rage. John Rothman had finally tracked Cleo down, and killed her. To shut her up. And to get revenge for the letter she'd written to Nick?

She looked at that face she'd believed she loved, that mobile face that could show such joy, could laugh and joke with the greatest charm, a face that could hide hideous secrets. She watched him perform, no other word for it. He was a natural politician, an actor of tremendous talent. To all the questions, Senator John Rothman said not a word. He stood quietly, like a biblical martyr as stones were hurled at him. He looked both stoic and incredibly weary, and older than he had just a month before. She couldn't see any fear leaching out of him; all she saw was pain, immense pain. Even she, who knew what this man was, who knew what he'd done, what he was capable of, even she could feel it radiating from him. If she had been asked at that very instant if he'd killed Cleo, if he'd ever killed anyone or tried to kill anyone, she would have said unequivocally no. He was the most believable human being she'd ever seen in her life.

He continued to say nothing, didn't change his expression at any of the questions, whether they were insulting or not. All the questions seemed to just float past him. Finally, and only when he was ready, Senator Rothman took a single step forward. He merely nodded to the shouting reporters, the people holding the scores of cameras, made brief eye contact with many of them as he gave a small wave of his hand. Immediately everyone was quiet. It was an incredible power he had, one she'd always admired. Even before she'd met him she'd wondered how he did it.

Senator Rothman said very quietly, making everyone strain forward, shushing their colleagues so they could hear him, "The police notified me just last night that they'd found my former wife's body, that it looked like she'd been dead for some time. They don't know yet how long, but they will do the appropriate testing to find out. Then, we hope they'll be able to ascertain what happened to her. As you know, I haven't seen her in more than three years. I would like to ask for your understanding for the grieving family and friends."

He took a step back, raised his head, and nodded to the reporters.

"Your wife's name was Cleo, right, Senator?"

"That's right."

"You were married how long, sir?"

"We were married for five years. I loved her very much. When she left, I was devastated."

"How did she die, Senator?"

"I don't know."

"Did she tell you she was leaving you, Senator?"

"No."

"Are you glad she's dead, Senator?"

Senator John Rothman looked at the woman who'd asked him that. A very long look. The woman squirmed. He said finally, "I will not dignify that question with an answer. Anyone else?"

Another TV-news reporter yelled out, "Did you kill your wife, Senator?"

He didn't say anything for a very long time, just looked at the reporter, as if he were judging him, and the conclusion he'd reached wasn't positive. He said, his voice weary, resigned, "It's always amazed me how some of you in the media, in the middle of a crisis—large or small—are like a pack of rats."

There was silence, some shuffling of feet, some angry whispers and outraged faces.

Nick stared at the man she'd come so close to marrying. Some of the reporters who were furious at what he'd said started to yell out more questions, but stopped. Everyone was looking at him—his face was naked, open, the pain stark and there for everyone to see. She saw tears streaming down his face, saw that he tried to say something but couldn't. Or pretended to. He shook his head at the straining group, turned, and walked away, his aides surrounding him, a barrier between him and all the reporters. Tall, stiff, a man suffering. The reporters, all the camera crews watched him. And the thing was—no one yelled any more questions at him. The sound of the cameras was the only noise. She watched him walk out of the room, a man in pain, his head down, shoulders hunched forward. A tragic figure.

Nick was shaken. She'd never seen John Rothman cry. She felt a moment of doubt before she quashed it beneath the rippling fear she'd felt when she'd awakened from that dream and known, all the way to her soul, that all three attempts on her life had been made by the same man, the man John Rothman had hired to murder her.

The fact was that John Rothman had also tracked down his ex-wife and murdered her in cold blood. Or had he hired the same man to kill Cleo Rothman? The autopsy would show that she'd been dead for no longer than four weeks. That was when Cleo had written the letter that had saved her life. Only Cleo had died.

A local reporter turned and said with great understatement, "Senator John Rothman appears very saddened at the discovery of his wife's grave by a hunter's dog yesterday. Cleo Rothman's remains were identified this morning. We will keep you informed as details emerge from this grisly case."

Nick walked slowly to the TV and turned it off. She started shaking, just couldn't help it.

She looked up to see Dane watching her from across the room. He was leaning against the door, his arms crossed over his chest.

She hadn't heard him come in. And that was a surprise. She'd become very attuned to him over the past week. Only a week. It was amazing. She tried to smile, but couldn't manage it. She said finally, "Did you see it?"

"Yes."

"There's no proof, Dane. Nothing's changed. I know you must have found out that there's no missing-person's report on me because I did have the sense to write to my dean at the university about a personal emergency."

"And your point would be?"

He didn't move, just said when she held silent, his voice very low, "It's time to tell me all of it, Dr. Campion. There are no more distractions to keep us away from this. Linus is dead. Detective Flynn is with the district attorney deciding what to do about Captain DeLoach, and Weldon will survive. How is Senator John Rothman connected to you, Nick? I want all of it. Now."

"Up until three weeks ago, he was my fiancé."

"He was what? Jesus, Nick, I want to know how you could get caught up with a man old enough to be your father. I can't believe that— No, wait, I want to know, but not just yet." He crossed the space between them, jerked her against him, and kissed her.

When he let up just a bit, he was breathing hard and fast.

Nick's eyes, once tear-sheened, were now vague and hot. She said into his mouth, "Oh, God. Dane, this is—" She went up on her tiptoes and grabbed him tightly to her. She was kissing him, nipping his jaw, licking his bottom lip, her hands in his hair, pulling him closer, closer still, pushing into him, wanting him. She groaned when his tongue touched hers.

"Nick, no, no, we can't—oh hell." He wrapped his arms around her hips and lifted her off the floor, carrying her to the bed. He'd never wanted a woman like he wanted her. There was so much, too much really. His brother, all the death, and now the damned senator, more confusion, more secrets. No, he couldn't do this, not the right time, not the right place. He pulled back, lightly traced his fingertip along the line of her jaw, touched her mouth. "Nick, I—" She grabbed him, pulled him flat on top of her.

"Don't stop, don't stop." She was kissing him all over his face, stroking him, reaching to touch all of him she could reach.

"Oh hell." He wanted to cry, to howl. He didn't have any condoms, nothing. He wasn't about to take the chance of getting her pregnant. Okay, okay, it didn't matter, getting himself off wasn't that important, at least not now. Nick was what was important. She'd been engaged to that damned senator? That old man who looked like an aristocrat, the bastard? Well, no matter, she wasn't going to marry him, she wasn't going to marry anyone.

He stripped her jeans down her hips, off her ankles and threw them on the floor. She was trying to bring him back to her, but he held her, looked a moment at the white panties she'd bought that were French cut, and he had those off her in a lick of time. She was beautiful, he couldn't stand it. He was breathing hard, so hard, and he was panting. "It's okay, Nick. Let me give you pleasure. Just hold still, no, don't try to strangle me. Lie back and let me enjoy you." He had her legs open, and he was between them, kissing her belly, then he gave her his mouth and within moments she screamed and went wild. God, he loved it, just loved it, and gave her all he could.

When at last she fell back, her heart pounding nearly out of her chest, breathing so hard she wondered if she would survive, he came up over her. He was harder than the floor, harder than the damned bedsprings, and he hurt. He also knew it was a good thing he had his pants on, otherwise he'd be inside her right this instant. But it just wasn't important, at least not now. He wondered if there was a drugstore nearby. Hey, a gas station, anyplace that sold condoms.

He pulled himself over her and began kissing her, slow, easy kisses, and he knew she could feel him. It took a long time before he slowly pulled away from her and sat up on the side of the bed. He looked down at her long legs, flat white belly, and slowly laid his palm flat. "You're beautiful," he said.

She gave a small moan, looked surprised, then smiled up at him. "So are you."

He grinned. It didn't hurt quite as much. He was getting himself back together. He forced himself to concentrate on pulling her panties back up, then working on her jeans. Just before he zipped up the jeans, he leaned down and kissed her belly again. Oh God, he wanted her. No, no. He spent several minutes easing her upright, straightening her clothes.

He paused for a moment, leaned forward, and cupped her face in his palms. "This is just the beginning. You're wonderful, Nick. But I can't believe you were engaged to John Rothman."

"At this moment, I can't believe I was either," she said, and kissed him.

She leaned forward, resting her face on his shoulder. He stroked her back, up and down. He shouldn't be surprised, he thought, but he was, closer to floored, actually. "John Rothman is far too old for you. Why would you ever want to marry a man who's close to the age of your father?"

His voice sounded back to normal, and so she got herself together and pulled away from him. "John Rothman is forty-seven in years, but much less in the way he looks at things, the way he feels about things. At least that's what I thought."

"If he paraded around naked in front of you, I can't imagine that you'd be licking your chops, would you?"

She was so surprised by what he said that she hiccupped. She said, smiling, "I don't know. I never saw him naked."

"That's good."

"Why would you care?"

"It's really very simple, Dr. Campion. I decided about three days ago that your next fifty years are mine. I saw that they found his wife's body?"

"That's right. Fifty years might not be enough."

"He told everyone that she ran away from him? Three years ago? We'll begin with fifty years, then renegotiate, all right?"

"Yes, he told everyone she ran away. His senior aide was gone as well, a guy named Tod Gambol, and everyone believed she ran away with him. Yes, all right, we'll start with fifty years, then go from there."

"Was Tod Gambol found with the dead wife?"

"Evidently not."

Dane said slowly, "What happened? Did you find out that she didn't leave him?"

"Oh no, Cleo left him, all right. I believed that, no doubt in my mind at all. She'd been gone three years, and he'd divorced her, although she'd never responded, couldn't be found. Of course I accepted it. I loved him. I was going to marry him."

"But she didn't leave him. He killed her."

"Nope. Fact is, she did leave him."

"How could you possibly know that?"

"I also know that she was alive up to four weeks ago."

Dane crossed his arms over his chest. "How do you know that for a fact? Did Senator Rothman assure you that she was alive and well and screwing around with his aide?"

"No. The bottom line is that Cleo Rothman wrote me a letter. She hasn't been dead for three years—just for a month, at the most, and the tests they'll run will prove it. No, John Rothman didn't kill her three years ago."

"Why did she write to you?"

"To warn me. She told me about the first girl John'd planned to marry, way back just before both of them graduated from Boston College. He killed her because Elliott Benson, a rival, had seduced her. He got away with it, she said, because he was smart, and who would ever begin to suspect a young man who was engaged to be married of suddenly killing his fiancée? The final police verdict was that it was a tragic automobile accident. She said that John cried his eyes out at her funeral, that her parents held him to comfort him."

"How could she have found out about that? Did he talk in his sleep? Don't tell me he confessed it to her?"

"No, she found a journal in the safe in his library. She wrote that one day she noticed that the safe wasn't locked. She was curious and opened it.

"So when she opened it and found the journal, she read it. He wrote all about how he'd killed a girl—Melissa Gransby was her name—how he'd planned it all very carefully and gotten away with it. A simple auto accident on I-95, near Bremerton. She must have written at least a half dozen times in that letter how smart John was, how I had to be careful because I was going to be the next woman he killed. She wrote that John had come to believe that I was sleeping with Elliott Benson, too, just like Melissa did, that I was betraying him, even before we were married."

"Who is this Elliott Benson?"

"He's a powerhouse in Chicago, a very rich and successful businessman, an investment banker with Kleiner, Smith and Benson. He and John have been rivals for years and years.

"Cleo wrote that she didn't know if he'd killed other women, but she knew he would have killed her if she hadn't left and she knew he was going to kill me and I should run as far away as I could, and quickly."

Dane, frowning, said, "Why would a man who's supposedly so smart keep a damned journal where he actually confesses to a murder? And leave that journal in a safe in his own home, for God's sake, and then, to top it all off, he leaves the safe open? That's really a long way from being smart, Nick. This whole thing's a stretch. It just doesn't feel right."

THIRTY-FOUR

Nick said, "I thought the same thing at first. But listen, Dane. I knew Cleo Rothman, I knew her handwriting. The letter was from her, I'm positive about that. She told me she had the journal, that she took it with her, to keep John at bay in case he wanted to come after her. It was her only leverage."

"Why didn't she just go to the police with the thing? It was a confession, after all."

"She wrote that John had many important, powerful friends, and that many of those powerful people owed him favors. She said she could just see him saying that as his wife—she knew his handwriting, of course—she had written it herself, that it was all an attempt on her part to ruin him. I could practically taste her fear in that letter, Dane, her sense that she was a coward, but that everything was against her, that she had no choice but to run. Do you think the cops would have believed her, launched an investigation?"

"They would have looked into it, of course, but it wouldn't have helped if they believed she was vindictive, that she wanted to ruin a good man, and there was no other proof but the journal. Anyway, John Rothman wrote that he killed this Melissa Gransby because she cheated on him with this Benson character?"

"Evidently so. John couldn't forgive her. The pages were full of rage, over-the-top, unreasoned rage, and Cleo wrote that she could see that Melissa's unfaithfulness had changed him, twisted him, made him incapable of trusting a woman.

"She wrote that it did make a bit of sense since his mother had cheated on his father, and it hurt him deeply. Evidently he told her this when they were first married."

"Did he tell you this? About his mother?"

She shook her head. "No, he's never told me anything."

"So Cleo Rothman found his journal, read his murder confession, and she just up and left him? With this aide? Jesus, Nick. Ain't a whole lot of credibility here."

"No, no, she wrote that she didn't leave with anyone. She said she didn't even know where Tod Gambol was. She was never his lover, had never been unfaithful to John. She loved John, always loved him, but she was terrified, and so she just ran. She became convinced that he was going to kill her, too, because she'd heard rumors that she was sleeping with Elliott Benson. Knowing this, knowing that he'd already killed a girl because she'd supposedly cheated on him, she knew he would believe the rumors and try to kill her just like he did Melissa.

"When she heard that I was going to marry him, then she

heard the rumors that *I* was sleeping with Elliott Benson, she wrote that she didn't want to see me end up dead, like Melissa, and God knows how many other women."

"Okay, Nick, something else must have happened to make you go to San Francisco and become homeless."

"Just before I got her letter, someone tried to run me down. A man with a ski mask over his head, driving a black car. It was dark and I was walking just one block from the neighborhood store back to my building."

Dane stiffened. "What," he said, "were you doing out in the dark walking to the store? In Chicago? That's really dumb, Nick."

She poked her finger in his chest. "All right, you want to know every little thing? Okay, it was my period, if it's any of your business."

"Well, I can see that you wouldn't want to wait. But, you should have had the store deliver."

It was so funny, really so unexpected, all this outrage over something so very insignificant, that she laughed. And laughed again. Here she was telling him about one of the most frightening experiences of her life—until a week ago—and he was all upset because she'd walked to her local store, by herself, in the dark.

On the other hand, given what happened, maybe he had a point.

She cleared her throat and said, "As I was saying, I was walking back when this car came out of a side street and very nearly got me. There was no way it was someone drunk or a stupid accident. No, I knew it was on purpose. Then there was his sister Albia's birthday dinner. Supposedly it was food poisoning. It was really close. If I'd eaten more I would have died. The second I got that letter, I took off to his apartment to confront him about it."

"What happened?"

"I waved the letter in his face, asked him how many women he'd killed. He denied everything, said the letter couldn't be from Cleo, he just wouldn't believe that, demanded that I give it to him. Then he came at me and I thought he was going to strangle me. He got the letter, shredded it, and threw it into the fire, then turned on me. I pulled my gun out and told him I was leaving. That night, I woke up because I heard someone in my condo. I saw this guy from the balcony, running away, and realized that he'd set my condo on fire. I got myself out in time, but it was too close. I got away with my purse and that was it. I ended up in a shelter. Since I'd lost everything, since I didn't have a shred of proof, since I knew he'd try to kill me, just like he did Melissa, just like he'd wanted to kill Cleo, I decided being homeless wasn't such a bad thing. Talk about disappearing—and it would give me time to figure out what to do. That's how I ended up in San Francisco, how I just happened to be waiting in the church for Father Michael Joseph."

"So you went to San Francisco and just hid underground. You knew you couldn't remain hidden there, Nick. What were you going to do?"

"I hadn't yet decided. Believe me, I was in no hurry. Despite where I was, I felt safe until this happened."

"Who is Albia?"

"She's John Rothman's older sister. They're very close, always have been."

"What is she like?"

"Albia is some seven years older than John. After their mother died in an auto accident, Albia more or less became his mother. As I said, they're very close. Once I asked her about the family, and she told me about their mother, that she'd died tragically, that their father had died about five years ago of a heart attack."

"Lots of automobile accidents in this man's life."

"Tell me about it."

"So Albia didn't tell you about her mother being unfaithful to her father?"

"No, would you?"

"Maybe not."

"But there was something. At Albia's birthday dinner, before I got really sick, I gave her a scarf. She started to talk about how their mother had had a scarf like that and then she looked like she'd swallowed something bad. She shut up like a clam. They explained it to me that it was a touchy subject."

"No explanation at all."

"Not really."

"Nothing much there. Is that it?"

"No, there's more, and this is something I know. I remember John told me he was in love with Cleo within minutes of meeting her. When she left him, he was devastated, just couldn't believe it. He wondered and wondered why she hadn't spoken to him, told him what was wrong, but she'd just up and left."

"Hmmm," Dane said again.

She said, "You know, Dane, it was really hard for me to believe that John began murdering women just because his mother cheated on his father. Do you think it's remotely possible that he might have killed his own mother?"

"I think it's possible that someone did."

"But who else could it have been?"

He just shook his head. "There's lots here to process, Nick. Let's get Savich and Sherlock involved. MAX found out that you're Dr. Nicola Campion quickly enough. They're primed to help."

"I think that's a great idea."

The four of them met in the Holiday Inn coffee shop.

Dane said, "Maybe you guys could consider stopping off in Chicago with us before going back to Washington."

"Actually," Savich said, "Sherlock was just about ready to call you, Nick, get all the details out of your mouth and not from MAX."

"It's a real mess," Nick said. She talked and talked, slowly covered again all that had happened, answered many of the same questions, though many of them had a different slant, refreshing her memory for different things. She realized she was being questioned by experts. It was quite painless, actually. Finally, both Savich and Sherlock fell silent. Savich was holding his wife's hand, stroking his thumb over her palm, slowly and gently.

Nick watched Savich sip his tea, frown. He said as he gently sloshed the tea around in the cup, "It's very flat, no taste at all."

Sherlock patted his hand. "I think we should start traveling with the tea you like."

Dane, impatient, said, "Well? What do you guys think?"

Savich smiled at Nick and said, "I want to cogitate on all of this for a while. But first, I need to make a phone call."

He pulled out his cell phone, dialed, waited. "Hello, George? It's Savich, and I need a bit of help."

"Who's George?" Nick whispered to Dane.

Sherlock said, "It's Captain George Brady, Chicago Police Department."

Savich waited, listened, then said into the cell phone, "Here's the deal, George. I need you to tell me about Cleo Rothman."

Two minutes later, Savich pressed the off button on the phone. He looked at each of them in turn, then said directly to

Nick, "I'm sorry, Nick, but Cleo Rothman wasn't killed a couple of weeks ago."

Nick said, "What do you mean? I don't understand. I got the letter from her not more than a month ago."

Savich said. "Captain Brady said the medical examiner was just about ready to announce his findings. Fact is, Cleo Rothman was murdered at least three years ago."

THIRTY-FIVE

They spent the entire late afternoon and evening in meetings with Jimmy Maitland, Savich's boss and an assistant director of the FBI, Gil Rainy from the LA field office, and LAPD Chief William Morgan and his staff, including Detective Flynn. They had time for only a brief good-bye to Inspector Delion before he flew back to San Francisco late that evening.

The DA wasn't going to press charges against Weldon DeLoach, recognized that the man had lost his son and would probably be *persona non grata* in Hollywood. Besides, Weldon was going to show them where his father had buried all the discarded bloody clothes from so many years ago. That was, they decided, enough punishment for any man. As for Captain DeLoach, they'd tried to get details from him, but he'd acted utterly demented. Was it a game? No one knew. The fact was, though, he was dying. No one could see putting the old buzzard in jail, but the questions would continue to be asked. They would see if any were ever answered.

With Jimmy Maitland's blessing, the four of them flew to Chicago the following morning. They survived the usual hassles that accompanied traveling by air now that the world had changed. Their FBI shields were studied, their paperwork read three times, their fingerprints closely scrutinized until, at last, they were cleared through.

They rented two cars and suffered through the snarled traffic—which still didn't measure up to Los Angeles traffic—and it took them a good forty-five minutes to reach The Four Seasons. It was a treat, Savich told them, and one that Jimmy Maitland had approved. He'd told Savich they'd done such a good job with the script murderer that the sky was the limit, given, of course, that they realized the sky consisted of two regular rooms, which were still very nice in The Four Seasons. They managed to snag two adjoining rooms.

They ordered up room service first thing. Over club sandwiches, Savich's minus the turkey and bacon, he said, "Okay, I've given this lots of thought, talked it over with Sherlock and Dane on the airplane. Here's what we think, Nick: It's just possible that Senator John Rothman isn't the murderer here."

It was like someone punched her in the gut. She lost her breath. She gaped at the three of them, all of them nodding at her, said, "No, that's just not possible."

"Think a minute," Savich said, very gently, because he knew that her entire world was based on her belief that this one man had tried to murder her. "John Rothman is a very powerful man, true, with lots of clout, lots of friends who owe him favors, but despite that, he's got a lot on the line. Not just his political career, but his life. His life, Nick. For a man like him, with his skills, his place in the world, to really be that screwed up because his mom had an affair when he was a teenager, it just doesn't make sense, for any of us." He smiled at her. "Fact is, we're thinking that it just might be Albia Rothman."

Dane smiled, didn't say a word, just took another bite of his sandwich, which was quite good.

"Albia," Nick said, her voice blank, sandwich forgotten. "What on earth do you mean?"

"Well," Savich said, "to be honest here, it socked me in the face when you first mentioned her. That's why I said I wanted to think about it, discuss it with Sherlock and Dane. I'm not saying that we shouldn't immediately speak to John Rothman, because we have been known to be wrong before. Just maybe we'll change our minds. But I want us to give serious consideration to his sister as well."

Nick could only stare at each of them in turn. She drew a deep breath, took a bite of her sandwich, chewed, then said finally, "I'm not following you guys at all here."

Dane said, "Here's the deal: Older sister and younger brother are both hurt badly because of mother's infidelity. Older sister believes to her soul that she's her little brother's protector. Maybe she kills her mother, or maybe not, maybe her death just makes it all that much worse. She becomes her younger brother's biggest supporter, realizes she can't bear to ever let him go to another woman, and so when he meets someone in college, she kills her, making it look like an accident."

Nick was shaking her head. "But how can you possibly know if any of that is even close to the truth? It was all this Elliott Benson, this friend of John's who's always gone after the women John loved or wanted.

"Also, there's the inescapable fact that John married Cleo. They were married for five years. Why wouldn't Albia have killed her before John could marry her if she wanted to keep him to herself? To keep him safe from other women?"

Sherlock said, "It's likely that Albia simply didn't have enough opportunity before they married. We'll see about that. I'll bet you the last quarter of my club sandwich, though, that it was probably a whirlwind romance, and Albia didn't have a chance to stop him from marrying. So Albia had to bide her time, had to go underground with her feelings. After all, she couldn't just knock off his new wife; there would be too many questions raised. And certainly the last thing she'd want is to have her brother a suspect in the death of his wife, supposed accident or not."

Dane said, "Here's the clincher. You said that Cleo was the one who told you about Elliott Benson. Well, Cleo didn't write that letter. It's got to be Albia."

Nick looked thoughtful, her eyes on the crust of her club sandwich, all that was left. She said at last, "I know Albia, or at least I thought I did. She's always been kind to me, not chummy, because she's not like that with anyone. She's very dignified, very together, restrained."

Dane said, "Would she go to the mat for her brother, do you think?"

Nick pictured Albia Rothman in her mind, slowly shook her head. "I just don't know. I remember once in a meeting, though, Albia didn't agree with a political stand John wanted to take. She laid out her reasons, but he didn't change his mind. I remember thinking that I agreed with her. I also remember the look she gave him was vicious, but she didn't argue with him anymore."

"You said that Albia was married once, for just a short time?" Savich asked.

"That's right," Nick said. "Oh, God, her husband died very suddenly, if I'm remembering right. You don't think—no, oh no." Nick dashed her fingers through her hair. "This is very difficult. I've believed it was John from the very beginning. When he came at me that last night, his fingers curved toward my neck—and I swear to you, I saw murder in his eyes—I knew he was guilty. Not a single doubt in my mind. I was terrified. The thing is—why would he come after me if it was Albia who killed the women?"

"Maybe he didn't mean to hurt you," Sherlock said. "Maybe he just wanted that letter from his ex-wife. And he wanted it very badly, enough to attack you to get it. Nick, his career is on the line here. All he cares about can come tumbling down around his ears. He had to get ahold of that letter. Now that raises a good question, doesn't it?"

"Yes, it does," Dane said. "Did he already know that Cleo was long dead?"

"No," Nick said. "He was saying that there was no way Cleo would ever hurt him like that, no way at all. Oh, I don't know. This is too much. You guys really believe then that it was Albia Rothman who tried to kill me in Los Angeles?"

"Probably," Sherlock said. "I'd for sure bet she arranged setting fire to your condo. As for the man on the Harley, maybe she hired someone she trusted, someone from Chicago."

Nick was shaking her head. "Actually, I figured it all out in a dream a couple of nights ago. The guy in the car who tried to run me down, the guy who set fire to my condo, the guy on the Harley—I realized that they were all the same man. I'm really sure of that."

Dane said, "That makes sense. Maybe a lover, someone she felt she could really trust."

"Maybe," Savich said. "And once Linus sent your photo to the media, and she saw you on TV, recognized you, she knew just where you were. It wouldn't be hard to locate where you were staying, and to have you followed. And when the Harley attempt failed, she just didn't have time to execute another plan."

Nick leaned over and took a bite out of Dane's sandwich.

Savich said, grinning as he sat forward, "That's interesting behavior, Nick. First you bite Dane's shoulder and now his sandwich. This appears to me to be serious aggression. Can you handle this, Dane?"

"I'll manage," Dane said, and smiled at Nick even as he touched his fingers to his shoulder. "She's too skinny. Let her bite anything she wants."

"Hmmm," said Sherlock, and gave her husband a look that nearly had him shaking. It was the same look she'd given him the night before, just before she kissed every inch of him and sent him to heaven.

"That's enough of that," Savich said, both to his wife and to Dane. "Let's get back to Cleo Rothman. She's been dead three years. I'll wager that senior aide, Tod Gambol, is dead as well. Now, who else could have sent you that letter, other than Albia Rothman? Is there anyone else remotely possible that you can think of, Nick?"

Nick shook her head. "I can't think of anyone else. But listen to me, all of you. I was absolutely certain that it was Cleo's handwriting."

Sherlock shrugged. "That's no big problem. It just means that Albia had copies of Cleo's letters, memos, whatever, and copied them. It's a real pity that John Rothman destroyed the letter. We could have run tests, figured out who wrote it, once and for all. Maybe she wrote you the letter to scare you off. Maybe she didn't want to kill you, maybe she did. Maybe she'll end up telling us. But she wanted you gone, thus the letter and the story about the journal."

"You don't believe there's a journal?" Nick asked.

"Oh no," Dane said. "It never made any sense that John Rothman would leave a journal in which he confessed to a murder, in his study safe, and the damned safe is left open accidentally. Nope, Albia made up the journal to terrify you, to get you the hell out of Dodge."

Savich said, "Regardless, it wasn't Senator Rothman who wrote the letter. He'd have to be beyond nuts to do that. Albia wrote it because she wanted you to break things off with her bro. When it didn't work, she got real serious about killing you."

Sherlock said, "Well, Rothman could be nuts, but listen, Nick, if it turns out that it's his sister who's behind all this, do you still want to marry the senator?"

Nick didn't pause for a second. "I have other plans."

Dane said, "She can't marry the senator. She bit my shoulder a second time. Not to mention my sandwich. I figure that's a really big step toward commitment."

"Sounds long term to me," Savich said.

Sherlock patted Nick's arm and smiled up at her husband. "Last night I was feeling just a touch let down, what with all the excitement over. Well, not let down in certain things, just the contrary, as a matter of fact." She gave Savich another look to make him shake, then shook her head, cleared her throat. "And now we have a bit more to keep us occupied. Then it's home to Sean. We've been away from our boy too long. He's very likely got his grandmother dancing jigs for his entertainment. Okay, what do you say, guys? Let's wrap this thing up today."

"She's an adrenaline junkie," Savich said, and hugged his wife against his side, kissed her ear. "Hey, after we see Senator Rothman, how about we go work out?"

Sherlock said, "The way this works is that Dillon will work out until he's nearly dead, then he'll smile at me and have the whole thing figured out."

Dane said, "You mean it's plain old sweat that solves your cases? Not sugar?"

"No sugar. Just sweat and pain," Savich said. "Let me call Jimmy Maitland, tell him what we're up to, see if he wants to notify the police commissioner here in Chicago. Sherlock, why don't you call Senator Rothman's office, see if he's in. I'd really like to pop in on him, just like we did with Linus Wolfinger."

Nick sat back in her chair, arms crossed over her chest. She looked from one to the other and marveled. "I just don't believe you guys."

They all ended up going to Hoolihan's Gym on the corner of Rusk and Pine because Senator Rothman was in Washington and not due to arrive at his office until late afternoon.

At the gym, they watched Assistant FBI Director Jimmy Maitland on the big overhead TV, flanked by the local FBI field office people, local LAPD, and the press, in Los Angeles.

Savich said, "I told Mr. Maitland that we didn't want to be part of the hoopla. He's really good at handling that sort of thing."

They watched the media pushing and shoving, all of them yelling questions at once. At least six reporters wanted to know where Dane, Sherlock, and Savich were. One even asked about the homeless woman—the supposed eyewitness—who hadn't managed to identify Linus Wolfinger.

Nick booed the TV.

Jimmy Maitland said, fanning his hand, "Sorry, people, but the special agents in question are already involved in another case. As for the homeless woman, she did just fine. She put her life on the line for us. Next question."

Delion had gone back to Los Angeles for the press conference, after being the main rep for a huge media ordeal in San Francisco at City Hall. Both Delion and Flynn were there now, standing together, smiling, Flynn's hand moving up and down like he was dribbling a basketball, freely telling the main facts of the case. All questions about Captain DeLoach were referred to the DA.

A spokesperson from Premier Studios expressed owner Miles Burdock's shock, surprise, and deep regret. He informed everyone that *The Consultant* would eventually be rescheduled. No one wanted the stars to be penalized for something they'd known nothing about.

He didn't say it was just possible that everyone would want to watch the show now, that it would get its highest ratings ever. He didn't say he was planning to use the profits the show generated to help cover the host of lawsuits the studio was sure to face from their scripts being used as models for murder by their own chief executive.

Belinda Gates and Joe Kleypas stood behind the spokesperson. It was obvious they were very pleased. The spokesperson announced finally that Frank Pauley would be assuming Linus Wolfinger's position as president of Premier Studios.

The four watching at Hoolihan's Gym in Chicago high-fived one another when the press conference was over. "Belinda was the only one who ever helped us," Sherlock said, "but even she let us down."

Savich said to his wife, "That reminds me. I haven't pulled those rollers out of your hair yet," and kissed her.

"I'll buy some tomorrow," Sherlock said.

THIRTY-SIX

An hour later the four of them were at Senator Rothman's office on Briarly Avenue in downtown Chicago. Press were hovering about in herds. "I feel sorry for the poor soul who just happens to be walking near here today," Nick said, and led them to the back of the building. "It looks like the reporters haven't found out about this back entrance just yet."

Savich said, "It won't take them long. I saw security people in the lobby. At least they can keep the vultures out of the building."

The secretary, Mrs. Mazer, jumped to her feet when she saw Nick and yelled, "Oh goodness me, you're all right! Oh, Dr. Campion, the senator will be so pleased to see you. Even though he hasn't said anything, I know he's been dreadfully worried, particularly after we all saw you on television and realized you were involved in that horrible script murder case. We all thought you were visiting your family. Oh, come in, come in. Who are these folks with you?"

"It's good to see you, Mrs. Mazer. Is John free for a moment?"

"Oh, yes, certainly. He will be so pleased to see you." She paused a moment, looking at Dane, Sherlock, and Savich, a gray eyebrow arched.

"It's all right. They're with me, Mrs. Mazer."

Mrs. Mazer said nothing more, opened the senator's door, then stepped aside.

Senator John Rothman was standing in the middle of his large office when Nick walked first into the room. She stopped, said, "Thank you for seeing me, John."

He stood stiff as a lamppost. "Nicola," he said politely. "Who are these people?"

Nick introduced each of them in turn. "Did you see the press conference?"

"Oh yes, I saw it all," Senator Rothman said. "Mrs. Mazer, please close the door and see that I'm not disturbed."

When the door was quietly and firmly closed, Senator John Rothman turned to Nick. He tried to smile at her, flanked by three FBI agents.

"It's good to see you, Nicola. Like everyone else in the world, I saw your photo on television. It was a shock, as you can imagine." He paused a moment, searching her face. "There was the fire in your condo. I was frantic but I couldn't find you. You simply disappeared. I called the university. The dean told me you'd written a letter stating that you had a family emergency, but that was a lie, wasn't it?"

"Yes, it was a lie," Nick said.

"I had no idea where to find you. I didn't think it was a good idea to call the FBI and demand information about your whereabouts. And now you've come back. Why?"

"First of all, to tell you I'm sorry about Cleo."

"Yes, I am, too. The thing is, some people believe I killed her, but I didn't. I'm sure my lawyers think they've died and gone to heaven, they're going to make so much money off this mess. Listen, I didn't hurt anyone, Nicola." His eyes never left her face. "I didn't try to hurt you."

Finally, he broke the moment, turning, when Savich said, "Senator, as Nick told you, I'm Agent Savich, this is Agent Sherlock, and Agent Carver. Since Nick helped us out on the murder cases in California, we've decided to help her out with her involvement in this particular mess."

"It is a mess," said John Rothman. He ran his fingers through his beautifully styled salt-and-pepper hair.

Dane, who'd said nothing, stood quietly behind Nick, eyeing this elegant aristocrat. He wanted to kick the man's teeth down his throat.

"John," Nick said, "do you remember that night I asked you how many women you killed?"

Dead silence.

"Yes, of course I would remember when the woman I love accuses me of being a serial killer. I assume all these Federal agents are familiar with what you think of me, Nicola?"

She nodded. She realized in that moment that she was now perfectly safe. No one could hurt her again. She drew herself up even taller.

"Did you know there was an attempt on my life in Los Angeles?"

"Of course not. How could I possibly know that?" He paused a moment, then said, "Should I have my lawyer present?"

"I don't believe so," Savich said. "Why don't we all sit down and talk this over?"

The lovely pale brown brocade grouping was expensive and charming. The coffee served in the Georgian coffeepot was fresh and quite excellent. It was Nicola who served them. Dane saw that she was very comfortable in these surroundings, pouring the damned coffee from that exquisite silver coffeepot. He'd be willing to bet Paul Revere had made the thing. He didn't know if he ever wanted to see Nick in the senator's penthouse, damn that man's sincere and honest eyes.

Dane sat forward, clasping his hands between his legs. "Nick has told us that your mother died in a car accident some three months after she confessed infidelity to your father. You were sixteen at the time. Is this correct?"

Rothman said slowly, "Why are you asking about my mother? It is absolutely none of your business. It's no one's business. It has nothing to do with anything."

"Senator, we're here as friends of Nick," Sherlock said. "Of course, our superiors also know that we're here. We rather hoped we could clear everything up today, informally." She gave him her patented smile, which no human being alive could resist. He found himself smiling back at her, taking in her brilliant curly red hair. He said, "I appreciate that, Agent. But of course I haven't killed anyone. I don't know what's going on, any more than you do. Nicola, I told you that my mother was dead, that she died in a car accident. But what does that have to do with anything? Why the questions about my mother?"

"It was in Cleo's letter," Nick said. "The one you tore out of my hand and hurled into the fireplace."

Senator Rothman looked utterly bewildered.

"You do remember shredding the letter and throwing it into the fireplace, John?"

"Yes, of course. I was very upset that night. A letter from Cleo—I simply couldn't accept that. Throwing the letter into the fire, it was an impulse, and one that I now regret."

Dane hated it, but he believed Senator Rothman. He'd really hoped, in a deep, black spot in his heart, that the senator was so guilty he'd stink of it, but he didn't.

Dane said, "Senator Rothman, perhaps we can end this very simply. Could you please show us your journal."

Senator Rothman looked blank.

"You do have a journal, don't you, sir?" Sherlock said.

"Yes, of course, but it's more like a recording of events over the years, nothing personal, if you know what I mean. Actually, I haven't written in it in a very long time."

"May we please see it, sir," Dane said.

Senator Rothman rose, walked to his exquisite bird's-eye maple desk, opened the second drawer, and pulled it out. He handed the journal-sized notebook to Dane.

Sherlock said, "You don't keep it at home in the safe in your study?"

"Oh no, I've always kept it here. I'm hardly home enough to leave it there. As I said, I haven't written in it in a very long time, since before Cleo left—no, before someone murdered Cleo." He winced.

Nick said, "Cleo wrote that you confessed to murdering Melissa."

"Murdered Melissa? That is absurd. I wish I hadn't destroyed that damned letter. Listen, Nick, whoever wrote you that letter, it wasn't Cleo."

"We know that now," Savich said. "Cleo's been dead since she supposedly left you."

No one said anything. Dane opened the journal, a rich dark brown leather with a clasp that wasn't locked. He skimmed through it.

Rothman said, "As you can see, Agent Carver, it's more a recording of events and appointments, nothing at all sinister." He paused, said, "No, Cleo didn't write you that letter, Nicola. God, she was dead, dead all along, and no one knew." He put his face in his hands, his shoulders heaving, struggling to keep control.

No one said a word until he got himself together again, drank some of his coffee. "I apologize."

He said finally, "What the hell is going on here?"

"Haven't you wondered who wrote me that letter since Cleo has been dead for three years?" Nick asked.

He splayed his hands in front of him, didn't say anything.

"You kept insisting that last night, John, that Cleo hadn't written the letter, that it was impossible. It occurred to me that you must have known she was dead, that it was impossible for her to have written to me, that it had to be someone else."

"No, I had no idea Cleo was dead. What I simply couldn't believe was that Cleo would slander me like that, that she would make up that story about a journal and what I'd written. There was no way she could have believed that I killed Melissa, would have killed *her* as well, and now even you. All because of some rumor that you were sleeping with Elliott Benson?"

"That all three of us slept with Elliott Benson, beginning with Melissa back in college."

He shook his head. "That's absurd. Elliott is a friend, not an enemy. He's a man I trust, a man I've always trusted."

Nick looked away from the man she'd planned to marry just one month before. Now he and Elliott Benson were the best of friends? She didn't know, just didn't know.

She rose and walked to the huge window that gave onto Lake Michigan. The water was whipped up by a strong wind. She could tell it was cold and blustery from there, on the twenty-second floor of the Grayson Building. She said over her shoulder, not looking back, "I never heard any rumor about me and Elliott, did you, John?"

To her surprise, he slowly nodded, saw she still wasn't looking at him, and said aloud, "Yes, I did hear some rumors. I actually spoke to Elliott about them, and he denied them, of course. I remember I was about to leave when I turned and saw that he was smirking behind his hand. Then it was gone, and I believed I must have imagined it. Elliott would never hurt me." He rubbed his knuckles then, and Savich knew that the restrained aristocratic senator had been thinking about hitting Elliott Benson. Because he believed he was the enemy? Did he believe that Nick would do such a thing?

"Why do you think he would slander Dr. Campion?" Sherlock asked. "If, of course, he actually did."

"I don't know. He's occupied a unique position in my life, sometimes a friend, sometimes an enemy. It's been that way since we were in high school. I do know he wanted to sleep with Cleo, I know that for a fact. But she didn't want him. She told me about it." He paused, looked down at his hands, at his fingers rubbing against his palms. "But of course there was Tod Gambol."

"Who still hasn't been located," Dane said.

The senator said, "Maybe Tod's the one who killed her. Or maybe it was Elliott and he's the one who started the rumor about

Nicola because he wanted her to leave me. Maybe I've been wrong about him all these years. But would he go that far? Jesus, I don't know. Do you know why he would say such a thing, Nicola?"

"No, I have no idea. Did you believe him when he denied the rumor about me, John?"

"Good God, yes, naturally."

"Are you quite sure?"

"Of course." But he dropped his eyes. He said, "Those references to my journal, to what I'd supposedly written, listen to me. I didn't write any of that, so that means she lied, but now we know it wasn't Cleo who lied, it was someone else."

"Yes," Savich said. "Yes, we think that just might be the case, Senator."

Senator Rothman looked pathetically eager. "Really? And just what exactly do you think, Agent?"

"We need to speak to you and your sister, Albia Rothman, sir," Sherlock said. "Could you perhaps arrange a meeting?"

"I'm sure Albia would want very much to see you again, Nick. Why don't all of you come to dinner tonight at my home?"

"That would be fine," Nick said. "Thank you, John."

"What's this about Albia? You think she's got something to do with this? You think she wrote the letter to Nicola, made up that journal?" His face was flushed. "That's nonsense, absolute rubbish."

"What time, John?" Nick asked.

They were all seated at the magnificent dining room table, which was set for six. Senator Rothman sat at the head of the table and Albia at the other end.

Dane thought she was a beautiful woman, as charming as her brother, though perhaps a touch more calculated. It was obvious to him that her brother hadn't mentioned the letter or the journal to her.

Albia Rothman had cried when she first saw Nick, hugged her, told her over and over how very worried they'd been about her, that she was utterly distraught that Nick had believed such horrible things about John.

"My dear, I cannot tell you how much both John and I worried about you. We talked and talked but nothing seemed to make any sense to us. Then you were on TV with this man here—this Federal agent—and you were some sort of eyewitness in that script murder. However did all that come about? We heard that the murderer killed himself. It must have been a horrible time for you, Nicola."

"Yes, it was very bad, Albia," Nick said.

Nick's voice was soft, a slight musical lilt to it. Dane saw that she wasn't wearing anything he'd bought her. She and Sherlock had gone shopping at Saks on Michigan Avenue, and both of them looked expensive, and, to Dane's eye, utterly beautiful. Nick's black dress was short, showing off very nice long legs, but conservative, very appropriate for these surroundings. Once again, he thought she fit perfectly in this environment. He could easily picture her as a powerful senator's wife. It made him sick to his stomach. He realized, as he looked at her, that he never would have met her if Michael hadn't died.

It was over the artistically arranged Caesar salad with glazed pecans set precisely atop the lettuce, nestled in among croutons, that Nick said, "Albia, did you write the letter to me? The letter that Cleo supposedly wrote?"

Albia Rothman raised a perfectly arched brow. She looked

markedly like her brother with that expression. She frowned, just a bit, hardly furrowing her brow, and shook her head. "No, I don't know anything about a letter. What letter are you speaking about?"

Nick said, "John didn't mention the letter I received from Cleo, warning me that he was trying to kill me, that he'd also tried to kill her and that was why she ran away?"

"Good God, what a novel idea. A letter from Cleo? How very preposterous. John try to kill Cleo? Kill you? That is utterly absurd. John, what is going on here?"

Senator Rothman merely shrugged, methodically picked a pecan out of his salad, never looking at them. "The FBI agents are the ones with all the answers here, not I."

"You realize, I hope," Albia said to the table at large, "how very absurd that is. John is a very kind, intelligent man, a man to admire, a man who will make this country a better place."

Dane said, "Ms. Rothman, let's get back to whether you were the one who wrote Nick the letter."

"That means you were trying to warn me, Albia," Nick said. "You were trying to help me. Or were you trying to get rid of me?"

"Do eat your salad, Nicola. I didn't come here to discuss this nonsense."

Savich said, "We need your help, Ms. Rothman."

Albia said as she carefully laid down her salad fork, "If your friends—these Federal officers—are pushing you to do this, Nicola, then I do believe that I don't even wish to stay." She rose as she spoke, said to her brother, "John, I'm leaving. I have no intention of trying to digest my dinner with these people accusing you of murdering women. If I were you, I'd call Rockland and have him come represent you. I would also consider asking them to leave. Nicola, you have really disappointed me."

And she walked out of the dining room.

John Rothman said nothing until he heard the front door close quietly in the distance. "Well, whatever it is you were trying to achieve, that was disgraceful. Good evening to all of you."

Senator John Rothman rose, tossed his napkin over his uneaten salad, and walked gracefully out of the dining room.

They all stared at one another when they heard the front door close a second time.

"Well," Dane said, "I do enjoy the unexpected. The salad is delicious."

THIRTY-SEVEN

Dane said, "Jimmy Maitland asked us to a meeting with the police commissioner and several other nervous politicians, all of it regarding the Rothman case. Nick, you're not invited to this meeting. You're going to stay with Sherlock. She's agreed that you're more important than this meeting, so just Savich and I will go. You're to go nowhere alone, you got me?"

"I got you, but it's not fair to Sherlock."

Savich said, "Think of this as a good-old-boys butt-covering meeting. The SAC of the Chicago field office will be there, maybe even the mayor. It's all under wraps, at least it will be until the six-o'clock news."

Sherlock said to Nick, "I really don't enjoy watching a group of men in a pissing contest. But, guys, if anything outrageous is said, I'm sure you'll tell me about it." She kissed her husband's ear and gave him a little wave as he and Dane walked out of The Four Seasons lobby.

"We've got better things to do, Nick," Sherlock said when they'd reached the street. "We're going to go see Senator Rothman. Oh yes, my husband knows, but he didn't want Dane to know. Dane is very protective of you, Nick. Actually I'd have to say that he's terrified that something will happen to you if he doesn't stick to you like Grandma's toffee. You could probably have six cops with you and he'd still worry himself sick. But it'll be all right. You've got me."

Nick grinned, rubbed her hands together. "I can't imagine anyone needing more protection than you."

"I sure hope you're right about that. Okay, let's go see what we can find out. I'd much rather do this than go to a meeting, anyway."

Nick watched her check her SIG Sauer, then smiled when Sherlock said, "Dillon always says that if you aren't one hundred percent sure of what's going to happen, you just get yourself prepared."

They were at Senator Rothman's office by 9:30. Mrs. Mazer raised an eyebrow when she saw the two of them.

"Where are the big boys?"

"They're out playing with other big boys," Sherlock said.

Nick smiled, shook Mrs. Mazer's hand. "It's just us this morning. I'm here to see John, Mrs. Mazer."

"He'll be back in just a bit, maybe twenty minutes or so. I'm sure he'll want to see you, Dr. Campion. I hope you managed to avoid the media."

Nick nodded. "Yes, we came in through the back delivery entrance."

"I'm surprised they haven't found it by now," said Mrs. Mazer, and Nick didn't tell her that the media already had. "Oh dear, all this grief from the media. Senator Rothman is a very fine man, and now there are all these questions about the former Mrs. Rothman."

"The fact is, Mrs. Mazer," Nick said, "I'm really not sure about much of anything. But hopefully everything will become clear soon. Do you mind if I wait in his office?"

Mrs. Mazer wondered whether Dr. Campion wanted a few minutes to search the senator's desk. Who was she to say no? She'd left Dr. Campion alone in the senator's office many times. She said after a moment, "Why not?"

"Agent Sherlock, would you like to go with Dr. Campion or would you like a magazine?"

"What I would really like is to speak to any staff who might be here."

"Did Senator Rothman okay it?"

"I'm sure it will be all right," Sherlock said.

Mrs. Mazer pressed an extension on her phone. She spoke quietly, then raised her head. "Matt Stout is the senator's senior aide. He'll be out shortly to speak to you." She nodded to Nick, pressing a buzzer just beneath her desk. "Dr. Campion, it shouldn't be long." Was there a warning in her voice? Nick didn't know. A few minutes would be enough.

She said as she opened the office door, "Thank you, Mrs. Mazer." Nick stepped into the big office, knowing exactly where she was going to start looking. Not in his desk. One day she'd seen him kneeling in front of the drink cart, seen a flash of papers disappear through a small opening in the bottom of the cart. She walked straight to it.

"Hello, Nicola. I'm very surprised to see you here. In the camp of the enemy."

Nick nearly dropped in her tracks she was so startled. She jerked about, nearly losing her balance, to see Albia Rothman standing by the huge windows, dressed in one of her power suits, a rich charcoal gray wool with a soft white silk blouse. She looked quite elegant, rich, intimidating.

"Albia! Oh my heavens, you scared me. What are you doing here?"

"I think the more significant question is what are you doing here, Nicola? I spend a great deal of time here, but you? You ran away, left John without a word, just ran. And now you're back to try to hang him. He is a good man, a man this country needs. He is a visionary, a man of ideas, and here you are, trying to ruin him. I really won't have it, Nicola. I won't."

"No one wants to hang John," Nick said, facing the woman Savich, Sherlock, and Dane believed to be a killer. She wasn't afraid simply because she wasn't alone, not really. Sherlock was outside, as were a dozen people. All she had to do was yell and people would come running. No reason to be afraid of Albia. She could take Albia, all sleek in her three-inch high heels and tight skirt. She didn't have much maneuvering room, but she was in better shape than Albia.

Most important, there was Sherlock, her biggest weapon. She said, "But it's clear to everyone that since Cleo's body was found, and she'd been struck with something on the back of the head—there are questions that have to be answered. Cleo was John's wife. All of us have to face that reality. People think John would have had to know. Some people think John may have killed Cleo, Albia."

"How did you get in here without the media attacking you?"

"I slipped in through the delivery entrance. It was real close going, but I was lucky. The media guy who was supposed to keep his eye on it was having a coffee break. I saw him go into the deli across the street. John told me about that entrance a long time ago." Actually, both she and Sherlock had come in through the delivery entrance, but Nick didn't want to tell Albia about Sherlock just yet. She wanted to make Albia feel safe, make her feel in control. Just maybe she'd say something, admit to something.

Albia said with a shrug of her elegant shoulders, "Vultures, aren't they? But why did Mrs. Mazer let you in here?"

"I told her I wanted to see John. She suggested I wait in here, that he'd be back soon. Of course, I've waited for him many times in his office. I would have thought she'd tell me that you were here, but she didn't."

"That's because," Albia said, as she took a step toward Nick, "she doesn't know I'm here."

Nick forced herself not to move an inch. "How did you get in?"

Albia smiled at her, waved a graceful hand in dismissal. "When John took the lease on this building some ten years ago, he had the architect design a private entrance that led only to this office. Most people in his position have alternate ways of leaving their offices, in circumstances just like this one. I wonder why John didn't tell you about the private entrance? I wonder—perhaps when it came right down to it, he didn't really trust you, Nicola. Perhaps he did come to believe that you really were sleeping with Elliott Benson. You know, of course, that Elliott has always wanted any woman that John has, and vice versa, I might add. It's been a competition between them since before they went to college. And they pretend to be close friends. Did you know that Elliott was in love with Melissa, the girl John was engaged to? Turns out she wanted both of them, stupid girl. She slept with both of them until she died in that car accident. It was a terrible thing for my poor brother."

"Did he know she was sleeping with Elliott?"

"I have no idea. As for Elliott, I don't know what he felt about Melissa's death. It was a very long time before John became seriously interested in another woman. But he did, finally, and he and Cleo married. It wasn't long before Elliott got to Cleo, screwed her brains out, and everyone knew—but not John, not until after she left. I suppose she was sleeping with Tod Gambol, too, since he left when she did."

"But everyone knows now that she didn't run away with anybody, Albia. Someone murdered her. And buried her, hoping her body would never be found."

"Isn't that interesting? Nicola, did you sleep with Elliott Benson?"

Nick didn't answer her immediately. She was remembering how she once wondered how John had arrived at his office without her seeing him. A hidden private exit, what a good idea. Nick said, "Sleep with Elliott Benson? That's a novel thought. Another man old enough to be my father. Oh, he's as polished as an Italian count, as sleek as both you and John, but I'll tell you the truth, Albia. Whenever I see him I am reminded of a Mafia movie character with his pomaded hair and his expensive Italian suits. Whenever he looks at me, speaks to me, I want to go take a bath."

"Cleo didn't think he was bad at all. To be honest about this, I didn't believe so either, at least not at first. Yes, he was my lover for a time as well. Too bad it wasn't because he adored me, no, he just wanted something else that belonged to John. I suppose I'm included in that group. And, fact is, he's not a very good lover. Sure, he maintains his body well, and says all the right things, but he's selfish. He's used to expensive call girls who lick the bottoms of his feet if that's what he wants. He has difficulty remembering to give as well as receive when he's with a woman he isn't paying. And like I said, the both of them still pretend to be friends. What games men play."

"Albia, do you think it makes any sense at all to sleep with another man when you're engaged to be married? Why would you even be engaged if you wanted to sleep around?"

"Any number of women do it all the time. They want the power, the money that marriage would bring them and they want the excitement a lover brings. It's not a big mystery. Don't be coy, Nicola."

Nick walked over to John's desk, sat down in his big, comfortable leather chair. It steadied her, sitting behind his impressive desk. She picked up a pen and tapped it against the beautiful maple. She remembered Linus Wolfinger doing the same thing until everyone wanted to strangle him. She tapped the pen again, then once again. She said, seeing the look of annoyance on Albia's face, "Did you spread rumors about me sleeping with Elliott Benson?"

"Of course not. It was common knowledge."

"I see. How odd that I didn't know. I do know you are the one who wrote me the letter supposedly from Cleo. It couldn't be anyone else, and you also wrote with great detail about Melissa."

Albia was framed by that beautiful window, the sun surrounding her. She looked powerful, otherworldly, her stance, the tilt of her head identical to John's.

Nick felt the sudden taste of sour bile in her mouth. It tasted like fear, fear of this woman whom everyone saw as an elegant creature they admired and respected, a woman who was powerful in her own right. They didn't see Albia Rothman as a person who could have started off her adult life murdering someone. For John, for her little brother, whom she adored.

"I didn't write you anything, Nicola."

Nick let it go for the moment. What had she expected? A confession? She said after a moment of silence, "I can't believe Cleo ever slept with Elliott Benson. Nor with Tod Gambol. She loved John."

"Oh, but Cleo was a little harlot. John wouldn't believe me until I finally showed him photos that I had a private investigator take of her and Elliott, all cozied up in his small house on Crane Island. It's all private, you know, the nearest neighbor is a good half mile away. I might add that he and John both have used that house. If they happen to have each other's woman at that house, they make sure to leave a small token, a small trace of it. Perhaps you've been there, Nicola?"

Nick shook her head. "I don't believe it. I knew her. I really liked Cleo. She loved John, I'm sure of that." She realized that only about fifteen feet separated them. She said, "Albia, it's time to admit that you wrote me the letter, that you made up that journal confession to save me, to make me leave Chicago and leave John. You did it to help me, didn't you? Please tell me. You wanted to protect me, didn't you?"

Albia shrugged. "Yes, all right, no reason to lie about it now. Yes, I wrote you the letter, for all the good it did. You're back and now you want everyone to pay. John didn't try to kill you, Nicola."

Nick's heart was thudding so loudly she believed that surely Albia would hear it, that Albia must know she was so scared she was ready to pee in her pants. The words just came out, she couldn't stop them. "If it wasn't John, then was it you, Albia?"

A perfectly arched eyebrow went up a good inch. "Me? Goodness, no."

"You hired someone to try to run me down, to burn down my condo, with me in it."

"It strikes me, though, that just maybe you were the one to set fire to your own condo."

Nick laughed, couldn't help it. "That's idiocy."

Albia shrugged. She took a step back, leaned against the window, crossed her arms over her chest. She looked mildly amused. "So it was your lover who tried to kill you. It was Elliott Benson. I called him, you know. He told me all about you, told me that poor John had picked the wrong woman yet again. And he laughed then, a very pleased laugh."

"Albia, who killed Cleo?"

"Tod Gambol. After all, he was the one to run away, wasn't he? As I said, Cleo was a slut. John has always been so innocent, so trusting, so unsuspecting. They say people always search out the same sort of person again and again, doesn't matter if that person is rotten. John's the classic example. Melissa, Cleo. Then he chose you, and just look at what you did."

"I didn't do anything, Albia. Did you have the same man come to LA to kill me while he was riding a Harley?"

"I'm really tired of all this nonsense, Nicola. All this will blow over. John didn't kill Cleo, he didn't try to kill you, and neither did I. I want you to leave now. I honestly believe you should take yourself as far away as possible. I did my best to get you away from here. You should get away again, Nicola."

"No, I'm staying this time, Albia. I want to know who's trying to kill me."

Albia examined a beautifully manicured nail a moment. "You're not very bright, given all your education. I have no idea about any of this. However, I saw last night at that ridiculous dinner you and your FBI friends set up how you and that one agent were looking at each other. You've already taken another lover. John saw it as well. He knows you're sleeping with that Federal cop. That's really sad, Nicola. You're not at all worthy of someone as fine as John Rothman."

"Probably, from your point of view, no woman is good enough for him, Albia."

"Well, that's probably true. I've taken care of him since our mother died."

"I've wondered if your mother really died accidentally?"

"What a ridiculous thing to say. You're nothing but a little bitch with a big mouth. I'm glad you'll soon be out of our lives. And you will be, one way or another." And with that, Albia walked across the room, pressed her finger against one of the wall panels, and watched it silently open. Then she was gone, just like that, gone without another word.

Nick looked at that blank wall. What was Albia going to do? Figure out how to kill her again? Obviously she couldn't do it here, not with so many people just a short distance away. She wasn't stupid. Where was the man she must have hired? Nick's heart was still pounding. She felt a headache building over her left eye. It was time to fetch Sherlock, time to see Dane, to tell him everything Albia had said, which wasn't much of anything except for all this stuff about Elliott Benson.

First, though, she wanted to see where that hidden entrance went. She walked to the wall, found the nearly flat button, and pressed it. The panel slid silently open. When she stepped through, she saw that she was in some sort of narrow passage. Her heart nearly dropped to her stomach when the door slid closed behind her. She was alone, and it was dark as a moonless night. There had to be a light somewhere. She started feeling the smooth wood wall, and stopped abruptly when she came to the end of the passage, turned to the right, and suddenly there were lights set above an elevator door.

She nearly ran into Albia and a man she'd never seen before. He was holding her, stroking her hair, her back, whispering to her.

She must have made a noise. The man looked up and stared at her. Very slowly, he eased Albia away. "Would you look here, Albia. We have an unexpected guest."

He was wearing a black leather jacket. Dark opaque sunglasses hung out of the breast pocket. His hands were large, fingers blunt—strong hands.

She turned and ran.

He was on her in an instant, grabbed her arms and twisted them up and back, hard, and she groaned with the pain.

He leaned down and whispered in her ear, "Whatever are you doing here, love?"

"Darling, bring her here."

"Looks like she followed you right through the hidden panel, just like a little Alice in Wonderland." He twisted her arms again, but this time Nick didn't make a sound.

He dragged her back to where Albia stood, looking unruffled and elegant, her arms crossed over her chest. "My goodness, Nicola, you are a bad girl, aren't you? I rather hoped you'd come after me and you did. You've been trying very hard to muck things up and I really can't allow any more, now can I?"

The man eased his hold on her arms. He turned her slowly

to face him. He was older, his face seamed from years in the sun. He pushed her face up, his fist beneath her chin. "You're very pretty. I always thought so, but not smart, even with all those diplomas you have. But you know what, love? You were lucky, very lucky. I've always believed that luck ranked right up there with brains."

Nick stared up at him. "You're the man who tried to kill me."

"Well, yes, I did, and it was quite a blow when I didn't get you. Albia was very upset with me."

"Of course I was upset. You know, Nicola, you had more than your share of luck," Albia said. "Poor little Cleo, she didn't have even a lick of luck. Just as well that Dwight here sent her to her great reward. She was looking quite old there at the end. John told me that he used to love to touch her, her skin was so soft, but there, toward the end, he thought she was getting old, her skin becoming coarse."

"I thought she felt pretty nice," Dwight said.

Albia laughed. "John is very choosy. He told me he loved touching Nicola, that her skin was so very soft. He prayed that she wouldn't become coarse for a long time."

Nick jerked, felt Dwight's hand tighten around her arm. "Don't think about yelling, love, this area is soundproof, the senator's office as well. No one can hear a thing."

Nick whispered, "It was you, Albia, all along it was you."

"Yes, dear. You want to know something? You're nothing, Nicola, nothing at all. Dwight will make sure that no hunter's dog finds you. You've caused me a lot of trouble, but this will be the end of it. Yes indeed, it's so fortunate that you followed me through the wall panel. Now, that's what I call luck—for me."

Nick knew what fear tasted like, but this was more. This numbed her brain, made her shake. She didn't want to die.

There was nothing close to her, no weapon, nothing. If only she had Dane's SIG Sauer again. But Dwight was here, ready to grab her again if she even twitched.

She didn't think, she just screamed and screamed again as she shoved her fist into Dwight's belly and tried to pull free.

"That's quite enough," Albia said, and brought the butt of a gun hard on the back of her head. Nick didn't see points of light, just instant, nauseating black. She sank to the floor.

THIRTY-EIGHT

"When did you say the senator would be back, Mrs. Mazer?"

"He should have been here by now, Agent Sherlock. I wonder if he came in through his private entrance?"

Sherlock went *en pointe*. "What private entrance?" She didn't wait for an answer. She was around Mrs. Mazer's desk in an instant, her hand on the doorknob, turning it, but nothing happened. It was locked.

"It locks automatically when it's closed from the inside," Mrs. Mazer said, rising, alarmed now. "Some years ago a reporter forced his way in, so the senator decided to make the lock automatic. What's wrong, Agent Sherlock? Oh dear, is it about Dr. Campion?"

Sherlock knocked on the door, yelling Nick's name.

"Here, Agent."

Sherlock ground the key into the lock, twisted it, and the door opened silently.

The office was empty. "Where's the private entrance? Quickly, Mrs. Mazer."

"In the back wall."

Sherlock pulled her SIG Sauer out in a flash, even as she yelled over her shoulder to Mrs. Mazer, "Call the police. Tell them your Senator Rothman has taken Dr. Campion. Hurry!"

It took Sherlock a moment to find the small button, built in nearly flat against the wall. She pressed, and the door silently eased back. She stepped into a dimly lit passage that was oak-paneled, the floor carpeted with two small Turkish rugs. She paused, listening. She thought she heard something, movement, a man's breathing.

She went forward slowly in the darkness. The corridor turned once, then ended. The whole thing wasn't more than six feet long. She was facing a narrow elevator, its silver door barely visible in the dim light.

She heard the low hum of the elevator motor. He was taking Nick down. But Sherlock didn't know where the elevator let out. She punched the button again, then a third time.

And while she punched, she pulled out her cell phone, dialed Dillon's number. He answered immediately. "Hello?"

"Dillon, hurry. Rothman's building. He's got Nick. It isn't Albia. Oh God, hurry—"

The elevator door opened silently and smoothly, and she jumped inside, punched the only button. Dillon was no longer connected on the cell phone. It didn't work inside the elevator. No, it was all right, she'd said enough. Every available cop in Chicago would converge on the building within minutes.

The door opened and she stepped out slowly, fanning her SIG. She was in a dark area of the basement. There was the low hum of equipment all around her. She paused for a moment, listening. Where could he have gone? How big was this damned basement? How could he begin to hope he'd take Nick out of here without being seen? There were media nosing around.

Sherlock stood quietly for a few more seconds, but she simply couldn't hear anything except the sounds of the equipment motors all around her.

When the gun barrel slammed down, she collapsed to the floor, her SIG hitting the concrete and skidding away from her.

Her first thought, when she opened her eyes, was that she had a bitch of a headache. She felt the pain slash through her head. Not a moment later, Nick remembered—Albia had struck her with the butt of her gun. She tried to raise her hand but couldn't.

She heard the sound of an engine, loud, but that didn't make any sense. She realized she was tied to a chair, arms and ankles, really tight. The pain in her head made her nauseous, and she swallowed repeatedly until she knew she wouldn't vomit. Then she heard a moan, but it wasn't from her.

She looked up. She was in a small room, lots of wood, cramped. She looked to her left. There was Sherlock, tied to another chair, her head slumped forward.

The room lurched. Moved. She realized they were on a boat and the boat was moving fast, the engine pushing hard. She smelled the water and the diesel, heard the powerful engine, felt the boat bounce and rock as it sliced through the waves.

Boat?

"Sherlock, wake up. Sherlock? Please, come out of it. You can do it."

Silence, then, "Nick?"

"Yes, I'm all right, just a horrible headache. He got you, too. I'm so sorry."

Sherlock got herself together, closed her eyes, tried to get her brain back in gear. "Nick, I'll be okay, just give me a minute."

The boat slammed down and Nick's chair nearly toppled.

"We're in a boat, going really fast," she said.

"Yes," said Sherlock. "I can feel it. I'm very sorry I let him get me, Nick. At least I'd already called Dillon. Every cop in Chicago will be looking for us, count on it."

"We're on John's boat. I've been out on it a couple of times. It's good-sized, a sixty-three-foot Hatteras Flybridge yacht. It's really fast, Sherlock. He used to brag that it could do twenty-one knots."

"It feels like he's nearly at maximum. The man's nuts, Nick. I can't understand how a United States senator could do something like this. I can't imagine how he got both of us out of the building and here on his boat, all without being seen. He's a very well-known man."

"It isn't John, Sherlock. You guys were right, it was Albia. The guy who's driving the boat is Dwight, the man who tried to kill me three times."

Sherlock digested that. "You know something? I don't feel all that smart that we figured out Albia was behind it."

"I wonder where Dwight is taking us?"

Sherlock didn't say anything. She was afraid she knew. Dwight was going to take them to the middle of Lake Michigan, weigh them down, and toss them overboard.

It's what she would have done if she were nuts and in a hurry.

"Crane Island," Nick said suddenly. "Maybe he's taking us to Crane Island. Albia said that John owns a house there, really private."

Fat chance, Sherlock thought, unless he wanted to kill them and bury them there. She wasn't about to say that to Nick. She got her breathing and her brain together, shook her head just very slightly so she wouldn't be sick, and raised her head. "You're right, there's the boat logo over there. My cell phone, Nick, it's in my pocket. We've got to get loose and use it. Nick, how tight are your wrists tied?"

Several moments passed before Nick said, "Real tight, but my ankles aren't too bad."

"Mine are tight, too. Okay, do you think you can move yourself closer to me, Nick?"

"Yes, Sherlock."

Nick was nearly there when the boat hit a big wave and she toppled to the side. She hit her face against the thin carpet on the wood floor. She was winded, lay there a moment trying to get herself together.

"Nick, you all right?"

"Yes, but I don't know if I can still get over to you, Sherlock."

"I've been working on my ankles, they're a bit looser, maybe. Let me see if I can't get over to you."

It took time, so much precious time, but finally Sherlock was right next to Nick. "Okay, no hope for it. I'm going to have to topple myself and hope that I'm close enough to reach your wrists."

Sherlock's chair went over. She looked over her shoulder. She was too far from Nick's wrists. She wiggled, pushed, as did Nick. Finally, she could touch her hands. She was panting hard, pain shooting up her arms. "At last. Just a bit closer, Nick. Hurry. That's good."

Sherlock went to work. They were both aware of time, and too much of it was passing too fast. Dwight could stop the boat any minute, come down the wooden stairs, and shoot them. Oh God, it was all her fault. She'd been arrogant, so sure of herself— oh God, she felt low as a slug. She thought of Sean, of Dillon, and knew, knew to her soul that she simply couldn't die. She wouldn't.

She concentrated, focused. The knot was loosening, finally. "Nick, get the rope off your hands, quick. We don't have much time."

Nick pulled her hands free, got her ankles untied, then went to work on Sherlock's wrists. She was panting, but not with fear now, with hope, urging herself to move quicker, quicker.

The boat was slowing down.

"Hurry, Nick!"

Done, her wrists were free. Both of them untied Sherlock's ankles. They both pulled themselves to their feet. But they were uncoordinated, numb from being tied so long. "He took my cell phone," Sherlock said, panting. "Blast it."

The boat was coming to a stop.

Sherlock managed to get to the galley area, pulled out drawers until she found the knives. "Here, Nick," and handed her a knife. "Can you move now? Damn, I'd rather have my SIG, well, no matter, at least it's a steak knife, with a nice sharp serrated edge. The boat's stopped. We're not in the middle of the lake.

We're at a pier. I was sure he'd just shoot us and throw us overboard. Do you think we're at this Crane Island?"

"Yes, we're at Crane Island," Dwight said, walking down the stairs. "Come to think of it, I wish I'd buried Cleo here. No hunters allowed, you know? Well, well, would you just look, both of you free. How very efficient of you, Agent Sherlock. Ladies, put those knives down. I want you to come up the stairs, slowly, your hands on your heads. Do it or I'll shoot you right here. Oh yes, you're going to die in a beautiful place. I'm going to bury you beneath some ancient pine trees at the back of Senator Rothman's property."

Nick dropped the steak knife. She put her face in her hands and started crying, low, ugly sobs.

Dwight laughed. He'd taken off his leather jacket. He was wearing a black T-shirt, khaki pants held up with a silver belt with a big turquoise buckle, and sneakers. He laughed, watching her fall apart. "I knew once you realized that you weren't long for this earth, you'd break. I expect more from an FBI agent. No, I'll wager she won't shed a tear.

"Pull yourself together, Nicola. I'm not going to kill you right away. Think of all the trouble you've caused me and poor Albia. I've got to punish you for that. I promised Albia I would. I'm going to let the two of you wonder about the end I've got planned for you."

"What plans?" Sherlock asked.

"You'll see," he said. "I want you to go up the stairs first, Agent."

Sherlock nodded to Nick, turned, and began climbing those nine wooden steps up to the deck.

Nick just nodded, and sobbed some more. She felt his hand

pushing against her back, and trailed after Sherlock. Once on deck, she kept her head down, kept the choking sobs coming from her mouth. She saw they were docked at a long stretch of wooden planking. There was a narrow strip of beach, tossed with driftwood. The land looked wild, all thick pine forests as far as she could see.

"Welcome to Crane Island. Albia assures me there won't be any interruptions. It's a perfect place, just what I needed. Come along, Nicola, don't hang back like that. Pull yourself together. I expected more from you. Even Cleo didn't carry on the way you are."

But Nick was crying harder now, completely out of control. She dropped to her knees and crawled to Dwight. She clutched at his feet, his ankles, sobbing, "Please, Dwight, let us go. I swear I'll never say a word. I'll run and never come back. Don't kill me."

"God, you're pathetic. Get up!"

But she didn't, just kept pleading, trying to grab his knees.

He leaned down to grab her and pull her upright when Nick suddenly wrapped her arms around his knees and jerked him forward. He yelled, off-balance, and tried to hit her with the gun. Sherlock, who had been waiting, straightened and turned, smoothly sending her foot hard into his left kidney. He went stiff in agony, then yelled. He turned the gun on her, but Nick was hitting his knees, trying to jerk him down again. He struck Nick's cheek with his fist, then whirled on Sherlock. He tried to back up, but her leg was up and she kicked him in the ribs. He didn't dive away, ran straight at her and managed to grab a fistful of her hair. He twisted, pulled. Sherlock yelled in pain and rage, and first slammed her fist into his gut, then her foot into his crotch. He yelled, bent over, his finger pulling the trigger of his gun. Two shots went wild. Nick threw herself at his knees, shoved him backward with all her strength. As he fell, Sherlock grabbed his wrist and twisted it hard. He dropped the gun to the deck and fell on his face. Sherlock scooped it up.

Nick dove on top of him, hitting his face, his neck, yelling, "I'm not pathetic, you murdering jerk! I wouldn't beg you for anything, you murdering son of a bitch! We got you and you're going to rot in jail for the rest of your miserable life."

Sherlock stood over them, the feeling returning to her hands and feet. "That was quite an act, Nick. Well done."

"It was, wasn't it?" Nick said, and grinned up at Sherlock.

Then, suddenly, Dwight moved, lurched up, knocking Nick backward.

Sherlock said, "Thank you, Dwight," and she kicked him in the head.

He crumbled back onto the deck.

Nick scrambled to her feet, yelling, "You bastard," and hit him in the belly, then rose and kicked him hard in the ribs.

She looked over at Sherlock, grinned until she thought her mouth would split, and dusted off her hands.

"We're good."

Sherlock hugged her close, then leaned back. "We are good, Nick. We're very good."

"No one to match us," Nick said.

"Let me get Dillon," Sherlock said and went to the boat radio. She got the Coast Guard, which was just fine.

Twenty minutes later, when the Coast Guard launch pulled up to the Crane Island dock, with both Savich and Dane ready to leap onto Rothman's boat, it was to see both Sherlock and Nick leaning over the side, waving to them.

"Why am I surprised?" Savich asked to no one in particular. "Thank God."

"I've got to start breathing again," Dane said. "Damn, I've never been so scared in my life. Just look at them, grinning from ear to ear. Is that Rothman lying facedown on the deck?"

"Oh no," Nick said. "It wasn't Senator Rothman. You guys were right all the time. It was Albia, and this is the man who tried to kill me three times."

"Four times," Sherlock said.

Dwight groaned, then slumped back on the deck.

"Hey, Dwight," Nick shouted to him. "Am I lucky, or what?"

Dwight didn't answer. With a scream of rage, he jerked upright, grabbed a knife out of his boot, and went after Nick. She froze. That knife was up, coming toward her, arching downward to her heart, and suddenly she was thrown to the deck onto her back. Dane was on him, both hands locked around his wrist, shaking, tightening.

Dwight screamed in his face, "You're the Fed cop. Hey, I nearly got you once, I'll do it again."

"Oh no," Dane said, let Dwight draw him in closer, then he drove his knee up into Dwight's groin. He screamed, fell back. Dane slammed his fist into his belly, shoved him down. He was on top of him, slamming his head on the deck. Vaguely, he heard Savich call out. He saw the blur of the knife, realized he'd let his own rage get the better of him. He rolled off Dwight, came up, and when the man came at him again, crouched over, still in bad pain, Dane kicked him in the jaw. He went down like a rock.

This time he didn't move. They all watched the knife slowly fall from his fingers.

"Good move," Savich said, and squeezed his shoulder. He watched, smiling, as Dane turned, looked at Nick, then slowly brought her against him. They didn't move for a very long time.

Sherlock said, "You know what, Dillon? I want to go buy some fat rollers this afternoon. We've put it off long enough, don't you think?"

Savich laughed.

EPILOGUE

She watched Dane place the single white lily on top of Father Michael Joseph's grave. He straightened, his head down. His lips were moving, but she couldn't hear what he was saying to his brother.

Finally, he raised his head and smiled at her. He said simply, "Michael loved Easter, and that means lilies." He paused a moment. "I will miss him until I die. But at least he's been avenged."

"It isn't enough," she said. "It just isn't enough."

"No, of course not, but it's something. Thank you for coming with me, Nicola."

"No, please, just call me Nick. I don't think I ever want to be called that other name again."

"You got it. Whatcha say we go take Inspector Delion to lunch?"

"I'd like that." She took his outstretched hand. He turned once to look back at his brother's grave. The single lily looked starkly white atop the freshly turned dirt. Then he looked back at her and smiled.

Nick said, "Inspector Delion told me about this Mexican restaurant on Lombard called *La Barca*. Let's go there."

He grinned down at her. "You mean all I've got to do is give this girl a taco and she's a happy camper?"

They walked in silence to the rental car. He said, "I just heard from Savich. Albia Rothman's hearing was this morning. She pleaded not guilty. And you know what? Dwight Toomer isn't rolling on her, at least not yet. We'll have to see how tough the DA is. You'll have to testify, Nick. It won't be fun."

"No, but maybe we can get justice for Cleo."

"It'll talk a long time to come to court. Albia Rothman's got big-tag lawyers. They'll stall and evade and file more motions than O.J.'s lawyers. But it will happen. She will go down. It's not enough, but it's all we can do. Now, what are you planning on doing, Nick?"

"You know I resigned from the university."

"Yes, I know," he said, and waited, and thought of the huge box of condoms he had in his briefcase. He smiled even as she said, "I've been thinking I'd like to come east, maybe to Washington, D.C., see what's available for an out-of-work college professor."

He stopped, lightly touched his fingers to her cheek, smelled the fresh salty air, and said, "Yes, I think that's a fine idea. Given your record for getting into trouble, it's probably smart of you to get as close as possible to the biggest cop shop in the U.S."

"I sure hope you're wrong about that. I don't even plan on

getting a parking ticket. Dane, remember you wanted the next fifty years?"

"Yes, and then we'll negotiate for more. I was thinking that someday Sean Savich will be a grown man and just maybe, if we have a girl, she and Sean could get together. What do you think?"

"Good grief. We're not even married and you've already got our daughter married! Hmmm. To Sean Savich. We'll have to speak to Savich and Sherlock about some sort of nuptial contract, what do you think?"

He laughed, took her hand, and felt a bolt of happiness fill him, deep and bright. He turned back once more to see the lily atop Michael's grave lightly waving in the salty breeze.